GROWING

UP

RICH

Also available in

SCRIBNER **SIGNATURE** EDITIONS

SOUTH STREET *by David Bradley*

WHAT I KNOW SO FAR *by Gordon Lish*

DEAR MR. CAPOTE *by Gordon Lish*

VOICES AGAINST TYRANNY *edited by John Miller*

COOL HAND LUKE *by Donn Pearce*

BLOOD TIE *by Mary Lee Settle*

THE KISS OF KIN *by Mary Lee Settle*

THE LOVE EATERS *by Mary Lee Settle*

20 UNDER 30 *edited by Debra Spark*

STATE OF GRACE *by Joy Williams*

GROWING

UP

RICH

Anne Bernays

SCRIBNER**SIGNATURE**EDITION

CHARLES SCRIBNER'S SONS · NEW YORK
1986

This novel is a work of fiction. Names, characters, places and incidents are either the product of the author's imagination or are used fictitiously. Any resemblance to actual persons, living or dead, events or locales is entirely coincidental.

Library of Congress Cataloging-in-Publication Data

Bernays, Anne.
Growing up rich.

Reprint. Originally published: 1975.

(Scribner signature edition)
I. Title.
PS3552.E728G7   1986   813'.54   86-11902
ISBN 0-684-18648-9

Originally published in hardcover by
Little Brown and Company.

First Signature Edition 1986

Printed in the United States of America.

Cover art "Treasure Ox" by Rodney Alan Greenblatt.
Courtesy of the artist and Gracie Mansion Gallery, New York.

For Joe

1
The
Invisible Axis

DURING THE TIME I lived in his house with his wife and two kids, Sam London, when he roused himself to display any curiosity about me at all, would sometimes ask me to tell him about what he called my marzipan life. The more details I gave him the better he liked it. It wasn't that he hadn't touched it firsthand himself but that *I* had been in the center of it. I knew it like the shape of my own horribly bitten fingernails.

To me it was simply the way I was brought up, and the way you are brought up is never so interesting as the way someone else is. How on earth could Sam possibly find my mother's and stepfather's art collection or dinner party guest list exciting? To me it was the same old dreary thing: day after day of marzipan, silk velvet, Steuben glass, butterballs.

I had no idea then that the fact of being immensely rich makes you automatically interesting even if you have a boring personality. It's like having a supernumerary nipple.

My mother wasn't a celebrity the way Hildegarde or Mary Martin was. She was, in fact, quasi-private. Still, she was the object of great curiosity. If you were as rich and visible as Mummy was, people thought they could ask her anything. I suppose they thought it was like asking a local monument how much its pedestal was worth.

Sam London is not now and never has been known for tact.

Furthermore, he's as proud of being a Russian Jew as my mother
and stepfather were of their German origins. Silly, isn't it? Sam's
point is that the only real cultural contribution made by German
Jews is the department store. Sam says that the majority of
American-Jewish writers and artists are Russian: Mailer, Mala-
mud, Roth, Baskin, Lipschitz, Miller, Tovish, Bernstein, Perel-
man, Kazin, and so on. You can count on the fingers of one hand
the German Jews who have produced anything very lasting:
Hellman (two of them), Untermeyer, Kronenberger, Sondheim.
Who else?

Put this way, Sam's case is fairly persuasive. The Russians have
the brains and the passion, the Germans have the *gelt*.

My mother's name was Marguerite; most people — with the
exception of her lawyer, Donald Snyder, and her mother-in-law,
Oma Lucy Stern — called her Fippy. Fippy suited her. It had the
right WASPY sound. Mrs. Stern made Mummy's first name sound
like an operatic aria — Mar-ghee-your-eat. The name Fippy was
given my mother during her first week as a student at the Seeley
School. Mummy, one hundred per cent Jew, looked like a shiksa.
She had a Scandinavian forehead, an Episcopalian nose, a Beverly
Farms accent, and a debutante slouch. The funny part is that,
though I am only half Jewish, the only thing they ever called me
at the Seeley School was Stern, my surname. I just didn't have the
right psychic equipment to "pass."

My mother married my stepfather, Alfred Stern — Freddie —
during one of his Navy leaves; that's also when Roger was con-
ceived. Before that she had played the Gay Divorcée for all it
was worth for four or five years. She might have been gayer — in
the obsolete sense — had not all the men remaining at home been
either too young, too old, or too queer. The men who squired
my mother during the war either made me laugh or made me
sick. Young as I was, I knew a bad thing when it was sitting on
the living room couch making goo-goo eyes at my mother. One

was a sheep farmer from Australia, probably a secret agent. Another was a lieutenant commander from California who I knew was married because he hadn't bothered to remove his wedding ring when he came calling. A third was the pansy conductor of an orchestra that played Mendelssohn and other loose melodies over the radio.

When my mother married Freddie she stopped being a blossom and became a full-blown flower. It was the way of life she had always wanted. Out of his naval uniform, casting around for something to do with his time and money, Freddie discovered Griffin House, a small publishing firm on its last legs financially and in every other way. He bought it lock, stock, and backlist and began to publish the kind of books few other firms would touch: medieval and contemporary poetry, anthropology with a Jungian tinge, novels he only dimly understood. It was Sam London's job to understand and recommend the difficult books, the esoterica. Thus Sam was indispensable to Freddie. My stepfather could not have found a more appropriate outlet for his energies and yet he wasn't satisfied. Right up to the day he died Freddie couldn't believe in himself.

My mother was three years older than her husband. This discrepancy gave their marriage a lopsided, slightly wicked look. Most people thought they were deliriously happy. I suppose, given your average marriage, they were.

Freddie looked like a Jewish Abraham Lincoln, who always looked Jewish to me anyway. He had those same high, prominent cheekbones, that same melancholy expression. But Freddie was handsomer than he should have been; his interior was not nearly so striking as his exterior. He fooled a lot of people into thinking he was an intellectual. Maybe that's one reason he could never believe in himself.

My mother and stepfather rarely fought with one another. There was one fly in the ointment: Sam London. My mother couldn't mention Sam's name without getting red in the face and her mouth tightening. Sam was an invisible presence in the house on East Seventy-third Street; I knew he was there long before I laid eyes on him. There was the almost nightly ritual of Freddie's long distance call to Brookline, Massachusetts, where Sam London lived. This call generally took place just before the cocktail hour. Freddie would retire to his immaculate, leathery study on the second floor and put through the call.

"Operator, I'd like to place a person-to-person call to Mr. Samuel London," etc.

It drove Mummy crazy. "Why," she would ask me, "does he make it person-to-person when he knows perfectly well Sam is expecting him to phone?"

My mother would wait impatiently in the living room in her long, just-us-family velvet hostess gown and say to me, "Listen to him. You'd think they were having an affair or something. Be a dear, will you, Sally, and ask Kathleen to fill the ice bucket. It's not even half full."

I think my mother really believed that Sam London had a mysterious hold over her husband, something like blackmail, the basis of which Freddie was afraid to reveal. Freddie was always citing his friend the professor, Sam London, as a reference for all kinds of literary and extraliterary matters. He did, I have to admit, make Sam sound like Svengali. I don't blame my mother for getting irritated.

"If you're just talking about business," Mummy said to Freddie, "then why don't you call him from the office?"

He may have been seething, but Freddie was compassionate with Mummy. "Because I know I won't be interrupted here. You know I can't conduct any real business at the office. Besides, this is the one time Sam can give me his complete attention. He works all day."

"So do you, sweetie," Mummy said. "I wish you weren't so

dependent on that man." She was the sort of woman who, if she had something on her mind, brought it right out without caring whether she hurt anyone's feelings. She could never sit on anything.

Freddie denied being dependent, although he did admit Sam was useful. "He's got contacts in places I haven't even heard of," Freddie explained. "He knows who's writing what and who's about to produce a novel. He's got a toehold on the grapevine. I suppose you think I should be up there too? Well, I'm not. I'm too rich. It sounds funny, doesn't it? Being too rich to be in the right place at the right time?"

"You're damn right it does," Mummy said, wagging her glass of gin and vermouth so vigorously that drops spilled on her skirt where they were immediately absorbed into the deep green velvet. "Sam's an intellectual snob. He tries to make you feel inadequate."

"If you've got to be a snob," Freddie said, "I suppose that's the one to be." I suspected that his cavalier answer hid some hurt.

"I thought snobbery went out with America First and Senator Burton K. Wheeler, my love," Mummy said archly.

"I wish you'd drop it," Freddie said, emphasizing each word. That's about the worst thing he ever said to her — "I wish you'd drop it." "Shut up" and "bullshit" were not in Freddie's vocabulary.

As a matter of fact, by bringing up the subject of Sam London, my mother had touched her husband where he lived. With me right there. Sometimes they would go on talking as though I weren't present. Other times I would be sent from the room, such as when they were about to launch into one or more of the taboo subjects — death, cancer, adultery, big money, sex, unspecified sin, or being Jewish. You didn't talk about being Jewish; presumably if you didn't mention it, it would go away. Not so with Oma Lucy, but I'll get to that later.

Naturally the taboo subjects occupied my thoughts and my fantasies far more than my mother realized. What you know is not nearly so interesting as what you suspect.

Soon after Freddie finished his nightly call the phone rang. Mummy says, "Let Kathleen get it."

Moments later the maid's head appears at the doorway to the living room. An indirect light, designed to enhance the Picasso watercolor, throws a glow on her pink cheeks. I suspect that she is raising a crop of subcutaneous bumps. "It's for you, ma'am," she says, close to a whisper.

"Who is it?" my mother asks. She has trained Kathleen to ask the caller's name, but Kathleen sometimes forgets.

"It sounded like Dr. Baum, ma'am."

"Thank you, Kathleen. In the future will you please try to remember to ask who's calling?"

"Yes, ma'am." I look for some sign of smoldering resentment in Kathleen's face and see nothing. I have been reading a lot of books about people with smoldering resentments and have got it into my head that anybody who works for anyone else and takes orders from them is about to burst into a terrible flame. All I see now is a young Irish girl in a black silk uniform and lace cap from Bloomingdale's, waiting, like a schoolgirl, to be excused.

"Damn!" my mother says. "I guess I'd better take it. It's not like Pop to call me during his bridge hour."

While Mummy is in the corner talking to her father, Freddie chats with me. Freddie never allowed himself to get into a serious discussion with me. He chatted, he made small talk, he asked a lot of questions, but I don't think we ever swam underwater together. This particular night it was school, another it might be my piano lessons or what book I was reading, or what concert his mother had most recently dragged me to in the course of my private musical education.

"You won't believe this," Mummy says, throwing herself

gracefully onto the couch. "Pop's having a seventieth birthday brawl" — she sighs — "at The Club."

"Who's giving it?" Freddie says. "You're not going to tell me he's giving it for himself. Even *he* wouldn't do that."

"Not on your life. At least not for public consumption. His former medical students — about twenty of them — are giving it for him. That way they share the expense. They're going all the way. You know, the book of tributes solicited on the qt, the speeches, the telegram from the President . . . no, I'm just kidding, it'll be the telegram from the Surgeon-General. Naturally, Pop's creating the guest list, the menu, the seating. Can you see him letting anyone else do it?"

I'd better explain or you'll think Mummy was some kind of Goneril or Regan. Her father was the legendary dragon, Theodore Baum, M.D., F.A.C.S., etc., the only Jewish surgeon on the staff at P & S, a man so egomaniacal and brutish that he would save people by removing their diseased organs and then send them into a suicidal depression by his postoperative manner. His wife had shriveled and died during the war — he had no close relatives left to torment except an older despised sister and my mother. I was supposed to call him Opa Teddy but I thought that made him sound much too nice and bearish. He called me Little Lady and sometimes he looked at me as if he had never seen me before.

"What does he want from you?" Freddie says. Freddie was her ally in the cold war against Opa Teddy; he was his wife's ally in most things.

"He claims he wants help with the menu. Of course if I suggest anything that doesn't please him it'll be the usual 'any color so long as it's black,' " Mummy says.

"Are you going to help him?" Freddie says. Whenever my mother tried to do anything with her father she'd stay angry for days.

"I have to," she says. "How can I not?"

The Club was the way its members referred to the Orange Club. Housed in a massive banklike structure a few yards from Fifth Avenue's mica-specked pavement, the Orange Club was a stronghold of respectability. Inside, it was hung with weighty velvet curtains and carpeted with thick crimson rugs — from front door to service entrance. The Orange Club, like a deodorized delicatessen, was about as Hebrew in character as the Royal Pavilion at Brighton. It was as hushed as a surgeon's waiting room. Silence seeped up and down the wide stairwells and filled the halls. The idea behind this absence of noise was the members' answer to the accusation that Jews are noisy and pushy. Also, since Jews are vulgar, we'll decorate the place in subdued Mauve Decade. Jews smell funny. So we'll seal off the kitchen and keep odorous food off the tables, no sour pickles, no herring, no garlic, no knishes. Since all male Jews have long curls and comic accents, the members of the Orange Club will be all but indistinguishable from their gentile counterparts, the lawyers, book publishers, doctors, and businessmen they daily did business with. There wasn't a beard or an accent to be seen or heard on the premises; likewise there were no Epsteins or Kaminskys, only names indigenous to Germany, Spain, France, or England — Strauss, Loeb, Kahn, Freund.

Protruding from the walls of the dining room a safe several yards above the diners were the chopped-off heads of moose, mountain goat, and water buffalo. The ladies' lounge served up pink porcelain and Elizabeth Arden powder. There was so much waste space at the Orange Club that if you happened to be there during an off-hour, say three in the afternoon, you might think you had stumbled into an empty palace kept immaculate by an overzealous staff waiting for the imminent return of the royal residents. To me The Club was the stuffiest place in my entire world.

Freddie, not unreasonably, felt warmly at home in the Orange Club. For one thing, he'd practically grown up in it. When he had a drink at the Oak Bar on the third floor he would rub elbows with his Horace Mann or Yale classmates. When he dined under the water buffalo he could see his counterparts from other Jewish publishing houses like Viking, Simon and Schuster, and Random House. When Freddie was at lunch at The Club with agents or authors or once in a while Sam London, he would catch sight of his doctor, his lawyer, and his broker, sometimes all three at once. Whenever I went to The Club with my mother and Freddie, I wore regulation white gloves which buttoned over my wrists, and sterile white socks.

My mother, too, had practically been brought up at The Club; her parents had eaten there every Thursday night, Cook's Night Out. The only time she stopped going was when she was married to my father, William Sanderson, and that didn't last very long.

For Opa Teddy The Club really was a home away from home. Especially after his wife died. He ate there almost every night. This is the sort of thing on the menu, but scorned by Opa because of his vanity: breaded veal cutlet, mushrooms in cream, sauerbraten, chicken paprika with spaetzle, apricot tarts and schnecken baked on the premises. Cold salmon or chicken in wine jelly when the season turned. Opa Teddy was a man loathed, feared, and prayed to. He would receive gifts from grateful patients, for Christmas, things like an entire case of Chivas Regal (even during the war), twenty-pound turkeys smoked in the Virginia backwoods, glass ashtrays from Steuben. The family referred to and laughed at these gifts as the "annual loot." Opa Teddy would have died if the stream of loot had dried up. My grandfather felt about women the way he felt about Polish and Russian Jews, namely, that they belonged to a lower order. I once heard him tell my mother that the reason there weren't more women surgeons was that female eyes were not properly connected to their brains. If you'd asked me, I would have said Opa Teddy and the Orange Club were made for each other.

Sam London was fascinated by the most trivial details of Orange Club life. For instance, the fact that although you could ask for — and get — matzos during Passover, The Club went all out during the Christmas season and threw an elaborate kids party late in December. My mother simply assumed I wanted to go this party and never bothered to ask me. Had she bothered to ask, I would have told her that the party, far from being fun, was an ordeal. I was dressed like a little doll, the kind they bought for my birthday at F. A. O. Schwarz. My dress was velvet or heavy watered silk that stood out stiffly, all by itself. My shoes were Mary Janes, black patent leather with a strap across the instep, buttoned by a hook with an ivory handle which my mother kept in a drawer full of things like suede brushes, unopened boxes of miniature pillows filled with perfumed powder, silver and gold chains, ancient fans, and other odds and ends. My mother or Fräulein Kastern tied a ribbon around my thick hair which had been brushed one hundred times. My gloves were inspected for spotlessness. Someone — Kathleen or Fräulein or my mother if she wasn't busy — would deliver me to the front door of The Club and drive away again in the family buggy, a huge hearselike Cadillac with Rooney at the wheel. Delivered, or, as I tended to think of it, *dumped* and given a shove in the direction of the weighty glass and wrought-iron doors of the Orange Club. There was no question of pretending to go in and then hightailing it as soon as the car disappeared around the corner. I was the sort of child who did what they told me to, not necessarily without complaining but certainly without entertaining alternatives.

If you looked at it objectively, there was no reason for me to be as miserable as I was at the Orange Club parties. They were really quite good.

A typical annual Christmas party was the one I remember when I was around ten. All the children are seated on spindly red chairs with gilt legs and crimson seats. We cross our white-socked ankles and applaud as this year's magician takes five snowy rabbits from his silk hat and makes green water turn red. I don't see anyone from my class at school — Renata Paul's mother wouldn't dream of sending her off to a kiddy party and the other two Jewish girls have gone South for the vacation. I am momentarily distracted by the magician who asks for volunteers and points to me. Embarrassed, I answer his summons. He makes me the butt of a disappearing penny trick. I blush and feel stupid. This is the second time this has happened to me. The other children clap enthusiastically. I shrink back to my seat, still blushing.

I burn through the rest of the act. Refreshments are served. Two waiters with familiar faces stand behind long tables. I see punch in an enormous cut-glass vat, silver platters of sandwich triangles: chicken salad, egg salad, ham salad, cream cheese and olive, tongue, and something spicy I can't identify. I try them all, being a great finder of peace in food. There are piles of little wet cakes coated with pink and white and light brown sugar hardened into a crust. And metal ice cream goblets filled with tricolor ice cream so cold you can hardly cut into it with your spoon. There is nothing "Jewish" about the spread except its lavishness. It is about as ethnic a snack as mashed potatoes. I am unaware that it is odd for a Jewish club to throw a Christmas party, to display a Christmas tree surrounded by false presents and holly boughs and pine branches at strategic locations. Another year we had a treasure hunt all over the building with a music box from Tiffany awarded to the winner. Another year The Club hired a Rumanian dancer to come and teach us folk dances.

Most of the children — who, unlike me, had a good time at these parties — went to Horace Mann, Fieldston, Ethical Culture, New Lincoln, or the Dalton School. I was a Seeley girl and that

started me off with two strikes against me. The gap between me
and them was unbridgeable. We simply had nothing to say to each
other; furthermore we regarded each other like the Germans and
the Russians. Once I thought I saw a cousin of my mother's but
when I looked for her face again it had melted into the mob of
ignoring faces.

When my mother married the handsome bachelor Lieutenant
Commander Alfred Stern, she moved into a house they bought
jointly on East Seventy-third Street between Park and Lexington.
(Long after I moved away someone asked me where I grew up,
and when I said "the East Side" they assumed that I meant the
Lower East Side, where everybody else's parents grew up.) The
day wartime building and renovation codes relaxed, Mummy got
to work on the house. She sheared off the brownstone stoop and
brought the front door down a story, so that you entered at
basement level, a few feet below the street. You didn't refer to
this floor as the basement, however, but as the ground floor. My
mother had gone to the Cordon Bleu as a young girl and now she
exploited her talents like a prostitute released from jail. She became a famous cook and hostess, introduced garlic, oregano,
telicherry pepper, cardamom, and coriander to people who had
been content with catsup until they learned better from her. My
mother cooked with wine and herbs where other women used
canned tomato sauce or library paste. Her recipes were printed in
the *Tribune* by Clementine Paddleford. When she gave one of
her famous parties, the guests were invited to come down into
the kitchen, which she had furnished with a restaurant-type stove
and other unusual equipment, and they watched her at work. She
was like Isadora Duncan in the kitchen: creative, innovative, brilliant, and somewhat ad hoc. There was always a maid standing by
to wallop the pots and pans when she was through creating. That
way her hands stayed smooth and her fingernails long, almond-

shaped. I don't think I ever saw my mother hold anything under the faucet except an onion.

It sounds like a cliché, but my mother had the sort of beauty that people remember like a punch in the mouth. She looked a little like Hedy Lamarr, although she didn't like being compared to anyone. Next to my mother I felt like a cow. I was overweight; my clothes never seemed to sit right. My blouses were always ruching out of my skirts, my socks collapsed around my ankles, zippers bulged and collars rode unevenly around my neck. I was no Snow White and my mother didn't need to ask a mirror which one of us shone the brightest. It was all too painfully obvious. It's awful to have a mother so beautiful that people sigh when they see her and then cough nervously when they catch sight of you. My mother, incidentally, never told me that beauty was only skin deep because she didn't believe it herself.

The third member of the broken triangle that was my parents was my father, William Sanderson. I adored him out of all recognition. I idolized him the way my classmates idolized Tyrone Power and Van Johnson. I literally prayed to him at night in bed with the lights out. When I didn't hear from him I went into a depression which my mother recognized and teased me about. The more Mummy bad-mouthed her first husband, the stronger became my passionate attachment to him. I had hundreds of photographs of Daddy, from boyhood in Newport, Rhode Island, to Air Corps to Tennis Club. It was for his love that I chiefly existed. For him I endured the torments of school, dancing class, piano lessons, schedules, meals with my family, homework, the dentist's drill and the doctor's checkup, dress fittings, loneliness, and being forced to play with the children of my mother's friends.

I was born in 1933 and barely remember Pearl Harbor. I *do* remember V-E and V-J days because everyone acted as if they were going crazy; everyone, including my mother, was hysterical and gave up all pretense — for twenty-four hours — of leading a normal life. I remember the day Roosevelt died because my mother was uncharacteristically emotional. I came home from school and found her sitting in the kitchen — Mother *never* sat in the kitchen — crying with the cook, I think her name was Bessie. They were both blubbering like children. It made me uneasy. I said, "What did he die of?" I needed to know exactly.

"He had a stroke, poor man," my mother said, sniffing.

"Died like a prince," Bessie said. "And his wife not with him. I feel so sorry for the poor soul."

"What's a stroke?" I said. The two women looked at me as if my curiosity was too morbid for consideration. I didn't understand what a stroke was; I thought someone must have hit him.

"It's something that happens inside your head," my mother explained. "With the blood vessels."

"Will it happen to you?"

"Good God, Sally, go upstairs and do your homework." I had annoyed my mother again. I imagined blood bursting loose inside her skull. It made me feel faint.

The party for Opa Teddy started gradually, with people drifting in for cocktails around six o'clock in the fourth floor bar. The drinks were served by waiters in black pants and white jackets. The hors d'oeuvres were fat and thick — chicken liver on black bread, black caviar on melba rounds, smoked salmon and sturgeon carved before your very eyes and placed on small plates with silver forks, little all-beef hot dogs tucked in "blankets" of crispy dough, egg salad, chicken salad, and, yes, ham salad between slices of crustless white bread. I can list just so much food without feeling like getting sick, no matter how good it sounds. Lots of goodies to eat, plates piled high with them, but not before you were shunted through the reception line to greet Opa Teddy on his seventieth. I was in the line, wedged between my mother

and Freddie. Mummy was dressed to the teeth in one of last year's dresses — as she said, zippering herself into it, "God knows, none of Pop's friends has seen it on me."

The great surgeon stood surrounded by an invisible halo of self-esteem. I knew it was there because I could feel its moist heat creeping around like a radiator in a room that's already hot enough. Opa Teddy gave each of his guests a bone-shattering handshake and a bromide of a greeting and then passed him on. Some of the people he had known as long as he'd been in business — colleagues and underlings from the hospital and medical school, former students who had their own bronze nameplates along Park Avenue and Fifth Avenue, a liberal scattering of grateful patients, some with only one lung, stitches in their arteries, or colostomy bags well disguised by Brooks Brothers suits. He acted just like the King of England. It made me slightly ill with disgust to watch him loving himself so much. I noticed that my mother wore a mask of amiability which she didn't remove once during the proceedings. Freddie looked distracted, as if he wished he were somewhere else. Opa Teddy wore a new dinner jacket and a cummerbund. He looked extraordinarily polished. He was a fitness nut, did calisthenics every morning, didn't smoke except for one Havana cigar after his evening meal, and dieted like a movie star because, as he was apt to tell anyone, letting yourself go is an unforgivable indulgence. Many of Opa's guests had never been inside a Jewish club before. You could tell by the odd way they looked at things, full of wonder and curiosity and whispering. They acted a little like unbelievers who had sneaked into Mecca and were fascinated by it; on the other hand, they were not quite sure someone was not about to come up behind them and stick a knife between their ribs.

After nearly an hour of eating and greeting, the guests are herded down the carpeted stairwell and into a large private dining room with a head table and twelve round tables seating eight

people each. Like Mark Twain's famous birthday party. The
seating plan has been carefully worked out so that no wife sits at
a table with her husband, no doctor sits with an immediate col-
league, and the nurses all sit together. I am not at the head table,
thank God, but shunted off with relatives, a couple of cousins
who are just out of my age bracket and talk about boys and an
aunt who makes goo-goo eyes at Opa's lawyer and asks him for
free legal advice. I amuse myself by watching two elderly ladies
across the table. They didn't look like anyone on Opa's side of
the family — and he has the kind of physical traits that *always*
show up, that are always dominant even though genetics say they
shouldn't be. This pair have identically dressed blue hair, identical Roman noses, and tons of burnished and sparkling antique
jewelry around wrist and neck and ladled onto bosom like some
elaborate life-saving device. Later, when I asked my mother who
they were, she said only, "Oh, they're special friends of your
grandfather's." Did she mean *girlfriends?* Both of them? Or just
women he played bridge with in the long frosty evenings high
above the noise of Fifth Avenue buses? Or some kind of wicked
ladies and he had given them the jewels? My mind went racing off
with each possibility and still was not satisfied.

My mother and stepfather are at the head table along with the
other VIPs in Opa Teddy's life: his chief-of-staff (the only man
in the room to whom he defers and even then it isn't much of a
deference), his own doctor, an old New Yorker of impeccable
Dutch extraction, his ugly old sister and a few people I didn't
recognize. I'm only guessing, but one was probably the medical
editor of the *New York Times* and another the dusky queen of a
remote Pacific Island whose face he had rebuilt. The food is
wonderful, the length of time almost intolerable. No child likes
to sit still for long unless it's at the movies, and I am no exception,
despite my professional training in deportment. Immediately
after the ice cream with chocolate sauce people begin getting up

on the hind legs and paying what are known as "handsome tributes" to Opa Teddy. It seems to me we sit for nearly two hours
listening to lies and half-truths. These graceful little speeches
— the kind of thing that must be delivered as if ad lib but actually have been rehearsed for days — sound more like eulogies
over a coffin than anything said in the subject's living presence. I
know my grandfather is a mean, old, selfish, insatiable bully. *They*
say he is "generous to a fault," "selfless," "brilliant" (I concede
this because I know nothing to indicate the contrary), "witty,"
"charming," and so on, deep into the land of make-believe.
Witty? My grandfather is as witty as a chicken. Why are
they doing this? Selfless as a crab crawling along the sand. Is it
mass hysteria? Generous as a newborn baby. I can't believe it.
But Opa Teddy can. He smiles modestly, nodding ever so
slightly, once in a while casting his eyes into the chocolate soup
in the bottom of his sherbet cup. He is eating it up, he is swallowing it whole, it is feeding him power and life, it is better than
whole blood. I look at my mother. Her lovely slim hands point
heavenward. Her chin is almost but not quite resting on them.
Her eyes are half-closed as if she is sharing her father's humility.
I know she must be thinking but she betrays nothing. She is a
goddess. For a moment I am overwhelmed by admiration for her
cool beauty, her self-control.

It was at my grandfather's party that it began to dawn on me
that most adults go through life faking, thinking one thing and
showing another. Being heavy with hate or disgust and smiling all
the while. Desperate to fuck but pretending to listen to music.

A book is held up. It is school notebook size, bound in crimson
leather with gold letters embossed on the cover. I can't read what
it says, but it is probably something like Theodore Baum, M.D.,
F.A.C.S., the greatest man in the world not excepting Winston
Churchill and Dwight D. Eisenhower. Everybody applauds and
Dr. De Hooch, Opa's doctor, reads ten telegrams of greeting and

ceremonial sentiments, including one from the Surgeon-General
regretting that he cannot be present at this festive and crowning
occasion. It is time for the great man to respond. The guests rise
and applaud at chin level. My grandfather takes out a clean white
handkerchief and dabs at his eyes. He thanks us from the bottom
of his heart. This evening has been sufficient reward for the years
of labor. He will treasure this moment so long as he lives. His cup
runneth over. I wonder who he is imitating. The only person I
can think of is Dr. Elias, the Rabbi of Temple Joshu-a.

I am embarrassed but nobody else seems to mind. Opa Teddy
does a chronological survey of his career. This takes about
twenty minutes. My fanny has gone to sleep and I need to go to
the bathroom like anything, but I daren't get up for fear that
everybody will look at me. I pray for the end. I pray like I've
never prayed before — for it to be over. Opa Teddy sits down at
last, the guests clap again. There is momentary indecision in the
room. Is it all over? Can we go home now? All of a sudden
something is wrong, something bad has happened. I look toward
the head table. My grandfather's face has turned the color of
green mayonnaise. His eyes are bulging like Red Skelton's. His
arms fly up symmetrically, and then, boom, his head smashes
down into his dessert plate. His baldness looks out at us, a blank,
featureless face. Immediately disorder fills the room. One or two
woman scream, there is a general shoving and pushing and talking,
all at once, and milling around. I am frozen with fascination.
I think I'm the only person in the room standing absolutely
still. I watch as two men lift Opa Teddy out of his chair and
put him on the floor. Someone takes off his jacket to place
under his head, so it doesn't have to touch the red carpet. The
two blue-haired ladies are carrying on as if they'd been forced to
witness a hanging. I am beginning to get scared. Has Opa had a
stroke like Roosevelt? Is the blood going to burst clear through
his skull? Is he going to leave The Club feet first, never to get up
again? Everyone is talking and a few are sneaking out; it's getting

late, and tomorrow is a working day. Where's Mummy? I can't see her anywhere. I come out of my trance and race to the head table.

"Mummy, what's happened to Opa?"

"We don't know yet, darling," she says, half whispering. "Dr. De Hooch is examining him now. Come away." My mother takes my arm and tries to lead me away so I won't see anything interesting. I resist.

"What are they going to do?"

"Don't you worry, Sally," Freddie says, putting his arm across my mother's shoulder. She acts as if she doesn't know I am there. People's voices start out on a strident note and stay there. I am shivering slightly. I can't tell whether I'm cold or scared. They bring in a stretcher for my grandfather, whose head is limp and whose hands hang like two wet cloths. I'm pretty sure he's dead. Which makes him tremendously interesting and even a little attractive.

Freddie took me home and Mummy went off with her father to the hospital. The fact that the diagnosis — acute indigestion aggravated by stress and transitory angina — was an anticlimax was not exactly his fault.

My mother put it this way. "He did it on purpose, the old frog." She was glad, I suppose, that he hadn't died then and there, but she saw his performance as running pretty much true to form. Freddie was stuffy compared to my mother. He looked shocked at this but said nothing. It wasn't important enough to make a fuss about. It seems to me that in general Freddie thought very few things were worth making a fuss about, and maybe that's why he and my mother got along so well.

Do you know what a kike is? A kike, according to Otto Kahn, is a Jewish gentleman who has just left the room. The thing about my stepfather was that he almost never left the room. He

had so much money and his family had been in the right places in
New York for so long that people accepted him almost the way
they would a real white man. He was in commerce but book
publishing didn't truly fall in the "business" category. He knew
most of the important artists, writers, musicians personally and
entertained many of them at his house, regularly mixing them up
so the talk would be livelier. The Stern house was a well-known
watering place for people passing through town and looking for
high-class fun. Though not the rowdy sort; if anyone got really
smashed Freddie would ask the hired butler to see the guest to
the door. The fact that Freddie was excluded from membership
in the Union League Club, the Century Association, and the New
York Athletic Club may have bothered him on some very deep
level, but you would never have guessed it from the way he acted.

It was Freddie who determined the course of my life. And yet
I always thought him neutral, a sponge, a receiver rather than a
giver.

2
Getting Things Straight

PEOPLE WHO HAVE BEEN or still are rich never use the word "wealthy." They say "rich." There's no point in not calling a spade a spade.

If you are as rich as Freddie and Marguerite Stern everything in your house is either extremely heavy and substantial — like Shetland wool, solid silver, porterhouse steak — or else fragile, delicate — antique lace, crystal stemware, chocolate soufflé. That's it; there's nothing much in between. No dreck. Or "drecky," as my mother used to say. Dreck is anything made from inferior materials or a combination of two things or something that's made to look like something else such as wood-grained plastic or marbleized asphalt tile. Also books hollowed out and stuffed with a radio, or a plastic toy that falls apart after being played with twice. Dreck is tasteless, not worth the money, tacky. A knife with a handle made from something other than bone or ebony and a pillow stuffed with anything but down is drecky. It was kind of nice the way most things in stores were simply out of the question for my mother.

Whenever Mummy picked up the phone to call Gristede's and chat with her friends the butcher, the grocer, and the cashier, she always, as a matter of course, ordered more than she needed. This was so that if Freddie brought someone home for dinner unexpectedly she — or rather the cook — would not be caught short-

handed. When Kathleen passed the platter of chicken breasts or
lamb chops there was always at least one that went back to the
kitchen, where it was either eaten by the help or served to my
mother for lunch the next day, depending on her schedule. Once
in a while it was chucked out, along with the plate scrapings.

During the war my mother suffered badly. She was like an
addict suffering withdrawal symptoms. She wasn't used to small
portions or large shortages, she was used to gobs of things, lots of
whipped cream, steaks as thick as the Manhattan telephone direc-
tory, sugar to make caramel icing with, a pair of shoes for each
outfit. I have no doubt that she was, in fact, more deprived than
the poor, who were already accustomed to being hungry, or at
least to not having their appetites satisfied. And this, in spite of
the fact that when she felt compelled to, she patronized the black
market and had laid in a healthy supply of canned goods and
staples like rice and sugar just before shortages got beyond the
joke stage.

In our house on Seventy-third Street we had a Degas dancer in
the dining room, an Arp in the foyer, Boucher, Rembrandt,
Fragonard, and Tiepolo drawings along the staircase, a Calder
mobile and a fantastic Braque over the living room fireplace. In
this built-in museum — a regular stop on the college house tour
circuit — I was surrounded by objects both heavy and fragile, by
exquisite taste transformed, via U.S. currency, into furniture and
furnishings, leather, rosewood, marble, antiques of various kinds,
and a kitchen which had made the pages of *Life, Town and
Country,* and *The Saturday Evening Post.* It made me terribly
aware of "things," of possessions, of their care and feeding. I
remember once when I damaged a painting by accidentally
scratching it with a pen, I thought they were going to have me
put away for the rest of my life. You didn't go around touching
things in my house.

The Calder mobile was my favorite. This structure swung

gently from the end of a thin steel wire attached to the ceiling at the top of the stairwell. Its disks were half- and crescent moons, blue, black, and crimson. Every time the front door opened our giant bird flew gently and tamely on its tether above the second-story landing, turning silently on an invisible axis.

The Calder, much to my dismay, went to the Museum of Modern Art. Actually, though grieving, I was mad as hell when I found out because I didn't see why they shouldn't have passed it on to me. After all, they had it in *their* house, why shouldn't I have it in *mine*? I would have been willing to pay personally for copies to hang in permanent collections of museums all over the country, where anyone who wanted to could look at them until closing time. I would have taken good care of the original.

My mother and Freddie produced one child, Roger Lucien Stern, who was born the same year his parents were married, 1942. He might have been an unexpected dividend, but accident or not, his parents treated him like a little prince. He got away with all kinds of things I was never allowed to get away with, because even at the tender age of three there were rules for me not to break. Roger had a nurse, Fräulein Irma Kastern, who made my life more unpleasant than it might have been.

If you think it's strange for a Jewish family to hire a German nurse, you are wrong. The German nurse was as standard a feature in the German-Jewish household as the service entrance. Every once in a while a Swede or a Scot would appear in Central Park rolling the baby carriage or pushing young master on a swing, but mostly there were good sturdy Germans — Krauts, as I thought of them. The echt German nurse went along comfortably with rigorous theories about behavior and health.

When I think of Fräulein Kastern — just plain Fräulein — I think of red rubber enema bags, licorice-flavored laxatives, menstrual cramps, huge feet, and a voice that sounded like a couple of men with drills working on the street outside the house. Fräulein adored Roger with a frank passion, and Roger, who spent more time in her company than in his mother's, adored Fräulein. She slept in his room, like Mary Poppins, behind a portable screen. In every other respect Fräulein was not like Mary Poppins; she was a walking outrage.

I went to the Seeley School every weekday morning unless I could convince them I was sick. Kathleen, the maid, would come into my room, draw the curtains back, shut the window, and announce, "It's seven-thirty, Miss Sally." I don't suppose I bothered to thank her. I would dress quickly, looking in the mirror as little as possible. The sight of my own face caused me more distress than I chose to deal with before breakfast. Then I went down to the dining room where Kathleen would serve me orange juice, eggs, three slices of bacon, toast with marmalade, and milk, except during the war, when I got only one slice of bacon. Before I left the house I would go up to my mother and stepfather's bedroom where Mummy would be having her breakfast off a tray in bed and Freddie, dressed and ready for work, would have his at a table across the room. My mother rarely got up before ten; thank God she didn't have to. After accepting a ritual kiss from her which left me no different post-kiss from pre-kiss — except perhaps the feeling that I had been made to do something which wasn't my choice — I left the house to wait for the Seeley School bus. It was like waiting to walk the plank. In all the years I went there I never missed out on that fresh sweep of dread coming over me every morning like a storm warning. My mother assured me "A Seeley education is your passport to the world, honeybunch, you can go anywhere after you graduate, Wellesley, Vassar, even Bryn Mawr, although I trust no daughter of mine would want to turn herself into a greasy grind." "But I hate it," I'd say. "Nonsense," she'd answer. "How can you hate the Seeley School? I went there. It's a perfectly *mar*velous place, I never had so much fun in my life. You don't hate it, Sally, you just think you do."

"Yes, Mother."

There's no use trying to convince her I ought to switch to another school. Do people jump around from one religion to another? I had figured out what my mother was telling me even though she would have died rather than tell it to me straight: A Jewish girl at the Seeley School has an unrivaled opportunity to mix with the crème de la crème, the families so socially secure that their names don't appear in the papers unless one of their black sheep relations happens to be running for public office. It was Mummy's goal to have me so homogenized and absorbed into the bland cereal of American white Protestant culture that you could not tell me apart from a little Vanderbilt or a medium-sized Whitney. Until I went to live with Sam and Judy London I thought all Jews wanted to be mistaken for gentiles.

There were, in fact, several Jewish girls besides me at the Seeley School, but only a few, scattered judiciously and with a light hand, like the toffee-coated peanuts in a box of Cracker Jack. Well-behaved, straight-haired, blondish, button-nosed ersatz shiksas. We steered clear of each other, careful not to bond.

To be objective and fair, the Seeley School was not a bad school. In many respects it was an admirable school. It sent most of its students on to the Seven Sister Colleges, it made use of the city's museums, and it mounted excellent stage productions, like *Medea* in Greek, *The Magic Flute*, *The Skin of Your Teeth*, and *Caesar and Cleopatra*. It was nice if you could act — I couldn't. It was a decent place; it just wasn't the place for me and that was what my mother would not admit. You don't have to love every minute of every day of every week you spend in an educational plant, but you shouldn't hate it so much you feel like throwing up. The Seeley School was my blacking factory.

My one friend was a girl named Nancy Short. We clung together like two mute orphans thrust into a big noisy family. Nancy was Catholic. There weren't many of her kind either, maybe about five or six to a class, which varied in size from around thirty-five to almost fifty. The year I'm writing about now there were five Catholics and four Jews. Me, Connie Stix, Polly Keyser, and Renata Paul.

My academic performance at school was nothing to write home about. I managed a B-minus average while resisting almost every aspect of the learning process. Languages were especially hard; somehow case endings, irregular verbs, declensions, even simple vocabulary ran from me like a cat from the vet. Math was not only mysterious but ugly and mysterious. Each time I solved a problem in algebra I felt as if I had done the impossible; each problem took a concentrated and major effort. Instead of seeing my teachers as learning aids I saw them as tormentors. I can remember only one or two teachers whom I could talk to; one or two made an impression on me that I could bear to think about in retrospect. It wasn't their fault; it was mine. I daydreamed endlessly. Not very interesting dreams. I thought about how I would like to look if given a chance to have a complete physical overhaul. I thought about my mother, I thought about my father, I set my mother and father in various stances of opposition. My father would always win. It would end with my mother crying and saying she was sorry, she would never do it again. I deliberately repressed all memory of my father being drunk and shouting at her, which was real. I preferred my version, where she was the villain. No wonder I couldn't listen to my teachers. I had three-act melodramas going on inside my head most of the time.

Occasionally I would come out of my stupor and listen to instruction. "*Alors, mes vieux, conjugez 'lire.'*" My God, we're having a quiz. How come everybody but me is writing?

"Salleee, why is it you do not have your paper out?" Mademoiselle Gargin is an ancient lady weighing in at less than one hundred pounds, with hair like steel wool. "Is your hearing deficient this morning? Or perhaps you did not get a proper night's sleep and are dozing at your desk? Come-come-come-come, get out your paper now, *vite, vite, vite,* you are keeping the rest of the class waiting." The blush of shame, the wanting to jump out of the window, taking Mademoiselle Gargin with me. Anyway, I can't conjugate *lire* because I haven't done the homework. She snaps several more irregular verbs at us. I know approximately half the answers — not good enough. Beside me Janet Salisbury is scribbling away fiendishly. What all can she be writing? I look down at my desktop. Years of initials are gouged and smoothed into the wood. B. R., K. M., S. S. Who are they? Did they like this school? Did they do well? Did they have millions of friends? Bet they did. They grew up and married non-Jewish bankers, doctors, and horsemen—half the girls in my class take riding lessons on Saturday mornings, the other half are learning how to be little Sonia Henies. Maybe B. R. is Bunny Rabbit. K. M. is Katharine Mansfield, an unknown writer I have recently discovered on my own. Mademoiselle Gargin is breathing on my shoulder, waiting for me to hand in my paper. How long has she been standing there? "You are asleep in your seat, Sallee," she says. "Do you feel well, would you like to visit the nurse?"

"I'm fine," I tell her. "I'm sorry."

"If you are quite well, then pay attention, if you please. *You* cannot afford to sleep through class." The implication is not lost on me — or on anyone else. I am stared at briefly. The dummy, the dunce. Will she put a huge ice cream cone upside down on my head and make me stand on a high stool?

The next class is Music, taught by the only Jewish teacher in the school, Miss Gisela Bloch, a refugee from Germany. Whoever hired Miss Bloch could not possibly have disregarded the fact that she was a natural victim. She had watery tan eyes on the verge of flooding, and a thin, quavery voice like a melancholic old woman, although she couldn't have been more than forty-two or -three. Miss Bloch didn't know anything about adolescents, about American schools, or about teaching. All she knew was music. She played the cello and when she sat down to play in assembly she spread her legs as if — the story went — she was waiting to be screwed by a hippopotamus.

Miss Bloch had no sense of humor; she couldn't tell the difference between a joke and a stab in the back. When I think of how I sat in her class, hour after music hour, and watched distantly as she was put through the wringer by my classmates, these splendid young girls with beautiful shining straight teeth and lovely warm woolly sweaters and Sunday school diplomas, or whatever they give you from St. James's Episcopal Church on Madison and Seventy-first Street, I have to excoriate myself: I should have stood up and said, "Do it to *me*, I won't mind so much. Don't torture Miss Bloch, she lost her sister and her mother in a concentration camp. She was going to be a concert cellist, and here she is teaching a lot of musical morons and snots who don't know a chord from an arpeggio and couldn't care less." But if she was a natural victim, I was a coward. I could no more have helped her than I could have joined the bullies. I was in the middle, just watching and feeling sick to my stomach.

Whatever Miss Bloch did was compounded by the way she sucked up to Renata Paul. Renata was the daughter of the most famous violinist in America — a refugee who had made good. Renata was so sophisticated that even girls like Molly Sawyer and Katherine Schirmer who had fur coats and went to the theater on opening nights thought she was sophisticated and left her alone. She also knew almost as much about music as Miss Bloch and wasn't very nice to her either, but for other reasons. She probably suspected that Miss Bloch was dying to meet Paul *père*, which was, of course, out of the question.

Buffy Carter starts off this particular session by dropping her pencil at the moment Miss Bloch asks her to define a triad. This is the signal for Tip Browning, the class actress, to begin coughing. Tip's eyes bug out, her face turns crimson. Miss Bloch, deceived, gets flustered and tells Tippy she may be excused to get a drink of water. Stuwie Jones gets permission to help her friend to the water fountain. Another girl insists she must help too. The class is in confusion. Miss Bloch's hands have begun to tremble and flutter. She looks at me, meets nothing encouraging, then to Renata, who is writing something down; Renata is no better than I am. The three girls leave the room. Miss Bloch tries the triad question on Bunny Warner. Bunny pretends to be deaf. "I have a cold in both ears," she explains with a straight face. "The doctor told Mummy I may need an operation." "Oh dear," Miss Bloch murmurs, "you poor child."

Two girls start a discussion which grows in intensity and drowns out Miss Bloch's lecture on the augmented seventh. Totally at a loss, Miss Bloch sends them from the room. They leave, giggling. Miss Bloch is a wreck, I am sick with baffled sympathy.

Caroline Harvey asks a question that has nothing to do with music. Miss Bloch scowls at her. Barby Frick waves her hand back and forth like a drowning swimmer. "Yes, Barbara? What is it? Do you want to be excused?" The teacher's speech is sibilant, clipped. She sounds as if she had learned English only this morning.

"Do you like Frankie, Miss Bloch?"

"I don't know any Frankie, is there a Frankie in this class?"

"Frankie Sinaaaaatra!" Barbara shouts. "Haven't you ever heard of Frankie Sinatra? *We* all think he is a very good singer. You ought to hear him, Miss Bloch, he's div*ine*."

Miss Bloch shakes her head. Her eyes are threatening again. Renata snorts and recrosses her legs. She's the only thirteen-year-old I know who sits with her knees crossed. The rest of us sprawl. Miss Bloch sniffs and takes out a balled white handkerchief. The bullies have triumphed. By now I have so identified with the victim that I cannot look at her. No one learned anything in this class, nobody did anything with music; some girls had a very good time.

Arabella O'Conner had one short arm. It stopped somewhere below the elbow, but since she always wore long-sleeved dresses no one could be quite sure where the arm actually ended. Miss O'Conner taught Latin and was Director of Admissions at the Seeley School. In my whole life I don't remember running up against anyone who had as much bad in her as Miss O'Conner. Being in her class was an education in itself. To begin with, she had absolutely no sympathy with the slow learner. The slow learner was a mile beneath her notice. She would dash through a lesson or a passage like an unarmed Gaul running before Caesar. Miss O'Conner had her favorites and these she frequently manipulated against the rest of us. Her pets were those who had a flair for Latin plus a dash of slavishness. These girls were given the cream of Miss O'Conner's affection — what little there was of it. The rest of us she treated as if we were cats being taught to use the litter box.

Miss O'Conner's least favorite girl was Renata Paul. First of all, because she was, as Oma Lucy would have put it, "an M.O.T." and Miss O'Conner was an anti-Semite. But worse than that, Renata never bothered to disguise what she thought of Miss O'Conner; she didn't even bother to hate her, she merely tolerated her, the way you do a particularly long run of hot weather or rain. Renata didn't have much use for me either. Come to think of it, Renata didn't have much use for anybody at school. She was the kind of child who always seemed to have a bigger, more thrilling home life than anyone else; although school took up most of her waking life, it made a very small dent on her.

This same day Renata asks me, "What are you doing winter vacation?" Her voice is soft and low, modulated like an adult's.

"Nothing much," I answer, wondering if she wants me to ask her the same question back. "What are you doing?"

"I'm going to Cleveland with Ernest and Muriel. Ernest's doing the Brahms there." Ernest and Muriel were Mr. and Mrs. Paul.

"That's nice." Just that morning I have overheard someone saying, "Renata thinks hers is ice cream."

"The Brahms what?"

"The D-minor, of course." She gives me a withering look. It suddenly occurs to me that there isn't a soul at the Seeley School, with the possible exception of Miss Bloch, that Renata can talk to in her own language.

"My father tries to take me along whenever he goes on tour. It's educational for me." Renata was absent from school more than anyone else, yet she never fell behind in her work. She was a superbrain, the kind of person who could solve almost any logical problem and do figures in her head, remember dates and case endings without trying, and synthesize disparate information. She was asked to be a Quiz Kid on the radio, but she declined the honor.

I look up at the wall clock, which has just brought us a minute closer to Latin class. "If Miss O'Conner asks where I am, will you tell her please that I'll be right back. I have to go to the john," Renata says. I nod. Renata was the first girl in our class to start having her periods.

The bell rings, the whole school settles, you can hear chairs scraping in other rooms, doors closing on other floors. Miss O'Conner materializes, my stomach constricts. She is stick-thin and expensively dressed. Miss O'Conner lives with a Seeley family and acts as a sort of housekeeper-nurse for the three children of a divorced woman who always seems to be away on a vacation. I pity the children. The class quiets down. The girls, most of them, have their heads bent like novices at prayer service. Miss O'Conner looks us over. "Where is Renata? Has anyone seen Renata Paul?"

No one has seen her. Tentatively I raise my hand.

"Sally?" Her voice saying my name sends ice water squirting through my blood vessels.

"Renata asked me to tell you she'd be right back." I'm mad at Renata for making me her messenger. I ought to mention that Seeley is the kind of school where you are at your desk when the bell rings. Also you stand up when an adult walks into the room. You do not run in the halls or up and down the stairs. You greet your homeroom teacher each morning with a handshake and say goodbye to her in the same way.

Renata's shadow grays against the pebbled glass of the class-room door. The door opens softly. Renata stands briefly in the doorway, gives Miss O'Conner a look that could be read either as contempt or amusement. In any case, it's not the usual pupil-to-teacher look. Miss O'Conner's little eyes narrow. "Take your seat, Renata, you are two minutes late."

"I'm sorry," Renata says. "I was in the bathroom." A gasp escapes from the seated girls.

Miss O'Conner blanches. Seeley girls do not talk about bath-rooms. "I am marking you tardy," she says, taking up her tardy book and putting a mark in it. "You will stay after school and clean the blackboards on this floor."

Renata does not respond satisfactorily; she takes her seat. "Did you hear what I said?" Twin spots of red appear on Miss O'Con-ner's cheeks.

"I did. I didn't know you were asking me a question."

"That's enough." Miss O'Conner looks as if a chunk of meat is stuck in her throat. Her eyes shoot invisible flames. "Will you young ladies take out your *Gallic Wars* and read to yourselves pages 57 through 59 inclusive and be prepared to answer written questions on the text. You have fifteen minutes." Miss O'Conner slides into the chair behind her desk. Her hand is trembling, maybe her stump is too. I sense that something unusual is about to take place. There is anxiety in the room. It hangs over us like the cloud of smoke in the faculty lounge. I dive into my Caesar and read three pages which are exactly like the preceding three.

For a few minutes the only noise you can hear is a slight shifting in seats, a page turned from time to time, once or twice a sneeze. No one is passing any notes today or sharpening any pencils.

"Renata!" Heads shoot up as if we are all simultaneously elbowed in the ribs. "Renata," Miss O'Conner repeats. "Will you kindly take this book down to Miss Smythe's office. Do you know where Miss Smythe's office is?"

Renata says she knows where it is. She walks up to Miss O'Conner's desk and takes the book from her without touching her fingers. They are both now so mixed up in this thing between them that you can't tell from their faces what's on their minds. If Renata smells a rat she's not letting on.

Miss O'Conner waits for the door to close behind Renata and then she walks to the middle of her room. Behind her on the blackboard are bits and pieces of algebra left over from another class. Her audience is rapt. Miss O'Conner has a fine sense of theater; she knows exactly how long to stand staring at us in this portentous way, with her mouth sucking poison and her good arm ending in a clenched fist. She is the Wicked Witch of the West; I expect her to start cackling.

"Perhaps," she begins in a level voice, "some of you, the more perspicacious among you, may have guessed that I invented that little errand for Renata." She pauses and does something subtle with her body, a shifting, an adjustment that makes her seem more substantial and more ominous. "Under ordinary circumstances," she says, "I disapprove of saying anything behind anyone's back that I would not willingly say to her face. However, I believe these circumstances to be exceptional. What I am about to say to you, young ladies, is for your ears and your ears alone. I trust you not to repeat any of it, and most especially not to Renata herself. Can I trust you all?"

We nod dumbly, riveted. This has got fire drills beat all hollow. It's almost as good as a snow holiday.

"Well, then." Deep breath. "You all know, I'm sure, that Renata Paul is a member of the Jewish race." Oops, my heart begins to thunk against the muscles in my throat. Doesn't she know *I'm* here? I sneak a look at Connie Stix (blank) and at Nancy Short, my best friend (also blank). "And surely you must all be aware of how Adolf Hitler destroyed five and a half million of Renata's people in gas ovens and concentration camps. It was an act, you might say, of genocide, pure and simple. A madman, Hitler, a monster whose crimes make those of Attila the Hun and Ghenghis Khan pale in comparison. The Jews have known little but persecution and suffering since biblical times — the diaspora, the Spanish Inquisition. Think about the notion of the Wandering Jew, homeless and wretched." No one but me seems to mind that Miss O'Conner is laying it on with a trowel. I can feel my cheeks burning. This time I don't dare risk looking at my allies for fear I will start to do something awful like giggle or scream.

"The Jew has always been what you might call a tormented soul, a tormented people, unpopular, forced to flee or hide, excluded, shoved into walled ghettoes. Do you all know what a ghetto is?" No one knows what a ghetto is. Miss O'Conner gives a succinct, historical sketch of the ghetto. "There were many periods when Jews became converted to Christianity in order to avoid torture or death. I cannot say I blame them for this act of self-preservation. I cannot say that I myself would not resort to the same action. In their effort to escape punishment let us hope they found their true Maker.

"The history of the Jewish race" — inexorably, she continues, repeating the same offensive phrases over and over again — "is a classic story of persecution. Nothing, however, matched the diabolical cleverness with which Herr Hitler went about wiping out five and a half million European Jews. His methods were as scientific and efficient as the destruction of the yellow-fever mosquito by Dr. Gorgas. He had the motives of a fiend. Hitler was a Caligula, Caligula *de nos jours*." Miss O'Conner has warmed to her subject. I can't help but admire her skill. I begin to feel anxious about Renata's coming back in the middle of this.

Miss O'Conner is shifting styles. She takes an enormous breath for a small woman and looks at each one of us in turn, as if by staring at us she can pry us open to accept just a little drop more. Her voice is as maternal as she will ever be able to make it. "Now we all have our own private feelings about the people we know — our parents and our parents' friends, our classmates, the people who work for us, oh, the various men and women and girls and boys we are involved with in one way or another. Some of them we are deeply devoted to, some of them we like, and a few we have reservations about. This is one of the facts of life that cannot — and perhaps should not — be altered. We cannot love everyone with equal intensity. We love our fathers more than we love the milkman, we love our sisters more than we love the women who teach us to play the piano. Once in a while we find it hard to admit that we harbor these different feelings, we may even feel ashamed to have feelings we think of as un-Christian. Would it surprise you children to learn that adults, too, have the same 'un-Christian' feelings from time to time?"

This rhetorical device works. Our little thinkers are set in motion: what, grownups hate people? Revelation!

Miss O'Conner nods back at several heads which are nodding in muted agreement. "What I want to impress on you here is that while we can regret having these negative feelings, it is really how we *behave* that matters, how we act toward those very people to whom we feel the least kindly disposed. We are *not* Adolf Hitlers, we are civilized females living in a civilized country. Now I am sure that some of you do not particularly care for Renata. There is about Renata a quality that does not make for immediate or close friendship. Whether this is true because the Jews in America have never quite managed to fit themselves into the mesh of American society — in a sense they are still struggling to survive amid alien corn — or whether she possesses certain traits that are uniquely her own I am certainly not going to attempt to resolve. Whatever the cause, we must not, ever, by our actions or behavior give Renata the slightest reason to feel that she hasn't the right to an equal place in this exceptional school. Renata has a remarkable brain and she works hard. If she is different from the rest of us that is her privilege. Our duty is to adjust to her as far as we can. All of us on the faculty of the Seeley School count on you girls to help make Renata as much a member of the student body as she would like (however slight that may seem to you). There is one final point I want to make before Renata returns and we get back to our Caesars. I want you girls to listen very carefully." Here the voice drops. We all lean forward for the message. "What I am about to say gets at the root of most of the prejudice in the world. It is this: we must not dislike Renata merely because she is a Jew. To do that would be to betray the laws of God and His only Son, Jesus Christ. Remember this well: the Jews did *not* kill our Lord, it was the Romans who murdered Him, Pontius Pilate was a *Roman* judge, not a Jew. And it is on *his* head that the ultimate sin lies." Miss O'Conner ends with head bowed.

For several minutes we sit there, paralyzed by all the paradoxes. Renata, an oddity before Miss O'Conner's sermon, takes on a new glamour. She is not a Christ-killer but something weird, pitiful and stubborn. Whatever Miss O'Conner set out to do, she has made Renata into a blazing star.

Renata comes back. We all act as if nothing has happened. I am in a frenzy of guilt and shame. Should I tell Renata? Damned if I will, I don't even like her, and not because she's a Jew, certainly not that. Am I not a Jew myself? Well, not as much as she is, only half a Jew. Oma Lucy says half is as good as whole. "Hitler knew that. No use pretending to be what you ain't."

3

Disguises

THE YEAR the U.S. minimum wage was approximately sixty cents an hour — 1947 — my allowance was raised to fifty-five cents a week. The concept of my getting an allowance was a farce because if I wanted anything, all I had to do was ask for it. There were some things I was forbidden on principle, such as Batman comics (I went to Nancy's to read my comics), certain varieties of dreck candy, like Mars bars and Babe Ruths (I went to Nancy's to eat my candy; I'd give her the money in school, she'd buy, I'd go to her place), but almost everything else was mine for the asking. I had drawers full of sweaters, button-downs, cashmere pullovers, tennis sweaters, short-sleeved, long-sleeved. I had six skirts, four party dresses, three bathrobes — one for winter, one for summer, one for emergencies — four coats, an entire drawer of scarves. My room was like a specialty shop for overweight teen-aged girls.

Clothes I could have by the trunkful, trips to Radio City Music Hall to see Deanna Durbin or Walt Disney, books, records, you name it. It's hard for me to remember just what I did spend my allowance on.

Lucy Stern, Freddie's mother, insisted that I call her Oma even though we were not related. Oma Lucy was my favorite female except for Nancy.

Oma Lucy often seemed to forget that I was a child; there was something wonderfully insinuating about her conversation — which she pronounced converzation. She was, I suppose, a gentle bitch, and it was this that I responded to; if she thought someone was awful she'd say so and not hide behind euphemisms and excuses. She had opinions the way a stray dog has fleas. These opinions she expected me to buy wholesale.

Oma Lucy had been married to a founder of one of New York's biggest and best department stores; commerce, yes, but Oma's heart was in music. She had had a salon of a modest sort for musicians. She name-dropped Jascha, Artur, Mischa, Leopold, Ignatz, and Pablo the way my stepfather dropped Wystan, Tom, and Christopher. She dragged me to concerts and operas. (She insisted that we go properly, at night, over my mother's objections that it was a "school night, Sally needs ten hours' sleep." "Nonsense," Oma Lucy would say. "She needs to hear *Aïda* with Pinza more.") Sometimes it was so boring and noisy that I would fall asleep during a performance; then Oma would prod me awake with an elbow. She reeked of lavender water, which was her favorite and sole scent. You could always tell when Oma Lucy had been somewhere because she left behind her such a powerful, flowery odor. Oma Lucy "exposed" me, as they say, to so much music that I began to like it and look forward to it. It was Oma who found Miss Crabtree, my piano teacher, a lady who came to our house every Wednesday afternoon and who insisted I practice an hour a day even though I had no gift for the piano. Oma claimed that unless music were a part of your life you could not call yourself a whole person. She knew that Renata Paul was my classmate and could not understand why we were not friends. One of her opinions was that music creates the same kind of bond between people that sex does. Even if you were entirely different kinds of people and only played a few hours a day, if you played at all, that made you soulmates.

Oma Lucy's cavernous apartment was so high above sea level you couldn't hear traffic noises. Before this, she and her husband and only son lived in a stone fortress in the fifties, also on Fifth Avenue. The fortress had since been turned into a school for dumb rich girls who couldn't get into Miss Hewitt's or Seeley. She had some regrets about moving out, although she told me once that living there was like living in the Museum of Natural History. "If I put something down on a table, it might be weeks before I found it again."

Oma Lucy had a faithful retainer named Jonathan. Jonathan was the color of the hot chocolate you got at Gay Blades Ice Skating Rink, without the whipped cream. I had been assured that Jonathan was a full-blooded Indian from the American plains but I never wholly believed it; to me he looked like an ordinary Negro. He had a flat Negro nose and kinky Negro hair. I couldn't understand this discrepancy but I wasn't nervy enough to ask. Jonathan didn't wear sneakers, but he walked as if he did. He was always coming up in back of you like a thief in the night. He had the creamiest voice I've ever heard in a human being.

I always dressed to the teeth when I went to Oma Lucy's for lunch and she always laid on a spread as if I were a princess. We did this out of habit and because it was our way of trying to please each other. She gave me things to eat that Mummy thought unsuitable for a child. Things like lobster bisque (too rich), artichokes (too sophisticated), squab stuffed with wild rice (too extravagant), asparagus Hollandaise (nothing wrong with that), linzer torte (too rich), and strawberries out of season (too quixotic). Fish she ordered from Wynn and Treanor, a store she waggishly called "Tiffany-by-the-sea," and the meat from Shaffer's, the world's most expensive butcher. Oma Lucy said that sometimes you do get what you pay for and at Shaffer's you did. Oma Lucy indulged her own fussiness.

I am greeted by the elevator man in Oma's building.

"Good day, Miss, coming to see your grandmother again?"

"She's not my grandmother, she's my step-grandmother."

"Oh, I see, Miss," he nods. He eases the control handle around. We slide to a soft stop. "Well, here we are again, fourteenth floor and Grandmama's house. Hee-hee." The door slips open noiselessly. I stand in the vestibule. There is only one other apartment on the floor. They have an umbrella stand outside their door, choking with umbrellas. I ring the bell to 14–A.

Jonathan opens the door so fast he makes me jump. "Good day, Miss Sally," the Negro-Indian says. He is wearing his uniform: black serge trousers, starched white shirt, black bow tie, stiff white cotton jacket cut like J. Press. "May I take your coat?"

I slip out of my coat with Jonathan's help and thank him. "Where's Mrs. Stern?"

"Your grandmother is waiting for you in the library, Miss Sally."

The library is the reliquary. Mrs. Stern's favorite possessions from the past are crammed into this room. It is her personal museum. The rest of her usable stuff lies in airtight, waterproof, double insulated vaults in the Lincoln Storage Warehouse. Shards of a life of ease and affluence unaffected by the whimsical ups and downs of the U.S. economy are here in abundance. There are bits of wine-colored Viennese glass, miniature furniture in bonelike porcelain, silver cheese and cake knives with ivory handles too fragile to use, ecru lace antimacassars, cloisonné picture frames enclosing relatives dead and gone in quaint but stout costumes (there are literally hundreds of them), Lalique vases with dust-like finish. Her furniture was powerful — there wasn't a spindly arm or leg in the place; everything was on a heroic scale, from the Steinway concert grand to huge armchairs with arms as wide as a horse's back, sofas that could accommodate six people side by side, and massive refectory tables with Chinese lamps the size of ashcans.

Whenever I enter Oma's apartment I become Alice in her small phase or Gulliver in Brobdingnag.

Oma Lucy was built on a small scale (she wore size three shoes), but she didn't seem out of place, although the armchairs swallowed her. She dressed like a character. The clothes she wore in the house went clear to the floor and were cut on the bias so that they took the shape of her body, like the clothes Ginger Rogers wore in her Fred Astaire movies — except that Oma's weren't gaudy. She favored the color rose — most of her dresses and coats were rose-colored, a shade flattering to people with gray hair. She usually wore a little hat and carried a purse around, even when she had no plans to leave the apartment. This getup was as much her uniform as Jonathan's black pants and white jacket. When we went to a restaurant together, or a concert, Oma wore street-length dresses, always a little longer than was fashionable. She explained why she made this concession. "I don't want people to think I'm hopelessly old-fashioned. When I was a girl, everyone wore ankle-length dresses all the time. The calf was as hidden as the bosom."

I go over and kiss Oma's cheek. It smells of lavender and feels faintly powdery, dry but smooth. She has her hair done by Elizabeth Arden; sometimes she bumps into Mummy there and they have a little chat. I don't think Oma Lucy thinks all that much of my mother although she's grateful her son didn't marry something worse, like a real playgirl or an ugly duckling. Oma says that ugly women are a blight on the face of the earth.

"Have you read this, my dear?" She thrusts a leather-bound book at me and advises me that if I want to be a worthwhile person, I must read Jane Austen, that no woman writing since has had Jane's this and Jane's that, and her world view and her wit and sense and so on and so forth. Oma's literary lecture lasts a full five minutes during which I nod obediently.

"Come, come, sit down here by me and tell me what you have

been up to. Did you get to that Lehmann recital I told you about?"

"No," I say. "Mummy was too busy."

"That's a pity," she says. "Your mother doesn't care much for music. That's the trouble — you can't expect a child to grow up appreciating music if her family prefers the wrong Strauss."

Jonathan sneaks up on us balancing on his pink palm a large silver tray with two glasses on it, one a crystal wine glass filled with sherry and the other a miniature tumbler of V-8 cocktail. He passes the tray to Oma, bending low from the hips. "Thank you, Jonathan," she says. "Take some of these cheese biscuits, Sally. They're from Fortnum's. Not too sweet. Isn't it a pleasure to have these little luxuries again?" Oma takes a sip; her little finger is extended and crooked like a C.

I know she expects me to tell her what piece I have been given by Miss Crabtree. Later she may ask me to play it for her on the Steinway, from memory.

We get the required topics out of the way quickly. "I understand, my dear, that your father is thinking of remarrying."

"What?"

"That's no surprise, is it?"

"I didn't know," I say, barely able to form the words.

"I don't know why your mother doesn't tell you the facts of life," she says, glad to get something current on my old lady. "I believe she thinks there are two mutually exclusive classes of subject matter, one for the adult and one for the child."

I'm not interested in Oma's opinions or theories at the moment; I am too upset about Daddy. Why, if it comes to that, hasn't *he* told me?

"How do you know?" I ask.

"Alfred told me last night on the phone. There's been no formal announcement as yet but my understanding is that your father is engaged to a woman named Lorna Emerson, a young woman some years his junior."

Nancy and I are always talking about middle-aged men who marry their secretaries. We think of these types as dirty old men. I don't want to believe a word of what I'm hearing, yet it has, somehow, the sound of truth.

"That's awful," I murmur. "I mean, I wish he'd told me himself."

"Perhaps he's tried," Oma Lucy says. "Tell me, do you like Schnitzel à la Holstein, because that's what I've ordered for our luncheon."

"I don't know," I say. "What is it?"

"Well, don't tell anyone, but it's really just breaded veal cutlet. I suppose your mother thinks fried food is indigestible for children?"

"She says broiled or boiled is better for you." I say. My mind is not on food, for once. I want to go straight to the telephone and call my father and ask him what this is all about. Daddy has never betrayed me before.

We are summoned to lunch. Oma takes my arm. Jonathan pushes her chair up to the table, impeccably laid with linen and silver. Between us sits a silver plate under six pieces of homemade melba toast.

Oma wants to talk about Mummy: what time she gets up in the morning, how many times a week she goes out for dinner, what she's taught me about "morality."

"She's never used that word," I tell Oma Lucy.

"I daresay," Oma snaps. "Today we think young people simply absorb standards and ideals by osmosis. It's not so; young people must have it spelled out, they must be taught. My husband taught your stepfather. If Alfred were your real father, he would teach you. It's his ambiguous role, adoption notwithstanding, I'm certain, that makes him reticent. I can't imagine why your mother does not take a more active role in forming your character. I don't suppose she does much about your little brother, either?"

"They spoil him," I say, delighted at this chance to complain about the unfair treatment I receive at home.

"I am quite aware of that," she says matter-of-factly. "I have brought it up once or twice myself. They do not choose to listen, so there's little I can do. I do *not* want to cast myself in the role of interfering mother-in-law. That is the *last thing* in the world I want. I want your mother to feel I am her friend, not her enemy."

For a skinny woman, Oma Lucy takes in more food than any-one I've ever seen. She's helped herself to a second cutlet and has sent Jonathan out for more toast. I wonder how and where she burns away the calories that seem to be holding an everlasting national convention inside my own body.

"You are excessively fond of your father, aren't you, my dear?"

"Not excessively," I say. "I just love him. He's my father."

"I didn't mean to be critical," Oma says quickly. "I merely meant that you were extremely fond of him. There's nothing wrong with that, child."

Well, if there's nothing wrong with it, I tell her silently, why did you say it in that funny way. Why do you make me feel bad?

"My, aren't these avocados delicious," Oma says. "Good heavens, listen to me beating around the bush. I simply cannot imagine what it's like to be the issue of a mixed marriage. You've heard me say often enough, don't try to be what you ain't. Still, it must be quite difficult for you, with a father like yours. He does belong to every club in the book. He's a character out of Marquand or Edith Wharton. Quite frankly, I don't know why your mother married him in the first place; Alfred is patently more suitable for her." She smiles at this as if to tell me she knows she's exaggerating. "I would very much like to know something about which you don't have to tell me if you don't feel like it, my dear. My natural curiosity appears to have got the better of my natural tact. Don't you ever feel as if you were being pulled two ways at once — in spite of what I've told you about Jewish blood?"

"Well . . . yes. Sometimes I feel one way, and sometimes the other."

"Never both at once?"

I shake my head. "That would be like being in love with two men at the same time."

"Not so rare an occurrence as you might think," she says. "But never mind about that. I'm afraid I've had rather a shock today. You don't mind if I talk about myself for a moment, do you? I do it so seldom."

I nod noncommittally. She's going to tell me about someone's lingering death or bankruptcy or something else I'm too young to hear. Oma Lucy makes no distinction between adult and child, a change from home where I'm lumped in with my six-year-old brother who goes to bed at seven-thirty and isn't allowed to eat nuts or anything cooked with wine.

"My niece Virginia, you know her, she's the one who has all her clothes made for her by that anti-Semite Mainbocher. I daresay his taste is excellent, but even so one ought to have a certain amount of pride about these things. I will *never* hear that man Gieseking play again so long as I live; imagine his performing for Hitler. It's a wonder he's running around giving concerts in any country at all. The same goes for Schwartzkopf and that clown Chevalier, Axis collaborators, every one of them. Is the artist exempt from the same sort of scrutiny we give our politicians and soldiers? Ah, it would seem so." Oma makes a sour-lime face. "Where was I?"

"Your niece . . ."

"Quite right! You're a good girl to remember. My niece Virginia has managed to elude herself, so to speak." Jonathan comes in and replaces the salad course with a lemon soufflé as light as spun sugar. I taste it; how can anybody cook anything so good? I wish I could. At home I am denied access to any part of the kitchen except the icebox. Neither the cook nor Mummy sees any reason to teach me to do what they do. "Do you realize, child, that there are Jewish women in this city who will go to any length to hide behind one disguise or another? They all end up nameless, faceless, and wretched. They are ersatz gentiles and no longer Jews. They are nothing. They are like a piece of that awful cotton bread they're selling these days, with no taste and no texture and no nutrients. Poo-ee." She says this last word as if she were smelling dog-do. "My pretty empty-headed niece Virginia, who went to Ethical Culture like her brothers and sisters and attended services all during her childhood and went out with nice Jewish boys in high school and college — well, you know of course that she married Jim Fisk who is about as much a Jew as your father and I must say a great deal less simpatico. Well, my dear, she has got herself into the Foxglove Club and at the same time into the congregation of St. James's Episcopal whatnot on Madison Avenue. She's been boasting about it. Can you imagine — *boasting?* If I were her mother, I would tell her exactly what I think of her — thirty-three years old or not. She's a disgrace. I'm not sure I can bring myself to have her in my house again."

I can't see where niece Virginia has committed such an awful crime. If you want to be in the middle of things instead of always at the side or underneath I can't see why you shouldn't. What's it to Oma if Virginia Fisk says her prayers at St. James's instead of at Temple Joshu-a.

"If there is one thing I find intolerable it is disguise. I cannot abide disguise. That is why I could never really enjoy *Remembrance of Things Past* — so much camouflage."

She's losing me with her allusions to books I haven't read and people I hardly know. Besides, I am so distracted by the news about my father that I can't concentrate on her problems. How *could* my father go down to the end of the town without consulting me?

I sit silent while Oma takes angry sips of black coffee with a spoonful of whipped cream lolling on its surface.

Oma is lost in her outrage. I've never seen her so ruffled before. She acts as if her niece has joined St. James's as a deliberate affront to Lucy Stern. I decide to change the topic — maybe I can make her feel better.

"Oma, do you know Freddie's partner, Sam London?"

"I wasn't aware that Alfred had a partner," she says, alert once more.

"I guess I didn't mean partner, really," I tell her. "He's a sort of silent partner. Mummy says he's Freddie's what-was-the-name — Svengali or something like that. He doesn't even live here, he lives near Boston. He's a college teacher. They met during the war."

"You don't say," Oma answers. "Tell me more, Sally."

"Well, Freddie talks to him on the phone almost every night, long distance. He isn't like Mummy's and Freddie's other friends. He dresses differently and he has an accent."

"What sort of accent?"

"Well, Freddie says it's a Boston accent."

"I thought you were going to tell me he had a foreign accent. You know, like little Mrs. Nussbaum on that radio program."

"The Fred Allen show?"

"That's right. I listen to it every once in a while. I *enjoy* it."

"Not at all like Mrs. Nussbaum. He says 'peppa' for pepper and 'idear' for idea. Like that."

"Why did you ask me if I knew Mr. London?" Oma says. "I think we should go into the other room. Jonathan would like to clear." She gets up. In the fluid way she rises I have the impression that age hasn't done anything very bad to her body. She moves like someone who once danced or did something else graceful. My mother has pronounced her a very good-looking woman for a woman her age.

"I don't really know why I asked you except that Mummy doesn't seem to like him very much. That's putting it mildly. If Mr. London was a woman I'd think that my mother was jealous of him. You know, like 'the other woman.' "

"You've been going to too many movies, young lady. Too many movies and not enough concerts."

"No." I don't mind contradicting Oma because she doesn't seem to mind. "Mummy practically said so herself. She said 'Freddie acts as if he were having an affair' with Mr. London."

"*Tiens!*"

"But it's not like that. I mean Mr. London and Freddie . . ." I blush pink.

"Are not homosexual, is that what you're driving at? Goodness, child, it never occurred to me. I think I know my own son better than that." Her eyes are neutral and I can't tell whether or not I have overstepped the line.

Oh, Jesus Christ, how did we ever get into this? "I didn't mean that. I meant that my mother thinks that he is too important to Freddie. Oh, I don't know what I'm talking about, really. It's just that they so seldom have an argument, but when they do it's usually about Mr. London, and I thought maybe you could tell me why."

"It's quite obvious you know more about this than I do. Alfred doesn't talk shop to me, although I must say I would rather hear about his business than his health. My son, as you must have gathered, is something of a hypochondriac. When Alfred was a little boy he used to tell me over and over again that he would never live to see forty-five. I don't know where he picked up such morbid ideas — it certainly wasn't from me. The Sterns are notoriously long-lived and so are the Lowenthals. Only his poor father didn't die in bed, as you know." Oma's husband — as I knew — had died of blood poisoning from a pimple on the side of his nose. An ignominious end, as they said in the kind of books I liked to read.

It's true that Freddie is always taking precautionary measures against sickness and germs. Not so an outsider would think he was a nut — no handkerchiefs over doorknobs and not talking into unsterilized telephones, but things like not drinking out of public fountains, not going to movies or the theater during polio season, having hay fever shots and cold shots and a lot of other optional immunizations. He is a great believer in the yearly checkup and the biannual visit to the dentist. He won't drink out of a glass anyone else has used, not even his wife, and when Roger puts something in his mouth that has been on the floor, Freddie takes it away from him.

"Tell me more about Mr. London's background — curious that I've only heard his name once or twice. Curious, if he dominates Alfred's life, as you say he does." I think it's pretty curious myself. The fact that Freddie doesn't tell his mother about the things that are most important to him strikes me as the same kind of thing that is now going on between me and my father.

"I wish I could," I tell my nongrandmother. "All I know is that Mummy considers him, well, how can I say it without sounding like a snob . . . not in her social class or something like that. I think his parents came here from Russia."

"Dear, dear," Oma says.

"What's wrong with that?"

"Nothing wrong, just rather unusual." I sense from the way she answers that Oma Lucy would rather not get into this. Her prejudice is sticking out a mile. It's almost as if she'd opened up her dress and showed me her bare skin and all her equipment which, being sixty-plus years old, is not all that attractive.

Both of us now have noses out of joint. We do a little obligatory tour of the living room. All over the piano, like birds on a
telephone wire, are signed pictures of her beloved friends, the
famous violinists and pianists and conductors who used to flock
to her house and some still do. We say hello to Mischa and Sacha.
We blow a kiss to Leopold and Lilly. Oma Lucy sits down at the
piano and plays a Chopin nocturne, urgently, with a slight trem-
ulo. She asks me to play. It's a Bach Invention and I muff it
sufficiently to make her frown. This is not one of our memorably
good times together. Still, I feel sorry for Oma Lucy. I begin to
see that what people say to you can make you feel worse than
what they do to you.

I kiss Oma goodbye. She reminds me of the midweek concert
we are going to. "Please be waiting downstairs for me promptly
at seven forty-five. I want to see the audience come in." I assure
her I'll be there. I'm hardly ever late; Mummy says it's terribly
rude to keep people waiting, especially older people.

When I get home the house is quiet. I'm in an agony of impatience. I've got to find out about my father. I'm reluctant to call
him now: suppose it's not true? My mother, Kathleen tells me, is
out to lunch with her bosom pal Valery Gibson, née Velma
Greenberg, the chanteuse who sings at the Plaza and the Maison-
ette. I don't like Velma because she has a fake laugh and always
stands on her tiptoes. Freddie is away for the afternoon. Boston?
"I think so, Miss. Your mother said he would be home in time for
dinner. They are having a party."

"Another one? What's for dinner?"

"Chicken fricassee for you, Miss, and your baby brother."

"What are the grownups having?"

"Veal birds. Your mum's going to cook."

"Natch," I tell her. I'm tired of having the baby menu. I'm
thirteen, for Christ's sake.

"Did you get your letter, Miss?"

"What letter?"

"I put it on the hall table for you, Miss Sally."

I gallop out to the hall and there's the envelope, cleverly hidden under the evening *Sun*. I curse Kathleen, who always hides my things. I rip open the envelope. It's from Daddy. Here is how it goes:

My dearest little Princess—

It seems an age since I wrote you last. You are my favorite correspondent and there's simply no excuse for my letting so much time go by between letters. Mea Culpa.

What's he talking about? I got a letter from him not six days ago. He's always writing and calling me up. But not seeing me, because he's not allowed to do that.

But I think that after you read this you will understand and forgive me; things have been happening at such a fast clip that I've hardly had time to breathe, let alone sit down and write to my favorite little girl. Here's all the news, but not necessarily in order of importance.

1. You'll be pleased to hear that your father and his old buddy Skitch Bond won the men's doubles at the Club. Not bad for an old man of forty-one. We're sharing the trophy. Six months in his house, six in mine. Rather like *our* little arrangement, though not so lopsided.

Daddy is referring to my two months a year with him at his house in Princeton, En-Jay.

2. Your father has finally got himself hooked again after all these years. The lovely lady's name is Lorna Emerson (no relation to the essayist). She's twenty-six but looks eighteen and she plays tennis like a man. As a matter of fact, I met her on the courts. Her backhand could knock a man's eye out. My sweet selfless girl works three days a week in New York Hospital on the pediatrics floor. She adores kids and wants loads and loads of them. I just know you two will take to each other — everybody she meets loves her on first sight. My fiancée — you'll see the announcement in Sunday's papers — comes from Oak Park, Illinois, and she's still somewhat timid about the Big

City. You and I will have to give her our special Sanderson tour of the high points one of these days. We plan to have a quiet wedding, only family and a few friends. Of course you'll be there — with bells on. We haven't named the day yet; we both feel there's no special hurry. It will probably be some time in the spring. I'm going to get you two together as soon as is humanly possible.

3. This is not the best news in the world. I have to go into Lenox Hill next week for a few tests. It's nothing serious but I'll have to stay there a couple of nights. Will you please ask your mother to relax her iron-clad rules just this once and allow you to come and visit me at the hospital? Even *she* can't be so cold-hearted as to refuse.

Until I see you my sweet darling girl, be good, get enough sleep, and practice that forehand!

With love and an ocean of kisses from your devoted

Daddy

Inside the letter is a new ten-dollar bill.

I am too upset to appreciate the gift. I don't know what to concentrate on first: the ominous-sounding tests or verification of Oma's sick-making news. I have to sit down. My legs have suddenly gone limp. I want desperately to talk to my mother. Where the hell is she? It's past three and she's not home yet. She's probably decimating the custom department of Bergdorf's. I pace the various floors of our house, look in on Roger sitting on the immense lap of his nurse, being read to from a book of morbid German fairy tales.

Fräulein Kastern tells me I better not stick around because Roger has a bad cold and may be catching. I take the hint.

I speak to Nancy briefly on the telephone, but I hear her mother ordering her to stop talking and get busy cleaning her room; Nancy's mother has a big thing about Nancy cleaning and cooking and so on. It's because she's Catholic and has strong feelings about the virtues of housework. Nancy is a natural slob which makes this very hard on her, but we live in an age where you don't defy your mother's orders. Nancy has assured me that when she grows up and has children she will never make them clean their rooms.

I have the opposite problem: I have begged and pleaded with Mummy to let me take care of my own room because Kathleen has this compulsion to hide my things. She's always moving the box of my father's letters from one location to another and misplacing precious objects on purpose. I know she does it but I can't prove it, and of course Mummy won't believe me. Nor will my mother let me assume responsibility for my own room. "Kathleen is paid for cleaning your room, and that's what she must do." I tell my mother I *like* to run the vacuum cleaner. "And dust? and wash the windows and change the bed every week and clean out the closet, wipe down the walls, shake out the rug? No, Sally, it's a full-time job, you have your homework and your practicing, and besides Kathleen is a professional. I think — I really believe — she would be hurt if I asked her to stop."

"Oh Mummy . . ." I know she's lying through her teeth.

I can't win. It seems I don't ever win. I wish I lived with Nancy's mother. No, I don't either, because I'd have to go to Mass every Sunday and wear a hat and pretend there was no such thing as a boy. At nineteen, Nancy's sister Dorothy still has to come home from a date by eleven-thirty and then take a bath in live steam.

"Yoo-hoo, I'm ho-ome." My mother's voice comes floating up the stairs. I'm sitting on her satin bedspread using her telephone. I jump up. She doesn't like me to sit on her bed when it's made and I don't like to sit on it when it's not.

"Bye, Nancy, speak to you tomorrow," I say, and run out to meet my mother. Her face is as beautiful as usual, although she's a little flushed. The two sides of her face match perfectly — even her hair is alike on both sides of her head, which doesn't happen very often. My mother looks as if someone with a symmetrical imagination had invented her.

"Hi ho, darling," she calls up on seeing me. "I've been celebrating your father's engagement. Oops, I guess I forgot to tell you."

"It's okay, I know. He wrote me."

My mother hasn't got a drinking problem — I think she was permanently turned against alcohol by my father's excesses — but she looks as if she'd had at least a couple of martinis before lunch. *Celebrating.*

"Don't look so down in the mouth, pet," she says to me. "Your father's got himself a nice clean little Junior Leaguer from Chicago. She's got the proper pedigree and I understand she plays a mean game of tennis. Of course, she's about twenty years younger than his nibs, but so what? If that's what she wants . . ." My mother smells like Femme, the only perfume she ever wears. She buys it in eight-ounce bottles. Whenever I smell that perfume now I feel dizzy. I wish I didn't ever have to smell it again — it reminds me of her and of my sadness, which I sometimes forget.

"Not twenty, only fifteen years," I say through my teeth. Mummy usually refers to her ex-husband as *le cochon.*

"I won't quibble about five years," she says airily. "Have it your own way."

"It's not my way," I say, coming to a boil. "It's the way it *is.* *He's* forty-one and *she's* twenty-six. That's fifteen years, not twenty."

"Sally, you'll be the death of me." She sighs as if I were just *too* much. She pulls her hat off and throws it on the bed. I've followed her into the bedroom. Though I can't stand about half of her mannerisms, a lot of which she drops when there's nobody but me around, I'm fascinated by the way she moves, by her nineteen-year-old figure, by her corporeal perfection. I am her, perverted: everything that's beautiful on her is skewed on me, I go in where she goes out and vice versa, I am rough where she is smooth, I am dull where she sparkles.

"Of course," she babbles at me from the bathroom over the noise of sink water. "Of course I don't think your father *ought* to be married. Some men make good husbands and others are rotten at it. He prefers his booze and his manly pride to whatever feelings may lurk deep in the heart of a female — and little Miss Emerson will find this out sooner or later. He shouldn't be asked to compromise or accommodate — it's too much for him. No, I see your father as the ideal extra man at a stuffy dinner party. His chitchat is quite good and he knows his wines."

"*Don't, Mummy*." Each time she goes for Daddy's jugular I want to go for hers.

"Sorry, pet. I forgot how touchy you were on that subject. How was lunch with *la belle mère*, by the way? What abomination did she feed you?"

"It was very good, Schnitzel something." My mother raises her eyebrows but says nothing. "She was mad at her niece Virginia Fisk because Virginia had got herself into some fancy non-Jewish club and then joined St. James's Episcopal Church. Oma doesn't think she ought to do things like that. She was very angry. She kept talking about people who try to disguise themselves. I couldn't understand why it bothered her so much."

"Oma Lucy has very firm opinions about 'passing.' She thinks it's a sin. It's her hobbyhorse, dear. Of course she's the ultimate snob herself. Did you know that when she refers to any Jew who isn't the acceptable kind — not German or Spanish — she always uses the word *little* in front of their name. Little Mrs. Steinberg, little Mrs. Epstein. It's a dead giveaway. I don't think she's aware she does it. Oh, she'd be horrified to hear what I'm telling you. And don't you go repeating it back to her either."

"Of course I won't."

"Well, I can't be too careful. I don't want to get on the wrong side of Lucy. There's no point in it. She's a pretty good sort and she's got taste and she's not depressed all the time like some women her age who have nothing better to do than play bridge and get their hair done. She likes you, doesn't she?"

"Yes, Mother, is that so cuckoo?"

"Oh Sally, do go away, you're really impossible this afternoon. Go away and let me nap. There's a mob coming and I've still got to cook the dinner. By the way, what club was it?"

I tell her the name.

"Jesus," says my mother, collapsing on her bed. "I wonder how she did it."

4

Wising Up

"NO, DARLING, people like your father don't get cancer," my mother says to me. "Their livers rot or they get gout or ulcers. Never cancer. Cancer is what people destined for tragedy get." My mother did a brief stint on a woman's magazine as assistant to the beauty editor; she came away with a head full of loony ideas.

"That doesn't make any sense," I say, vaguely relieved anyway. I thrived on superstition, so long as it went my way.

"Maybe not," Mummy tells me. "But that's the way it usually happens. If your father were seriously ill, I would know about it. Donald Snyder would have told me, he's such a ghoul." Mr. Snyder was Mummy's lawyer; he got her her divorce mostly on her terms. "What he might be is seriously ill in the head for thinking of marrying again, but we've been over that ground, haven't we?"

I'm convinced they're lying to me about Daddy. I'm afraid of doctors and hospitals, not that I've had that much experience. My appendix came out when I was six, which was no picnic, but I don't remember it well enough to account for my being as frightened as I am. The smell of hospital makes me sick to my stomach.

I excuse myself from the table, though I haven't finished my dinner, and go upstairs to my room on the third floor and shut the door. I have homework in French, math, and science. I turn on the radio. I live inside my radio. I know just what Fibber McGee's kitchen looks like; I can see the lines on Lamont Cranston's face and the crease in Mr. District Attorney's trousers. I can smell the beer in Duffy's Tavern. Sometimes the people who speak to me in the dark as I'm lying in bed are more alive than my own mother and father. Certainly more real than most of the teachers and the girls I go to school with. I'm listening to Archie right now. Fräulein barges in without knocking although I've asked her a thousand times to knock before she barges.

"Are you doing your homework, young lady? Your mama says to make sure."

Fräulein Kastern's not my nurse, she's Roger's. Technically she has no jurisdiction over me, but she's a busybody and she can't keep her nose out of my business. I can't stand her. I think my revulsion started the day I went into the bathroom we share and saw her corset with its laces like a swarm of pink intestinal worms, hanging on the towel rack, drying, dripping all over the bathroom tiles. Whenever Fräulein has her period we all know about it because she walks around with a hot water bottle belted to her midsection under her uniform. She has an amalgamated smell: part underarm odor, part female, part sweaty shoes, part Germanness. Even Mummy says she smells. I can't understand why my mother doesn't invent some tactful way to tell her for Christ's sake use some Odorono.

Fräulein has a pure German accent. She sounds like a Nazi villain in the movies. When she walks in the house she is the opposite of Jonathan. She sounds like a battalion of paratroopers. Altogether there isn't an ounce of sensitivity, grace, passivity, or doubt in Fräulein's hefty body. Still, Roger loves her passionately.

Fräulein acts as if my mother were the Grand Duchess of something or other. She says things like, "How lovely Madame's

hair looks today" and "Oh, isn't Madame shust like a young girl."
It makes me want to puke. Still, she's devoted to Roger, as if he
were her own son. I don't know what she would do if anything
happened to him. This is not a subject I'm apt to lose much sleep
over; actually, I think Roger and Fräulein Kastern deserve each
other.

Fräulein asks me a second time about my homework. I tell her
I've finished it and she seems willing to believe me. "And please
don't come in again without knocking."

"What are you hiding, young lady?" she says in a voice coated
with German chocolate.

I turn self-conscious and pull my bathrobe tight over my
minuscule breasts. Fräulein hasn't missed this gesture and smiles
at me knowingly. "You have got nothing to hide *there*," she
says.

Silently I consign her to German hell. "Please, Fräulein, go
away and let me go to sleep. I'm tired. I'm going to turn out the
light now."

"*Guten Abend*," she tells me. "I wish you pleasant dreams in
spite of your saying so rude things to me. I am surprised you two
children come from the same mother."

I don't know why she hates me so much. It hurts my feelings
to see her face go sour every time she looks at me. It never
occurred to me that I might have been part of the trouble; I don't
think I have ever said anything nice to Fräulein Kastern.

The weirdest thing happened. I couldn't understand it and neither could my mother. Freddie somehow got it into his head that
he ought to make the Orange Club accept Sam London as a
nonresident member. This was comparable to placing Mabel
Mercer on the board of U.S. Steel. I'm not exaggerating — no
one is as "exclusive" as a Jew who assumes he's at the top. He's a
much more zealous excluder than his non-Jewish counterpart.
That's why Freddie got so urgent. It never bothered him that

maybe Sam London didn't *want* to be a member of the Orange Club, resident or nonresident, absent, present, permanent or temporary.

Freddie would say to my mother, "In your book the world stays frozen in the last century. That's how it ought to be. Am I right? Isn't that the way you feel?"

And Mummy would answer, "Look, sweetie, The Club was practically my home away from home. I ate there every Thursday night for twelve years. I know how each john in the ladies' room flushes, I'm one of the few people who's ever seen the kitchen, the maitre d' is my oldest friend. You can't tell me The Club is about to let down the bars to some unknown academic whose parents landed at Ellis Island instead of Pier Ninety. Why should they?"

Freddie looks at my mother as if she were a helpless moron. "Just because things have always gone one way doesn't mean they always will. As a matter of fact, I proposed Sam myself, today. Charlie Taub agreed to second him."

"*Tiens,*" my mother says. "And I suppose Sam put you up to this?"

"Sam doesn't even know," Freddie says.

"You're kidding." Kathleen pops her permanent waves in at the living room entrance. "Dinner is served, Madame."

"Thank you, Kathleen," my mother says. "We'll be down in a moment. And please remind Marie" — that month's cook; they never stayed very long because they didn't like having Mummy muck around in their kitchen. Either she cooks or I cook was their attitude. I can't really say I blamed them. It was an impossible situation. "Remind Marie to put the plates in the platewarmer before you bring them on. Remember that, Sally, when you grow up and have your own home: *Never* serve hot food on cold plates. Where was I?" Freddie is looking glumly at his martini.

I know where she was; I'm fascinated to see my mother and

stepfather on opposite sides of an issue. It doesn't happen all that often.

"You accused me of kidding," Freddie says, eyeing his olive.

"Oh, come on, sweetie, don't go gloomy on me. I just can't believe you haven't told Sam about what you've done. What if he doesn't want to be proposed?"

"Now you must be kidding, Fippy. Of course he wants to."

"You're so certain," she says. "People don't usually want to go where they're not wanted."

"There's this joke I heard on the radio last night," I pipe up. "This man says he wouldn't want to belong to any club that would want *him* as a member." My mother and stepfather look at me as if I'd said shit.

"Not very funny," my mother says. "And you're interrupting. I think we ought to go down and eat. The soup will be either cold or burned. That woman doesn't know how to keep things on the simmer."

"Call Fräulein and Roger, will you, Sally?"

Fräulein and Roger ate with us when it was just us happy family. Fräulein had an appetite like an elephant, and when she chewed it sounded like a hippopotamus with his feet in the mud. Roger had terrible manners, but he was only six and my mother had decided that she wouldn't try to teach him directly, that is, by telling him not to put his elbow in the butter or eat with the wrong end of the fork. Instead, as she put it, she was going to teach him "by example. When he sees us eating properly, he'll follow our example. You don't need to tell a child how to eat. All he has to do is watch."

"But you told *me*," I protested. "You still do. You're always nagging me about my table manners."

At dinner the discussion about Sam and The Club is tabled. I guess they don't want to talk about it in front of Fräulein. Instead, there is this awfully fake conversation during which my mother and stepfather try to include Fräulein, but since they have few topics in common, the talk is limited to the Central Park Zoo, Gimbel's, where Fräulein shops on her day off, and the various things you can do with sour cream. I sit quietly and properly, aching to leave the table. These dinners are for me what church is for Nancy. I decide that when I grow up my children can eat standing on their heads or listening to the radio, if that's what they want. They can eat bologna sandwiches, potato chips, and ice-cream-on-a-stick every meal if that's what they like. They can eat whenever they're hungry, alone if they want to, in the bathroom if that's where they choose.

Roger takes up his milk glass and pours the contents over his capon, broccoli, and potato puffs. The milk sloshes over the sides, forming a white moat around the plate.

"Mummy . . ." I protest. "Look what he's doing!"

"Now *Liebchen*." Fräulein starts sponging with her napkin.

Mother tinkles her little crystal bell for Kathleen.

Freddie, showing a rare flash of pique, says, "Fippy, can't you teach that child any manners? He does that every time we sit down to dinner."

My mother's face clouds over, then clears. She's considering whether to go into battle.

"Roger, you really mustn't do that," she says in a tone that suggests a blue ribbon instead of a slap.

"Jesus Christ!" I yell, going out of control. "I can't stand it."

My mother's face cracks open, her eyes widen, and her hand goes to her mouth.

"What did you say?"

"I'm leaving," I say wisely. I get up and run out of the room, up the stairs two at a time, dash for my room, make it, slam the door. What's the matter with me? I have never done anything like this in my whole life.

Suddenly I feel a pain like a steel hand squeezing my gut. I double over and fall on the bed. It's God, killing me for swearing, for swearing at my mother. I'm dying and I'm glad. Life is hell-

ish. I don't care if they cry and feel guilty. Serve them right. I
drift off into semisleep and have a seminightmare. About an hour
later something wakes me up. It's wet and sticky. I think I have
wet my pants. That's impossible. I haven't wet my pants in
twelve years ("You were trained very early, darling, you were
really a very good little baby." Swell).

I go to the bathroom. I've got it! I've got my first period. It
doesn't ooze out, it pours like an arterial wound. It's pouring
down the insides of my legs. I touch it, expecting it to be different. It isn't, it's just like blood. It *is* blood. But it isn't quite the
same either. Is it thicker? Maybe. Redder? A little. I smell my
bloody fingers. It's odorless. What's all the business about menstrual blood stinking?

I won't tell my mother. I'm determined not to tell her anything
private about me. If I tell her, she'll take over and manage it for
me. I have a box of Junior Modess and a belt ready and waiting
on the top shelf of the linen closet in the bathroom. It's been
there nearly a year. Why are my hands shaking as I put them on?
I'm not scared but my hands are shaking. I decide I ought to take
a bath. I run water into the tub, take off the napkin — which isn't
like a napkin at all, more like a wadded-up diaper — and get into
the tub; the water pinkens briefly.

"So this is it," I say, feeling foolish. Have I changed merely
because I am bleeding?

My mother finds out, I don't know how. I'll bet Fräulein finds
the evidence and tells her. It's just like Fräulein to go running to
my mother with her little tales. I am furious that Mummy knows.
It's none of her business.

"You're a woman now," she says to me, trying to ruffle my
hair. "Freddie, your daughter became a woman last night."

I color. "Don't tell him," I say. Freddie looks trapped.

"Nonsense, Sally, it's nothing to be ashamed of. Freddie wants
to share your secrets, don't you, sweetie?"

"Sure, Fippy, but maybe it embarrasses Sally."

But I'm already out of the room. How can she be so thick? I am certain she was never a child herself. If she had ever been thirteen she wouldn't say and do the things she does. My only solace is a phone call to Nancy. I tell her what it's like to have the curse. Already, after twenty-four hours, I'm an expert. She hasn't got hers yet. She says that Jews start earliest, look at Renata Paul. I wonder how that can be true. What does your religion have to do with whether you start to menstruate in June or December?

"I don't understand that," I say. "I don't believe it."

"Daddy told me." Nancy's father is a doctor. If he says so it must be true.

"What about Catholics?" I ask.

"Late, I think," Nancy says. "Did you tell your mother?"

"She found out," I say. "She always finds things out. This stupid house is full of spies. Kathleen's a spy and so is Fräulein. I think she pays them extra for information."

"That's pretty funny," she says. "But what did Mumsy say?"

"Oh God, listen, you mustn't tell anyone. Promise not to tell a soul. It was so awful. I think she says things just to make me feel rotten."

"Yes, yes, I promise. What did she say?"

"She turned to Freddie and said" — I do my heavy Tallulah Bankhead imitation — " 'your dahling daughter is a woman now.' I could have strangled her."

"Barf," says Nancy. "Your mother uses you. You shouldn't let her use you that way."

"Any suggestions as to how?"

"Don't tell her anything."

"I don't," I wail. "She always finds out."

"You could stop her," Nancy tells me. "I don't tell my mom *any*thing."

"But she makes you do things that she wants you to do, like go to Mass and confession and wear hats and tell her where you are every single minute when you're not at home. So *she* uses *you* too." I'm sitting on the telephone chair in the hallway, third floor, outside my room. I can't, even now, be sure that Fräulein isn't eavesdropping.

"You really think I tell my mom where I am every single minute when I'm not at home? Catholics have very good imaginations, didn't you know that? We're famous tellers of tales."

"You mean you *lie* to her? Do you do things even *I* don't know about?"

"Of course not, silly, I just lie to my mother so I can keep my self-respect. It's important for me to have a private life, even if it doesn't amount to very much. You think I go down to Times Square and pick up sailors? Hey, not a bad idea, Sally. Want to try it with me sometime?"

"Sure," I tell her.

The Club thing with Sam London dragged on for weeks. Freddie grew more determined as he sensed the opposition mounting force and gathering strength to head him off. He considered it a personal battle — he began to feel that they weren't so much against Sam London as against Alfred Stern.

It was light years later, when Sam London told me about being blackballed by The Club's Admissions Committee, that I started lining up my experiences there against my own ideas, especially ideas about the ways I would eventually like to live my own life. Maybe those early experiences gave me my taste for the bizarre. But it took a long time to surface. Children absorb, they rarely analyze. Ask a child to tell you why he hates something and he'll tell you that "it's icky." He can no more tell you *why* it's icky than he can tell you how to make wine from cornflowers.

Sam told me that when he found out about it he was mad as hell at Freddie for putting him up for membership in The Club.

He wasn't merely neutral about it; the whole idea of belonging to the Orange Club was an outrage. "It was a half-assed thing to do, proposing me without asking me first," he said. "I could have saved him a hell of a lot of tsurus by saying thanks but no thanks right at the beginning. It was his money's fault. His bread and his almost incredible social ease. He was loaded with money and culture, he couldn't believe anyone might not want to fight the battles he fought. No, that's not true. As you well know, there *was* another side to Freddie, the side that sent you and Roger here to live with us. But that didn't operate more than a few times in his whole life. The thing that kept him functioning most of the time was the Jewish Rockefeller thing. You have to be at the center of the action, you have to use your money and position like a club — no pun intended — you have to push for reform and change, but always within the system. You have to live the ideals of a liberal — all the time. I don't think your mother was cut from the same bolt of cloth — maybe, but I don't think so. She was too busy having fun. Or am I wrong?"

"You're not wrong. Mummy sometimes made fun of him. He'd look as if he was going to cry."

"Freddie," Sam said, "for all his avant-gardism was really a very straight guy."

I don't want to get off the time track too far. Freddie's character is part of this story, but it doesn't operate for a while.

Sam London was turned down. Freddie hit the ceiling. He wrote a letter to the Board of Governors calling them fossils. He wrote a letter to the *New York Times* which he read aloud to us during the cocktail hour one night. Fippy advised him not to send it; her advice was academic because they never printed it. He went around groaning one minute and raging the next. For all the noise Freddie made about injustice and bigotry, you would have thought that all the Negroes in America had been rounded up, herded into concentration camps, and shot. I wasn't curious enough about the whole thing to start wondering why they had turned Sam down. What struck me as peculiar, however, was how angry Freddie got. He nearly resigned from The Club.

"If you feel so strongly," my mother said to him, "Why don't you quit? Why don't you write another letter, one that burns right through the envelope, and tell them you don't want to be in a club that only accepts clean Jews?"

Freddie looks startled. Is it possible this has not occurred to him? "I'll think about it," he says somberly. "I really think I might just do that. It's what they deserve. I'll take it under advisement. I will, Fippy, that's quite an idea. I honestly hadn't thought about it."

"You think about it," my mother says. She is fed up with the whole business.

The sky grayed and grew heavy. Snow began to fall. It fell and fell. Schools closed early and the snow fell relentlessly, like rain, muffling noises and stopping cars. People skied down Park Avenue and across Seventy-second Street. The city's pulse fibrillated, then died. The opening of a musical Mummy had front-row-center tickets for was postponed. She was furious. "And nothing in the house to eat except canned hash and leftovers," she wailed.

And it wasn't anything the Republicans had done. God did it, or whoever manages the earth's weather. I was delighted because the Seeley School shut down. The city was unearthly quiet — it was quieter than our house in Maine because here there were no birds, no waves. Mayor O'Dwyer was stymied, so was NBC and the *New York Times* and *Life* magazine. It was an epic blizzard, not ranking with 1888's probably because in 1948 nothing happened that was nearly so dramatic as a horse up to his knees and thrashing in a snowdrift.

"You never know what's going to happen in this crazy town," my mother told me. She was chopping shallots for a sauce for the leftovers. "Smell these," she says to me. "Don't they smell like spring?" Marie the cook is sulking, slamming drawers, banging pots and pans, and glaring at my mother, who pointedly ignores her.

"You never know what's going to happen at all," I say. "Who knows what's going to happen?"

"My little philosopher," my mother says.

"I wouldn't want to know what's going to happen — unless it was good. Suppose you found out that you were going to die on May twelfth or something. What would you do?"

"Where do you get such morbid ideas from?" Mummy says severely. "From the radio, all those scary programs, no wonder. And those so-called comic books. They're about as comic as Goebbels. I wish you wouldn't read them, Sally."

"Oh Mummy!"

"Don't 'oh Mummy' me, young lady." Sometimes I think my mother thinks that being a mother is like playing a role in a stylized play, like *Everyman*. When you're playing the role you say things like "young lady" in a special way. When — and if — I am ever a mother I will never say "young lady" to my daughter, if I have one. I will never tell her to stop being so silly. I will never make her feel stupid or clumsy. I will make her feel that it's all right to try things even if I'm sure beforehand that they are going to end in disaster.

My mother doesn't sound like a Jewish mother. A Jewish mother shrugs and holds her head and calls on God to witness the torments inflicted by an ungrateful child. A Jewish mother is fat and tells you to eat, eat. A Jewish mother goes into the bathroom with you to make sure you do your business. She has thousands of female relatives always swarming over the house and making suggestions without being asked. A Jewish mother talks funny and claims to be ignorant of prevailing cultural trends. Well, my mother *was* a Jewish mother; genetically she was more Jewish than I. But you wouldn't have recognized it unless you were expert at picking up the subtle messages that identify one acculturated Jew to another. For one thing, they are usually preverbal and for another they are so subtle as to be frequently unread. Americans think all Japanese schoolchildren are identical; non-Jews lump Jews together and dispose of them thus. The only generalization you can make about Jews is that no Jew is or probably will ever be an astronaut.

I received permission to visit my father in the hospital, though not without a certain amount of bitching on my mother's part. She was convinced he had cirrhosis of the liver and didn't mind my hearing her say so. She made remarks, also, about the rigors of having an athletic girlfriend and so on. Every biting sentence made me angrier.

By Saturday I have worked myself up into a lather of indignation. I grab my camel's-hair coat, pull on my boots, cover my head with cap and scarf, put on my rabbit-skin mittens, and head off through the muddy and melting snow. I have left the house without saying goodbye. They can go jump in the lake, Mummy and her handsome publisher, my adopted father, with his fifteen suits and his leather-bound novels and his membership in the Orange Club, not to mention the Grandview Country Club, the Yale Club, and the Lotos Club.

I nearly keel over from the ether smell pouring out the front door. I have to sit down in the lobby for a minute before I am sure of my legs. I buy some violets in the hospital flower shop and, squeezing them by the stems as if they were a snake about to bite my hand, I go up to his room. Outside the door I pause, hearing a strange woman's voice say something arch about someone called George. For a minute I think I've got the wrong room. Then I hear Daddy's voice laughing faintly, as if he were far away. I take a deep breath and knock.

"Come in."

"It's me Daddy!" I cry with the depressing heartiness of a gym teacher. I steel myself and look: there is my father, tattletale gray and looking as if he's just been licked in straight sets. He is lying against a bank of pillows piled against the cranked-up bed. His hands, which always have seemed large and muscular, are limp on the sheet like two moribund animals. They remind me of chipmunks. There are no tubes visible, either coming in or exiting. Thank God. "Oh Daddy," I cry, because I'm so relieved about there not being any tubes.

"Hey there," he says. "I'm okay. Look at me, I'm fine."

"What did they do to you?"

"They snipped away a little piece of my stomach. It's called an ulcer. It's a nasty, nasty thing. I'm going to feel much better now. It was very nice of your mother to let you come and see me." One of the chipmunks reaches out for one of my own hands. I let it. His hand is soft and sloppy; it has no muscle in it.

"Sally, darling, I want you to meet Lorna." For the first time I take my eyes off my poor father and look at the fiancée. "Lorna, my sweet, this is my lovely princess. Isn't she a treasure?"

Lorna is Miss Young Protestant Upper-Class America. I've seen hundreds like her — she's the older sister of half my class at school and the stepmother of the other half. She has wide-set blue eyes, clear, faintly freckled skin, a perfect blond pageboy tucked into an invisible hairnet. She is wearing a blue wool suit from Peck and Peck, with a circle of gold stuck to it over her small left breast. Her nails are manicured and covered with colorless polish. Her right hand is almost as large as a man's. It confused me to find Lorna indistinguishable from her many sisters; it would have made me happy if she had been odd in some awful way — big nose or bad complexion, or the wrong lipstick or the Old Look instead of the New. Something to objectify my distrust.

Lorna sticks out the giant paw and grinds my fingers together.

"I'm just thrilled to meet you, Sally. Your dad has told me so much about you. I'm sure we're going to be the very best of friends." She may have a grip like a man but her voice is like a little girl's.

I nod at her implausible prediction and mumble something polite.

"Lorna's been here day and night since my surgery. She's the best medicine a man could ask for, far better than a nurse, that's for sure." He smiles weakly at his girlfriend and then at me.

"How long are they going to make you stay here?" I say.

Lorna answers for him. "Oh, not more than ten days at the very outside. Your dad's doctor — you should meet him, Sally, if he isn't the most debonair creature you've ever laid your eyes on, then I can't tell one man from another — your dad's doctor says they are getting postoperative patients right out of bed, practically as soon as they come down from the recovery room. Of course Willy had all these awful tubes coming in and going out of him for a couple of days, so they really couldn't get him out of bed, but since yesterday he's been in that chair right there twice, haven't you, sweetheart? Why, I think it's just amazing. I remember when I was a little girl and they took my appendix out, why, I lay in bed for simply days and days, bedpans and everything. I distinctly remember the morning they let me out of bed — it must have been at least two weeks after the actual operation. My poor knees just turned to water and I fainted, I actually collapsed. It was a pity . . ."

"Lorna," my father interrupts.

"Yes, sweetheart?"

"Sally just wanted to know how long I was going to be here." He thus slaps her down and then smiles sexually at her so that she won't know which end is up. She smiles back, clearly untouched by the slap. I stare at Lorna, disbelieving. My father is marrying an inexhaustible fountain of words, words that will flow and

gurgle and splash and overflow unless someone deliberately turns
her off.

This eccentricity of Lorna's makes her a less dangerous adver-
sary. But it doesn't make me like her any more than I did before I
met her. Next to Lorna even *I* sound sensible.

I wait for Daddy to make his usual sarcastic remarks about
Mummy — they're always cutting each other up in front of me
— but he doesn't seem to be in a cutting-up mood. Everything
he says is hopelessly sentimental. He asks me about school and
then gives me a lecture on how to be a good student without
making the other girls distrust me. He has no idea that I am
lumped in with the other Jewish girls in my class. Not being
Jewish, he assumes that I am more *him* than my mother at all
times. If my father were suddenly with the minority I think he
would die of a smashed heart. I don't think he would know what
to do. I think he would feel so weak and helpless and mind the
closed doors so much that he would just give up. He believes in
Darwin in the social sense. But what happens when the weak
suddenly become strong? What happens to people like my father?

My father tells me that now I am about to have a stepmother
(fond gaze toward object of choice), he feels like a family again
after all these years. He's looking forward to next summer. I
don't know what to feel about *that;* Lorna will make it different,
that's the only thing I can say for sure.

When it is time for me to go, Lorna kisses me on the forehead.
"I am a lucky creature getting a wonderful man and a lovely
daughter all at once. My cup runneth over. Now I know I'm just
a stepmother to you, but I want you to promise you won't think
I'm wicked, like stepmothers are supposed to be, because I
haven't a wicked thought in my whole body, have I, sweetheart?
You maybe won't believe this, but I used to be so innocent my
friends back home called me Gullibulorna. I guess I believed just

about anything anybody told me. I believe in the goodness of all people. I certainly can't tell when someone's lying to me. To this day I can't tell. Isn't that amazing?"

"Lorna, honey," my father says. "Nobody ever accused you of being wicked."

"That's what I've been trying to tell Sally," she says in her nine-year-old voice.

My head is spinning. She may not be wicked — though I am going to withhold judgment — but she is hopeless. Living with her would be like living with an electric drill in your ear twenty-four hours a day. I don't see how Daddy can stand it. I know I couldn't. Inside the space of forty-five minutes, my summers with Daddy have been destroyed, my refuge (Daddy's house, Daddy's devotion) have been monkeyed with so badly that I'm not sure I even want to take advantage of it anymore. Lorna Emerson is worse than wicked.

What does Daddy see in this unbelievable lady? Not her figure: she's built like an athletic teen-age boy. Not her face: there are a million prettier, softer, more intelligent.

It must be her forehand.

5

Departures

"WELL, BABY DOLL, what was she like?" my mother asks, jabbing long-stemmed glads into a crystal (heavy this time) vase and then standing back, à la Susan Hayward, to measure her success. "*Bon*," she says. "*Ça suffit*." Mummy likes to throw a little French around from time to time. She hasn't been in France since long before the war.

"Okay," I tell her expansively. I look at my fingers. They're grimy again. I want to wash them but it means going upstairs to my own bathroom. Mummy doesn't like me to use hers. She claims I leave the soap gray and drip water all over the rug.

"What's *okay*? What does *okay* mean? Sally, you can do better than that, with your head. Besides, we send you to that expensive school to learn, among other things, how to express yourself like a civilized human being. *Okay* doesn't tell me anything except that Lorna Emerson doesn't have two heads or webbed feet. What I want to hear from you is, what does she look like, how does she act with *le cochon?* What was she wearing? I'll bet she buys her clothes at Best's. And, for heaven's sake, stop biting your nails, you won't have anything left!"

"Well, she has a pocketbook a little like your alligator one except hers is grayish." It's hard for me to describe Lorna to my mother; whatever I say will make more static than I care to hear. "She talks a lot."

"So did I," my mother says. "To keep myself from going ga-ga. Is she smart or dumb? Probably dumb. Your father has to feel superior."

"I don't know," I tell her, beginning to be sorry as hell that we got started on this.

"Anyway," my mother says breezily, trying the vase on dressing table, desk, bureau, windowsill, and, finally, occasional table between the windows, where she leaves it with a little sigh of satisfaction. It's amazing how much time I spend with my mother, when being with her hurts so much. Why can't I go off and be alone more often? Read? Practice the piano? Walk in Central Park? Shop for clothes? *She* likes shopping for clothes so much, why don't *I*? Listen to my Artie Shaw and Benny Goodman records? No, I stick to her with dogged perversity. Maybe if I stick with her long enough I can understand why it is she makes me feel so lousy.

Now my mother is occupied in taking clothes out of her bureau drawers and dumping them on the bed. Femme is everywhere: she's inserted it in sachet pillows and powder, in cologne —she sprays it on the walls. It's in the soap in her bathroom. It clings to the sheets and blankets. When I leave her room, *I* smell like Femme.

"What are you doing?" I ask.

"Freddie and I thought we would go to San Francisco next Saturday. Freddie's got someone to see and I thought I'd just tag along for a little vacation." This is incredible. As far as I can see my mother's whole life is a vacation. She hasn't got a job, she doesn't keep house, she's got a nurse for Roger. What is this vacation *from?*

"Can I come?"

"Now, really, Sally, you'll make me sorry I mentioned it. No, darling, you can't come. We're staying at least a week. You wouldn't want to miss that much school, would you?"

"Winter vacation starts Wednesday so I'd only be missing two days." Private schools have a holiday in the dead of winter. It's very convenient for skiers.

"Two days is still two days. If you were an A student that might make a difference. But you're not. I mean you can't just go skipping days of school because you feel like taking a little vacation."

"Renata Paul does," I say. I can feel my face beginning to burn with frustration.

"What sort of marks does Renata get?"

"You're punishing me for being stupid," I accuse her.

"Good heavens, Sally, that's about the silliest thing I ever heard you say." She shakes her head like a horse trying to get away from the flies. "Punishing you? I'm not punishing you. I simply don't think you ought to cut school."

"I got A— in English," I tell her. "And a Very Good in dance."

"Dance!"

"You just don't want me to come with you," I say coldly.

"That's not true, Sally, we'd love to have you. Look, I promise, the next time we'll schedule our trip so you won't have to miss school. We'll make it coincide with a vacation. Then you and Roger and Fräulein can all come along. We'll be a big happy family — more like a medieval caravan or something. How does that sound?"

It stinks. "Okay," I say. "But I think it's terribly unfair. Renata always goes along with her father."

Mummy's face stiffens. "In the first place, Miss Complaint, you know it's no good using other children as examples — you know perfectly well that I don't do things just because someone else does them. In the second place, *that* family. I'm surprised Renata isn't *enceinte* already. They let her drink champagne and stay up till God knows what hour of the morning. If you ask me, Renata Paul is heading for deep trouble."

"How do you know what they do?"

"Oh, everybody in our crowd knows. They're such a public family anyway. Muriel Paul falls into a depression if her picture hasn't made one of the slicks for six months." I am amazed that she knows so much about the Pauls. I don't think they have ever set foot in our house.

"I still don't understand why you don't want me to come."

"Really, Sally, you're awfully dense this afternoon. Do you know who Norman Baker is?"

"Of course," I say, though I'm not all that sure.

"Well, now listen to this — Sally put your hand in your lap — it's possibly the most exciting thing that's happened to Griffin and to Freddie. But you must promise not to say a word till the thing is settled. You know that Svengali of Freddie's, Sam London? Well, for once he's earned his way. He's found out — God knows how — that Baker has the manuscript of a novel almost finished. And Sam has somehow got him to agree to show it to Griffin. Actually, Baker's other things are so filthy that no American publisher in his right mind is willing to take the chance of being sued for obscenity. But apparently this book is no dirtier than *Forever Amber* — the old man is mellowing, or something. Sam told Freddie the only way to get the book for sure was for Freddie to fly out and meet Baker on his home ground and convince him to let Griffin publish it before Blanche Knopf or Jim Laughlin gets wind of it. Baker hasn't published a book in America for over twenty years. If it goes through it will be the most beautiful, delicious coup for Freddie, who really needs a boost at the moment, after that silly Orange Club mess. We've got to leave right away, to put it crudely — and since we're talking business I don't know why I shouldn't — to beat out the competition. We probably shouldn't even wait until the weekend, but I've got to get my hair done and buy a new pair of shoes to wear with my new evening thing, and you know your old mother — she's not exactly a last-minute sort of person."

This is undoubtedly the most extended and confidential speech my mother has ever delivered to me.

She continues. "Mr. Baker lives in a glorified cliff-dwelling or something, hanging out over the Pacific, just south of San Francisco. The rumor is — though you don't necessarily have to believe every rumor you hear — that he's got two women living with him, just like two wives. Oh dear, I shouldn't be telling you this . . ."

"Oh Muh-ther!" Good Christ!

"Well, he does have a reputation for being something of a ladies' man. I wonder if he'll make a pass . . ."

"Please take me with . . ."

"I said *no!*" She's back on her high horse and is getting ready to trample me. "Not this time. Now stop being a pest and act your age!"

It's hopeless. I am hurt, angry. Obviously she thinks of me in the same terms as Roger and the German hippo.

I lurch toward the door, bumping into a small table and knocking a pile of books onto the floor.

"Pick 'em up," my mother says, pulling her Rita Hayworth nightgown from the drawer and holding it up. The top part is as transparent as a window screen. I think she's disgusting about sex. She acts as if she were the first woman ever to go to bed with a man.

"I was going to," I say through my teeth.

My mother has made the understatement of the century when she boasted about not being a last-minute type. You'd think she was going on a year's African safari the way she lays in supplies during the succeeding days. She's not a one-nightie-in-an-overnight-bag sort of person either. Kathleen is sent once to the cleaner's and twice to Bloomingdale's. Fräulein is instructed to take Roger to the Museum of Natural History, the Museum of Science and Industry, and the Planetarium to keep him from getting underfoot. I am dispatched to Larimore's, the Cartier of corner drugstores, for an extra supply of Mummy's special soap and facial goo. I am sent to Tiffany's to pick up a monogrammed house present for their Peninsula hostess. Even the cook is sent, grumbling, on errands to the cobbler and the cleaner again. It's not quite pre-Waterloo in the house, but it's something that would make an infant jumpy. I am still annoyed as hell at being left behind, but I've begun to make my own plans.

Nancy and I are going to spend one whole day inside the Paramount Theater listening to Gene Krupa twice and some crummy movie in between and eating chicken sandwiches from a paper bag. My mother hates me to get squashed in the kind of mob that congregates inside the Paramount, but she can't give me a reason good enough to keep me from going. Whenever I go to a Broadway movie house she makes me wash my hands afterward before I touch anything. She always asks me if someone tried to do "something funny" and I always answer no, of course not, even though once or twice men did and I was so scared I was temporarily paralyzed. Men like to get up behind you and goose you. I really don't understand what pleasure they get out of it, especially through heavy winter clothes.

Anyway, Nancy and I are going to hear Gene Krupa who, along with Artie Shaw and Woody Herman and Stan Kenton, tops our private Hit Parade. I have thirteen Artie Shaw records which Freddie makes me play softly because he can't stand the sound. I am going to put them on the Stromberg-Carlson in the living room and turn up the volume so high it goes clear through the roof. Fräulein is going to try to take over and boss me, but I'm not going to let her. I'm going to tell her to mind her own business. I'm not going to eat any proper meals either. If they're leaving me behind, I'm going to be bad, bad, bad. My idea of sin is pretty pathetic.

On Saturday morning my mother woke up with a cold. It wasn't just a runny nose or sneezing, it was the red eyes, sore throat, and aching bones sort of cold that sometimes turns into the flu. There was a good deal of indecision about whether to postpone the trip. It was Freddie who tried to convince my mother to put it off and she who insisted on going.

"You won't get Baker," she says, "if we don't go now."

"Nonsense," he tells her. He's standing there in his gray flannel suit and foulard tie and small-brimmed hat from Chipp. He's got a handkerchief folded in his breast pocket. The barber at the Pierre has made his hair look like Cary Grant's. "We'll wait till you feel better and then go. Baker will understand. He's not going to give the book to Blanche just because we're delayed a week."

"But there's Polly Westheimer's party — I can't disappoint her. She's asked over a hundred people to meet you."

"To meet *you*," Freddie says.

"All right, Freddie, to meet *us*. Over a hundred people. And the caterer. We can't disappoint the caterer." My mother sneezes and shudders. She's got herself all dolled up for the trip: a travel suit of dark green wool, a long, swinging skirt, a frilly blouse, new alligator shoes, a tiny hat that balances on her crown, long gray kid gloves. Her bluish mink is thrown over the lot as if she didn't give a damn if she left it behind in some expensive restaurant.

"I don't like the way you look. Did you take your temperature?"

"Yes, it was ninety-nine."

"That's fever," Freddie informs her. "I'm not leaving."

"Oh, no," my mother cries, like a small child. "We just *have* to go. I've been looking forward to it so much. I'll be all right, I know I will — it's just a little cold . . ."

"I'm going to call Ben. If he says okay, then we'll go; otherwise we'll stay." Ben is Benjamin Tannenbaum, their Park Avenue M.D. He's an old Yalie classmate of Freddie's. My mother is crestfallen. I just wish they'd hurry up and leave so I can begin being bad.

My mother tells him to hurry — the plane is leaving in an hour and a half. Everybody — Kathleen, the cook, Roger, Fräulein — all shift from foot to foot waiting for the momentous decision. My stepfather comes back.

"Ben says it's all right, but you're to be sure to rest when you get there if you still have a fever. I'm not at all sure I agree with him . . ."

"That settles it," my mother says triumphantly. "If the super-cautious doctor says it's all right, then it's all right. Come on now, everybody out to the street to say goodbye." My mother leads the procession. Rooney, all spit and polish in his uniform and visored cap, takes the bags and stows them in the trunk of the Cadillac. My mother kisses Roger, who's shivering in his pajamas and bathrobe and fleece-lined slippers. He makes her promise to bring him not just a present but a "big present." My mother tells him she will bring him the most beautiful toy in Magnin's.

It's my turn. I am shy as my mother approaches. She's never been physical with me; when she sat me on her lap when I was still a baby, her knees were so bony they hurt my fanny. Her chest is more hard than soft, her arms more chill bone than warm flesh. I suspect that she's putting on a little act now, a goodbye scene for the benefit of . . . who? Kathleen? Fräulein? Freddie? The people who might see from their windows? Me? "Aren't you going to give your mother a goodbye kiss?" For once she looks me straight in the eye.

"Sure." We bring our faces together. I see tiny imperfections on her skin that indicate nothing more nor less than age. But they startle me. My left cheek meets her right cheek. For a moment we pause, stuck together, then we both draw back. Her lips have barely brushed my skin, yet I can feel them like a burn. I look down, embarrassed.

"There," she says. "That's more like it. What shall I get you, Sally?"

"I don't want anything," I say.

"Oh, Sally, why do you always have to say the wrong thing?"

"Fippy," Freddie calls. "If we don't leave right this minute we'll miss the plane. Come on, finish your farewells and get in the car."

My mother gives me a brief look of hurt. "I'll get you something anyway, something irresistible. Goodbye, everybody. Fräulein, take good care of Roger. Kathleen, you see that Miss Sally eats her dinner. Goodbye everybody." She waves her kid-gloved hands and folds herself, like a dancer, into the back seat of the car. Rooney slams the door discreetly shut. It sounds *thunk*, good and heavy. He gets into the driver's seat and starts off. My mother turns in her seat as the car pulls away down Seventy-third Street and waves through the back window. Her face grows smaller and smaller.

"I'm freezing," Roger cries. "I want pancakes for breakfast. And sausages. My mommy said I could have anything I want until she comes back."

Fräulein nods in agreement. Kathleen and Marie exchange a look of disgust seen only by me. I don't blame them — I don't see how they can go on working for us. We traipse back into the abandoned house. Up and down the street a few maids in overcoats emerge with their brooms and sweep the soot and scraps of paper into the gutter. The sun hits polished panes of glass, sending reflections bouncing back like stabs of lightning.

I'm going to bed for as long as I want. Then Nancy and I will have lunch at the counter of the drugstore on the corner of Eighty-sixth Street and Lexington Avenue and then we're going to see *The Seventh Veil* and a comedy with Donald O'Connor and a talking mule. Maybe I'll wait to be bad until tomorrow.

After the movies Nancy and I go to Schrafft's, where we each order a sundae with marshmallow and fudge sauce, hold the nuts. I love this kind of between-meal snack probably because my mother frowns on it. She is *always* on a diet. I know that it's getting dark and I ought to go home, but I don't want to. Something about my mother's being gone gives me an unpleasant pang; she's left before and I haven't minded, but now I don't like the idea of their bedroom remaining dark and the house filled only with the noises of Roger and Fräulein. I realize I don't mind all that much my mother and Freddie talking about Sam London and the stupid Club and Freddie's famous poets and my mother's rich art-patron friends and the villainies of William Sanderson and Henry Luce.

Roger is hard to take. But he's never really been given a chance. He was like a crown prince; people treated him as if he were fragile, as if something would happen to him if he were not kept under constant surveillance. Maybe they were afraid he would get ideas that didn't gibe with his parents'. They didn't want him to be self-reliant because he might strike out in a different direction. First sons in Jewish families like mine have nothing to do with Emerson. What they are is first imagined, then shaped to fit the image. They are a piece of sculpture, excellent or crude depending only on the talent and sensitivity of their parents, the people with the gelt and the chisels.

Nancy and I part on the sidewalk, promising to call each other the next day. To make myself feel a little less lonesome I put in a call to my father in Princeton. He's at home recuperating. The constant Lorna is spending the weekend at his place. I think it's peculiar of him to have her there without being married. He starts talking about spring wedding plans. This depresses me and I ring off.

I refuse my dinner. Fräulein accuses me of eating "garbage" between meals. She tries to make me feel terrible by telling me how much trouble Marie has gone to to cook my dinner. I tell her that Marie had to cook dinner anyway, for her and for Roger.

"You are a wasteful girl."

"I admit it. Why don't *you* eat it if you don't want it to be wasted?"

She is horrified. For some reason Fräulein's nagging heightens my sense of being abandoned — I feel like crying as we square off, challenging one another to make the most damaging statement. Above us the Calder hangs motionless like a benign bird. Roger comes along and tugs at his nurse's skirt, shrieking that he's hungry. She lets him yell.

"I'm going upstairs," I say. "I'll be in my room." I am not cheered up by my trivial bravado; there is a large hole inside me which has only partly to do with the fact that I am skipping dinner.

I think of my room as a sanctuary, despite my not being able to keep Fräulein's big feet out of it. It is mine, mine, mine. My mother almost never comes up here, although you can see her exquisite hand in the decor. Whenever Roger pokes his cute little head in the door I growl at him and he leaves. I deliberately don't have anything lying around that he might want to play with. It's the very model of a "teen-ager's" bedroom. As a matter of fact, a friend of Mummy's on the staff of a ladies' magazine wanted to feature it in the Christmas issue, and Mummy was all for it. But I put my foot down. "If you put my room in that stupid magazine I'll set fire to it."

My mother accused me of being selfish. I said that after I set it on fire I'd move into the sewing room, a windowless hole with pipes running down one wall.

My mother, sensing that this battle was too unimportant to win, retreated.

I had a fourposter bed with a canopy which Kathleen took off and laundered by hand once every two weeks. I had a large, soft, shaggy rug so thick it concealed my bare toes. I had a dressing table with a triptych mirror and a little upholstered stool. I had a Swedish bureau and matching desk. My curtains complemented but did not match the rug. Nancy thought my room was heavenly, and compared to hers it was. Compared to ninety-nine percent of the bedrooms of thirteen-year-old American girls it was.

I go up to my sanctuary and pick up my contraband copy of *Memoirs of Hecate County*, a book Freddie brought home and hid clumsily. It is the dirtiest book I have ever read; it tells me more about adult sex than anything or anyone else I have tried, even Nancy, who hears about it from her older sister. The book draws me into it like Alice's looking glass. Sometime later I am startled by the phone ringing. Kathleen, who generally answers with a clipped "Stern residence," is out for the evening. Marie has gone home. Where is Fräulein? I get up and poke my head out of the door. I can hear Fräulein splashing around in the tub like all of Mr. Popper's penguins. That means I'll have to get it.

For some reason — is it that I don't want Fräulein to sneak up on me? — I run downstairs to my mother's bedroom instead of answering the phone in the hall outside my room. It is cold in Mummy's room; someone remembered to turn off the radiators. It is cold and dark, a dark, perfumed cave. I grope for the phone and whack my shin against the footboard of their bed.

Sitting on my mother's slippery Carlin comforter, I rub my shinbone and say hello.

A man whose name I'll never forget — it's Orin Hughes, the only Orin I've ever talked to in my life — announces that he is a vice-president in charge of something at TWA, customer relations or public relations or something like that. In any case his job that particular night is not escorting VIPs to the landing stairs. He has to tell the relatives of fifty-seven people that their mothers and fathers and husbands and wives and children are lying

scattered all over the approach to the San Francisco airport. First
Mr. Hughes asks me if there isn't someone else he could speak to.
Then he gets confused about who I am and, through chattering
teeth, I am forced to go through it once more — yes, I am Mrs.
Stern's child, but my father is someone else, not Mr. Stern. I can
still reproduce my first startled feeling as he said, "Unfortu-
nately, only two survived, neither one of them your parents." It
was as if someone had given me a massive, head-jarring shake and
then pulled all my insides out through the bottom. I cannot
breathe, I gasp like a boated fish trying to take enough air in. The
idea that my mother was dead hit me first as a physical insult
and then, much later, it took something enormous away from me.
It was the bodily thing that makes the deepest impression on my
memory; the sense of having my interior ruptured and taking
repeated, dull blows. A sense of having been, in fact, knocked
silly. The reality was so overwhelming that I didn't believe what
I heard. "I'm extremely sorry to have to tell you this, but your
mother has passed on." Passed on? The euphemism makes me feel
like vomiting. I will never see that beautiful woman, my mother,
again.

The man named Orin Hughes tells me that investigators from
the Federal Aviation Agency are already on their way from
Washington and that it is their job to come up with the answers.
I'm not sure what the question is, but it gets through to me,
through my fuzziness, that they're concerned with finding out
how it happened. "We can't, at this moment, say anything definite; just before the descent our man radioed that everything was
routine, he had clearance to land . . ." I can't let Orin Hughes
go on.

"I'll get my nurse," I tell him, throwing the receiver away
from me.

Even though I shout at her, it takes Fräulein several moments
to emerge in her cloud of bathroom mist, her plaid bathrobe taut

around her immense middle and secured by a satin rope. She is bewildered, annoyed at being removed from the bath before she's ready.

The stupidest mechanical things impede her. First she thinks it is a man in the house who wants to talk to her. Then she can't find her slippers. Then she's afraid of waking Roger so *she* has to go downstairs too. I'm sure Orin Hughes has hung up by this time. Then I remember that it does not in the least matter whether he's hung up or not. I haven't told Fräulein what has happened, not because I don't want to but because I can't pry the words out of my head — they are stuck there, going round and round.

Fräulein's reaction — I can hear it from where I have stationed myself outside the door — is explosive. First she says *"Nein"* about a hundred times, then she demands to know why the man on the telephone is playing jokes. Then, finally, when it soaks in, a flood of German pours from her and she starts to blubber. I am not crying. No tears are in my throat. It is a hollow, nauseous, sick feeling but not a stormy one. Fräulein, on the other hand, has turned on the waterworks, the flood. She is helpless. She hangs up the phone and announces that she is going to wake Roger to tell him the news.

"Don't wake him up," I say fiercely. "I'm telling you, don't wake Roger up!"

We have shifted roles. I am now Fräulein's boss, but I am too scared and sick to enjoy it. Fräulein insists that Roger be told now. I say, what good will it do? It's not going to change anything — let the poor child sleep. Fräulein thinks we are putting something over on him by not telling him. In the back of my mind it occurs to me that she wants *him* to comfort *her*, not the other way around. She is impossible. The phone rings again. For a moment I convince myself that it is Orin Hughes calling back to say it was all a terrible mistake; it was another plane that crashed.

Or it will be my mother, calling to say she is all right, even her cold is better, and the weather is fine — she's going to bring me the most beautiful present she can find and carry it to me in her arms. I answer almost eagerly. The bottom falls out again. It is Mr. Snyder, the lawyer, asking if I would like him to come over.

"What for?" The black sickness hits me harder. I have actually convinced myself that it was all a mistake. Fräulein apparently has the same idea, for she's tugging at me, asking "Is it your momma?"

My question confuses the lawyer. He admits he doesn't know what good he could do but assures me he will be here first thing in the morning. I am too stunned to ask him why. He asks to speak to Fräulein Kastern. She is sobbing so heartily she can barely talk. We are quite a pair. I don't know where my head is and she's forgotten her English. She jabbers German over the phone, then hangs up abruptly. "He says I should give you a powder." This strikes me as hilarious — she does not know how funny this sounds because she's never bothered to learn any slang. "I don't want to take a powder." I say, starting to giggle. She looks at me as if I am crazy.

"To sleep . . ." she says. I think I've frightened her. "A sleeping draft."

I can't stop laughing. Pretty soon I'm having hysterics. Fräulein takes my shoulder in her two big paws and gives me one great shake. I stop and look at her dumbly. "You must sleep," she says. "I will find some sedation." She heads for my mother's bathroom.

"Don't go in there!" I shout. "Please don't!" I want us both to leave the room because it has turned into my mother's grave. I am afraid of death. I am afraid that if I stay in this room something will happen to me.

I am better off than Roger. I am only half an orphan, while he's a whole one. I still have Daddy, Roger's got no one. They can't put me in the orphan asylum while I've still got Daddy. This thought licks at me like a tiny flame. They can't put me away so long as I have a real father.

"I don't need anything," I tell Fräulein. "I'll go to sleep by myself."

6

No Heart

I WOKE UP the next morning feeling nothing special, like a very sick dog who naturally has no idea he is about to die. It didn't take long for the truth of my new life to hit me, and I was forced to go through the whole thing once more: yes, my mother is dead — no, I will never see her again. Already she had altered. Her death had blurred her faults and flaws. In memory she had become a warm and rosy woman, soft and plump with large breasts and smelling like fresh bread instead of French perfume. As I lay in bed, I began to feel funny, slightly sickish, anxious, and hesitant, as if waiting for something brutal to happen.

"Oh, my God," I shout, jumping out of bed. "Roger!"

He is outside in the hall, yelling his head off. "You're lying," he screams. "She *is* coming back, she promised to bring me a present!"

"*Nein, nein, nein, Liebchen,* your mama is in heaven with your daddy, they are with the angels. Jesus took them last night." Roger starts to pound Fräulein's thigh with his little fists. I am amazed at how focused he is, for so small a child. Where did he find his strength?

"You big fat pig," he says to his beloved nurse, adroitly turning on her. I would have thought he would curl up in her lap and

93

cry, but instead he's slaughtering the messenger. "You're lying!"
"Roger!"

"Sally," he says to me, his eyes bigger than ever — and he has big eyes for a little boy. Big, brown Jewish eyes. "Make Fräulein stop lying to me. She says Mummy and Daddy are in heaven. She's a big fat liar. Make her stop!" He comes at me. I don't want him to hit me. I shout at Fräulein — it's a charming scene, all three of us losing control in different ways. "Why did you say that about Jesus? You know that's not true, why are you telling him those things? We don't believe in that stuff!" At this moment I could easily murder Fräulein, I hate her that much.

"He must find out . . ." Fräulein says, backing off. Her eyes are bleary and pink-rimmed, like a drunk's. I wish I could feel sorry for her.

"Roger," I say, trying to act calm. "Fräulein was wrong about Jesus, but she's right that Mummy and Freddie are not coming back. Oh God, what can I tell you? You see, they were in an accident. The plane they were in crashed and they were . . ." — the word "killed" sticks in my throat like a fishbone. I can't cough it up. I feel like I am choking. "They aren't ever coming back," I manage in a whisper.

"Then where are they?" Roger asks.

Good question, Roger. Where *are* they and what do they look like? Are they torn to pieces, are things broken, what happens to your clothes when a plane crashes? Are they burned to a crisp and do they look like charcoal? My mother like charcoal — I swallow hard to keep from being sick on the floor.

"They aren't anywhere, Rog, they're just dead." *There*, I said it.

"They're in San something," Roger says, reassuring himself. "They said so, they said they'd call up tonight."

"He doesn't understand," I say aloud, but not especially to Fräulein who is crying into a limp handkerchief.

"No Roger," I say.

"You're lying too. I hate you too!" he cries suddenly, denying the whole business. In a way I can't blame him.

"Roger," I shout, giving up any pretense of calmness. "You've got to listen. I'm not lying — listen to me!"

"I hate you," he shrieks. "And I won't listen." He runs into his room and gives the door a terrific slam. The house reverberates, then quiets.

I turn to Fräulein, who appears to be melting like the Wicked Witch of the West. "Fräulein," I say, and my voice scares even me, "Fräulein, if you ever talk to him about Jesus again, I'll kill you!"

"Heathen!" she says. "That poor orphaned baby has lost everything. All I was trying to do was help him feel better. He will feel better if he knows they are in heaven, with Our Lord and the angels."

"Stop!" I tell her. "It's not true. They're dead, just plain dead. Jews just die, they don't go to heaven or anywhere else. We don't believe in Jesus Christ!"

"We will *all* of us go to heaven when we die," she tells me. "Even you *Jews*." What she thinks of me personally shows clearly on her face. I look away, not caring. The doorbell rings. I want to speak to my father.

"It starts," Fräulein murmurs. She sighs, shuddering. Incredibly, she is beginning to open up like a dying flower.

"Who is it?" I say, wondering if I have time to call my father before dealing with whoever is ringing our front doorbell.

I lean over the stairwell and see the top of a head, hatless. Kathleen has just answered the door. She is crying and carrying on as if it were her mother and not just a lady she worked for. Mummy always said that Irish people are very emotional, especially about death. I don't recognize the head. For an instant I think it must be Mr. Orin Hughes coming to tell us it was a mistake after all. I want to scream. The head tilts. The face belongs to — Sam London. Why is *he* here? He sees me.

"Hello, Sally," he says.

"I'll be right down." I'm still wearing pajamas and bathrobe and I feel naked.

"I took the first plane out of Logan," he says. I nod.

"Why?" I ask. "I mean, I don't understand. Mr. Snyder, Mummy's lawyer, said he was coming and I thought you were him but you aren't. Why did you come down this morning?"

"Easy does it," Mr. London says. We stare at each other a moment. Then the phone rings. It rings and rings.

"Isn't anybody going to get that?" Sam London says.

"Kathleen the maid will," I say. Sam starts to say something, but Kathleen interrupts. There's a smudge of tear caking on her cheek.

"It's for you, Miss Sally," she tells me. "Your father wants to speak to you." She takes out a Kleenex and stuffs it against her nostrils.

I run to answer. It's my father, all right, and the way he talks to me says he is high on emotion, for once, instead of booze. He's absolutely looped on the idea of sudden death. Oh my poor baby, my poor little girl, who would have imagined . . . The expressions of shock and sympathy pour out like a Norcross greeting card. He completes his recitation by telling me about God — whom he probably hasn't given a moment's thought in the last thirty years — God giving and God taking away. The words in no way affect the way I feel; he might just as well be reading the menu at Chambord. "And," he winds up, his voice phlegmy, "just as soon as things have settled, we want you to come live with us — just as soon as we're married, that is. How does that sound? I've missed you all these years, princess, and though this isn't the way I would have chosen for us to be together, God knows, it's at least something to be thankful for out of this terrible tragedy." I don't really want to hear what he's implying; I can't face any of that yet. But the notion of going to live with him is like a peek at salvation for an awful sinner. Yes, I'll go, even if it means living with Lorna and her forehand. I've had the orphan asylum at the back of my mind ever since last night. My relief is so great it's almost a pain.

"Would you like to speak to Lorna? She's right here and wants to extend her condolences."

"Daddy," I say. "I can't talk anymore right now. I'll call you back after Mr. London goes." The last person I want to talk to in the whole world is Lorna Emerson.

"Who did you say was there?"

"Mr. London, from Boston. He's — he was — Freddie's business friend. He just came down this minute."

"What's he doing there?" Suspicion.

"I don't know yet. He was just going to tell me when you called."

"Run along, princess," my father tells me. "But please don't forget to call me back. I want to know what this London fellow has to say and why he's there. My God, I only heard the news myself an hour ago. You poor lamb . . ."

"Bye, Daddy." I hang up.

I have to look for Sam London and find him at last in Freddie's study with his nose in a book. "I wrote this," he says, snapping it shut as he sees me. He slides it back into its slot on the Friends' Shelf. The Friends' Shelf is reserved for books written by people Freddie knew personally. They are all archly inscribed and they have been specially bound in red leather with gold lettering on their spines. "It feels like an expensive pair of gloves," Sam observes. "I wonder if anyone's read it."

He takes out a crumpled pack of Camels and lights a cigarette. He inhales like there's no tomorrow. His skin is the same color as the smoke. I make one of my lightning-fast assessments. He's not a New Yorker, that's for sure. His clothes are wrinkled and his shirt is smooth and white, not like Freddie's, which were blue or pink rough cotton. He's got on rubber-soled shoes, the kind Dr. Singer, our dentist, wears. "You have no idea why I'm here, do you?" he says, looking at me like Miss O'Conner, at school. Shadows form patches on his face. He is one of the most unattractive, dirty-looking people I have ever seen. I think his underwear must smell. It did not occur to me at the time that Mr. London had lost something precious too. I was very busy thinking about myself.

I shake my head. Sam flicks the ash off his Camel. "It figures," he says, more to himself than to me. I notice that his fingers have a slight tremor.

"But then," he says, somewhat louder, "why should you, how could you?" He sits himself down in Freddie's chair. I am caught between admiration for the way he's taken over and revulsion at his arrogance. Freddie's chair is upholstered in natural cowhide; it swivels on soundless bearings and turns round and round like a piano stool. I often sit in it and give myself a ride. Sam tilts back, as if he owned the chair, the room, and everything in it. "Why don't you sit down, Sally," he says, indicating an armchair with his head. He crosses his legs. A stretch of white hairy skin emerges between socktop and pants cuff.

"How to begin . . ." he muses.

I am used to being patient with grownups. Most of them beat around the bush; even Oma Lucy does once in a while. I have the feeling that Sam London is the sort of man who doesn't like to start conversations on order. In fact, I have the strong feeling he would much rather think than talk.

"Sally, do you know what a guardian is?"

It's funny he should ask, because I've just been reading *David Copperfield* and I know all too well what a guardian is. A guardian is the alternative, as in "Please have this form signed by parent or guardian." No one I know has a guardian. Guardians, for their part, don't have sons and daughters; they have "wards" and they are mean as hell. They are cruel like James Mason who thinks nothing of smashing Ann Todd's fingers with a cane while she is playing the Pathétique for him. "I think so."

"Well," says the poor man, sighing with the effort of speech. "I am your brother Roger's guardian. As of last night. And yours too. If this is hard for you to swallow — and from the look on your face it obviously is — try to accept it slowly. Don't think about it all at once."

"I . . ." I can't finish. I don't know what he means about not accepting it all at once. How does a person do that?

"It's a little complicated," Sam says. "But since Freddie adopted you legally, he has some say in the matter of your immediate future. Naturally, the thing will have to be thrashed out in court, but I can't think there's going to be any real trouble."

"My father — " I interrupt him.

"He can object, of course, and the judge might rule in his favor, but we were hoping you might want to come with us . . . just for a while, you understand. Nothing permanent."

"I'm going to live with my father," I state flatly. No stranger is going to tear me from my father's embrace. I look at Sam London's face and find nothing in it to admire.

"That's your decision," he says, and his eyebrows shoot momentarily up, then settle again.

"Did Freddie say he wanted me to live with you? I don't understand."

"You ask some of the right questions," he says, putting his cigarette out by smearing it around the bottom of a massive brass ashtray.

Thanks a lot for nothing, I tell him silently. Does he think I will be flattered by the great compliment? If so, he has another think coming.

"All this must be quite a shock for you."

Now *there's* an original observation. Although it is not especially hot in Freddie's study, Sam is sweating. He has a sweat mustache. It occurs to me that he may be frightened of me. Why should he be scared of me? I'm just a thirteen-year-old orphan.

"Freddie never said a word to you about this arrangement, did he? I thought not. Why should he? The chances of anything like this happening were a mathematical long shot, to put it mildly. I guess I should be candid with you and tell you it took quite a bit of persuading on his part to get *me* to agree — it was late last spring, nearly a year ago — to be your and Roger's guardian if things went that way. I thought he was in a distracted mood at the time. The whole thing seemed strange; frankly, I was troubled by it. What healthy man in his thirties goes around doling out his children? He tried to convince me it was his lawyer's idea. You make a will, why not make an arrangement for your children? Maybe it was Snyder's usual brand of caution, but I don't think it was only Snyder. Sometime, when I know you better, I'll tell you about Freddie's mood. I don't really see any point in it now. Freddie was cautious too — you must know that. He never started out on a trip where he'd have to pay tolls without filling his pockets with dimes to give Rooney. He was prepared for emergencies. Insurance. You don't seem to be very interested in this, Sally."

The words are coming at me, but I can't seem to put them in proper order — it's my brain that's scrambled. "It's hard," I say faintly. My fingers are tingling as if they had been asleep. "I know about the dimes," I say. I start chewing on a nail.

"The dimes," he repeats. "You know, Sally, I agreed to take Roger and you in case anything happened to him and your mother partly because I was sure nothing ever would."

You don't even *want* us, I accuse him, again in silence. He will have to put me on the rack to get me to tell him what I'm really thinking.

"I don't believe in clairvoyance, do you? It's being able to predict the future. What a way for a so-called humanist to talk!" He pauses and lights another cigarette. "Well, I don't believe in it any more than I believe in heaven. But I do believe in anxiety, and Freddie was anxious. I don't particularly want to speculate about that at the moment. Did you know, Sally, that he had this thing about dying early? It came up from time to time. Or did he hide it from his family?"

"I don't remember anything about that," I say, refusing to talk about it. It's too late.

"Freddie had to sell me. He said he was rich and bought insurance to protect his investments and property. So why not get insurance for his children? Incidentally, you may not be aware of this, but Freddie thought of you as his own child. My wife Judy and I are the policy. It makes a certain amount of sense. The fact that I haven't done the same for my own kids only indicates I'm sloppy where Freddie was meticulous. It's not at all uncommon, as a matter of fact, especially with people as rich as Alfred Stern."

"Yes," I say.

"Sally. There's something I know you're not asking me."

"What?"

"Why me? Why not your real father or Freddie's mother, or your mother's father or any one of a number of friends or relatives? Why this stranger from Brookline, Massachusetts, who can't make it into The Orange Club, whose father came from Poland and whose mother never learned to speak more than pidgin English. God help me," he says suddenly. "I can't believe he's gone!" His eyes are open and scared. His emotion embarrasses me. I look at my lap.

"Why didn't you answer my question before?" I say severely.

"What question is that?" he says, taking out a handkerchief and blowing his nose.

"Whether Freddie said I should live with you too? Not just Roger."

"Legally, you're my ward. On the other hand, you have a father, living. That sounds funny, doesn't it? Mr. Snyder thinks that with some fancy legal maneuvering it might be possible for you to go and live with your father after you've turned fifteen if that's what you want. In other words, we're not going to try and stop you because that way no one would benefit — you'd be little better than a prisoner in our house. No, the thing is, my wife Judy and I thought it might be easier for Roger if you came along and stayed with us for a while. He's alone. By the way, when *is* your birthday?"

"June," I say, beginning to get the lay of the land and not liking it one bit. "But Roger's not alone. There's Fräulein. Sometimes I think he must love her as much as — you know."

"That may be something of a problem," Sam says. I can tell he's uneasy because he isn't looking at me straight-on anymore.

"What kind of problem?" Almost everything this man says manages to have an ominous sound.

"Well, there's no telling how long Fräulein Kastern will stay with us."

"Why not? She's been here ever since Roger was born. Why should she leave now?"

"Simply put, Judy doesn't get along with Germans. As a matter of fact, she can't stand them. It's the war thing — she lost a lot of relatives during the war, you know; they just disappeared along with about five million other Jews. One day they were there. The next — no trace. She blames the Germans, all Germans, big ones, little ones, fat ones, thin ones, whatever."

"But Fräulein was here during the war."

"Won't make the slightest bit of difference to Judy."

"That's silly," I say, beginning to feel the trap's teeth around my calves. "She's taken out her first papers."

"It's all the same to Judy," he repeats. "I guess we could talk about irrationality for a long time. Is it rational to systematically kill off all the Jews in Europe?"

"I don't know what that's got to do with it," I say.

"Ah," he says. "I wish I had the means to make you understand . . ." He rubs his forehead. "Look, Sally," he says, leaning forward at me. "Fräulein is going to come and live with us, but that's all I can say. Whether she chooses to stay on, given the circumstances — I mean, you have no idea how Judy is about this. It's an obsession with her. She wants you children very much — you should have seen her face when she heard; she's always wanted a girl — but the Fräulein thing is something else. It's not going to be easy for her. I don't imagine Fräulein is going to feel very comfortable with us. That's how it is. I wish I could do something to change it."

Judy must be a disgustingly difficult woman. Difficult and self-ish. She might even be a shit. Fräulein isn't exactly the greatest person to have around, but, my God, she's Roger's second mother. How can this Judy be so selfish? Judy and her obses-sions. What right has she got to go hating people who never did anything to her, people she's never even met?

I say, "Roger and I don't get along all that well. I don't think he likes me all that much."

"But you're the closest thing he's got to a blood relative, aren't you?"

"I guess so," I say. Angry tears gather to make themselves visible. I don't want to cry in front of this man. The heck with it, I don't care. Let him see me all sloppy. I don't want to leave this house. I don't want to move. Yes, I do — I want to move to my father's house, but I can't stand Lorna. I don't think I can live with Lorna. No, it doesn't matter about her. It won't be so bad as

going to live with this cold-hearted Sam and his fishy wife somewhere, probably some smelly old house with broken windows
and a toilet that doesn't flush. Fräulein isn't so bad — she's just a
mess of sauerkraut with big feet and menstrual cramps — anyone
can put up with Fräulein if they really try.

"I'm truly sorry, Sally."

"It doesn't matter," I sob.

"Listen, Sally. I'm pretty sure we can arrange for you to go
live with your father, if that's what you really want. After a
while. It shouldn't be too difficult. I told you I've already spoken
to Don Snyder about it. All we're asking is that you come up to
Brookline with us and stay for a while. No, I don't know what
I'm saying. I'm afraid that at this moment you really haven't got
any options. No choice. But I don't want you to come to us
angry. It isn't what we planned. Freddie . . ."

"He's crazy!" I blurt out, believing it to the bottom of my
loafers.

"No," Sam says. "Romantic maybe. Maybe you'll understand
when you're a little older."

If there's one thing I can't stand it's people telling me I'll
understand when I'm older — it's so goddam condescending. I
bite my pinky nail viciously. "Maybe, but I doubt it."

Sam sighs, shaken.

I can see right away that Sam is the sort of person who doesn't
mind when a conversation runs out of fuel or stalls. He doesn't
feel silly or stupid, the way I do, just sitting there and not saying
anything. Silence makes me nervous, unless it's at a concert, between movements of a symphony. I try to remember what my
poor mother told me about this Judy person. She said, or she
implied (in a voice reserved for her inferiors: servants, trades-
people, magazine lackeys, secretaries, and Russian Jews), that
Judy was overdeveloped intellect and underdeveloped style. Low-
heeled shoes, last year's fashions, and hairy legs; bad posture,
cynicism, and a know-it-all, vulgar, Jewish sense of humor. Sus-

picious. Naturally, I wouldn't like her, nor she me. She would think me poor little rich girl, Shirley Temple before she gets her comeuppance, New York snob, sophisticated in all the wrong ways. My mother's profoundest indictment: Judy London carried the same pocketbook everywhere she went, whether it was the market, the dentist, or the Copley Plaza. According to Mummy it looked like a saddlebag and smelled like one too.

The doorbell rings, interrupting my fantasy.

"That's Snyder," Sam says. I can hear Kathleen opening the front door. And voices, loaded with sincerity.

In another second he's at the door. "I hope I'm not interrupting anything." He is embarrassed, the kind of man who would rather have to deal with *deceased, trust, will* than with *widow* and *orphan*. People on paper do not cry and carry on. He comes toward me like an undertaker — is his suit really black or is it just the light? — and takes one of my hands in both of his. "A tragedy, a great tragedy," he murmurs. "Who would have imagined two such vibrant human beings, snuffed out in a trice? They were so alive. Why, just last Friday I lunched with your stepfather at The Club. He was full of plans, enthusiastic about his coming trip, optimistic about Griffin House, his Fall List. He thought he might have a best-seller at last in the Mortimer novel. Poor Alfred and Marguerite. It's a fearful blow. Both gone. It staggers the mind. I'm sorry, my dear, for going on — I'm afraid I'm not really myself yet. Your parents were my friends . . . good friends."

I find his speechifying loathesome. I look at Sam to see what he thinks, but nothing shows.

"Has young Roger been told?"

"Yes," I say. "But he doesn't believe it. He won't believe me or Fräulein. We both told him."

The two men look at each other, at a loss.

"It's gotta be done," Sam says. His face is looking grayer. Well, I'm not about to feel sorry for *him*.

He dispatches me to fetch Roger. As I leave I overhear Mr. Donald Snyder mention funeral arrangements. At the word "remains" the blood drains from my head, sending me reeling. The remains of my mother, a body without a spirit, a piece of dead nothing, a lump of rotten meat. I feel my own life leaving me and sit down hard on the bottom step of the staircase. I have the choice whether to pass out or not; there's still a moment of vitality left in me. I drop my head and shove it between my knees while mysterious things stir within me, and I choose to remain conscious. I want this moment because it represents — God willing — the worst moment of my life. Nothing will ever match it for pure horror and despair. Everything after this will be recuperation.

I moan, I let out a musical "oh" that no one hears but me.

After several minutes I get up. My legs are shivering, my head aches. I feel as if I've had a close call. But close to what, I can't say. Perhaps close to an understanding whose clarity has never again been matched for me. If it is the shiver of truth, okay, or the shiver of death — that's okay too.

I have to search for Roger, calling his name. I find him and Fräulein playing one of their sadomasochistic games: he's throwing things around his room and she's picking them up, crooning at him in pidgin German at the same time. Which makes it especially hard for me to claim his attention. He doesn't want to come with me, certainly not to talk to the "nice man" who wants to have a word with him. No, he doesn't want to see anybody. He wants to throw his brand-new F. A. O. Schwarz paintbox with twenty-two different cubes of color and two sable brushes out of the window. Fräulein is his steadfast ally; she seems to have gone deaf.

"I said Mr. London wants to see Roger, Fräulein!"

"Then I will come with him," she announces at last. "Come along Roger, the nice man wants to see you." She looks daggers at me, and I wonder if she has any idea what is in store for her.

Fräulein makes a final sweep of the room with her big beefy hands, picking up wooden blocks, a toy car, tiny scraps of paper I can hardly see. She's absolutely maddening. "I'll be in my room," I say, seeing she's not going to hurry.

Finally I hear them head downstairs for the interview. I go to my room, having avoided my mother's bedroom as if it were a smallpox ward. It is filled with evil spirits, with death and decay, with the power to destroy. I come near this room and my knees buckle. I promise myself never to go in there again so long as I live. It is a place of terror and darkness, my dead mother, her smell and her dead eyes and her broken pieces of bone and scalp, her anguish, my sorrow.

There are motions and crosscurrents in the house as if it were alive. The phone rings over and over again — who is it and why don't they tell me? Kathleen keeps running up and down stairs. I hear voices I can't identify. I am a prisoner in this house. I will soon go to another jail farther than ever from my beloved father. Why did he let Freddie adopt me? Didn't he *know* what was going to happen?

I can't bear to be alone. I see Mr. Snyder on the stairs and ask him, "Do you know if the plane caught fire?"

"Oh, my dear. I really couldn't say. Well, I imagine it did, somewhat — they usually do." He looks away, abashed.

"Two people got out alive," I persist.

"That's what I understand," Mr. Snyder says, taking out his pocket handkerchief and wiping under his nose with it. "I believe that one of them is not expected to live." He fingers his tie clip, a plain thin bar of fourteen-carat gold.

I walk away from him. I wander around my house, feeling strange, as if I were on one of my mother's house tours. I don't recognize things: the lay of the couch is wrong, the picture over the mantel in the living room — I could swear I've never laid eyes on it before.

I ought to call Oma Lucy. I know I ought, but I can't; I just

can't — it's too hard. In back of me I hear Roger's voice rise on a
note of fury and denial. He screams and sends shivers of terror
up and down the back of my neck. I run downstairs again. I
haven't eaten but the idea of food sends bile into my mouth.
Maybe I'll lose some weight — ah, it isn't worth it. I'd rather be
fat and have Mummy.

I turn to my friend, the radio. Instead of Frankie I hear about
"the death of Alfred Stern, avant-garde publisher, socialite, and
noted art collector, and that of his wife, the former Marguerite
Baum, famed Manhattan hostess, in a plane crash that claimed the
lives of fifty-seven others, including Martin Boltin, vice-president
of Farmer Industries, and the pilot, veteran Captain James C.
Burnett of Oakland, California. The wealthy Stern couple were
on a combined business and pleasure trip to the San Francisco
Bay Area. According to a family spokesman, Mr. Stern had
planned to meet with the controversial novelist Norman Q.
Baker, author of *Hell's Seventh Hole* and *In the Course of Time*.
The Sterns, married during a wartime leave of naval Lieutenant
Commander Stern, leave a son, Roger, six, and Mrs. Stern's
daughter by a previous marriage, Sarah Agard Stern, thirteen.
The Sterns' New York residence is on New York's exclusive
Upper East Side. The passing of Alfred Stern was noted today by
. . ." I snap it off. *Ça suffit*, as my mother would say. Who
writes that stuff? Who in hell is the family spokesman? And I am
not thirteen; I am almost fifteen.

I want to cry but I am as dry as an unlicked stamp. My mother's death has already begun to alter me. I find I can now do
something I have never been able to do before: stand outside
myself and watch what I'm doing. With a terrible wrench I have
been torn apart. One half suffers, the other half stands aside and
marvels.

I doze off. The next thing I am aware of is the Battleship S.S.
Fräulein throbbing beside my bed.

"What do you know of this plan?" she demands.

"You mean going with him, Mr. London? I just found out this morning."

"I don't believe you!"

"Why should I lie to you?"

"Oh," she wails.

I end up trying to tell her it won't be so bad. She seems completely undone, coming apart, losing her head — all those things you hear about people but hardly ever see. She just can't swallow the message. She doesn't want to move any more than I do, but she's a grownup and she's making a terrific fuss.

"Fräulein, can't you stop?"

"He is a disagreeable person, he is a hard man, he looks like thunder, he is not a polite person. He said the change would be hard for me. I will not leave my *Liebchen* — he is all alone now."

"Nobody asked you to leave," I say. I've been lying down. Now I swing my legs over the side of the bed and sit up. I am so tired I can hardly maintain an upright position, but it is important to face her.

"Something is funny here. How do I know what it will be like? There are no servants. I will have to help with the housework. I am not a parlormaid . . ."

"Fräulein, I don't want to talk."

"Oh," she says. I can see the little gears turning in her head and reminding her that she is not the only person on earth.

"You will be there," she says. By God, I actually believe she needs me. The world has turned inside out.

"For a while," I say. "Then I am going to live with Daddy. After all, he's my real father. I'm not an orphan. Roger's an orphan but I'm only half."

Fräulein bursts into terrible German tears, much juicier than American tears. I get up and hustle her out of my room. I can't listen to her blubbering another second.

The inevitable telephone call comes: Oma Lucy, just before noon. She sounds funny, but it would be funny if she didn't. First off, she tries to console me. Then she says, "Of course you and Roger will come and live here with me. There is so much room, extra rooms — what does an old lady like me want with so many rooms to rattle around in? And Fräulein Kastern will come too and we will try to live our lives as your mother and Freddie would have wished. I'm not difficult to get along with, you know that. We'll go to all the good concerts and see a lot of plays and you can have as many of your young friends over as often as you want. I love young people. I love being around them."

"Oma?"

"What is it my dear? Oh Sally . . ."

"Oma, there's something you have to know."

"What is it?" she says, her voice getting messed up by sobs.

"Look, can I call you back in a little while? There's someone leaving now I have to say goodbye to. I'll call you back in five minutes."

"All right," she says faintly. We hang up.

I run, panicked, to find Mr. London. "Mr. London," I cry. He's examining the Degas dancer with a vacant expression on his face.

"Please, Sally, why don't you start calling me Sam?"

"All right," I say, determined not to. "It's Oma Lucy, Freddie's mother. She just called. She thinks we're going there to live — she's got it all planned."

"Hey, calm down, Sally. Mr. Snyder's on his way there this minute to tell her about it."

"Oh gosh," I say. "It's going to be awful for him."

"He did make love to his profession," Sam tells the dancer.

"What?"

"Oh, nothing. Sally, are you hungry? I'll bet you haven't had anything to eat today. Why don't we ask the cook to fix us a nice big plate of sandwiches and a couple of glasses of milk?"

"I'm not hungry."

How can he think of food? Because he has a stomach and no heart.

"I'm sorry to hear that," he says, heading toward the dining room. "But I think I'll have a bite myself. I haven't eaten since six this morning. No point in not keeping up my strength. I imagine I'm going to need it."

7

A Sparrow
Is on the Roof

SAM CLAIMS he saw an usher go up to a little old man sitting in the last row of seats during the funeral and ask him to remove his yarmulke. Must I explain that wearing a yarmulke in Temple Joshu-a would be like wearing the American flag on the seat of your pants to a DAR meeting? The little old man took it off, at least that's what Sam says, and stuffed it into his pocket.

Temple Joshu-a represented upper-class Jewish life in the forties. It was an emblem, an objective correlative. The works. The temple was the hub out from which all else spoked. It must be a paradox that the very place where religion was nurtured, where God hung out, so to speak, should embody a tone, a style, that was so secular. It was clear to me even then that most of the men and women who came to pay their last respects to the Sterns would have willingly relinquished a thousand shares of Eastman Kodak to have been mistaken for Protestants. When I was a child, in that place and in that time, Goldstein hid inside Gordon and Goodwin, Hirschberg in Hersey, Greenberg chopped his off and crawled inside Green, Shapiro took refuge in Chase. Katz became Gray (because all cats are gray in the dark). Garrulous turned into muffled and mute. Aftershave lotion from Saks Fifth Avenue replaced the beard.

The atmosphere inside Temple Joshu-a was as lustrous as Hattie Carnegie's dress salon, from the mink skins to the coiffed heads, from the felt hats to the kidskin shoes and gloves. The place was more like a Unitarian church than most Unitarian churches, all traces of Rome and Jerusalem having been successfully eradicated and replaced with a clinging purity: white walls, crimson upholstery, sparkling clean windows, pews up front with neck-high sides, brass fittings, waxed floors. It was as unobjectionable as it was lacking in true character. In a passion to be "accepted," assimilated, the German Jews who maintained the temple's upkeep and paid the Rabbi had pledged themselves to erase everything that might give them away as marginal oddballs; they had sanded their fingertips to get rid of the prints.

The Rabbi was never called "Rabbi." He was called "Doctor," and when he sermonized he sounded like T. S. Eliot reading *The Waste Land* on a Spoken Word record. He enjoyed the sound of his own voice and words, rolling them around on his tongue like liquid-center chocolates from Louis Sherry. He gave my mother and stepfather the top-drawer service, the one reserved for A, big donors or B, important parishioners (they were B). Also, I suppose, because there were two of them at once, a circumstance that seemed to stun everybody but made an obscure kind of sense to me. The audience — I mean those assembled—included family, friends, business associates, authors, servants, and service people of one sort or another, men whom Freddie and Fippy had aided financially, and a scattering of people who owed Freddie money. I might have sat with my father but Oma Lucy needed me more. Sam London was there, of course, with his Judy and her smelly pocketbook. Fräulein appeared in a coat that looked like a horse blanket, leading a confused Roger by the hand and plunking him down on the other side of Oma Lucy. Poor old Oma quivered like a tiny motor. She wore violet-colored kid gloves and every so often she would extend one of these and put it on top of my hand. It felt like talcum powder and smelled like flowers. I couldn't take my eyes off these gloves. They seemed to me the most unusual things I had ever seen; they were as strange and lovely as a Monarch butterfly on the subway.

Opa Baum was there, of course, the dragon himself, his fire temporarily quenched. He was as white as a sheet and he didn't recognize me. As a matter of fact I had forgotten his existence. It was a shock to see him because I realized he too might want us to go live with him. But then I remembered that he openly disliked small and middle-sized children; they were irritations to him, people who asked for things at the wrong time and interrupted you in the middle of a bridge game and sometimes wet the bed.

There were no coffins, but the presences of Freddie and Marguerite Stern were there, like the scent of Mummy's perfume. I tried to listen to what the Doctor was saying and was able to tune in for short takes from time to time. His sermon was sparked by predictable themes of unpredictable mortality, change, chance, destiny, mutability, Americanism, and the gross assertion that the best are taken first.

After about thirty minutes the Rabbi wound up. He ended his death speech on a note of uplift, which was difficult because, unlike Fräulein Kastern, he could not claim that Alfred and Marguerite Stern were playing harps and calling on Jesus at teatime.

"Magnified and sanctified be His great name in the world which He created according to His will. May He establish His kingdom in your lifetime and your days, and in the lifetime of all the house of Israel, speedily and at a near time; and say ye, Amen. Let His great name be blessed for ever and ever." The emphasis was not on the next world but on this. Which is about the only way my parent and stepparent deviated from their superrich, supersocial non-Jewish friends, with their Wellesley and Yale diplomas, their seats on the boards of a lot of museums and other cultural establishments, and their freewheeling use of New York watering places.

As for me, I was too numb to care much about what Dr. Elias said, and I certainly didn't feel much like praising God at that moment. If God had killed my mother, why should I have anything to do with Him for the rest of my life? And if He had nothing to do with her death, then why bring Him into it at all?

We stumbled up the aisle — I wasn't conscious of people looking at me with pity and awe, but I'm sure they were. I was a victim of fate; I was a bona fide curiosity. I was the statistical long shot, which meant that if it happened to me it probably wouldn't happen to them. I was stunned by the sudden light and noise of life continuing regardless on Fifth Avenue. I stood there blinking and trying to keep my balance while the minks and the dark flannels moved down the shallow steps to the street. A few people came up to me and told me how beautifully I was bearing up. They told me it was a tragedy. They told me my mother was a wonderful, beautiful human being. And all the time I was trying to find Daddy. I considered the fact that I couldn't find him a very bad sign, an omen. Didn't it mean that I would never find him again? In the middle of this morbid speculation I felt an urgent grip on my upper arm.

"You'll drop by the apartment and have a bite with me?" Oma Lucy tells me. She looks so thin and weak I think she's going to break in half. I can see in the strong light that her face is caked with pale pink powder, too rosy for her ashen complexion. The semicircles under her eyes are the same shade of violet as her gloves. She's using a cane; I've never seen her with a cane. It makes me uneasy. It reminds me that she's going to have her own funeral service soon.

"Yes, thank you," I say. Jonathan, in his chauffeur suit, pearly gray with Cecil B. DeMille boots, takes her gently by the elbow and guides her down to where her Lincoln saloon car with two jump seats sits purring at the curb, waiting for her. "I'll just go tell the Londons," I say, still hoping to see my father before we have to leave.

"Darling, if you don't mind, I haven't asked the Londons," Oma says. "Just family and a few close friends."

"But Mr. London was one of Freddie's closest friends."

"Surely not," she says. "Or I would have met him years ago."

"I think I'm going to live with them for a little while."

"So I have been informed!" Her anger is pure ice. This fury seems to give her strength, like Geritol for tired blood. She straightens and takes her weight off the cane and at the same time shakes off Jonathan's arm. "I am not yet resigned to it. I understand there will be a hearing. I have not yet decided whether to fight for you. But whatever I decide, I want you to know I consider the arrangement highly unusual, highly inappropriate. This London fellow is a professor with almost no income. I am told he has two small children of his own. I cannot understand how Freddie erred so grievously in his judgment. He might have lost his senses for all we know about it."

"Do you think you're going to fight?" I say.

"I haven't had an opportunity to talk to my attorney yet — everything's happened so fast. Naturally I shall follow his advice, do what he recommends. I am not one to hire an expert and then pay no heed to what he says. But I will never approve of this bizarre arrangement. Why, it's like sending Princess Margaret" — my God, how does she know? — "to live with the Australian aborigine." She takes Jonathan's arm which is hanging patiently in the air, waiting for her. "Are you coming, Sally?"

"Well, at least let me tell the Londons I won't be home for lunch. They'll worry."

"Run along then, but please hurry."

Probably, if I'd had my wits about me, I would have been horrified by Oma Lucy's behavior. I can't say I blamed her for resenting the Londons. After all, they were going to whisk away her beloved grandchildren, take them off to some undistinguished middle-class suburb in New England. They were Russian Jews. There was no telling what evil things would happen to Prince Roger and Princess Margaret, I mean Sarah. Would they acquire funny accents, would their breath smell of potato latkes and kishkas, would they get hairy and forget to bathe? The lurking fears must have risen to the surface. Oma Lucy had had less to do with Russian Jews than Mrs. Roosevelt had.

Her ferocious snobbery was Oma's outstanding flaw. Everyone has a flaw, but when I was thirteen years old it was a surprise each time I discovered one in an adult. It took rather a long time for me to adjust to the fact that most people have a streak of something bad which doesn't fit in with the rest of their personality or behavior, something like a thread of sadism or sloth, a drinking problem, or a compulsion to clean their ears in public. Although her lawyer advised her against trying to get us away from the Londons, Oma Lucy lived her last years nursing her hatred for them, a hatred out of all proportion to how bad or good they actually were. Long afterward, Sam showed me a letter Lucy had written him, accusing him of using "Communistic tactics" to force Freddie into making him our guardian so that "your pitiful standard of living and your social position might thereby be raised without your having to lift a finger." That nice old lady with her devotion to Mischa and Sasha and the Philharmonic and starving musicians and her true, honest musical sensitivity. That nice old lady could be as rabid in her way as Father Coughlin was in his.

For all its exclusivity, Oma Lucy's postfuneral lunch party was no great shakes. Not that I expected it to be like a wedding breakfast. But everybody was crinkly and formal, as if they were afraid of me or afraid I would do something embarrassing. Nobody cried or moaned, nobody made a fuss, but there was whispering, and whispering made me uneasy. The way people whisper, for instance, in a doctor's waiting room. It's not a library, for Christ's sake — you're just waiting to have your blood pressure taken or your warts removed.

Once inside the apartment I was suddenly ravenous. I hadn't really eaten for two days and now my hunger reasserted itself. I ate like a maniac. I was glad the meal was a buffet — that allowed me to pig it without anybody noticing. I piled ham and turkey, wild rice, chutney, green beans with almonds, avocado salad and endive, buttered rye bread and spiced crabapples onto my plate like a fat man at a Chinese restaurant. I took my plate into a corner to eat like a squirrel afraid the other squirrels are going to grab his nuts. When I had wolfed this down, I went back and got a double helping of strawberry shortcake topped by a huge cloud of whipped cream. My eating like that stuffed away the empty sick feeling I had had ever since the "accident."

While I ate and ate, Fräulein tried to coax Roger to swallow his meat and vegetable so he could have some lovely shortcake. Roger was still fighting the truth; he was too occupied with this battle to eat. Fräulein should have known.

"I don't like that turkey, it tastes funny."

"That's silly, Roger," I say. "It's yummy. I had some. It's very good."

"Mummy makes it much better. This tastes like dirt."

Fräulein shoots me a very significant look and shrugs tearfully. Freddie's cousin Dorothy comes up to me and tells me how well I'm bearing up. She makes nice-sounding noises about my coming to stay with her on Martha's Vineyard next summer. I know my "cousins," her children, don't like me. They're two and four years older than me and they go out with boys. They're slim and pretty. They have button noses and straight hair. I say that would be nice, knowing I'll never accept her invitation. She coos at Roger and puts her hand on his gleaming brown hair. He looks up at her as if she smelled bad. She withdraws her hand and invites him to come and see her too. Roger says, "I don't want to go." Dorothy backs off. Orphanage has made him nasty.

Several other people make an effort to establish some sort of contact with me. They think they do but I know they haven't.

After a while I decide I can go home without its looking like eat and run, which is precisely what I've done. Fräulein is certainly not going to mind; she's up to her ears in Roger. The others won't mind either, because they won't even think about it. I look around for Lucy; she's not where I saw her last, sitting and poking food with her fork, so pale she seems bleached.

"Jonathan, where's Oma Lucy?" Jonathan's back in his butler jacket and black pants. His head, with its rivulets of hair plastered down with goo (even *I* know that Indian hair is straight as seaweed) catches the lights from the chandelier over the dining room table. His eyes flicker nervously. "She's retired to her room, Miss Sally."

Relieved that I don't have to stage a parting scene with her, I ask Jonathan to tell her that I will call her later and I make my getaway. I belch. The food rises and hits the back of my throat, stinging. I am a pig. I have eaten so much I disgust myself. How can I eat when my mother is barely cold in the ground? I decide to walk home, down Fifth Avenue. The wind makes whipping passes at my bare legs and sneaks underneath my camel's-hair coat. I hate the cold. I know it's going to be colder in Brookline.

After a few blocks I cross over to Madison, then Park, and finally, via a random snakelike pattern, to my house.

Later, the people who bought the house violated my mother's beautiful sense of balance, order, and grace. They covered all the hardwood floors with asphalt tiles or wall-to-wall carpets in urgent shades of purple and green. They replaced the fantastic restaurant stove with one equipped with a dozen dials and self-timers. I know about this because Sam told me about it after a trip to New York and a morbidly motivated visit to my old house.

He was amused by what he found, but I'm glad I never saw it; it would have made me feel even worse.

The first thing I did when I got inside the front door was call my father. I'm in a sweat of anxiety; why didn't he wait to see me? My poor luck holds — Lorna answers the phone.

Lorna oozes, she drips pity, condolence. I smell the garbage a mile away. It's funny how when a person uses too many of the right words you begin not to believe them. Protesting too much. Or giving more than one reason for not being able to do something. Lorna overdoes everything. I don't think she could ever come right out and say, "I'm sorry, Sally," and leave it at that. No, it's got to be "tragedy," "sorrow," "loss," "time heals everything," and "we're here to help you in your bereavement." Well, I know that bereavement is an adult state of mind. I try to get her to stop, but the button's been pushed and there's no way of stopping her till she runs down. I tune out until I hear her say, "Your father's here. He wants to talk with you, darling.

"He's heard from this man named London and from your mother's lawyer, a Mr. Snyder? Yes, Mr. Snyder. It's funny, I never even heard Mr. London's name mentioned before except maybe once by Willy but I'm not really sure even about that. Well, this London person talked to your father this morning, before the service — wasn't it a lovely service? I mean if you've got to go through that sort of thing, and you do, of course. You just can't say goodbye to someone you love without having a little ceremony, don't you think? Don't you think it was perfectly lovely the way the Doctor read that passage from Psalms? I don't remember exactly which number Psalm it was — I always get them mixed up, one hundred and one hundred and four, how do people keep them straight? It's a mystery to me, I just never can. Anyway, it made the hairs on the back of my neck stand straight up when he read that part about the poor little sparrow

all alone on the roof. I couldn't help thinking of that poor orphaned child, your poor little brother . . ."

I can hear the phone being wrenched from Lorna's hand.
"Hello, my poor princess, how are you? How are you bearing
up?" It's quiet in the background. He must have killed her.

"Where *were* you, Daddy? Why didn't you talk to me after
the funeral?"

"I tried to find you, princess, but by the time I spotted you I
was beginning to feel rocky on my pins. You know, I'm still not
quite up to fighting form. I'm sorry, Sally. I meant to see you. I
wanted to talk with you."

"Yes." I'm beginning to lose the full feeling from lunch.

"Well, partly about what Mr. London had to say. I must say, it
all came as a terribly unpleasant surprise. You see, Lorna and I
were counting on your coming down here to live with us."

"He told me I could come. He seemed to think it would be all
right with the court or something if I wanted to leave and come
down and be with you. He said he wouldn't stand in my way.
Doesn't that sound funny?"

"He's your guardian, my sweet. I don't know why I ever
agreed to let Stern adopt you. I must have been out of my mind."

"Yes, Daddy."

"It's water under the dam, but I'll never forgive myself." I can
hear Lorna's shrill voice in the background though not what she's
saying. My father, holding his hand over the mouthpiece, says
something back to her. His tone is impatient. "Nevertheless,
London said that if you were determined not to stay with them,
he would do whatever he could to effect your moving in with us.
You're perfectly right. He will not stand in your way. Decent
fellow."

"He's okay," I say, guardedly.

"As I said," my father goes on, "I find everything about this
extremely odd. I can't imagine what got into your stepfather's

head, passing you on to a complete stranger whose standard of living, to put it mildly, is hardly what you're used to. I foresee that for your brother it will be like putting him down on the moon and expecting him to behave normally. I just can't understand what made him do a thing like that. There are any number of more suitable places for you to live — any number of friends and relatives of your poor mother. I mean, what's the sense of sending you up to a suburb of Boston, like that?"

"I wish I didn't have to go," I say, almost choking on my own words.

"We're going to fix up some rooms for you," he says. "You know the top floor of the house, all those nasty dark little rooms? They used to be the servants' quarters. Well, Lorna has had this nifty idea to get in someone to do a real overhaul, tear down a couple of walls, paint the place, make a suite of rooms for you and your friends. She's very excited about this project. The way I have the situation figured is for you to go with London for a couple of months, just to prove that we're willing to be reasonable, and then, when our place is ready, say around summertime, you come down to us. Then we'll live happily ever after. How's that sound?"

"It sounds like you don't want me right away," I tell him.

"Princess . . . How can you say a thing like that? You know your daddy is living for the day when he can have his little girl with him again. But you wouldn't want to desert poor Roger right now, would you?"

"Daddy!"

"What is it, princess. What's upsetting you?"

"Never mind, I don't want to talk about it. It's all right, Daddy, honestly. I just feel sort of lost. When are you going to get married?" I don't know what I'm saying — I'm in a daze.

"Now, that's a nice cheerful thought to cheer us all up. We were planning it for a couple of weeks from now, but since what has happened has happened we thought it wouldn't seem right to go ahead right away. Probably in May sometime. We expect you to come down and be part of the ceremony. Well, not exactly in the ceremony but — isn't there a book — *Member of the Wedding*?"

"I don't know." Numbness has replaced agitation. And fatigue. I feel as if I could sleep for a month, if not forever.

"I have an idea. Why didn't I think of it before? Why don't you ask the chauffeur, what's-his-name, to drive you down here? You can spend the night, spend a few days with us, just rest and get your bearings. How about it, princess?"

"Maybe, Daddy," I say. "Actually, I think I'd just rather stay here. I'm awfully tired."

"It's a short drive, princess. Once you get here you can sleep to your heart's content. Why, we'll even give you breakfast in bed. Room service, just like at the Ritz."

Like at a hospital, you mean.

"Thanks, Daddy, but I think I'd rather stay here." Did I say that before?

My father's flipflopping from one position to another is as baffling as his disappearing after Mummy's funeral. Is he trying to tell me something?

I begin to be aware that my father's words have been overlapping slightly and some of the consonants are getting lost en route. Yes, he's been swilling the booze again. I don't want to talk to him anymore.

My father asks me to reconsider.

"I will," I tell him, as much to get him off the phone as to tell the truth. We mutually hang up. I wonder what Lorna was saying to him. I think of them as mixed up together like twins or a long married couple, people who can't separate themselves from one another. I can see Lorna as the kind of wife who insists on helping her husband make all his big decisions, such as whether to

change jobs or how much to sell in a falling market. I go upstairs
to take a nap. I never questioned the blessedness of being able to
fall asleep just when my world had split and shattered.

The first thing I heard when I woke up was Fräulein, mooing
and lowing. She blew her nose continually and kept crushing
Roger against her enormous bosom. Apparently what had been
worked out was that Fräulein was to come up to Brookline with
Roger and me and stick around until either a replacement was
found for her or Roger felt he could manage without a nurse. It
was perfectly clear to both me and Fräulein that nobody had a
nurse on the street in Brookline where the Londons lived. Nor in
their crowd. I wondered how long she would last in that alien
place. She was a big-city girl herself, even more than my mother.
She loved the subway, she was devoted to Gimbel's. Fräulein's
idea of the country was the Sheep Meadow in Central Park. She
got hay fever from flowers and chilblains from standing on a
corner for five minutes. I wondered how long she would last in
the frozen tundra.

This day was taking a long time. It was all *now*, with the past
and the future always out of reach.

The next thing I heard was Judy London, Sam's wife, talking
on the telephone. I could hear her using the phone in Freddie's
study and it made me feel very funny, violated. There was something so proprietary in the way she was telling the person at the
other end that she'd be "here for a couple of days. Please see that
the boys eat a good breakfast before they leave for school. Oh,
and don't forget to call Dr. Jackman for me and change my
appointment. Thanks a lot, Charlene, you're an angel." I walk up
behind her, she senses me and turns around, startled.

"Oh, Sally, I didn't hear you."

Obviously.

"We let you sleep. You seemed to be sleeping very soundly.

Would you like some dinner? We've all just eaten but there's plenty left. My, it was good."

"No thanks," I say. "I'm not hungry." Well, that's a partial lie. I'm not starving. But I'm gaining points by refusing food. It puts her on the defensive.

"Okay," she says. "But if you do get hungry, I'm sure Marie will have kept your portion warm for you."

"Thanks," I say. "Who's Charlene? I thought you only had boys."

"Oh, Charlene's the baby-sitter. She's neat — you'll like her. She lives across the street. You've never been in Brookline, have you?" She smiles eagerly, but I can tell the smile is an effort — she's trying to "reach" me.

"No."

"Well," she goes on. "All I can tell you is, it's not a bit like East Seventy-third Street. Oh, not at all."

"That's what I thought," I say. Here we are. Are we supposed to do something together? Is there some ritual we could perform that would make both of us more comfortable? That would start us out properly in this peculiar relationship. She's my guardian. Well, all I can say is she's not one bit like Marguerite Baum Sanderson Stern. Not at all. Thus I launch into what will be weeks of odious comparing in which she will emerge holding the short end. It isn't really fair, things, events, memories, and guilts have stacked the cards squarely in my mother's favor.

Mummy was slim. This woman doesn't care about her body; she's carrying around at least ten pounds she doesn't need. Her hair is long and heavy, like a girl's, and hopelessly out of fashion. She's got bangs. There isn't a single girl in the Seeley School who wears bangs, nor a single model in *Harper's Bazaar*, nor a single movie star. June Allyson with bangs? Rita Hayworth with bangs? The bangs are also a little too shiny for my taste. How often does she wash her hair? Her clothes are hopeless. A sweater and skirt. Skirt too short — not the New Look, the old look — prewar, as a matter of fact. I can see the shape of her hips too clearly. She's wearing pumps: that's okay, but the heels need an uplift. Stockings much too orange. Not enough makeup, just a pale shadow of pink. Her fingers are stubby, and the only ring she's wearing is a thin, absolutely plain gold band. Mummy had emeralds and rubies and sapphires which she wore, according to her mood or the weather or something, on her long, smooth fingers. Her hands looked like a Camay ad — they should, she posed for one. Mrs. L. slouches. Mummy stood up straight. My mother's face knew; this face in front of me asks questions. Mummy smelled of Femme. If Mrs. London smells of anything, it is last night's meatloaf or pot roast clinging to the warp and woof of her skirt.

And so on. Roger walks in. You can see the remains of his dessert at the corners of his mouth. This is reassuring.

"We have a big yard and a new swing set," Judy tells him. "And a cat named Topper. Do you like animals?"

"I'm not going with you," Roger announces.

"If you like, you can start in the first grade next week. I've already called the school and they said they're looking forward to meeting you."

"Not going," Roger repeats. Fräulein appears. Her nose is swollen and her eyes look as if they had been soaked in hot water. "It is the child's bedtime," she informs Judy London. "He is very tired."

"So soon?" Judy says. "We were just about to have a nice talk."

"He always goes to bed at seven-thirty, and first he must have his bath."

"Well," Judy says. "I guess we shouldn't mess up his schedule."

Roger says, "Don't want to talk." Fräulein shoots her a triumphant look. "Say *gute nacht*," she tells Roger, who doesn't.

"Pleasant dreams," Judy calls. When they have left, she turns to me and tells me that she hates schedules. "I never wear a watch," she says proudly.

I should care whether she wears a watch. My mother has — had — a watch that is hidden inside a tiny gold lid you can flip open with your fingernail. Probably Judy London wouldn't be able to open it. I bite my nails, but that's standard for an anxious girl. Judy bites hers, and that's not right.

I have the feeling she wants me to ask her about life in Brookline. But I really couldn't care less.

Judy is restless and wanders around the room. "I don't really feel I belong here," she admits. The understatement of 1948. I notice that her shoulders are broad and her legs somewhat bowed. She carries her arms away from her body like a musclebound athlete. Cataloguing her breaches of appearance and taste only makes me feel worse than I did to begin with. Meanwhile Judy tries to engage me in conversation and tests topic after topic, each of which falls flatter than a soufflé concocted by a monkey.

I wonder where Sam has gone but haven't the energy to ask. If I ask she'll probably go into a long song and dance about it. I lie back on the couch, wallowing in self-pity and gloom. It never occurred to me to try to guess what was going on inside *her* head. She hadn't asked for me and Roger any more than we had asked for her. We were smashing into her cozy little family and cracking it open like a stubborn walnut. She couldn't have been deliriously happy either, about us. I never stopped to consider Judy or the Londons. I only resented her as I would a teacher who insists on the right answer when she suspects you don't know it.

Judy has hair on her face, fuzz on her cheeks and the suggestion of an adolescent mustache over her mouth. My mother had her facial hair removed by electrolysis at Elizabeth Arden's salon on Fifth Avenue. She said it was excruciating but worth it — it wasn't right to go around offending people.

Judy looks at me, baffled. "It's like a museum in here. I wonder what's going to happen to all of this." She sweeps her arm in an all-encompassing gesture, taking in the pictures, the rugs, the furniture, the Degas dancer.

Sam appears, as if to answer her question. "It's going to the Museum of Modern Art. Freddie wanted most of it to go there. The rest goes to the Whitney."

I want to say, "Don't I get any?" but I realize it would sound bad. I keep my mouth shut although I want to complain about how unfair it is that every last piece of art is going to spend the rest of its life being stared at by strangers.

Sam goes on. "I think he left a couple of smaller things to you in trust, Sally. You'll get them when you're twenty-one."

"That's nice," I say, knowing it won't be the Calder, which is the only thing I care about. "The Degas?"

"I'm afraid not," Sam says. "Her skirt's too fragile. She's going to the Met, as a matter of fact. She's in a class by herself."

I always liked the look on the dancer's face. My mother said dancers and singers were stupid. But this dancer doesn't look stupid to me; she looks as if she felt herself to be supreme. Wouldn't it be wild if I could take her to Brookline with me and keep her in my room? God, I don't even know if I *have* a room.

"She's priceless," Sam adds unnecessarily.

"You know something funny," Judy says. "When I was a child I always thought priceless meant that it was worthless. It had no price — you could get it for nothing."

"Ah," says Sam. They're talking as if they have forgotten I'm there, which is standard for me. I bite on my third nail, right hand. It's close to the quick and I hurt myself. There's something pleasurable in the sting.

"You've decided you want to come with us?" Sam says, looking at his wife.

"You mean me?" I say.

"Nobody else."

"Yes," I say. "Daddy thinks it would be a good idea. They're going to fix up his house for me. Can I really go to him later?"

"It's up to you — and the court. If we can convince the court."

I remember Nancy. I haven't thought of Nancy since it happened. My God, I haven't spoken to her, although she's checked in and left a message with Kathleen.

I call Nancy. She sounds tight. I'm not used to her not being play-sarcastic. "Nancy," I tell her. "You don't have to change because of what happened."

"I haven't changed," she says, clearly awed by my parents' death.

"I'm not any different," I assure her.

"I know you're not."

"How's your sister?"

"She's fine," Nancy says.

"That's unusual," I say. "What's the matter with her?"

"She said to tell you how sorry she was," Nancy says.

I tell Nancy that I have to leave New York. She doesn't believe me at first. I have to go into the gory details. Finally she's convinced. "Who am I going to tell dirty jokes to?" she wails, sounding more like herself now. "Who am I going to share my movie mags with? Oh, Sally, *why* do you have to go?"

If she doesn't stop I'm going to break down. "I can fly down on weekends. It's only an hour away. I can come and spend weekends with you and you can come up and visit me. Besides, I'll be back down, at least to Princeton, by summer."

"Sure," she says. "It's only an hour from here to Princeton."

"I'll write you a letter as soon as I get there," I promise. "You've got to promise you'll write back and tell me all the foul gossip from school." I like to pretend that I'm part of the right crowd at school.

"I promise," she says. She sounds very sad. This is flattering, of course. It's nice to think your friend really cares for you. But I know I'll never have another friend like Nancy. Your first friend is your closest, your best. And, in my case, my only. I'm as angry at having to leave Nancy as I am at being dragged to another world.

"Jesus, I wish I didn't have to go."

"Run away," Nancy suggests.

"They'd only find me and lock me up," I say. I have recently read *Darkness at Noon* and can picture myself chained to a wall.

"Change your name," Nancy says. "Maybe I'll come with you. I can't stand it around here anymore — they're always nagging me. By the way, my mom says to tell you how sorry she is. She's written you a note."

"Thanks," I say.

The conversation winds up. "Don't forget to write me," Nancy says.

"I won't," I repeat. "Oh hell, I wish I didn't have to leave."

"Oh, me too, Sally. I don't know what I'm going to do."

8

House-Proud

I DIDN'T CARE what it was like, the place they were taking me to. It really didn't matter. My curiosity, usually the size of a mountain, had shrunk to a dried pea. Probably I was just protecting myself from my own worst fantasies. Whatever it was, I felt myself a criminal being whisked from freedom to jail. And what had I done to deserve this? Nothing, absolutely nothing — it had all happened *to* me, I had no part in shaping anything. I was almost glad when it was time to board the plane at La Guardia, because I was certain it would crash and finish off the rest of the Stern family. I think Fräulein was thinking along the same lines because she clutched Roger's hand as if it were a ripcord. Her fear was communicated to Roger who simply howled the way he did when Dr. Lehman gave him a cold shot. Sam London looked pained, although it was obvious to me he was trying to rise above the noise of women and children. Judy London just seemed anxious to get home to her two pets, her two darling little boys who had been so brave to stay alone with the baby-sitter. When the plane took off Roger shrieked and cursed and Fräulein talked a blue streak of German. The stewardess tried to give Roger some Chiclets which he pushed away. Judy, who was sitting with me, kept up a stream of trivial talk and I just sat back and waited for it to happen. Each strange noise in the engine said my time had come; I was stoic, I waited and

waited for the inevitable. I was first in line at the dentist, the
French test was next period, my music teacher was ringing the
doorbell this minute, the sky was falling, the plane is falling —
there it goes . . . Nothing happened.

I came to gradually. I remember being struck by the provincial
monotony of the landscape we taxied past on the way to the
Londons' house. New York was sharp and high — this was like
Queens, the place you pass through on your way to La Guardia
Airport. One-story shops and four-story apartment houses lined
both sides of the street. Certainly nothing you'd want to look at
twice — no snazzy store windows or glossy displays. The women
were dressed as if they didn't give a damn if anybody saw them
or not. It was not like Fifth Avenue, where every woman begged
to have her picture taken and put on the cover of *Life*. Or
Madison, where they worked either for the president of a broad-
casting company or the editor of *Coronet* and bought their
clothes in the Young New Yorker Shop or at Bendel's, if their
daddies were rich enough, and threw out or gave away everything more than six months old.

These women I now saw pushing baby carriages or carrying
paper bags with string handles had covered their bodies all right,
but you couldn't tell exactly what with. I had unconsciously
taken over some of my mother's worst, most snobby habits and
was giving them free rein. Again, I tried to feel more secure by
comparing and ended by feeling worse. But I didn't learn from
this. I went right on doing it for months.

I bit my thumbnail and looked at what I'd done. A rather clean
job, if I did say so. My head began to ache, one of those head-
aches that fit you like a low-lying wool cap, almost down to your
ears.

"Why are you frowning, Sally?" says sharp-eyed Judy.

"Am I frowning? I'm sorry."

"Don't apologize," she says. "Look, there's the best bakery in New England. Their devil's food is out of this world. I'll bet you like chocolate cake."

Roger makes a face.

"He does not eat chocolate," Fräulein says.

"Oh really, why not?" Judy says. "I thought all little boys loved chocolate."

"It looks like poo-poo," Roger says.

Fräulein's face reddens. I am delighted; Judy asked for it.

"Well," Judy says. "That's too bad." Sam, riding up front with the driver, either has not heard or has chosen not to let on that he's heard. "They also make good ladyfingers," Judy says, getting in the last word.

The driver is talking to Sam about the Braves and spring training. I don't think Sam's all that interested in baseball, but I could be wrong. Sam's mostly a mystery.

We wind around, stop for lights, climb a hill, turn several corners. Shops disappear and suburb takes over. The houses are large and squat, the streets flanked by neat rows of sleeping trees. It looks like a movie to me, since I've never seen anything in the flesh to compare it to. Andy Hardy is going to come swinging down the front path of that house and Judy Garland down the next. I sigh. "Here we are," Sam says, and the driver brakes. Fräulein makes a funny noise in her nose. Judy shifts eagerly in her seat and bends forward. The cab stops, Sam jumps out, pays the driver, and they both begin unloading our suitcases, Roger's, Fräulein's, and mine, from the trunk. I am scared to look. Slowly I turn my head. It's gonna be home, baby, you better get used to it, I tell myself, talking tough like Lauren Bacall. I can't believe what I see. Not that it's much different from the rest of the houses around us, but the idea that I will penetrate into its bowels, so to speak, exist in it, wake up and go to sleep in it, bathe and wash my hair in it, make telephone calls and eat my dinner in it — I have to take a huge jump. The house is what I would call large, although it's standard on the block. It's about twice as big as the New York house, spreading and groping, stained dark brown, shuttered, and, well, deformed somehow, a shape unknown to the laws of symmetry. It has odd extrusions and random eaves and a partial porch like a girdle someone forgot to hook up. It is the sort of house I have always before — being completely ignorant — associated with rundown neighborhoods, crime, dirt, venereal disease, and hopeless dreams.

To Judy 101 Hancock Street is home sweet home. She is ecstatic. Like a girl she jumps out of the cab and runs up the cracking cement walk that splits the lawn in two. Roger is reluctant. Fräulein tries to pry him out of the automobile.

"Come, come," she says.

"I don't want to."

"But you must, *Liebchen,*" she urges.

At that moment I catch sight of a female face staring at us out of a window in the house next door. To this face I answer with my most devastating, withering, New York look. The face shrinks back, wounded. I don't know what makes me do things like this; I'm not really unfriendly.

Roger finally debarks. He looks at the house and pronounces it unacceptable. "It's ugly. I don't want to go in there."

I feel like beaning him. He's being such a terrible brat I've almost given up feeling sorry for him. Yes, yes, I sympathize with his problems — losing both parents at the same time, being removed from home and dumped somewhere else, but still, does he have to act like a *mon*ster?

Judy has disappeared into her house while Sam waits to escort us in. He urges us forward. We don't know what lies beyond, the tiger or the other thing.

As I walk through the front entrance tears threaten. I am no longer one of us — I am now one of *them,* and I understand this not in any abstract way but by having to enter, to become part of their household, in however temporary a way. I'm not coming to visit, I'm coming to stay. I have been as sharply cut off from my past life as Jews taken from the ghetto and placed in concentration camps. I am now a member of what my mother waspishly called the unwashed middle class. I'm not ready yet; it's too soon after the accident; I am not yet used to being motherless.

Sam shuts the door with more noise than is really necessary. The smell inside the house is overpowering: cooking gas (a nauseating odor), beef or lamb stewed too long, old books, dirty socks, dusty curtains and corners, cats. This anthology turns my stomach. My stomach more than my nose relays the message that it is a dirty smell. *Our* house smelled clean, fresh as a slice of melon, clean as the inside of a lemon, squeaky clean, like your hair when you've rinsed it well. My mother once fired a cook because she didn't clean the oven the same night she roasted a leg of lamb.

I take a deep breath, hoping that I can keep my lunch down. Judy appears with her two children, one a boy about Roger's age and his brother a couple of years younger. She has one each by the hand, like an exhibitor at the dog show. Oma Lucy would have said that these two children had "the map of Israel all over their faces." Charming expression. There's nobody quite so direct as an anti-Semitic Jew. The London kids have sharp, pointed chins, deep-set eyes, full, rather feminine mouths, and skin that looks as if it saw the sun about once a month. It was weird, too, because the boys don't look alike; but they both look Jewish. They stare so hard their eyeballs are going to pop clear out of their sockets. Roger shifts uneasily — he knows when he's being given the once-over.

It is a standoff. No one wants to make the first move; we are natural enemies. Whatever the Londons do will not be enough.

Judy breaks the silence and says, "This is Danny London and

this is his brother Joseph — Joey. Guys, these are Sally Stern and
Roger. Joey, you and Roger are just about the same age." I'm
afraid she's going to say, "Isn't that nice?" but mercifully she
doesn't.

The staring contest intensifies. No chance of love at first sight.
"What's that funny smell?" Roger says.

I draw in my breath — the kid has nerve. "I guess that's just
our house's smell," Judy says. "Everybody's house has its own
smell, just like people. Ours is different from the one you used to
live in."

"It stinks," Roger says. "It makes me want to barf."

"He means puke," Danny explains to his little brother.

Joey makes the appropriate noise.

"Come on, you three," Judy smiles. "I'll show you where
you're going to sleep. Fräulein, I'm afraid you'll have to make do
with the living room couch for a while. Actually it's very comfortable. It opens out into a bed — it's almost a double." Fräulein
looks as if she's just been hit with a whopping menstrual cramp.
"The couch?" she repeats, trying out the idea. She looks devas-
tated.

"Yes," Judy repeats. "Listen, my own mother is crazy about
that couch and she's very hard to please." Now *that's* going to
cut a hell of a lot of ice with Fräulein.

"Where is the couch?" she murmurs. Is she going to start
crying again?

"In the living room," Judy tells her again. "But first I'd like to
show the children their beds. You don't mind, do you?" I can see
that life with Judy and Fräulein is not going to be a picnic.
There is a natural antagonism that goes much deeper than this
faceoff. More than Judy's German phobia there is Fräulein's
monolithic personality and the fact that some women — in this
case Judy — don't like having strangers clutter up their house,
using their bathroom, clumping around the kitchen opening

drawers and crying for more orange juice. Mummy never had to deal directly with the mechanics of keeping Fräulein alive and well. Judy will have to.

We deposit Fräulein in the living room and continue the tour —"the grand tour," as Judy puts it. I haven't yet heard the term house-proud, but I can sense it in Judy. She loves her house to pieces. She loves every shabby stick of furniture, every streaked window, the worn linoleum under the kitchen sink and the place you put your feet when you sit on the toilet. She loves the tiny back porch with old milk bottles perched on it like dead birds and the curtains in the dining room which have been shredded by the cat. She is more openly pleased by this house than my mother was with hers — and with far less reason. Of course everything she points out to me I dislike. And when it came time for me to be shown my room I nearly collapsed in despair. My bed, a sort of cotlike thing with no headboard, stood on a sleeping porch that wasn't insulated. In the corner there was a large electric heater with a circle of wicked coils and a thick snake of wire disappearing into the wall. The wind shook the loosely hung windows and sent drafts of New England chill in through the obvious and not so obvious cracks. Judy was brisk in her apology. "It's only for the time being," she explains. "We'll probably add on or maybe we'll move. We want you to have your own room here, Sally, or else I'd put you in the hall. Would you rather be in the hall?"

"No, this is okay," I say, faintly. There is neither closet nor easy chair on my little porch. But there is an ancient chest with sticky drawers and an unpainted desk with matching chair so that I can be a good girl and do my homework in peace and quiet. The desk is a little too high for me — a compliment, I suppose — and the chair a little too low.

"It gets drafty in here sometimes," Judy says. "So I've given you a few extra blankets."

"What should I do with my dresses and skirts?"

"There's a closet outside the boys' room I've emptied for you. Yell if you need more hangers." I've brought one suitcase with me. The rest of my stuff is being shipped by Railway Express, all three trunks of it. My God, I'll bet the entire London family could get all their clothes in fewer than three trunks.

"Why don't you unpack that suitcase and then come on down for a cup of hot chocolate or something?" Judy rubs her hands over the top of her head. She reminds me a little of the Seeley School nurse but not so starchy. She reaches out and tries to touch my arm. I don't want her to; if she touches my flesh she will think she has rights and perquisites with me. "Where's the bathroom?" I say.

"Across the hall. I'm afraid the lock is broken. Just close the door. Nobody will come in."

This is the last straw. Why in hell don't they get the lock fixed? Is it such a big deal to fix a lock? I am in a state of outrage. In a sense, this outrage keeps my feet firmly planted in reality.

In the London house the only place that seemed reasonable to me was the living room. It was clear that the children were discouraged from using it. Its two massive sliding wooden doors were kept shut most of the time and it was a lot neater than the other rooms. Everything inside it was new and modern. Modern was the thing immediately after the war as Scandinavia, under a shroud for years, became the furniture capital of the world. Smooth, swooping lines, brilliant scratchy upholstery, oiled teak and unvarnished birch, dining room tables, occasional tables, couches, lamps, beds — it might have been trendy but it was a huge relief. Even American-made imitations had the virtue of this simplicity. The fact that the rest of the house contained leftovers, hand-me-downs, and stuff bordering on junkyard antique apparently didn't bother the Londons at all. It was skewed but dramatic. The thing I found most astonishing, however, was the

Paul Klee over the mantelpiece. It was exactly like the one in my
mother's living room in New York.

I mentioned the coincidence to Judy. "Your mother had the
original; this is a copy," she said. "It cost nine-fifty in Cambridge.
It's hard to tell them apart, isn't it?"

I was ashamed for her; my face burned for her. My dead
mother's voice came back to me. "Don't ever buy fake anything;
it's drecky. Be honest. If you pretend, you'll only end up fooling
the wrong people. If you can't get the real thing be satisfied with
something else." For my mom it was emeralds or nothing.

"Oh," I managed to say to Judy. "It's very good. How do they
do it, so it looks so real?"

During that first afternoon I wandered around and tried to
keep out of everybody's way. I especially did not want to talk to
Fräulein, who complained in a loud voice that she had no place
to hang her clothes, that she had to walk up a flight of stairs to use
the bathroom, that the curtains in the living room did not give
her enough privacy, that she was too far away from Roger if he
needed her during the night, that this-and-that until she threatened to drive us all nuts. Even Roger seemed to want to stay out
of her direct path.

I went into the kitchen, which was about as much like my
mother's as Filene's Basement is like the custom salon at Bergdorf's.

Judy was at the stove, stirring something in a pot.

"Mrs. London?"

"Hey," she said, looking up. "You're supposed to call me
Judy. Nobody but my gynecologist calls me Mrs. London."

This is not the kind of talk I'm used to. "I'll try," I say, aware
of how hard it's going to be. I'm going to say "you" for a while
and avoid names altogether.

"What can I do for you?" Before I can answer that I would
like to call my father and is it all right to use the phone, she goes
on. "By the way, I forgot to tell you that everything here is for

you to eat or sit on or use. If there's something I'm saving especially I'll let you know. This is *your* house. If you want to use
the phonograph, it's in the living room, next to the bookcase.
We've got hundreds of books and lots of old magazines, so just
read anything you please. The only thing is, if you take a book
from the shelf, please try to remember where you got it from.
Sam's bound to notice and be annoyed if you don't. You don't
have to ask if you want a snack or something — just go ahead and
help yourself. No, I *mean* it. I couldn't bear to think that you feel
obliged to ask every time you want some peanut butter or a
saltine. I'll show you where the linen closet is, so you can help
yourself to clean towels and sheets. You make your own bed,
don't you? Good, that's a help. Now. Did you want to ask me
something?"

"Can I call Daddy?"

"Of course you can. You don't have to ask me that."

"It's long distance . . ."

"Of course it is. Oh, Sally, I forgot the most important part."

"What's that?" It sounds ominous.

"Sam's study. The only place in the house that's off limits. He
doesn't like anyone to go in there. Not even me. I think it's
because the place is littered with so many dirty socks and cigarette butts. It's a filthy room anyway. I'm sure you wouldn't
want to go in. But he's weird about it. It's private property — his
— and we all stick to his rules."

"What does he do in there?"

"Works and thinks. He's writing a book."

"A book? What about?"

"Oh, the postwar mood and American fiction. I'll bet you
hoped I'd say he was writing a detective story."

"No, I didn't," I tell her. She doesn't know me very well. I
don't care.

9

Everything I've Got Belongs to You

TOPPER, the Londons' cat, had long silky hair, lush like a whore's, and a tail like a feather boa. Underneath all the fur was a fat old body whose contours were mostly hidden. You had to hold him on your lap and stroke him in order to feel what his shape was like. His eyes were split emeralds.

"I never had a pet," I tell Judy somewhere near the beginning of my first week in the house. Things have settled somewhat. I have an appointment with the high school principal. The routine of the Londons' establishment is beginning to make some kind of crazy sense to me. I've begun, just begun, to eat again — the food is all unfamiliar, gluey and bready and with flavors I can't quite identify.

"Children should have pets," Judy says. She is supremely confident in her own assumptions.

"Mummy wouldn't let me have any. She said cats destroy the furniture and dogs shouldn't be locked up in a city."

"Cats *do* destroy the furniture," Judy says without bothering to explain the contradiction.

Topper is asleep on my lap — at least his eyes are closed. He's purring like a well-oiled motor. He's warm, his blood is warm, and so are his padded feet. His skull is too big for my hand all at once. I imagine the bone underneath and shiver.

"That animal is nine years old," Judy says to me. She slides the onions she has been chopping from the cutting board into a frying pan where they hit in a hissing cloud. "I don't know what I'm going to do when he finally croaks," she says. "The boys think he's immortal."

I figure it's nail-biting time again, but there's nothing left to bite. Judy must have the sensibility of a cow, talking like that about the cat's croaking. I examine my left hand. Revolting. How can I do this to myself? Fräulein appears. She demands to know where the Vaseline is. Judy tells her it's in the medicine cabinet, in the bathroom. Fräulein says she's looked there and it isn't.

Judy says, "Would you like me to look?"

"If you would be so kind," Fräulein says. Her voice drips scorn and helplessness. Judy gets up and goes upstairs; Fräulein clatters after her in her big ugly shoes. I don't see how Judy can stand it.

A few minutes later Judy comes down again and resumes cooking. "It was right there," she says. "Behind the Lavoris." Mouthwash is something glamorous, like Scotch whiskey. Along with cheap toilet water and chocolate sprinkles for ice cream, my mother considered it of dubious benefit and wouldn't allow it in the house. I've already sneaked some of the Lavoris — it's delicious, like Dentyne chewing gum.

"What are you making?" I ask.

"Meat sauce for spaghetti. I was raised on gefilte fish, latkes, and tsimmes. That's why I cook so much Italian and Chinese stuff."

Is *that* what it is? Her Italian cooking doesn't taste like Fippy's veal Marsala or mixed fish fry at all.

"Your mother was considered a gourmet cook," Judy says unnecessarily. "I never ate one of her meals. I'll bet they were great."

"They were okay," I say. She's making me miss my mother again. The missing has left the vague, generalized phase and now pinpoints itself onto very specific things, such as foods and smells and the sound of a spoken word. The odor of the cooking onions is getting to me; my stomach is doing a ritual dance of protest.

"I'm adequate in the kitchen, but that's all. I just can't get up the proper enthusiasm, I guess. I start daydreaming just as the sauce starts to curdle. Then I have to throw it out and start all over again. It's very wasteful." In fact, Judy has a small bookcase in the kitchen. I figure she'd rather read than stir any day. "Want to hear something funny?"

I nod.

"I once tried to make a chocolate soufflé and it came out like a piece of moist brown blotting paper on the bottom of the cas-serole. Sam had to run down to the drugstore to get some ice cream. We had guests, and you can't serve your guests blotting paper for dessert."

That's not funny — that's pathetic.

"I think I'll go to my room, if you don't need me." We had both adopted the convention of calling my porch a room. I know it's horrible to feel sorry for myself but sometimes I can't help it. I can't help connecting the fact of my mother's death with the chill that slips under the covers early in the morning before I get up, with the wire hangers that make a mark on my skirts, with the high carbohydrate content of Judy's food. Mother dies, daughter subsequently suffers from chilblains and obesity. As if I were being punished. For what? For being alive when she's dead? For being far from an ideal person? For harboring fantasies of murder, suicide, rape, masturbation, and so on?

Judy excuses me. She's been asking me to help her set the table for dinner, but suppertime is still a long way off. I resent the fact that she won't ask Fräulein but asks me instead.

Why doesn't she have anyone to help her in the house? She doesn't even have part-time help. *I'm* her part-time help.

As I climb the stairs I suddenly start itching all over — it's worse than poison ivy or prickly heat. At the same time I cough and sneeze and feel like a large tube having its insides squeezed out.

I crawl to the porch and shut the door. There I lie, gasping like a boated fish, until the attack or whatever it is subsides.

Which it finally does, but it leaves me weak, the way you feel after you've thrown up. I close my eyes and immediately my mother swims into view. I see her swinging down the staircase of our house, in a long crimson taffeta skirt with yards and yards of material shaped into a large bell. I loved that dress. I think she took it to San Francisco with her. Now the worms. The worms crawl in, the worms crawl out, they crawl all over your something snout. They eat your eyes, they eat your nose, they crawl all over your slimy toes. Some of the words are wrong, but the plot is right. My mother is a worm's meal — maybe there's nothing left already. Nothing but her hair and skeleton, her fingers shredded, disintegrated, peeling off like banana skins. I force myself to go into this horror, stumbling and blind but knowing perfectly well where I am. I am perspiring as if I had a fever which had just broken. My forehead is damp and sticky. My mother, meanwhile, is lying in her grave on Long Island and turning green and soft like rotten cheese.

I've *got* to stop this. Even *I* know it's bad for me. I turn on my best friend, the Philco radio I brought up with me. A voice is telling me about the Cardinal dedicating a parochial school in a place called Waltham that I connect only with watches. I haven't been here very long but already I know that Boston is a Catholic town. New York is Jewish and Episcopalian, Boston is Irish Catholic. Oma Lucy was absolutely hair-raising about Catholics. She called the Mass "mumbo jumbo" and informed me with quiet authority that nuns don't bathe. I took in some of what she said, but I couldn't quite swallow the whole thing. I had the feeling that, like Jews, Catholics were a little strange — after all, there was Nancy, who liked me, so she must be strange — and, in adult form, psychological imperialists. Catholics go out and capture the minds and hearts of naked savages and make them wear clothes. Jews perform ritual murder on little Christian babies.

But if Boston was Catholic, Brookline — our part of it — was a small Jewish enclave. A ghetto without walls. And in a different way from New York. For instance, the butcher that Judy patronized had a neon Hebrew sign in his window. I was so awed by this sign that I couldn't take my eyes off it. I couldn't imagine what it said, but I was sure it was something secret and awful. Judy told me the liquid red letters translated into "Kosher Meat." I was disappointed. Half of me didn't even believe her.

I lie on my cot in the frigid porch in the Londons' house and try to keep my mind off those worms. The worms are active and agile; they can go anywhere they please; they are contortionists extraordinaire. What are the quintessential differences between a Jew and a Catholic — not counting Nancy who is exempt? Catholics are pale and sickly, overexposed photographs, while Jews are vivid, with the darks almost black and the light patches almost white. Catholics are fuzzy, Jews are sharply in focus. Catholics are the semiclassics under Andre Kostelanetz (never mind that his wife sings with the Met), while Jews are Bruno Walter doing Mozart's *Jupiter*.

But then there are Jews and Jews. Oma Lucy is one kind, the Londons another, and my mother and stepfather still another, more saucy than the other two. Which am I most like? Who knows? Certainly I don't. If I was invisible in my mother's house, here I am a cracker crumb in the bed, a tiny little crumb, but oh, do I irritate them while they're trying to get to sleep.

Why am I here? I am stringing a necklace of questions. I cannot make out why Freddie did this to us, to me and Roger. Had he lost all his marbles during a critical interlude? Or was he simply meting out punishment? But if that was true, what were we being punished for?

The answer to my final question could, I suppose, be answered

handily by my guardian, Sam London, but I don't want to go to
him. He's a rude man. He's preoccupied, distracted. He isn't
civilized like my stepfather and my real father. In comparison to
both these excellent gentlemen, Sam London is Caliban. I
wouldn't ask him the time of day.

During dinner that night Roger made an unholy fuss about the
food and ended by dumping his plate of spaghetti and salad onto
the floor where it sat like something already ingested. Fräulein
cooed and clucked and started wiping up the mess. Judy talked
over the fuss and Sam pretended he was on another planet. Joey
and Danny London were beside themselves, bug-eyed with the
fascination of violent novelty, a boy spilling his meal on the floor
and then demanding a double lamb chop.

"Tomorrow, *Liebchen*. Fräulein will buy you a nice thick
chop. Now be a good boy and drink your milk. You will get a
nice bedtime story."

"*Struwwelpeter?*" Judy said.

"No child should read that book," Fräulein said. "We do not
even have that in the house. We *did* not."

"We have that book," Joey says. "He falls into the water. He
burns himself to a crisp. Oh boy, he gets into a lot of trouble."

"It is not for children, that book," Fräulein says.

Sam cannot stay out of this arena. "It was written for children,
Fräulein. It's a fairy tale. A little heavy on the allegory, maybe,
but all in all it corresponds faithfully to what kids have in their
heads."

"Disgusting," Fräulein says. "Roger, you must have something
to eat. Would you like Fräulein to make you a nice sandwich of
bread and butter?"

Roger nods. He seems nonplussed by his accident. I myself find
the sauce awfully good. I'll bet he wishes he hadn't done it. There
is a smudge on the floor, a smear.

Judy changes the subject. I've noticed she often relies on subject-changing as a means of reducing tension.

"I got a letter from Mama today — she's coming for a visit."

Sam's eyebrows shoot up, land back with a jerk. "My God!" he says. "Where in hell is she going to sleep?"

All eyes fly to Judy, whose mouth, for once, drops open in uncertainty. "We'll get her a room at The Major."

"That fleabag?" Sam says. "Well, it's your mother."

"They've renovated their rooms," Judy says. "They've put real towels in the bathrooms. The windows have shades. The doors close. Some of them even lock."

"How do you know so much about it?" Sam asks.

"I read the local paper," she says. "You don't. They've been doing a terrific image-building campaign. You might think they were running for President."

"Wallace," Joey says.

"That's right, dear," Judy says. "What a smart boy."

"Truman," Roger says. "You're a dummy."

"I'm not a dummy," Joey says. "You're a dummy. You don't even know how to light the stove."

"Why should I?" Roger says.

"*Liebchen*, please!" Fräulein says, handing him a bread and butter sandwich. The butter is so thick it looks like a slab of yellow bologna. He takes a bite and asks her why there are crusts on the bread. "You used to cut them off."

"We don't throw away food around here," Sam says in a threatening voice. I feel itchy again. My entire body itches from scalp to soles. I feel like tearing off my shoes and my clothes and scratching wildly.

A few minutes later Roger complains there is skin on his chocolate pudding. Judy tells him it is magic skin. "It will make you grow big and tall, it will make your wishes come true, it will give you strong arms, a red pony, and a happy smile."

"You are putting ideas in the child's head," Fräulein accuses her.

"What else would you suggest putting into his head?" Judy says.

"I mean," Fräulein says with a stammer, "you are putting fairy tales into his head."

"I know it isn't magic!" Roger shouts. "It tastes too icky."

"You won't let us say we don't like the food," Danny shouts.

"Oh my God," Sam says. "What *is* this?"

"This," Fräulein says triumphantly, "is what comes from putting ideas in children's heads." She rises, making the chair squeak as she gets up. "Come, Roger, we will go upstairs to read."

"Fräulein," Judy says in a steely voice. "I could use a little help cleaning up."

"This is not my understanding of what my job would be when Mrs. Stern hired me," the nurse says with an access of misconstrued dignity. "I am not a waitress or a cook. I am a qualified nursemaid with twelve years experience in good homes. I do not do the family dishes or take out the garbage. I am sure you understand this."

"You helped me yesterday and the day before," Judy says quietly.

"I felt sorry for you."

"Ah," Judy says, her eyes bitter.

Sam looks as if he were thinking of letting the rage inside him burst through.

Judy lets her go. We are left with their absence, like something you can touch. The two little boys grin at each other shyly but say nothing. Sam is fuming but also quiet.

"I'll be goddamned," Judy says. "I don't know if I can live with it. I really don't know."

Her husband says, "We'll talk about it later." He looks at me briefly. I must be the reason they can't talk about it now. Dinner breaks up into little pieces. The boys run off to listen to their radio, Sam slides into his study, Judy and I head for the kitchen with the dirty dishes. Judy drops a glass on the floor; it shatters. "Oh hell," she says. She looks at me and continues. "I'm sorry, Sally, this has nothing to do with you. It's Fräulein. I guess we weren't exactly made for each other. You understand, don't you, that some people just have incompatible chemistry?"

I nod. Should I stay in the kitchen with Judy and listen to her grownup explanations for what seem simple matters of like and dislike, or should I slip back into my own thoughts? Maybe it's just coincidence, but what I'm remembering is a scene out of my fourteen-year-old past. My mother is still married to my father. That was the marriage where the honeymoon was over within twenty-four hours. We live in a large house with marble pillars flanking the doorway; to me it was Buckingham Palace. There was a lot of marble and stone on the floors and footsteps would echo through the house like dull bells. My mother, later, referred to this house as "the ancestral home," meaning it was in the Sanderson family for some time before she and Daddy took up residence there. She hated it, mostly, I suspect, because it reflected someone else's taste in furniture, art, mood, kitchen, and light. She must have felt more like a tenant than an owner, and it was important for Mummy to own her own things.

I remember my mother running down one of the corridors on the second floor, starting out from one room and making for another at the opposite end. She was running like she was on fire. It wasn't just a matter of getting from one place to another, but of escape, survival. I was standing in her path, but this fact did not slow her or deter her one bit. She hit me broadside, knocked me flat on my bottom, and kept right on going, reached her destination — the room she slept in alone — and slammed the door as hard as she could. Chips and pieces of paint broke loose and went floating to the floor like the last leaves of November.

The noise of the slam went echoing in the house. The noise went in waves and subsided. I sat there, baffled and wounded, indignant and chastised. My father ran up to me.

"Did your mean old Mummy knock you down, you poor little princess? Are you hurt, my little baby doll?" He picked me up and rubbed his cheek up and down against mine. It felt like a scrub brush. His boozy breath filled my nostrils with dragon fumes. He whispered a bad word that astonished me, looked in the direction of Mummy's closed door, and told me that what was behind it was no better than a wild animal. Then he carried me down the wide sweeping staircase to the coat closet. We both got somberly into our coats and left the house holding hands. He bought me an ice cream soda at Schrafft's and smoked while I ate it, looking at me soulfully the way I would later gaze at photographs of him. He gazed at me like thick soup, like tears, like kisses. I was embarrassed. I wanted him to stop. Neither of us mentioned Mummy.

This was my first exposure to marriage.

My second — Freddie's and Mummy's — was sex-drenched. In one sense it never really had a chance to get out of the honeymoon stage; the only thing that riffled its surface was Sam London. During its brief duration Mummy played sex kitten. She out-Rita-ed Rita Hayworth. She liked to act out the role of dumb sex kitten married to big, strong, silent intellectual. It worked — somehow, it worked.

This was my second experience of marriage.

I was now going a third round, which was pretty good for someone not yet fifteen. I was getting to be a real woman of the world. The Londons didn't seem to be "in love" the way Freddie and my mother were. They had some unspoken communication going back and forth — you could sense it the minute they were in a room together — but they didn't touch each other much. Their meetings took place on an island invisible to the rest of us.

There was little of what Oma Lucy might have referred to as "vulgar display." I had seen Sam touching Judy's bottom as if he owned her, lock, stock, and genitalia. That's it. There's no other evidence that they even recognized the other's corporeal existence. And I was very aware of these things.

Aside from that occasional caress, more in passing than as a premeditated act, the Londons went, each one, in his own way. His way was usually into the study. Hers was into the kitchen. It wasn't until I moved into the Londons' house that I realized how much of a woman's married life was spent in the kitchen. It's amazing how often the kitchen is a bad room: cramped, crowded, not enough light or air, no comfortable chairs, the floor a mess and the walls bleeding old grease and smudge from the stove. Except for my mother's showplace, most kitchens were the place you would be least likely to take a guest. Judy's was pretty bad, but she had put in it a rundown old couch with protruding intestines. This couch was the repository for stray mittens, orange peels, candy wrappers, and pencils as well as for human bottoms. I liked the idea of a couch in the kitchen, but not *that* couch. It was revolting, and I never sat on it.

Judy would come into her kitchen and start peeling onions or scrubbing potatoes or washing coffee mugs. I had the feeling that Sam thought he was Dr. I.Q. and deserved to be left alone to think. Judy encouraged him. What was it about women that made them believe it was their duty to make their husbands think they were all Albert Einsteins? My mother was the same with Freddie. Not just sex kings but brain kings too. I was amazed when I heard Judy talking about how Sam's students thought he was so great. They were always calling him up at midnight to read him their poems or ask his advice about VD. I didn't think she ought to talk to me about VD, but apparently she didn't make the sort of distinctions my mother thought so important.

The funny thing about Judy's attitude toward Sam was that

my own mother had dismissed Judy as "one of those aggressively intellectual females who let their armpit hairs grow to show that they're not merely silly. Some women, Sally dear, think that they don't have to be attractive physically as long as they can feel superior about their heads." So far I had seen little to indicate Judy's aggressive intelligence. She seemed compulsively occupied in housewifely functioning, shopping, cleaning up, cooking, making beds, finding things that were lost, raising her voice, and creating mounds of garbage. The only sign of the intellectuality my mother disdained was the bookshelf in the kitchen and a pile of books on Judy's bedside table; out of seven books only one was a novel.

Danny and Joey brought up the subject of grandma the next morning at breakfast. Joey said, "Bubba doesn't have to go to a hotel. She can sleep in the same bed with Roger." This sent him and his brother into fits of dirty laughter. Roger looked furious.

"My mother's a nice old lady. Now you leave her alone!" Judy says.

"Do you like being pinched?" Danny asks me.

"Do you like halitosis?" Joey asks.

"Do you mind if someone asks you a million nosy questions?"

Joey takes up the beat. "Have you ever seen a bosom you couldn't fit in a trunk?"

Sam and Judy let them go on. I am surprised they don't stop them.

"You'll like her if you like big bottoms," Joey shrieks. This prediction galvanizes Sam. "That's enough," he says in a way that would shut anyone up, even Mussolini.

Judy looks a little sad. After all, it's her only mother. Fräulein is doing some ironing. She claims Roger doesn't have any pressed shirts, but the way I see it it's any excuse not to sit down with *them*.

"Belle's got to meet Sally and Roger," Judy says.

"I thought her name was Bubba," I say. Immediately, shrieks of laughter. They're laughing at me, no mistake; you can always tell when someone's laughing at you. "Bubba means grandmother," Sam says, trying to put his face back together. Oh boy, I really asked a stupid question. I burn with embarrassment, I can feel my face sizzling. "We call our grandmother Oma," I say, trying to locate a crumb of dignity for myself.

"That's German, dear," Judy tells me. "Bubba is Yiddish."

"Well," I say. "I don't see how I was expected to know that!"

"We're sorry we laughed," Judy says.

"I'm not," Danny says. "It was very funny."

"Who's ready for school?" Judy uses that maddeningly fake cheerful voice mothers use when they're navigating from one subject to another.

There is something of the Mad Hatter's tea party in this. They are dunking the dormouse in the teapot and I have the weird feeling I'm him.

The two London boys leave the house. Fräulein goes off with Roger for a walk; she is a believer in fresh air so long as it's not too cold. Also in getting out of this house which is hardly growing on her. It seems that every day she spends here is more depressing for her than the last. Sam is blowing around the house looking for something. He's nervous and he's making me nervous. He comes into the kitchen where Judy and I are working on the breakfast things and picks up a cup, pours coffee into it, and then spills it on his leg. "Shit!"

"Sam," Judy says gently.

"Sorry," he says, flashing me a look of nonrecognition. He puts down the coffee cup and leaves.

"He's preoccupied," Judy says, plunging her arms into a sinkful of bubbles. It's no wonder she's got rough red hands. She's got the hands no man loves to touch.

"Why?" I say. Actually I couldn't care less.

"They've asked him to be chairman of his department. There's all kinds of pressure being put on him to take it, but he doesn't want it. He loathes administration, it's the last thing on earth . . . He has a hard time saying no."

Not to me he doesn't. He's always saying no to me, even if it's a silent no. To my poor little mind, the mysterious people who want him to take this job must be out of their poor little heads.

"Of course he doesn't have to take the job," Judy continues, "but he feels obligated. Now he's going around in circles trying to decide. He wants *me* to decide for him, but that way lies disaster. I wouldn't get caught in that trap."

I gather that she's giving me oblique advice. About the man-woman relationship, that is. Still, I am startled by her claim that Sam is asking her to make up his mind for him. That's not the way I see it at all. As a matter of fact I don't believe he relies on anybody but Sam London.

"If it was me I'd go crazy weighing the pros and cons indefinitely. I think I'd just say no and have it over with."

Does she really think I'm interested in all this? "What are you doing?"

"I'm peeling potatoes for dinner."

"Dinner. But it's not even nine o'clock in the morning."

"I know, pet, but if I do it now I won't have to do it later." She sighs a shallow sigh, as if she didn't want me to hear it.

"Why not leave the peel on?" I say.

"Habit, I guess. Besides, you can't have peels in mashed pots."

Judy's string of housework is endless. It is a bottomless well, a horizon forever moving away, a terrible dragging chore with nasty little surprises and few rewards. It is a snake with its tail in its mouth. If it was me, I'd kill it with a forked stick.

It's funny, but I could not remember seeing potatoes peeled and dirty clothes removed from hampers and spots of grease removed from walls in my mother's house. Somebody must have done them but they were hidden. Maybe they should be hidden. I was thinking like my mother. Preparation and cleanup were secret things, like wiping your bottom in the bathroom. Of course preparation did not include my mother's virtuoso performances at home on the range. Those were exhibitions — they had theatrical style and even suspense.

"Is Roger spoiled, do you think?" Judy asks.

"I don't know, I hadn't thought about it," I answer, lying. I've thought about it a good deal — long ago I labeled my half-brother "spoiled brat." "They gave him anything he wanted," I added. "Especially Fräulein. Most of the nurses and governesses I knew were very strict, but Fräulein isn't. She acts like his slave sometimes."

"Well, he's had a rough time," Judy says.

"But she was always like that with him. Before."

Roger doesn't even have to tie his shoes. Fräulein ties his shoes and helps him into his little coat and practically goes to the bathroom for him. I wouldn't be surprised if she takes down his pants and plays with his little thing.

"What would you think if we sent him to school right away?"

"I don't know," I say. Why should Judy put me on the spot? If she doesn't know, how should I? I'm just his stupid older sister who never had much to do with him in the first place. "Why don't you ask him?" I say.

"Sally, would you mind getting me the large mixing bowl in that cabinet. No, not that one, the next one over. The red one. That's right, dear, the smaller of the two. Could I have it, please?" *Idiot:* she isn't saying, but we're both thinking, *idiot.* She doesn't hide her feelings very well; I almost wish I were in school.

"When do *I* start school?" I ask. The very idea of a public high school fills me with foreboding. For one thing, there will be boys.

"Monday," Judy says. "At least, we have an appointment with the principal."

"Why with the principal? Why don't I just go and join the class?"

"I guess that's the way they do it when someone comes in in the middle of the year."

I think I know what it will be like to go to school with boys. Hell, sheer, utter hell. They won't look at a lump like me. Their eyes will turn away but they will know my history and whisper about it. My history will make me an object of pathetic curiosity and ill will. Poor little rich girl, orphaned spectacularly, lives with a family she isn't even related to, has expensive tastes, and never talked to a Jew whose name was Epstein. The idea of high school chills my blood. There isn't a Chinaman's chance that I will be sent to the Boston version of the Seeley School. We have been all over that. At least *they* have, in consultation with Donald Snyder. The Londons have the final say. They feel it will be in "the best interests" of both their children and Roger and me if there is no distinction made between us. Past and present merge and blend. We are all the same. We will disregard the fact that in my trust fund and invested for me are several million dollars. Let's not talk about the money — here it means nothing.

"You've never been to school with boys, have you?" Judy says. Topper ambles into the room and scrapes his backbone against the edge of the swinging door which separates the kitchen from the dining room. He arches his back like a Disney cat trapped by the bulldog, trembles in the ecstasy of a stretch, then languidly paws at a scrap of food in the corner.

"Nice pussy," Judy purrs. "You're never preoccupied, are you? You don't have any trouble making up your mind." She throws it a piece of fat which the cat eats greedily. "He likes melon too, and Ritz crackers. Clever animal."

"There were boys at dancing school," I say, driven to confess, even though she's probably forgotten her question.

"Dancing school. You went to dancing school? I thought only people named Cabot and Van Rensselaer went to dancing school."

"Not this one," I say.

"Not a Jewish dancing school? Oh you must be kidding. A white-gloves dancing school for Jewish kids?"

"I guess so." Am *I* sorry I got into this.

"Well?"

"What?"

"Well, tell me about it. That is, if you want to. I don't want to make you tell me if you don't feel like it. But I'd love to hear, honestly." She acts as if I were about to let her in on atomic secrets.

"Mrs. Kahn runs it. She has this big house near Fifth Avenue and Sixty-fifth Street. It's a school. There are lots of classes, starting for ten-year-olds and going up to sixteen. She has about five teachers working for her. Everybody made fun of Mrs. Kahn. She's skinny as a rail but she has this huge bustline. The boys said she was topheavy . . ."

"Hmmm." Judy sits herself down at the kitchen table and is taking out a cigarette and lighting it with a stick match. There's something masculine in the way she does it. She uses her hands as if they were instruments separate from her body. She shakes the match out — my mother always blew hers out with an invisible and sweet vapor. "Were most of the kids German Jews?" Before I can answer she answers herself. "What a stupid question. Of course they were. If there was one German Jew they'd all have to be, wouldn't they?"

"I guess so." She's applying the hot wires to me again. Why do I stick around and let her?

"The same kids belong to The Orange Club," I tell her.

"It figures," Judy says, smiling and drawing in a murderous chestful of Camel smoke. This she releases through her nostrils. She reminds me of a horse on a cold day. "Do you want to hear something funny? When I was a little girl I started playing with a girl I met in the park near our house in Syracuse. I guess I didn't tell you I used to live in Syracuse. Anyway, I made friends with this girl. Her name was Myra and she had the most beautiful black hair and violet-colored eyes. She had a rabbit-fur muff. One day her mother found out that we were friends and that we went to the corner store for sodas together and bought books which we swapped. And her mother told her she must never see me again. I was heartbroken when Myra told me. We both cried, I remember, on a park bench. She got her muff wet."

"Why did her mother do that?" I'm the perfect end man.

"Because Myra was a German Jew and my mother and father were Russian. It was a geographical accident of the city that we had landed on neighboring playground swings. It was a terrible mistake. And you want to know something else funny? No non-Jew would believe this story. Or else, if they believed it, they would think it only happened just this once."

"I think that's terrible," I say. "It's stupid."

"Yes," Judy says.

"Did you ever see her again?"

"Well, as a matter of fact, a couple of years ago when I went back to visit some relatives I saw her in a downtown department store. We had tea together. She had turned out just like her mother, only worse. Her daughter went to the local Episcopalian nursery school. So it's probably just as well." This time Judy sighs grandly. Maybe she's telling me that the ways of the world are inevitable, dolorous. "Your eyes are all red," she says abruptly. "I'd swear you'd been crying if I didn't know firsthand that you weren't. What's the matter, don't you feel well?"

"They itch," I say. As a matter of fact my eyes itch so badly I want to remove them. And my breath is getting squeezed again. But I don't want Judy to see how miserable I am.

"That's odd," she says. "Are you sure you're all right?"

I nod. "Could I go upstairs for a while?"

"Of course you can, Sally," she says with some impatience. "Please, for heaven's sake don't think you have to ask me every time you want to make a move or go upstairs. This is *your* house. I'm not a jailer and I don't want you to act like that. It's not good for either one of us. Okay?"

I nod again. I stagger upstairs and hide in my room, my porch, and wait for the seizure to be over. For consolation I take out my white gloves and pull them on, admiring their thick, puffy white-ness. I catch in them the faintest trace of my mother's perfume.

10

No Time
Like the Present

IT TURNS OUT THAT Roger has been peeing without bothering about little things like toilets. Fräulein, who had him potty-trained at eighteen months, is beside herself with pity and rage. Roger doesn't seem to mind.

"A boy of six wetting his bed like a baby," she scolds. "What is the matter with you?"

"He needs diapers," I say in disgust. Fräulein is putting his pajamas in the sink where I wash my hands.

"I want diapers," Roger says. "I don't like wet pajamas."

"No diapers," Fräulein says, laying down the law. "Have you ever seen a grown man in diapers?"

"I don't care," Roger says. His tiny pink penis looks like something that belongs inside his body. He sees me looking at him and tells me to mind my own business. "Make Sally get out," he orders Fräulein.

"Gladly," I say and leave the bathroom to them. As a matter of fact they had walked in on me when I was sneaking a little Lavoris. They still haven't fixed the stupid lock.

"Roger's turning back into a little baby," I tell Judy. "It's disgusting."

"We'll get him some diapers," she says.

"Fräulein said no," I tell her. She's at it again, the housework. This time it's sorting and folding washed clothes. There are shirts

and jeans and socks and underwear and handkerchiefs. So much
faded old cloth cut and sewn into so many different shapes.
"Want to give me a hand?" she says. I don't, but I do it anyway.
Joey's shirts are so small they make me thoughtful, sad. "So
Fräulein says no, does she?" Judy says.

I want to ask who's the boss. This idea — who really *is* the
boss — was hanging over all of us in the house like the threat of a
storm, maybe even a hurricane. We know that the storm is going
to hit, but when and with what subsequent damage is anybody's
guess. Judy thinks about it. Fräulein chews on it. Sam confronts
it, Roger plays with it, I speculate. Even the two London boys
are beginning to feel it. Who's the boss of Roger: the Londons or
Fräulein Kastern?

Judy finds a rubber sheet and she and Fräulein remake Roger's
bed in contemptuous, cooperative silence. Roger is satisfied and
does not mention the diapers again. Neither does Judy.

Tomorrow Judy is going to take me over to the high school,
half a mile away. Just before I go to bed, Judy knocks on the
door of my porch.

"Come in," I say, echoing my mother's broadly inflected welcome, a welcome that she didn't mean half the time.

"I was just wondering what you planned to wear to school
tomorrow," Judy says.

"I guess a sweater and a skirt." I am amazed by her question. In
fact, I have been agonizing for days over which skirt, which
sweater, or whether it should be a dress instead, and the choice
between loafers and saddles and what I should wear in my hair
and so on. It's been ghastly. But Judy? I am convinced she can't
tell a dress from a slipcover, the New Look from the old. Why
should she suddenly care?

"That's good," she says. "Almost nobody wears a dress around
here unless they're going to a wedding."

Or a funeral? I'm not going to tell Judy that I own seven

dresses, one for each day of the week. They are wool, silk, linen, velvet, and if they have a belt it is leather-backed and if they have a lining it is pure silk. What am I going to do with these relics? Send them to the Costume Institute at the Metropolitan Museum of Art, the way my mother did with one of her custom-made jobs? "Street dress, fashionable New York teenage girl, circa 1948."

I'll wear them when I move back to the real world with my father. He'll take me to lunch at the St. Regis and I'll wear them there, one after the other, and then I'll buy some more. My nose is beginning to itch again and my eyes to water; my breath is going through a tunnel that's too small for it. I wish Judy would get out and let me die in peace.

"Well," she says. "I guess I'll get back to my book. Sleep well. I'll wake you in plenty of time."

"Thanks," I say, almost choking. She closes the door quietly. I wait until she's had a chance to get out of sight, then grab my pj's and run into the bathroom with them. I undress with my back against the door so no one will walk in on me. I'm wheezing again, like an old man whose lungs are filled with the smoke from a million cigarettes. What's happening to me? Thoughts of TB, lung cancer, or some dread parasite spin past as possibilities.

By the next morning I know I'm going to have to confess my illness. I can barely make it downstairs. Judy takes one look at me and calls the family doctor. "Milton says to come right over. Oh dear, I'll have to call the school and postpone everything. Sally, do you need any help?" I gather that I look like someone whose last day on earth has arrived. She doesn't want to talk about it but just to get me out of her house and into a doctor's hands before I die on her.

She chatters nervously and tells me that Sam's left the house for an early appointment with the dean, whoever that is. I start to cough, but it doesn't open up the breathing hole the way it should. My face turns red. I can feel the heat rising off me like steam. Tears dribble down my cheeks. "We're really in luck," she says, eyeing me nervously. "Dr. Fineberg had a cancellation. He's going to see you at 9:30. But we'll have to take the trolley because Sam's got the car, damn it. Or maybe we ought to take a cab. Yes, I'll call one right away." She trots off to phone for a cab and comes back swearing. "Hell, they're not answering. We're still in the middle of the rush hour. We'll have to take the trolley. Do you think you can make it? Would you like any help getting dressed?"

"Huhngggg."

"Good," she says, running off in another direction. I am, when I can stop to think at all, surprised by her panic but really too sick to care. It's all I can do to hold myself together; parts of me keep falling numb or floating off somewhere, like my head, attached by a thin, fragile string which grows longer and longer as each moment passes. This is how it would feel to drown.

As soon as we leave the house my dying recedes a little; the tide is going out. Judy takes my arm and we walk down to Beacon Street where we board a trolley. The motion of the car, that nice, silken, full-mouthed motion, helps me stay alive. I am a girl entirely surrounded and cut off by the corona of her own misery and I hate and blame and am ashamed of myself for being alive when my mother is dead, for having deserted my father, the only person I truly love in the world, for hating his Lorna as a bubblehead, for being paralyzed with dread over school, for despising Bubba without having met her, for feeling superior to Judy London because of her clothes and her messy hair and her funny pocketbook, and for feeling superior to Sam London because he's a grouch who thinks he's so great, and for wishing, in fact, that this thing, whatever it is that has got hold of my body, would just hurry up and get it over with and finish me off.

In less than an hour I find myself inside a huge metropolitan hospital. Judy knew where she was going, grabbed my hand and

pulled me after her like a little dog on a leash. Dr. Lehman, back
in New York, had an office you walked into straight off the sidewalk along Park Avenue and Seventy-second Street. I hadn't realized that doctors with private practices *had* offices in hospitals;
the very idea made me sicker. It assumed something I did not
want to face. Judy pushed through doorways, escorted me
around corners, up and down mysterious dark ramps, through
double swinging doors, up a couple of flights of stairs, past waiting rooms as cavernous as the main waiting room in Pennsylvania
Station, where row upon row of people sat placidly as cows in
their stalls. Many of them were Negro women with their kids
zippered to the chin in snowsuits or winter jackets, even though
it must have been over eighty in the building.

"You see all those people?" Judy whispers, dropping back a
moment to allow me to catch up with her. "They come from
miles away. And you know why? Because they've heard that
Jewish doctors are the best doctors. How do you like that? The
word's got around."

"How long do you think they have to wait?" I manage to ask.
My mother, in order to avoid sitting in offices and twiddling her
thumbs, used to phone ahead to the nurse to see if the doctor was
running on or behind schedule. She said that waiting, after you
make an appointment for a definite time, is a "frightful imposi-
tion. You don't keep *them* waiting. Why should they keep you?
Your time is just as valuable as theirs."

"Oh, some of them will be here all day, I suppose. It's a question of first come, first served. At least it's fair, everybody waits
his turn."

I don't like what she said about Jewish doctors. It sounds silly.
Besides, it couldn't be true. Daddy's ulcer doctor isn't Jewish,
and he's good. Most of the people Opa Teddy works with, if you
listened to him, were geniuses at the very least, and they weren't

Jewish. But I'm not going to ask Judy to explain herself; she's bound to make it sound even sillier.

"Look, that woman's brought her lunch." We're staring openly. A small group — a woman, another woman who resembled her, and two small children — are opening paper bags and extracting wax-papered bags and a Thermos. Each child is handed a sandwich and they all begin to munch mournfully.

"Isn't it awfully early for lunch?" I say.

"God knows how long they've been here." One of the women, a skinny figure with freckles on her cheeks and nose like a pale rash, looks at me with pale blue eyes, sees me looking at her, and flashes me a message of ruptured privacy. I look down, embarrassed for both of us. "Come on, Sally. We'll be late." The hand tugs at me again and we're off through more tunnels and annexes. I've never been in a building that was so complicated.

Was this the real world I had been reading about for years and years? Where had I been all my life? I had been sealed inside a germproof art museum, stuffed with cod liver oil, vitamins, and fresh orange juice, checked out yearly by doctors and twice yearly by dentists, baffled from the wind by camel's-hair coats and cashmere sweaters and from the rain by real rubber boots, handled with care, and blinded by the best of intentions. For the first time in my life, life sickened me.

The hospital began to reach me along other routes — the smells, the stuff they put on cotton before they swab you with it, the ether and the carbolic acid and other odors that penetrate your nose and reach clear into your brain and start you thinking about pickling and about death.

So that by the time we reached Dr. Fineberg's office I was a quivering wreck. He could have started to flay me with a dull instrument and I'm sure I wouldn't have been in worse shape than I was already. I took an instant dislike to Dr. F., mainly because Judy had oversold him. I had expected someone very Jewish-looking — big nose, kinky hair, and so on — but Dr. Fineberg surprised me. He had thick red hair and freckles, a turned-up nose, and a prominent Harvard Medical School diploma on his wall. He was wearing a pink button-down shirt under a tweed sports jacket and a thin black knit tie. He also wore an expression designed to put me at ease, a sort of we're-pals look that I didn't buy for a second.

"Well, Sally, suppose you tell me about it." He gives me a green light and I brake.

"About what?"

"Well," he says, unfazed, tilting back in his chair and caressing a spot on his ripe cheek. "About what brought you to my office."

"Didn't Mrs. London tell you?"

"Judy merely said you were sick. She didn't say what kind of sick. Is it something very private, something you find it hard to talk about?"

Like VD? He probably thinks I have VD up to the ears. That's the way he's looking at me, the goat.

"It's not the least bit private," I tell him.

"Ah," he says, obviously disappointed. "What then?" He sits forward now and leans his arms on the desk. His fingers have short red hairs on them, copper bristles.

"I don't feel well," I say.

"*Now* we're getting somewhere. Describe to me exactly how you don't feel well. Where does the feeling come from?" The mouth opens slightly, showing polished, straightened teeth. This man is hungry for symptoms, ravenous. I wish I could invent something to satisfy him, some zany thing like bleeding from the ears or fainting in the bathtub or seeing triple. But I lack the staginess to bring it off. The most interesting symptoms stay locked inside my head.

"It's sometimes hard to breathe," I say, looking at my left hand and deciding that the little finger is about ready. "And my eyes water and I itch all over. Not all the time, only sometimes."

"Ahah!" he exclaims.

"What is it?"

"I can't be sure," he says steadily. His mouth works on something invisible, then he swallows. "I can't diagnose anything on so little evidence. Why don't you tell me a little bit about yourself?"

That's the last thing I want to do. I know what he's getting at — he thinks it's all in my mind, he thinks I'm crazy. He asks me about school, about friends, about how I feel being motherless. How do you think I feel, you idiot? How would you feel having your mother killed in a plane crash when you were fourteen years old and then they took you and sent you to live with some family you'd hardly even heard of, let alone met the mother? He asks me if I've ever had a pelvic examination, and I have to ask him what a pelvic examination is; and when he explains I blush with embarrassment and blame him, and anyway, what has my breathing got to do with my pussy? And then he asks me about my weight and says wouldn't I like to "shed a few of those extra pounds," and I tell him I'm perfectly satisfied with the way I am, at which he puts on this silly face which says he knows I'm a liar. And are my periods regular, and I tell him I don't know, which is the truth.

"Why don't you keep a record? Just write it down on a little calendar."

"Why should I? Why is it important?"

"Ladies ought to keep track," he says.

"I don't," I tell him. "It doesn't matter. Just so long as they don't stop." I don't want to talk to a stranger about my periods. I didn't come for that.

The next step in the breaking down of Sally is the physical examination. He makes me take off my clothes and put on a smock that hits above my knees and ties over my back with two little twisted cotton strings. I feel nakeder than if I were really naked.

"You didn't need to take your underpants off," he says, feeling my tits with hands he has just dunked in ice water. I squirm and he apologizes for his cold hands. "Cold hands, warm heart," he says reassuringly.

"I thought you said I should take everything off," I say.

"Everything *but* your underpants," he says, palpating and kneading, then feeling under my arms for bubonic plague. "No, no, it doesn't matter, don't bother about them now, Sally. It doesn't make the least bit of difference."

It does to *me*. I want my underpants. I know he didn't tell me to leave them on — I would have remembered if he had. Underpants aren't something you take off like a hair ribbon. I'm burning with shame. My pubic hair seems very thick and very dark. If I ever get out of here I'm never going to come back. I'm never going to see him again so long as I live.

It's Judy's fault. She made me come. I'm so angry I feel like throwing something against the wall of the closetlike dressing room. But instead I catch my slip in the zipper of my skirt and have to tear it to free it. This makes me even angrier. The wheezing starts again and fury subsides into the mere effort to get enough oxygen to carry me out of Dr. Fineberg's life forever.

When I get back to his office I see Judy sitting in the other of the two patients' chairs. Judy and the doctor are chatting like two old ladies over cups of coffee. They both look at me as if I were something weird behind glass, on view to the public for the first — and possibly last — time.

"Dr. Fineberg thinks it may be a form of asthma," Judy says brightly.

"We can't be sure, of course," Dr. Fineberg says. "But one thing I am sure of — you're going to live."

Who asked you?

"He thinks it may be the cat," Judy says. She keeps her eyes from me. "You may be allergic to Topper."

"Judy tells me you haven't had any pets before," Dr. Fineberg says.

"No — I mean, that's right."

"Well, it's a relatively simple matter," he says, seizing the opportunity to conduct a sadistic experiment with somebody else's life. "All we have to do is to get the cat out of the house and see if this condition of yours clears up. If it does, then we've found the villain and won't need to conduct a lot of expensive and time-consuming tests." Oh, he's so pleased. My blood runs chill at the thought. They're going to hate me. That's all I need. They're going to kill me.

"What about Danny and Joey? It's their cat."

"They'll survive," Judy says. Still, she avoids my eyes. I can tell she hates me now too.

"In the meantime I want you to get this prescription filled. There may be quite a bit of residual cat hairs and dust in the house even after the animal is gone. Take a pill just as soon as you feel an attack coming on. They may make you feel a little drowsy, so no getting behind the wheel of a car, eh?"

Oh, what a humorist you are, Dr. Fineberg. I look at him with cold, blank eyes. "Just a little joke," he says, turning to Judy and giving her further instructions about my care and feeding. Judy is effusive in her goodbyes and thanks. She tells him how grateful she is for seeing us so promptly and so forth until he actually gets up and takes her arm to get rid of her.

But when we get out into the chilly April day, with the wintry trees trembling and a mean wind flicking at our necks, Judy promptly shuts down. I haven't seen her so quiet since the funeral. I know what she's thinking about. She is thinking about how she is going to explain — first the invasion from Mars (me, Roger, and the German hippo), and then the wiping out of Topper. I don't blame her; *I'd* be thinking too.

We board the trolley for home and sit side by side, me at the window, not touching flesh but touching coats. We pass solid stretches of what must surely be neighborhoods except that everything blends so anonymously it's impossible to tell where one leaves off and the next takes up. It is all shops, and three- or four-story apartment houses, office buildings behind glass instead of behind walls, so that you see people sitting at their desks in the Grumbach Realty office and Household Finance Company talking on the phone or gesturing at a secretary. It's all on a skimpy scale, almost as if they were children playing at realtor and banker.

Judy points out a new supermarket, big as an airplane hangar, where you push a cart around and pull anything you want off the shelf, paying for it just before you leave; the Orthodox temple she attends when and if the spirit moves her; a library; a pet store that sells sick birds; and a lot of other places that swim in and out of my view.

"What's a Spa?" I ask. To me "spa" means a place in Germany where they make you drink mineral water and take high colonics.

"A spa is where you get ice cream and frappes," Judy explains. "It's what you would call a soda fountain, I guess."

"What's a frappe?" I don't really care.

Judy describes it. "That's a frosted," I tell her with authority.

"Not here. Here it's a frappe. And your liquor store is a package store and the cleaner's is the cleanser's, and we're not a state, we're a commonwealth, and I'll bet you're thinking you're in a foreign country. We have funny, wrong names for everything, don't we?"

I look down. She's got my number; she knows exactly what I'm thinking. But does she have to go ahead and say it? There is grime on the outside of the window — tiny specks of black mixed with smoke and dried-up moisture smeared against the glass. I feel as if there were grime all over me too. I feel dirty and my underarms are sticky and no doubt stink. I've stopped taking a daily bath. Who wants to bathe when you can't tell who's going to burst in on you?

"Judy?"

"What, hon?"

"Are we going to get the lock on the bathroom door fixed, please?"

"Oh sure," she says. "Just remind me to buy a lock the next time I go shopping. I'm really sorry about it, Sally."

I'll bet.

The news of my allergy and its treatment went over like an announcement that school had canceled spring vacation. Judy apparently buffered me from the immediate howl of protest but things slipped through and continued for a long time: dirty looks, nasty teasing, "accidents," like spilling milk on me and stabbing me with sharp little elbows. "I'm allergic to you!" Joey said, catching sight of me as I stumbled down for breakfast.

And over the lumpy cereal and overdone bacon: "Why do we have to get rid of Topper? Why can't we get rid of *her?*"

"Joey!"

"I don't care. She's too rich to live here and she says she isn't Jewish. That's a lie, isn't it? She is Jewish, isn't she?"

"I never said I wasn't Jewish," I cry. "I said my *father* isn't Jewish. I *never* said I wasn't Jewish! He's not telling the truth."

"Both of you stop!" Judy cries.

"Dear Gott!" Fräulein says, rising to her ultimate, square, one-hundred-and-eighty-pound on-the-hoof dimensions. "This is too much."

"It's life," Judy murmurs under her breath. Sam looks as if he'd rather be beneath the North Atlantic.

Fräulein makes a dramatic exit — that is, her chair tips over backwards. Roger jumps up in alarm and runs after her, leaving Judy sitting there, her chin palmed, but not actually crying.

Dr. Fineberg's medicine made me gag but I could keep it down, which was the main thing. And it helped when I was drowning, which was the other main thing. The seizures became

less severe the minute the cat was sent across the river to Cambridge with a friend of Judy's. Evidence — it was the evidence
the doctor was after. His diagnosis was confirmed, although to
this day I harbor a suspicion he was convinced my attacks were
triggered by something in my head.

I wrote to Nancy frequently, two or three times a week, and
she wrote back faithfully. It was funny how the minute we were
separated our relationship changed. Naturally it changed — we
were apart. But it was not just the distance, it was as if we were
trying to make one another feel better and so put up a sort of
sassy front and made light of neglected terrible things. For instance, she never told me during that time that her sister had an
operation for cancer, never mentioned that they were all afraid
she might die, never wrote a word about how her mother went
into a six-month tailspin.

It was too bad, it was a greaty pity — friendship can't really
survive separation, no matter what anybody says. You can take
up again where you left off, but while you're apart the thing is
suspended, stops, like a TV that's had the plug pulled out.

"Dear Nancy," I wrote:

I had to go out and fill my prescription tonight because *he* was too
busy working to go down to the drugstore. He's always working. He
doesn't have any hobbies. They don't do any sports like tennis or
skiing, even though there's plenty of snow around here in the winter-
time and they don't do anything in the summer except go to Cape Cod
where a lot of their friends go. They talk about being Jewish. They
don't exactly discuss it like a topic, but they joke about it and I have
the feeling they think about it a lot even when they don't mention it.
Judy's always saying "Is so-and-so Jewish?" The other night I heard
Judy scolding Him for telling an anti-Semitic joke in front of someone
who wasn't Jewish and he got mad at her. Ha ha.
    I guess I forgot to tell you that the medicine I'm taking is because

I have this allergy to the Londons' cat and he had to be sent away. It was him or me, dear one, and guess who won? Isn't that a scream? They had to get rid of their smelly old cat because of little old me.

Tomorrow, dear one, I'm being dragged to the high school. You'll envy me when I tell you about all the gorgeous boys I'm going to take math with. There are more than a thousand kids in the school and it's just called High. He says it's one of the best school systems in America — God forbid he should have anything to do with anything that wasn't the best.

By the way, how is everybody at good old Seeley?

You and Daddy are really the only people from civilization that I hear from. Oh yes, and Oma Lucy who keeps sending me the programs from the silly concerts she goes to. What am I going to do with a lot of old Town Hall programs, for Christ's sake?

They have a perfectly good dining room here that they hardly ever use except when there's company. We ate in there at first, but for the last few days Fräulein has been eating first, before we get there. She and Judy can't stand each other. It's a riot. They talk through their teeth at each other. I'm waiting for the blowup. You should see Fräulein's face get red. It reminds me of Miss Oakland in Gym that day Bunnie kept dropping the ball and blubbering. Anyway, they have this dining room they don't use. We eat in the kitchen, which is OK because the food stays hotter. Actually the dining room is sort of gloomy. It's got two tiny windows, one of them with stained glass in it, and horrible dark wood that looks dirty all around the edges. You realize that I'm learning an awful lot about how the other half lives. I know it sounds stupid, but I didn't have the least idea how rich Mummy and Freddie were until I landed here. Not that the Londons are all that poor. I mean they're not like those pictures of really poor people in *Life*, where their eyes practically hang out and they're wearing rags. But the Londons do things I thought only people with no money did, like darn socks instead of throwing them away and pass clothes down from one person to the next and use leftover food for the next meal, made into something gluey, and lots of times don't eat meat at all but macaroni and cheese or melted cheese sandwiches and thick soup like the war was still on. It really started me thinking because if the Londons who aren't that poor do these things, what do very poor people do? They must starve. Don't tell anyone that I'm so dumb.

Please, dear heart, keep writing. I rely on you. As Ronald Coleman would say, you are my last link with the outside world. Let's not either of us break the chain.

I sealed the letter with a kiss, having put on some Orange Tangee and pressed my mouth against the back of the envelope. SWAK. I sighed as I sealed it; each time I wrote to Nancy she seemed to recede another mile.

Topper was the last straw for the two London boys while Fräulein was the last straw for Judy, and any of us, in any combination, were the last straw for Sam. So much for those up-lifting, heartfelt stories on women's pages, stories that describe the joy and warmth which invade a family along with war orphans and disturbed, black five-year-olds. These families seem to absorb another member without going through a period of tissue rejec-tion. One more person to use the bathroom. Two more sheets to launder each week, another pair of rubber boots to trip over in the front hall, another voice to raise the voice level, one less cookie in the cookie jar. The cat was the last straw for these two poor kids who already felt I was not much of a good thing. They decided to hate me for the cat and they couldn't forgive me. They let me have it in ingenious ways although Judy lec-tured them ad nauseam on the involuntary nature of allergy. I began to feel like a pariah.

Roger, meanwhile, had grown horns and a tail and breathed fire. If he was maddeningly difficult to live with before — an abso-lute monarch with a household of slaves — now he was impossi-ble. He had prickles all over him, he stank, he was a mess. One minute he'd be in a profound sulk, and the next something would make him explode and he would fall into a rage, break things, and use language so foul it turned your ears red. He would slam doors, knock glasses full of milk to the floor in a grand sweeping gesture, scream bloody murder and roll on the ground, make enough noise to fill a state-run orphanage. Then, inexplicably, he would go limp and gloom would circulate through the house like the fumes from a spilled bottle of ammonia. Fräulein was growing restless, you could tell. She would invent errands to take her out of the house by herself.

"I think she's had it," Sam says to Judy one Saturday morning not long after the cat left for Cambridge.

"Oh, no, she's just going out for a tube of hemorrhoid ointment," Judy says, smiling. "She's got plumbing problems."

"I think she's had it," Sam repeats. "I'm sure I'm right. She's got that scattered look in her eyes. She doesn't argue with you so much. She's about to make up her mind."

"She not going to quit," Judy says. "She's the sort of masochistic woman who thrives on adversity. The worse the situation is, the harder she clings to it. She's not a quitter. Fräulein Kastern is not a quitter!" Judy says it in a comic German accent I couldn't help smiling at. "Is she, Sally?"

"Not that I know of," I answer, delighted to be included in their conversation.

"Would you like to make a little bet?" Sam says. "I am willing to bet anything you like that she'll be packing her bags and be out of here within a week."

"Okay," Judy says, putting away the last of the breakfast dishes and surveying her kitchen for something else to clean up. I stand in front of the garbage pail so she won't see it is full and ask me to empty it. "What are the stakes?"

"You name it," Sam says, beginning to leave on the inevitable walk to his inner sanctum and a morning on the intellectual treadmill.

"A copy of the *New Oxford Book of American Verse* — the one that just came out."

"We'll get it anyway," Sam says.

"Not so soon," Judy tells him.

"You're on." He disappeared and didn't come out for three hours, and then he looked as if he'd been wrestling with the Swedish Angel and acted as if he'd lost the match.

Eventually I had to start school. All healthy American girls go to school, even ones without mothers and living in strange towns with odd families. Sooner or later life has to take up its regular beat; it can't stay arhythmic forever.

The day — "*Der Tag*," as Judy coyly called it — arrived unseasonably cold and gray. The wind had sheared off several branches during the night and they lay scattered over the street and sidewalks of Hancock Street like jackstraws shaken out of a giant box.

"It looks like a hurricane," I say as I help myself to scrambled eggs, toast, and hot chocolate.

"You gonna wear those real pearls to school?" Danny asks the catkiller.

"Are they real pearls?" Joey says, wide-eyed. "Lemme feel." He reaches at me. He's going to pull them hard enough to snap the string. I dodge. "I want to feel them," he repeats, looking at his mother for permission to snap my necklace. "They look like beads anyway," he adds.

"They're real," I admit. Judy looks around sharply.

"Have you got anything else?"

"I've got a little pin in the shape of a Scottie with my name on it. Daddy gave it to me two Christmases ago," I say. I'm embarrassed about the real pearls. "I'll take these off," I say, undoing the clasp and slipping them into my skirt pocket.

"The pin sounds nice," Judy says.

"She didn't let me touch them."

"Oh Jesus," Sam says, looking up for the first time from his *Transcript*. "Can't you kids manage to come down and have breakfast one morning without turning the place into a battlefield?"

"Excuse me," I say, and go upstairs to change the necklace for the pin. I am mortified, the way I felt when Mummy's chanteuse friend told me I ought to have my hairline shaved, it was much too close to my eyes. And when she said I should shave under my arms. And when she suggested I go on "a little diet." A little diet for her meant nothing but tomatoes, hard-boiled eggs, and a laxative so powerful it could blow a person clear into New Jersey. I hated her; she made me feel cruddy.

There is a funny look on Fräulein's face when we leave the house. Somehow, although I wouldn't call it either determined or tranquil, there is a quality of both on her features and in her voice as she wishes me "good luck at the school" and tells Judy that she and Roger are going to walk over to the elementary school where he will start next fall, "to watch the children when they are playing on the swings." This idea curdles Roger's mouth but for once Fräulein isn't listening.

All this flashed by me without meaning anything; it was only later that I could look back and say, "Aha, there *was* something fishy about Fräulein that morning I went off to school. Fräulein became a new woman, events were turning before my eyes. The changes were manifest." At that moment, however, all I was interested in was getting the ordeal of entering a new school over with.

There aren't many experiences in a person's life so bone-chilling as going to a new school in the middle of the term. Or, as in my case, when the school year was almost over. I can think of a couple of other experiences I'd rather not go through, such as a breast-tissue biopsy or hearing small children call each other mother-fuckers, but by and large the new school business is about as agreeable as root-canal work without novocaine.

My teeth were chattering. "Hey," Judy says, "It's not that cold. Why are you so cold?"

"Don't know," I say as I slip into the Pontiac's front seat beside Judy, who works the key into the ignition and guns the motor.

"Well, you've got butterflies. I understand," she says blithely. "Relax, it's not so bad, really, you'll get over the strangeness very soon, I guarantee it. It's really a friendly place."

How can she guarantee anything like that? Who does she imagine herself to be, Mrs. God?

I think it was the concept of "Public" almost as much as the concept "School" which had my teeth chattering and my heart beating like ninety. This is what Public School, fed by my mother's snobbery and my fake grandmother's fear of The Mob, meant to me. Hordes of loud-mouthed teen-age boys who slammed their lockers and bumped into you on purpose so they could feel your boobs. Girls who wore pointy bras and spent all their time talking about Frank Sinatra and Gene Krupa and their Saturday night dates. I'd seen enough June Allyson and Peter Lawford movies to know a little bit about Public Schools: teachers with strange accents who wore sweaters, spoke slang, and weren't very bright.

Public was other things as well. It was federal handouts and standing in line. It was noise and body smells. The smell seeping out from under the door of the ladies' room in the Central Park Zoo, near the bear cages, which my mother forbade me to use. "I'd rather have you wet your pants." The smell of wet wool on the Madison Avenue bus on a warm February day. Public was people jammed up against each other with parts touching and mouths breathing into other mouths. It was the sweaty, steamy insides of enclosed spaces like subways and elevators. (My mother used to hold her breath in elevators.) It was the way you felt when the circus was over in Madison Square Garden and the crowd moved as slowly as lava going backward. Public was endless lines waiting to see *Snow White and the Seven Dwarfs* at the Music Hall or the Futurama at the World's Fair and being pressed, like Sell's Liver Pâté, from in front and from behind. Well, to be candid, it was bad manners or no manners at all.

Somehow Oma Lucy had got it into my head that poor people — people who went to Rockaway Beach on the subway and ate out of paper bags — were not so high a form of life as people like her and me and Mummy and Freddie and even my father whom she normally didn't have very many kind words for.

But here's the secret. The poor may envy the rich but the rich are scared shitless of the poor.

Once inside the Public High School I would need a Public School Dictionary to understand my teachers and they would need a Private School Dictionary to understand me. The clothes I was wearing — my navy blue wool skirt and pink sweater, my white bobby socks and saddle shoes, even my little Scottie pin — were merely a disguise. Underneath I was the Private School Princess, the princess atop a perpetual pea, the child who would bleed to death if you cut her with a remark and would turn into melted butter if you asked her a personal question.

Mr. Turner, the man in charge, basking under the benign gaze of Harry Truman, asked me a number of personal questions, and I began to run at the seams. I distrusted him on sight, his fat tummy pressing against his vest with its watch chain stretched across the mound, and his rimless glasses, not round and not square either but an unknown shape, and his hair that looked as if it had been pressed by a hand heavy with Vaseline hair tonic, and his smirk. I hated the smirk most. I couldn't figure out why he was smirking at me, but there was no doubt in my mind that it was I who aroused the smirk.

"So, young lady," he says. "You come to us from the famed Seeley Academy?" He looks at me through the specs. His eyes are large and gray; they can pierce a person's skull.

I nod. Is it really "famed" or is he pulling my leg?

"I never understood the term 'finishing school,' myself. You're not finished, are you? Why, you've hardly begun. And what did you think of your teachers? And what, more importantly, did

they think of you?" Without looking at her, I can tell that Judy
is squirming. At that moment Mr. Turner's secretary knocks on
the door, simultaneously opening it. She walks across the carpeted floor and hands her boss a folder. They enter into an intimate conversation on the subject of something called Language
Arts Three. He looks at her backside as if longing to give it a
loving touch. She leaves finally and he turns back to me.

"I apologize for the interruption," he says, obviously pleased
with his power to keep people on the hook. "But school business
must proceed, mustn't it? Where was I?"

"You were asking Sally what she thought of her teachers,"
Judy says. "Does it matter really?"

"Just a form of chitchat, Mrs. London, and a way of getting to
know your charming ward." He sees me through lenses pasted
with $$$$ signs. I'll bet he doesn't know the names of three other
students in the entire school.

"I suppose," he says, studying me for clues that will reveal the
heiress in me, "I suppose that you've had three years of general
science, seven of French, two of Latin, perhaps a year or two of
Greek, and enough World and American History to turn out
several textbooks on the subject?"

"Really, Mr. Turner," Judy says, laughing.

I gulp. "No Greek," I murmur, "and not that much History.
You could take Greek in the eleventh grade." I am perspiring
lavishly.

"You didn't think I meant that literally, did you?" Mr. Turner
says. "I only put my question that way to let you know I'm quite
aware of the extraordinary reputation of the school from which
you come. How much Latin?"

"A year. We started Caesar."

"*Natürlich*," he says. "Everybody always does."

"And I suppose," he continues, patting his fat stomach lightly
with one hand, "that you think we ought to promote you imme-

diately into the sophomore class. Your superior reputation and all that. Well, I want to tell you, young lady, we don't do that sort of thing here in the Brookline School System."

I start to protest but he has the ball and is running with it for a touchdown. "Not at all. Once in a great while we may decide that a student is ready to take on an independent project, but skip a grade — never! Never, so long as I hold this job."

"I don't think Sally had that in mind," Judy says, clearly awed by the man across the desk from her.

"It doesn't matter," he says. "We will put her in the ninth grade, where she belongs. When did you say your birthday was, young lady?"

"June fourteenth," I say.

"Excellent. You will have Miss Fletcher as your homeroom teacher. Many people think she is the finest teacher in the school. A few disagree. We'll see, won't we? If you hurry now you can be in time for our regular homeroom announcement period." He checks his golden watch and smirks again. Mr. Turner's secretary appears on a signal that I neither saw nor heard — this unnerves me. Judy, too, seems uneasy.

"She's going to start right now?" she says.

"There's no time like the present, I always say," Mr. Turner tells her. "I am a man of action myself. You wouldn't think it to look at me now, sitting in this big comfortable office in this comfortable chair, but I am indeed a man of action. You probably wouldn't believe me if I told you I go to the 'Y' three times a week and work out with the medicine ball and swim thirty laps in the pool, rain or shine, winter and summer. I cannot tolerate inactivity for long. Rots the brain, you know."

"Why shouldn't I believe it, Mr. Turner?" Judy says, recovering her equilibrium.

"Ah," he says. I look at his stomach. Judy may believe it, but I certainly don't.

As he escorts us to the door of his office — but not a millistep further — Mr. Turner says, "You will undoubtedly discover sooner rather than later that our approach here is worlds away from what you have been accustomed to at the famed Seeley School. You will not be given individual attention unless you are failing — and then, alas, it may be too late. We cannot afford the luxury" — he lets the word, with attendant meanings, sink in a while before he continues — "of individual attention. Still, our graduates forge on to such venerable educational institutions as Harvard, Yale, and the other Ivy League schools. Bryn Mawr, Vassar, and the rest of the Seven Sisters, universities such as California, Chicago — the choicest. So, my dear girl, who is to say whose approach is ultimately the best? Miss Danehy, take this child to Fletcher's homeroom, please."

I gulp again. I feel as if I were being dragged off to view the circles of hell and then to be thrown, fully clothed, into one of them. I look at Judy. She catches the desperation on my face, makes a motion to pat my arm, but Miss Danehy pulls me away. Judy misses executing the ritual, comforting gesture. I look over my shoulder in time to see her turning and walking slowly toward EXIT, as if she had just glimpsed the last of Sally Stern. And as if she really cared.

I was determined to get through the morning without giving in to my terror and I entered the same mystical state I used to get myself in when my mother took me with her on a Saturday shopping safari, which frequently lasted from ten in the morning until closing time, with an hour out for lunch at Schrafft's. I would dig in, go under, turn inside out, to avoid being where I was and doing what I was doing. I had had enough practice to baffle the most important faculties, sight and sound. During my first day at Brookline High I saw no one, heard no more than a general adolescent hum, felt nothing but the warmth of the steam-heated air. I suppose I was stared at and maybe even made fun of, but to me I was invisible.

For some strange reason I can remember exactly what they served in the cafeteria for lunch: bright orange macaroni and cheese, cole slaw with tiny morsels of green pepper, and red Jell-O with pieces of slimy canned fruit suspended in it.

11

In the Long Run

ABOUT THAT TIME I became a compulsive; dreamy. There were rituals, habits, and procedures I had to carry out in exchange for another few hours of life. Things like touching the banister in three predetermined places when I came down to breakfast in the morning and went up to bed at night. And arranging my clothes and shoes in a certain inflexible position. I opened drawers, then shut them, fixed my window at the same level as the day before, and so on. The whole bedtime routine took ten minutes; I was in a state of anxiety until it was over with. Every night I went through the routine; nothing short of a fire could have stopped me.

In the grip of angst, I sailed unscathed through all sorts of real-life unpleasantness at school (the word had got around that I was filthy rich and a Private School Princess, and the kids stared at me as if I had two heads), a bout with the green death, and the end of Fräulein Kastern with only the slightest flicker of a response. I was emotionally inert. Urgency was saved for an interior chaos which, had I been an artist, might have produced pictures like Bosch's or stories like Kafka's. But alas, I was nothing but a troubled child whose creations were only ritual reassurances that she was still alive.

Fräulein's departure was no surprise to Sam, me, or Judy. But it stunned Roger, who was no more prepared for it than he had been for his parents' death. Fräulein was the kind of woman who believed that you must not drag things out by explaining or anticipating. She was the off-with-her-head, let's-get-it-over-with sort of person, mainly, I suspect, because she did not have the slightest idea of how — or why — to cushion blows. One minute, I love you; the next, I am gone forever. She had, it appeared, suddenly bought her plane ticket. She had "secured a place," as she told us anachronistically at lunch one Saturday. Roger was chewing on a tuna fish sandwich at that moment and didn't hear her. Judy tried not to let her pleasure show on her face. Sam went on eating. As usual Fräulein had eaten first and now was standing over us like doom in a governess costume. Sam eyed her and asked her where. Fräulein said, "With a Mr. and Mrs. Vanderbilt, on Long Island."

"Not really," Sam said. Roger is hearing something now. His little eyes look up and his mouth, half full of tuna fish mush, hangs open.

"They have three small children," Fräulein says. "Twins and a baby girl. I will have complete charge." She looks at Judy.

"That sounds very nice for you, Fräulein," Judy says, her eyes flashing happiness but her mouth straight as sin.

"*Ja*," she says. "I am looking forward to having my own room."

The two London boys are now aware of what's happening. The smaller, Joey, whoops and says, "She's leaving, she's leaving." Fräulein gives him a look designed to ream his insides out. Untouched, he jumps up from the table and starts dancing around it like what my mother would call "a wild Indian."

"What?" Roger says. "What did you say?" He grasps Fräulein's arm and gives it a terrific tug, nearly pulling her over on his lap.

"I am going, *Liebchen*. Tomorrow morning my plane leaves."

"Going where? When are you coming back?" The fear in his face looks like sickness.

"I will come back to see you soon," she says, evasively. Evasiveness is not her usual style, and she does it badly. Now Roger jumps up and confronts his nurse. "You can't go. I won't let you."

"I must go, *Liebchen*. This is your new life here, your new home. They will take good care of you. They do not need a nurse in this house — it is easy to see that right away. The momma here does all the things."

Judy, embarrassed, looks down. I start to bite number four on my right hand, tear a tiny shred of nail, and spit it out softly. I think Sam ought to say something but he remains silent.

Roger is in a panic. He's beginning to pound his fists into her hip the way he did when she told him his parents were dead and in heaven. She stands there, letting him hurt her, looking down with watery eyes. My God, even *I* can see the woman going through hell. All this occurs to me at a distance. I see it as if it were happening in a far-off room I am peering into through a telescope.

Finally, Judy puts in, "Are you sure you're doing the right thing? Oh, sit down, for heaven's sake, Fräulein. I can't talk with you standing and me sitting. Sit down and have a cup of coffee or something." Judy sweeps her hand through her hair. "Look, there's no earthly reason why you shouldn't stay here. At least a little while longer. Roger needs you."

"I prefer to stand, Mrs. London," Fräulein says. Things are going pretty much the way she planned them vis-à-vis Judy. She's going to make Judy feel bad for a long time. She's rubbing Roger's hair. Roger stands against her, motionless. I recognize his quiet as the prelude to a storm.

"I think this way is best for all of us," Fräulein adds. "Roger will start school in the fall . . ."

At that point Roger lets go in a display so spectacular that it is a pity his energy can't be converted into something useful, such as warming a house or sending a motorboat across Baffin Bay. He throws his plate to the floor. He grabs a candlestick and heaves it against the window. Sam comes to life and tries to tackle him but is thrown off balance as Roger adroitly sidesteps. He begins to shout obscenities at Fräulein, coming at her like a bull in the ring, smashing up against her bulk and kicking her legs. The London boys — one standing, the other still seated — watch agog, thrilled by the performance.

Sam turns and comes after Roger again, trying to peel him off Fräulein who is incapable of defending herself. It is amazing how much strength a little boy can galvanize when he's as angry as Roger. Sam has trouble. Roger is slithery, his legs are driven by fury, he's impossible to contain. I'm staring at all this in a mood of detached wonder, wondering vaguely how it has come to this, how events have linked themselves in a chain to produce a scene so chaotic and brutish. It reminds me of Daddy and Mummy a long, long time ago. I close my eyes, willing myself away. The moment freezes, then everything breaks at once. Judy jumps up to help her husband. I run from the room and go upstairs where I immediately fall into a trance; the events that have just taken place vanish from my mind and my memory and I take out the picture again.

The terrible picture. It shows Daddy and his Lorna standing on a flagstone walk with his lovely clean white house in Princeton as backdrop. The trees are bare but the ground is snowless; they are caught in the limbo between seasons. It suits Lorna, who smiles like a retarded angel. She is looking shyly, slyly at my father, whose left arm is missing. I know it. It has been cut off just below the elbow. There is absolutely no mistake — the bottom half of his arm is gone. I have been staring at this picture for two days. Why didn't they tell me? When did it happen? What is the matter with him? My anxiety is an unuttered shriek. I take out my stationery and start to write a letter. I complete one page, read it over, and, realizing how bizarre it sounds, mass it into a tight little ball and throw it away. I am perspiring and my heart is going crazy.

Finally, after several drafts, I manage to write a letter with the proper tone.

Dearest Daddy,

Thank you for the lovely jar of cashew nuts, the banana bread, and the tins of anchovies. I gave the anchovies to Judy and she served them to guests with cocktails the other night. They went like hot cakes. Honestly, the way you keep sending me food and stuff I think I'm at camp or in the army or something. Judy says to tell you she thinks you're a very generous father.

I can't wait for the two weeks to be over and your wedding! It's the one thing I've really looked forward to all year. Should I plan to stay in New York overnight? If you think I should, do you think I ought to let Oma Lucy know I'm coming and maybe she'll want me to stay with her?

In your last letter you asked me how things were going. Pretty well, I guess. The Londons are okay, at least Judy isn't so bad and she isn't always bossing me, telling me what to do and when to go to bed and things like that. I have to tell you Fräulein is leaving. Roger is having one of his tantrums right now. Judy does everything Kathleen and the cook and Rooney used to do. She does all the shopping and cooking and cleaning and making beds and vacuuming and everything. I heard Sam London tell her they had enough money to have a cleaning lady once in a while but she said she didn't want one. I don't understand her. She's taught me some things like cooking chocolate pudding and meat loaf and how to dry dishes so they're not all smeary. I don't mind it so much but I wouldn't want to do it as much as she does. Sometimes she acts like she's doing something wonderful and important and as if there's no difference between cooking a delicious meal and cleaning out the toilet bowl.

When I said she's okay I meant that I hardly know Him at all. He's always either off teaching or working in his study that no one can go into. He doesn't even allow his wife in there. I couldn't believe it when I heard it at first.

Do you still want me to come and live with you if the judge says it's okay? Because that's the one thing in the world that will make me happy. It's all right up here but it's not like being with my own family, my own father. I wouldn't want Him as a father; He's too grouchy and He doesn't ever say anything nice at breakfast.

Every once in a while I still dream about Mummy and when I wake up I find that I've been crying. Do you think that's normal? How much longer will that happen?

There are a couple of little things that are bothering me and since you asked me how things were going I might as well get them off my chest. The first thing is — and I know you'll think I'm silly — that I can't get used to the fact that the Londons are so different from you. I keep wanting to make you the same and I want you to like each other. I told you you'd think I was silly. It bothers me that He doesn't play tennis and doesn't own even one racket and you have four. It also bothers me that they're so Jewish and so many of their friends are too. He doesn't know how to dress well and they almost never go out to restaurants to eat. Judy says the food is lousy. Don't you think that's a little snobby of her? I do. I love going out to eat. Remember how you used to take me to Rumpelmayer's and the Plaza?

The reason I brought that up about them being Jewish is that I never used to think about it much but now I think about it a lot. I *feel* more Jewish here. It's like they put something Jewish in my milk. No, I'm kidding. They don't put anything in my milk but Bosco.

Anyway, I wish you and they weren't so different. I think about this all the time. It worries me because I can't help thinking that one of you must be right and the other wrong.

The last thing I want to write about is that funny picture you sent me of you and Lorna Emerson. Is there something wrong with your arm?

Here, my heart starts pounding in my ears and I am so agitated I can hardly hold my Parker Fifty-one steady enough to write with.

You'll think I'm silly again, but have you had some awful operation you haven't told me about? Don't worry, Daddy, I can take it. Just tell me the truth.

I hoped that this disclaimer would sound like I was joking — I wasn't joking.

School's okay. I don't like the boys. They make too much noise and they talk as if they hadn't been taught the English Language. Otherwise, I've made a couple of friends from the girls and the teachers seem all right, some of them. There's an awful lot of homework. When I told Judy she said she thought that was good. Sometimes I stay up till after eleven doing homework. I hate it. The sports program is nice and there's a good dance teacher.

I have to stop now. Homework in three subjects and a test to study for in French. *Bon nuit, mon cher papa. Ecrive moi s'il tu plais.*

Votre jeune fille, aimée,
Sarah

I made it a point never to send my love to Lorna.

I got a letter back from him in two days, which was some sort of record. I opened the envelope with shivering fingers and was so nervous I ripped the letter.

My dearest little-big girl Sally —

What a lot of things you have on your mind these days, I don't know when you find the time to do anything else but think — and brood. I hope you're not going to turn into one of those ladies who are always thinking.

But, princess, I am glad, really glad that you still confide in your old man. It is a very precious gift, to be able to tell someone else your troubles. Most people think it is easy but I know better. Please don't stop, don't ever stop bouncing your ideas, your doubts, your deepest feelings off me. I will be here as long as you need me.

Now, to get down to your questions, one by one, in order.

(But first — listen, my dear little girl, when I send you a gift, it is for *you*, for *your* enjoyment. When I send something to Mrs. London I don't expect her to go out and give it to the first person who comes along. Those anchovies were for *you* to eat and enjoy. 'Nuff said.)

1. I don't see why you shouldn't stay with Alfred's mother when you come down for our wedding on the tenth. Wouldn't it be nice if you could come along on the honeymoon with us? But I'm afraid

Lorna would find that just a bit unusual. We're holding the reception at Lorna's club in the city. It will be a small party, mainly family and a few friends. You'll love Lorna's friends. They're a terrific bunch.

2.   Of course I still want you to come live with us. We wouldn't have it any other way. We'll just have to clear up a few minor legal matters and then it's clear sailing to the seas of Princeton, N.J. Lorna didn't want me to tell you — wanted it to be a surprise — but I can't help it. The workmen have been tearing things down and building things up for a couple of weeks now. You wouldn't recognize the old place. The timetable says your apartment should be completed just about the time the school year ends. Keep a stiff upper lip, be a good girl. I'm glad you're helping Mrs. London in the house. It's splendid that you're learning the homely arts at last, arts which your mother, poor woman, neglected, for one reason or another, to teach you.

3.   This is a little more difficult to answer. My first recommendation is that you forget pronto about trying to make all people alike. Can you picture a world where everyone had the same taste in sports, in music, in food, in each other? It would be like a land of robots. Thank God, we haven't come that that, though what with the activities taking place down in Washington for the past fifteen years I sometimes wonder if that isn't what our benighted government has in mind for our country. Differences are *not* wrong, Sally. They are the spice of life. Rejoice in those differences. You know the saying "You can't square a circle." Don't try. Don't try to make me resemble Mr. London or Mr. London resemble me. It's impossible, one, and two, it's an unworthy goal. The important thing is not whether the Londons and your father are or are not alike but that they behave toward each other in a civilized manner. As you get older you will come to realize that people have varying values and like to do a wide range of things. There are differences in temperament, intelligence, taste, attitudes, etc. These differences are as natural a part of the human condition as blue and brown eyes, black and blond hair, thinness, fatness, and skin color. It follows, then, that we choose our friends on the basis of nothing more than common traits and interests. A black savage from the depths of Africa is not going to be very comfortable sitting down to tea with a member of the British Royal Family.

Now I have never had an extended conversation with Sam London and no doubt we could hold a polite, amusing chat. But as far as being lifelong friends, it just isn't in the cards. There is no use in my trying to make myself over to be like a Jewish college professor, any more than you would expect him to turn a somersault and become a squash player or an investment broker. If this sounds as if I were laying it on the line somewhat roughly it is only because I feel that I owe you an honest, candid, truthful answer. These are very basic questions about society and about people you are dealing with. What I'm trying to get across to you in my long-winded way is that it is not important for London and me to be buddies or to wear the same jacket. I get mine from Brooks Brothers and Chipp. The world, little darling, has bumbled along lo these many years without all its people being homogenized like Borden's milk.

Now don't I sound like an old uncle or Lord Chesterfield giving advice all over the place? Oh yes, I thought of one more thing in this connection and then I assure you the lecture will be over. If there's one thing I've learned in my long life it is that there is nothing to be ashamed of in good, honest bias so long as you can admit it to yourself and still act like a gent or a lady. Trust your good sense and your solid instincts and you will never go wrong.

4. Of course there's nothing the matter with my arm. Whatever put such a strange, morbid notion into your pretty little head? I want you to promise me you won't entertain any more ideas like that!

Lorna joins me in sending you bushels of love.

We are both counting the days until you are with us for good.

Your devoted

                                                                    Daddy

I was still trembling when I finished reading my father's letter. I had been so convinced that his arm was gone that I distrusted and ignored his reassurance. I couldn't get it through my head that he might be telling the truth. It took days before my good sense dominated and the idea that my father was mangled disappeared. I never told a soul but carried this dread around like a dead pet mouse in a coat pocket, knowing I should get rid of it but somehow unable to.

As for the rest of the letter, I promptly forgot it, which is probably just as well because I couldn't have swallowed it anyway. And he hadn't even answered my question about the night-mares.

Everything began to go like a car that has outlived its war-ranty. It became clear that Roger would have to be dealt with in some way a little more strenuous than Judy's and Sam's admon-ishments and their sons' righteous fury. After Fräulein left, Judy talked Roger's way into a play group which met three times a week under the guidance of rotating mothers. After four sessions, Roger was politely booted. Judy was told that he didn't blend with the group. It sounded as if he had a solo voice in a chorus composed of perfect choristers. I understood what it meant and I'm sure Judy did too.

She went to see the family doctor, my old friend Dr. Fineberg, who hemmed and hawed, had Roger in for a friendly hour of scrutiny, and suggested that Judy "seek outside help." You would think, given all the circumstances leading up to this little boy's breakdown, plus the fact that Judy wasn't his mother, that she would have accepted this proposal with relief and delight. But no, she took it personally. You could see her melt into a self-doubting, self-blaming failure before your very eyes. There were moments when I felt, for no plausible reason, triumphant: she is in fact more like the rest of us than the rest of us. She thinks she's so great, she's not so great; she's fairly small; look at her teary nose; look how her shoulders sag, how she's burned the potatoes, and scowls at her husband; hark how she snaps at her children. Hear the sense of failure in her voice. "It's my fault," she says.

Sam tells her they should have convinced Fräulein not to leave just yet. "It's my fault," Judy repeats like a child.

"For Christ's sake, Judy, I can't talk about this with you if you don't stop blaming yourself. Guilt never helped anything."

"No, well how about the Catholic Church?"

"Oh, come on, Judy, do you want to talk about Roger or

not?" I'm in the room with them, but as usual, when they're deep into something hairy and serious, they ignore me. So I hear all sorts of things my mother considered unsuitable for little girls. Maybe she was right. Who knows?

"I don't know why you keep shying away from the truth."

"And what's that?" Sam says.

"That I'm responsible for Roger's being in the terrible shape he's in."

"Horsefeathers. Bullshit." Sam is really angry. He's actually having a fight with his wife. I shiver with guilty anticipation.

"I don't want to talk about it anymore," Judy says. Her voice sounds like tears but her face is still dry.

"That's up to you," Sam says. I admire his managing, on every point, to get the upper hand. I'm not sure how he does it, but she is constantly at a disadvantage with him. What is his secret? And Mummy thought Judy was so smart.

The discussion ends. I slink away. Sam walks off somewhere, guess where. And Judy remains, another little piece of her broken off and flushed down the toilet.

Judy eventually joked about it. "You know what a psychiatrist is, don't you, Sally?" I shake my head. "It's a nice Jewish doctor who can't stand the sight of blood." Ha ha. They found a nice J. D. who couldn't stand the S. of B., a Dr. Gabriel Mintz whom I never saw but who became rather a prominent person around the Londons' house. To Judy and Sam he was the man who took the heat off them, and thus he became a kind of hero.

"Imagine, a six-year-old kid having a full-blown neurosis," I heard Judy say on the telephone. I thought she oughtn't to talk about him that way to an outsider. It was none of the outsider's business. Judy had obviously recovered from her prolonged bout of guilt and self-hatred, had come out of it completely unaffected. So much for learning from experience. I hated her cockiness in the light of Roger's equally obvious suffering. Each time the hour came around, Judy bribed him into the car with a promise of a Brigham's ice cream soda. But at least he went.

Then came the great shall-we-move crisis. And soon after that, Bubba. It was quite a spring.

The shall-we-move crisis evolved from an honest, realistic, however belated, appraisal of the situation. We were crowded. I should have my own room. There should be a place for guests, not just the living room couch. There was plenty of dough, tons of it, all the money on earth, in a fund set up to keep me and Roger comfortable, lolling in luxury's lap, not just stuck away on some drafty porch where early spring rain dripped in icy puddles and ran down into one corner. I'm not sure it wasn't Mr. Snyder who initiated the reappraisal. After all, he was being paid to look out for our interest.

"I know it's silly," Judy said, "but the idea of moving scares me. It makes me feel very sad."

"Change should make you feel good," Sam instructed her.

"It doesn't. It makes me think of death."

I thought what she was saying made a kind of morbid sense, but Sam wouldn't let her have it. He tried to convince her she was closing down. "Mustn't close down," he said. "You'll get old before your time."

"Maybe so," she said. It didn't seem to bother Judy that Sam always knew a better way of facing up to things than she did. "We could build on. There's lots of space out back. We could add a couple of rooms. And another bathroom. Then we wouldn't have to move."

"I thought we'd decided already," Sam says with a sigh.

"You have, I haven't," Judy answers, matter-of-factly.

"Well," he says, slipping down onto the end of his spine the way the posture teacher at Seeley said you should never if you want to grow up with a straight back and a healthy mind. "Let's just suppose it's settled. Where would you like to go?"

"How about Athol?" Judy says.

"Not a bad idea," Sam says. "Can you see us telling our friends

in New York and San Francisco that we live in a place called
Athol?"

"We could always pronounce it A-toll, like Bikini." I can tell
they've got something good going between them. It happens
every once in a while. It's as if they were playing in two different
orchestras and all of a sudden the conductors have started them
on the same piece.

Sam sees me and tells me what they're talking about, which I
already know because I've been listening for the last five minutes
without their noticing that I'm standing there. He turns back to
Judy. "What about Marblehead? It's such a quaint town, so picturesque, with all those little sailboats bobbing up and down in its
picturesque little white harbor."

"Marblehead?" Judy says. "That's what I am."

"Come to think of it," Sam says, picking up the upbeat, "we
have to pick the place for its name. Otherwise, why move?"

"I've always like the name of Chelmsford," Judy says. "A silent *l* and a dark *e*. Chelmsford."

"Peabody, Mashpee—very organic," Sam goes on. "Quincy—a
code in de head. Lincoln—another silent *l*. Barnstable, Sudbury,
North Reading—veddy English."

"Wellfleet—a healthy armada," Judy tells him. "Shirley.
How'd you like to live in her, Sam?"

"I'd have to meet her first."

"What about Cambridge?" I say. I like the sound of Cambridge because it's got Harvard.

"It's too expensive," Judy says. "Besides, if we lived in Cambridge we'd have to send you to private schools."

"Why?"

Judy looks uncomfortable, then mutters something about the
public schools in Cambridge not being up to snuff. She doesn't
want to talk about it.

Sam explains that most of the Harvard professors send their

kids to Shady Hill and Buckingham and Milton Academy and that left the public schools in the hands of the Town instead of the Gown. He said, "You think that's hypocritical, don't you?" I nod. "Well, that's the way it goes. There's a double standard in everybody's woodpile, even ours. You just have to look for it."

I wasn't altogether sure what he was driving at. All I was sure of was that it was baffling how one Public could be better or worse than another. Wasn't all Public the same? It was like some non-Jews believing all Jews to be the same disagreeable people.

Judy returns to the theme. "How about moving up to Fisher Hill with Mrs. Gotrocks?"

"You mean," Sam says, "Mrs. Gotrocksky. On gefilte fish-er hill." Judy laughs like a hysterical child. I don't see what's so funny. They've left me out again. It must be something very Jewish they're laughing at.

They change the subject and start talking about money. Judy says, "You don't mind if I fix these vegetables while we're talking, do you?" Sam says no, of course not. I grit my teeth. She's at it again, she never stops. Bubba is scheduled to appear later in the afternoon, and she's doing special little things, like peeling the cucumbers and putting cheese in the salad dressing.

Judy remarks that Freddie must have trusted Sam profoundly. "I don't know if I would have trusted you with all that dough. It might go to your head. And all those big decisions, God, you could do anything. What if you took it into your head to buy a racehorse or a complete set of the DAB and gave Sally and Roger gruel and water for breakfast?"

"Freddie may have trusted me, Jude, but Snyder certainly doesn't. Snyder acts as if I were Willie Sutton. He's paid not to trust me, that's his job. Sally knows I wouldn't give her water with her gruel, don't you, Sally?"

"I guess so," I say. Their bringing up the question of my money and racehorses makes me extremely uneasy.

Judy doesn't like what Sam has said either. "You mean that Snyder checks up on you like the FBI? Or the House Un-American Activities Committee? I think that positively grotesque. Can't you stop him? Why didn't you tell me this before?"

"I thought you knew all about it," Sam says, hardening. "Why do you suppose I get all those long distance calls? I don't understand you, Judy. I assumed you knew all about Snyder's going over expenditures."

"Maybe you assumed too much," Judy says. "I can't read your mind, you know." Now she's playing Bach and he's doing Moussorgsky. I feel the dissonance—it makes me want to leave the concert hall.

"I'm sorry," he says curtly. "Look, you can listen in on the extension next time he calls."

"Thanks a lot," Judy says. "You know what I'm going to do? I'm going downtown and buy myself a baby grand piano with my own money, and when he comes snooping and accuses me of using Freddie's dough for my own pleasure, I'll just show him."

"But you don't play the piano," Sam says.

"I'll take lessons," Judy says. "Very expensive lessons."

Sam smiles and gets up. "I'll see you later," he says.

"You know, Sally, I think we'll move around the corner. I don't think I can tear myself away from Mr. Greenberg."

Mr. Greenberg was Judy's butcher. They were having an affair of the heart. He gave her extra slices of all-beef bologna and called her Bubbala.

Bubba came at last. If you think I'm going to say that after the buildup she turned out to be an anticlimax you're wrong. She was every bit as vivid as I expected. It's difficult to describe how some people are more *there* than others; they may not make more noise or be bulkier but they emit something: electrical impulses, animal magnetism, something. You won't see this person come quietly into a room and sit down quietly. It doesn't work that way. They are sending out signals and picking them up at the same time. Part of the message says "notice me," "speak to me," "listen to me," "get out of my way."

Bubba Belle and reticence were strangers. The moment she walked into the house and plunked her fat suitcase down in the hall, she began to stare at me. Every time I was in the same room with her, those eyes, those eyes would follow me, asking questions, only some of which came out of her mouth.

"Sallee," she said, with the trace of a girlhood spent in another country, "tell Bubba about the high life in New York. How many maids did your momma have? What was the cook's name? Did you have one of those nannies to take you to the park? Tell Bubba—did your folks take you to temple? What temple did they attend? Temple Joshu-a? Am I right? I knew I was right! The Orange Club, the famous Orange Club—is it true they throw a Christmas party every year? I can't believe it's true. Sally, *you* know, please tell your Bubba everything. Did they make your bed for you? Oh, what a life you must have led. You're a good girl. She's a good girl, Judith, a sweet girl. Where's your brother, Sally? I never see your brother. Where does he hide himself all day? It's no good for a child to be alone by himself so much. Judith, Roger shouldn't be alone by himself so much."

"Yes Belle." Everybody but Judy called her mother Bubba. Judy called her by her first name.

"Sally, you look like a shiksa—did anyone ever tell you? Those blue eyes—look at her blue eyes, Judith. They look like big blue marbles, don't they? Except for the hair. That thick curly hair. No shiksa I ever saw had hair like that. Judith, it's just like your grandmother's hair. She could braid it and it would stay in braids without any ribbon to hold it. Now isn't that something — Sally looking like my mother, and they're not even related."

I'm blushing. I can hardly bear to be in the same room as Bubba. I've never liked being referred to in the third person. Judy reads my mind. "Belle," she says. "Maybe Sally would rather not be talked about in the third person."

"What do you mean? Sally doesn't like to be complimented on her beautiful hair? I don't believe it!" Bubba's eyes widen, like Molly Picon. In spite of her age she manages to extend a little-girl expression. "Judith," she says. "You don't know anything about girls."

Judy's mouth flops open. She's about to say something, then changes her mind. You're right, Bubba. Judy doesn't know very much about girls. That's because I'm her first, and she got me when I was middle-aged.

"Where are your sons?" Bubba asks.

"Out playing. Somewhere in the neighborhood."

"At this hour? But it's dark outside. They should be home by now, it's not safe after dark, Judith."

"They're always out till suppertime, Belle, they're with a bunch of neighborhood kids. Nothing can happen to them. This isn't Harlem, dear — this is Brookline, Mass."

"They'll get kidnapped. Don't forget the Lindbergh baby."

At this Judy starts to laugh. "Why would anyone want to kidnap Danny London?"

Bubba looks at me long and hard. Pretty soon we all understand what she's talking about. Thanks a lot, Bubba, for making me scared. It never occurred to me before — now I've got another thing to worry about.

"Belle, for heaven's sake, I've never heard anything so far-fetched in my life," Judy says. "What on earth are you trying to do — scare everybody out of their wits?"

"I'm only trying to be realistic. Those boys should not be out where you don't know where they are. They will be kidnapped." She doesn't actually say "mark my words," but you can tell she

means it. Judy is glum; her mother has a bad effect on her. It's as
if the mother took something out of the daughter and used it for
herself.

"By the way, Judith, do you think I should lose some weight?
Your Aunt Esther says five or six pounds, do you think she's
right?"

"What's five or six pounds, Belle?" I can see Judy does not
want to be drawn into a weight controversy.

"Five or six pounds is five or six pounds," Bubba answers.
"What do you think, Sally, should I take off a little here?" She
pats her hip. I've been watching her, trying to figure out whether
her dress was too small when she bought it, because it certainly is
now.

"Mother, don't ask Sally!"

"Why not — why shouldn't I ask? She's got eyes, hasn't she?
And a brain?"

"I dunno," I murmur. Bubba eats like a horse. She picks things
up between meals and pops them into her mouth. Cookies, crackers, fruit, even crumbs. This morning I saw her brushing crumbs
into her hand and popping them right in.

"Stay away from the latkes and the honey buns and you'll lose
it in no time," Judy says.

"You talk as if I ate too much. I hardly eat anything. A bird
would die on what I eat."

Judy catches my eye.

"How do you like this for a diet? I read about it in *Vogue*
magazine at Dr. Mirsky's office, my podiatrist. I was there last
week getting a corn removed — you should have seen it, Judith,
it was as big as a walnut. In the magazine it said you should
eat only grapefruit and hard-boiled eggs three weeks. And drink
a glass of lemon juice when you get up in the morning. Have you
ever heard of such a diet? If you ask me, only a goy would make
up a diet like that!"

"Belle, don't eat that cookie if you want to lose weight."

"One little cookie won't make any difference." In it goes. "Too dry, Judith. Next time try putting in a little milk." I'm sneaking out the door when Bubba pins me. "Sally, you had a chauffeur in New York? And a Lincoln Continental?"

"A Cadillac," I say. My personal wealth is becoming an unbearable burden. What good does it do me? It only makes me feel guilty and ashamed. I would like to give it away to those people I saw sitting and waiting in the hospital.

"Belle, dear," Judy says. "Don't you think you're being just a little nosy? I think Sally has had her fill of questions for the moment."

"Me? Nosy? I don't know how you can say such things to your mother. How can I make friends with your brand-new daughter without asking her a few questions? You don't mind my questions, do you, Sally?"

I just love them.

"Sally, how would you like to run down to the corner drugstore and pick up a quart of French vanilla? I forgot to get it this afternoon."

"I'd love to," I say, grabbing my jacket. As soon as I'm out of the house I feel freedom and solitude embrace me like two old friends. Imagine what it would have been like to grow up under *her* wing. I decide to sit down after supper and write a nice long letter to Oma Lucy.

12

Foods
for Thought

COMPARISONS BETWEEN Bubba Belle and Oma Lucy were
as inevitable as boys and girls together. Bubba. Oma. Two women
who had entered life within the same decade were as dissimilar as a
bagel and a madeleine. I prefer madeleines myself, though as I get
older I begin to appreciate the solid virtues of a bagel, especially
when it is covered with cream cheese and red caviar.

Bubba was the embodiment of the sort of vulgarity my mother
despised. Everything about Bubba was loud: her voice, the color
of her clothes, the way her feet thwacked on the back stairs. If
she was an outboard, Oma was a sloop. Oma was soft and whis-
pery, pastels, challis, silk, velvet, whipped cream. Bubba was si-
rens and burlap. Oma was Fauré and cashmere. I could do this
sort of analogue-listing forever when it came to the two women;
it was fun but it didn't make me feel better. The more Oma came
out on top, the worse I felt about Bubba.

"Hubbahubba, goodrich rubba, we all hate our big fat Bubba!"
Joe and Danny chanted this when they thought Bubba was out of
hearing range. What if she heard them? I trembled at the idea.
And I was sure they didn't hate her. They didn't exactly adore
her, but they didn't hate her either. She brought them presents —
three pounds of milk chocolate in jagged chunks, toy trucks
made out of molded plastic, a couple of framed pictures of Pi-
nocchio and Jiminy Cricket. She even brought a plastic bathtub

duck for Roger which he promptly stepped on and then sailed out an open window. And a bottle of eau de cologne for me, the kind my mother would have dismissed as "whore perfume" because it was strong, sweet, heavy and smelled like the ladies' lounge at the Plaza.

Bubba was ecstatic about the imminent move, having read it more or less correctly as a step up in the world. She was profligate with advice. "Don't buy a house without a modernized kitchen," she said. "It should have a built-in stove and a washing machine and one of those things in the sink that chews up your garbage. And fluorescent lights, every kitchen should have fluorescent lights — it's much easier on the eyes. It looks like a highway at midnight. Beautiful."

"I don't like fluorescent light, Belle," Judy says.

"You don't like fluorescent light?" Bubba says.

"No, it reminds me of hospitals."

"Well, you don't have to have it if you don't want it."

"Thanks," Judy says.

Undeterred, Bubba continues advising on number of bedrooms, exposures, size of rooms, attic space, hallway dimensions, privacy quotient, back yard fencing, basements. There was nothing about which she was not the resident expert. Judy suggests that she ought to start a newspaper column on interior decoration.

"I just read the magazines, darling," Bubba says with a shrug. "Anybody can pick up a little here and there by reading the magazines. What else have I got to do?" Actually she is being unfair to herself. With her sister Esther she owns and runs a women's undergarment store in downtown Syracuse.

Bubba tells Judy she shouldn't even bother to look at what she calls a "glass shoebox," meaning a contemporary house. Judy is taking it all in, and from the look on her face throwing it all out immediately. Bubba is staying for three weeks. She's going to have a lovely time looking at other people's houses. Before we looked at the first house Bubba went down to Beacon Street where she had her hair washed, cut, and set at Janine's Beauty Garden. She came back lacquered to a fare-thee-well and pleased as a kid.

"You're going to get yourself a schwartze, aren't you, Judith, with all the work in a big house?"

"I haven't decided yet," Judy answers.

"I will never understand you, Judith," Bubba says. "What are you trying to prove? With all your new responsibilities" — eyes swivel meaningfully in my direction — "and all the extra cooking and washing, you still want to do everything yourself. What are you trying to prove, that you're some kind of superwoman? You're going to wear yourself out. You'll be an old lady before you're forty."

"Oh, Belle, please! I don't want to talk about it."

It began to dawn on me that people — even smart people with high I.Q.s and a large quantity of common sense — worried and agonized about things that don't, in the long run, matter. John Maynard Keynes said, "In the long run we are all dead," and I say amen to that. What did it matter about fluorescent lights and garbage disposals and Judy's reluctance to get some help in the house only because it would make her a member of a class she despised — the idle rich? It was obvious that Judy would never be idle until she was downed by old age or a terrible disease. And as for rich, she didn't have it in her. No matter how much money she had invested in AT&T or Eastman Kodak, no matter how large her bank balance, she *thought* poor. She didn't have the flair to throw away bread crusts and socks worn at the heels. She couldn't buy a ring for herself merely because she liked the look of the gem. She could never have owned thirty pairs of shoes, the way my mother did, nor spend $45 on a cotton dress to wear in the city in August when everyone was away. Judy thought in terms of saving, not spending, which I discovered was the big difference. Almost, in fact, as big as the difference between your

German Jew and your Russian Jew. My mother was a spender, and she had such fun — oh, she had an absolutely lovely time spending oodles of fresh, sticky bills tucked away in their Mark Cross wallet until she was ready to snap them out. And all her little charge-a-plates, one for Saks Fifth Avenue, one for Lord & Taylor, and a dozen more for the best shops around town. (Around town for Mummy meant between Forty-second and Seventy-second streets and between Fifth and Third avenues.)

You wouldn't believe it — the long drawn-out boring conversations of this smart woman, Judy London, and her family about whether or not to hire a cleaning lady to help her do the chores. It was as if you had asked her to be a kidney donor or a subject in an experimental cancer project.

She called cleaning ladies slaves. Sam refuted this. He said they didn't have to do that kind of work — they chose it. Judy said a system that allowed other people to wash out your toilet bowl and scrub the ring from your tub and wipe away your muddy prints from the front hall was a rotten system and she would have nothing to do with it. Sam told her she could clean her own toilet bowl if she felt so strongly about it. Bubba hovered in the background offering wisdom, which always came out on Sam's side even though I could see that these two existed in a fragile truce situation at best.

I was diverted momentarily by house-hunting.

Judy thought it would be good for me to come along when she looked at houses for sale. She would wait until I got home from school, and then we would set off, Judy, the agent (usually a woman), Bubba, and me, the rest of the family left behind with a baby-sitter, a teen-age girl from across the street, Charlene Lipshutz, who wore a gold-filled Star of David from a chain around her plump neck.

The women who escorted us through the "better homes" of Brookline were kitchen-table agents, a self-explanatory label for their general age, circumstances, and hunger for what one of them referred to as "my pin money." Each time we entered a house they would make a sort of nonverbal signal to Judy implying that this house was the most desirable home on the face of the earth. Judy stayed distant throughout. She was impressed by ugliness and ostentation, nothing more. She didn't want to move — she loved her house; this was a form of punishment. The only times I saw her smile were when she met ugliness or ostentation face to face. One house we saw had a room upstairs, next to the master bedroom, for the dog. Just the dog. He had a wicker doggie bed and a fluffy carpet and a box of dog biscuits on the windowsill. Judy liked that. Another house had wall-to-wall carpet, pale green and thick as a porterhouse steak, hiding every last inch of floor. It ran down the cellar steps like a swollen green tongue, ending as it licked the feet of the furnace. Another house had a dressing room whose walls and ceiling were covered by shimmering rectangles of mirror. Why the ceiling? There was no bed in it — so why the ceiling? The same house had all black fittings in the bathroom — black toilet, sink, tub, shag rug, toilet paper holder. Judy reacted favorably but the agent was visibly uneasy and ushered us in and out of the bathroom as if someone was sitting on the black toilet. Bubba later called the owners "perverts," which made Judy howl with laughter. I went into a trance thinking about being on a black toilet and why that was such an odd idea. What was the difference between a black toilet and a plain old white one? Maybe Bubba was right.

We walked through houses that had bars outfitted like a Fred Astaire movie — with leather-covered, swiveling stools and rows of bottles on glass shelves like a shooting gallery. We saw pantries stocked like the gourmet shop at B. Altman's. It was staggering, the number of odd and expensive possessions people owned. But none of it reminded me of my mother or of New York. These things seemed to say, "Look at us." Mummy's things said,

"Know we are here but don't look at us." It was a subtle difference, but it made a strong impression on me.

Every last damn house had a den. Den was a word that made
people like Mummy and Oma Lucy squirm with displeasure, like
the word "drapes" or saying "don't mind if I do" when offered a
plate of goodies. "A den, Sally dear, is a lower-class word for a
library that has no books in it. *Never* say den."

She was right about no books. The only books we saw in our
extensive three-week house tour (something like twenty-five
houses in all) were a set of the Waverly novels, some *Reader's
Digest* condensed books, a couple of complete Dickens and
Shakespeare, and scattered mystery novels — and I mean scattered, like on the floor or in a wastebasket or chewed up by the
dog and lying there dead. I spotted a copy of Van de Velde's
marriage book on a bedside table and so did Judy. She made a big
thing about the absence of books: her scorn didn't need words.
She said, "A den is for when you want to sit down somewhere
comfortable and don't want to use up the living room furniture.
It's more *gemütlich* in the den. All those virile things like
meerschaum pipes and hunting prints and firearms — it makes the
men in the family feel good."

"What about the women?"

"It makes them feel all cuddly and dependent."

"Not me it wouldn't," I said.

"Not me either," Judy said.

The women who escorted us through these houses were un-
abashedly hard sell. They could have invented a glowing descrip-
tion for a septic tank, calling it something like a daisy waste-
master. One agent assured us that a cramped and windowless
dining room was "cozy." A bathroom with antebellum (Civil,
not Second World War) fixtures was described as having "charming, antique fittings." A hall black as a Stygian cave was
"intimate." While Judy took everything with several heaping
teaspoons of salt, Bubba took hers unseasoned. She was like

a kid from the Lower East Side set loose in F. A. O. Schwarz with a fifty-dollar bill. To her the most conspicuous object was the most breathtaking, and since there was very little of anything subtle to be seen, she was in heaven. If she had had her way we would have bought 'em all. This made it pretty sticky at home because Bubba couldn't keep her mouth shut. She told Sam how stupid Judy was not to adore such-and-such a house, which made Judy bridle and then Sam would ask her to explain.

"My God, Sam," she says. "It was pretentious!"

"What do you mean, pretentious, just because it had a conservatory? I don't see what's so pretentious about a conservatory. You should have seen the plants. Some of them were as big as an oak tree. It was gorgeous!"

"Not the conservatory, Belle, I mean the size of the hall upstairs and those huge pillars in the front hall. The scale of the place, all that egg-and-dart carving in the attic. I mean I just wouldn't be comfortable in a house like that."

"I see what you mean," Sam murmurs.

"How can you see," Belle erupts, "when you didn't even see it?"

"I'll just have to take Judy's word for it, I guess." Sam loathed getting between mother and daughter, a place where he was deliberately inserted by his mother-in-law. I didn't blame him.

"And not mine?" She lays down her fork and actually stops eating for a minute.

Sam did a little song and dance about trusting Judy in matters of taste. It didn't go over very well. Bubba fumed. The little kids, the three boys, were finding Bubba's visit more entertaining than they had counted on. They liked the fur to fly. Even Roger seemed to take a peripheral interest in what was going on.

"Judy's too fussy. If you ask me, Judith, you have too many funny ideas. Why can't you just walk into a nice house and see how nice it is?"

"Because, Mamma dear, what's nice to you may not be nice to me."

"That's nonsense."

I feel like screaming. She tells her mother what I could never bring myself to tell mine.

What I couldn't believe was that it was so important how big the freezer was or the precise age of the electrical wiring. They were doing the same thing as my mother only in a more urgent way — they were worrying themselves sick about Things. If there had been an earthquake, a tornado, or a flood all Things would have disappeared in a flash. And so what? What difference did it really make? The only person who didn't seem over-whelmed by things was Sam, and he went too far the other way. All he cared about was words and ideas and the intellectual food lodged between the covers of a book. He went around looking like a classic slob—I was sure he didn't even brush his teeth.

One night, Bubba announced she was emigrating to Israel. "I just got this letter," she said, waving the envelope. "Esther sent it on. It's from your cousin Mona, she wants me to come and pay her a long visit. I said to myself, Why not stay for good?"

"Belle, not really." Judy's eyes say I don't believe you.

"Why not? It's the answer to a thousand years of prayer, isn't it?"

"Yes, but it's just a desert, Belle. You couldn't survive."

"Of course I could survive. I don't have to have all the com-forts of home. Mona has an icebox. She said it's like heaven on earth. There's no reason for me to stay here now that you have your own family and I am reaching the twilight years."

"For God's sake, Belle," Sam says.

"Well, it's the truth," Bubba says. Judy looks as if there were nothing more to say. As for me, I found the implications of Bubba's proposal staggering.

Israel was the bitter end, the last resort. Israel was a country

populated by wretched refuse, the men and women other coun-
tries had booted out. It was the place people went when they
had no home: refugees, criminals, orphans, cripples, children
with black holes for eyes and coal black hair, hairy men and
gaunt women with scarves over their heads à la Ellis Island. Israel
had no language and an army composed of *zaftig* girls bursting
the buttons on their khaki shirts. Israel was a human dog pound.
My anti-Zionism had been picked up wholesale from Oma Lucy
(she once spotted a group of Hasidic Jews and said to me, "Don't
they look terrible — I wish they'd shave") and from my own
mother and her friends. God forbid that we should be associated
with refugees.

And Bubba Belle wanted to go there and live out her what?
Her twilight years. I couldn't believe it. I looked at her with
renewed interest but found nothing to suggest that she was either
demented or joking. No, she was telling it all straight, as if it was
the most natural desire in the world. My mother, meantime, was
spinning in her grave.

Judy objected. It dawned on me that her objections were not
mine. "Belle, listen," she says, her face intense. "Do you really
want to give up the girdles and all your nice friends and go over
there and live like a pioneer? You'll have to do your laundry on a
washboard!"

"It won't be the first time," Belle says. To my surprise she gets
up from the dinner table and starts clearing the dishes. She has
shed her calm and is clearly agitated. "And for what, may I ask
you, do you think I've been a lifelong member of Hadassah? A
dues-paying member who goes to all the meetings? Do you think
I was just playing games?"

"Mama, please, don't get so upset. I'm just surprised, that's all."
Sam wanders off, imitating himself for the millionth time.

Judy orders her boys and Roger to help their grandmother
and, rising herself, starts the inevitable washup.

"Well, you shouldn't be surprised," Belle says. "I've been thinking about it for a long time."

"They've got food rationing," Judy says. "You get two eggs a week and no meat to speak of. As for butter, forget it."

"You think I need these things?" Bubba says. I think she most certainly does, but I'm not about to say so. Judy clearly thinks she does too.

They found a house six blocks away as the crow flies but a thousand as the status rises. "You won't ever have to wait in line to use the can again," Sam told Judy, somewhat coarsely I thought.

"That's just great," Judy said. "I object to that street, that neighborhood. Fisher Hill ain't my style at all."

"It's gefilte fish-er hill, remember?" Sam told Judy, trying to make her laugh. She didn't.

"There's a lawyer and a doctor in alternating houses. And lots of people who don't do anything that isn't directly concerned with money," Judy said.

"Well, at least we're in good shape if someone comes down with pneumonia or breaks a leg."

"I don't like it. I wish we didn't have to leave here."

"Oh, Jude, not again!" She was getting to be a bore about moving — even *I* thought so. I liked the house they were going to buy although I was very careful not to tell anybody how nice I thought it was. It had fifteen rooms, some of them with odd shapes and bay windows. The back yard was huge and mani-cured, with a well-tended garden and a meandering flagstone walk. Money had been poured, soaked into the grounds and a real live gardener "comes with the house." My bedroom — the one I was given until such time as I left — was on a corner. It had three enormous windows and a walk-in closet almost as big as my mother's in New York. There was enough space in it for twin beds, a couple of chairs, and my personal, free-wheeling choreography of *Swan Lake*. The wallpaper looked as if something bloody and explosive had been thrown against it, but Judy assured me that they would strip it and put on anything I chose. I wanted the room white, dead white. I even had a working fireplace. Though my room was large, it was also cozy. I couldn't explain why. Maybe it had something to do with good proportions and the fact that the fireplace was centered in the longest wall.

Donald Snyder came up to approve the purchase before the final papers were passed. I could see this man lurking at the margins of my life until he dropped dead. The funny thing was, we hardly ever spoke. I rarely thought about him. Yet he watched out for me with a greater commitment than my own parents. Where I went to school, where I lived, what medical and dental care I was getting, whether I was properly protected against cold and ice, how my vacations were spent, what my money was doing, was it doing as well as it possibly could — all these caretaking duties were Mr. Donald Snyder's, a man with whom I didn't even like to hold a conversation. Snyder even got copies of my report cards. C in science. He knew about my C in science. And he wasn't even Jewish.

Judy was fascinated by Donald Snyder. "Did your mother like him, Sally?" she says. She's dumping clothes into a large carton and every once in a while discarding something hopelessly ragged or much too small to fit anybody in our house. Otherwise every last scrap was coming with us.

"Sure, he used to come to dinner a lot." Mummy adored his Yalie manners. You didn't have to show Donald Snyder which fork to use or hint when it was time to go home.

"He'll be here this afternoon. Do you think I ought to invite him to stay for dinner?"

"I don't know," I say.

"Well, I think I will. We're having lamb stew."

Donald Snyder brought an architect with him. Not one from New York but one he picked up in Boston on the way from the airport. The architect looked like Yale too. Together they went through the new house as if they were trying to see if it would do for Princess Elizabeth. They knocked on the walls and jumped up and down on the floors. They examined the wiring and the plumbing. They gaped at the furnace and the state of the basement floor. ("Looks like a little dry rot down there," the architect said. "But it's minor. Shouldn't be a problem if it's taken care of promptly.") The architect took out a little knife and cut through the top layer of wall in the living room and peered at the lathing. Judy looked as if she wanted to kill him but held her tongue and tried to smile at me. I realize it's all my fault that they're doing this to her. What they're doing, of course, is questioning Sam and Judy's ability to buy a good house — that's what it comes down to. The architect told Judy that a couple of the chimneys needed pointing.

"I know."

They glare at each other.

"He makes me feel like an ax murderer," Judy whispered to me. I am thrilled. The two men hold a conference and decide an engineer ought to be called in for consultation. "Now he tells me," Judy moans.

The engineer, summoned from a meeting in Boston, arrived breathless, carrying a kit of strange tools. Judy was dejected. "He's going to tell us the walls are made of cotton candy and the floors are just dried mud. Come on, Sally, let's leave them alone. I can't bear it."

The worst part, the really awful part, was the people who came to inspect the Londons' old house. I wouldn't have predicted I would mind. After all, it wasn't *my* house they were

poking through. I was just a transient. But I hated them. I hated
the nosy look on their faces, the way they opened up kitchen
cabinets and closet doors, not to see how they worked but to see
what was inside. They even opened the oven door (to see if it
was clean), the medicine chest (to see what kind of pills we
took), and the slop closet (to see if we owned an up-to-date
vacuum cleaner). I saw one woman open my bureau drawer
when she thought no one was looking and another slip a silver
spoon from the dining room sideboard into her purse in one swift
motion. I watched her, fascinated, not sure a moment later
whether I'd imagined the theft or actually witnessed it. I mentioned it to Judy. She hit the ceiling.

"You saw someone take a spoon? Why didn't you stop her?"

"I don't know."

"Sally, that was my grandmother's silver spoon, she brought it
over from the old country in her pocket. You should have
stopped her!"

"Oh, Judy, I'm terribly sorry . . ."

"Which one was it? Which woman?"

I described the thief. I felt terrible. I felt as if I'd stolen the
spoon myself. Judy called the real estate agent, the agent called
the woman, the woman denied it, the spoon was gone forever. It
was my fault. Judy said, overcarelessly, "Oh, hell, it was just a
thing, just an object. Don't fuss so over a little thing."

You should talk.

Oh, the people who trooped through the house, peering and
prying and lifting things, tapping, thumping, opening and shut-
ting, spreading street dirt all over the rugs, using the bathroom
and asking for drinks of water, dropping gum wrappers in the
wastebasket and snide remarks about how "chilly" it was on my
porch. All these people had Jewish names: Greenberg, Steinberg,
Levin, Goodman, Pinsky, Minsky, Epstein, Kaplan, Gross, Gold-

berg, and Skolnick. I had never heard such a splendid collection.

"They all have Jewish-sounding names," I say.

"That's because they're all Jewish. Except that one O'Connell family, I wonder how they slipped in."

"Do nothing but Jews live here?" Where I lived in New York it was different — cosmopolitan, my mother called it. And then Freddie would say, "You know about Pease and Elliman, don't you? Elliman waits on the gentiles and Pease on the Jews."

"We cluster," Judy said. "It's got something to do with real estate and something to do with retail stores. Read *Gentleman's Agreement* if you want to find out more about it," she says.

"Don't you mind?"

"Unh-unh," she says. "Why should I? I like living near my own kind. Oh my God, will you look at this — somebody threw tangerine peels in the corner. What pigs!" Judy squats and picks up the peels. I'm not sure whether she meant it or not, about liking to live with her own kind. It sounds like an inside-out joke.

"Isn't it against the law not to sell or rent to Jews?"

"Well, it really *is*, pet, but there are so many ways to get around it that the law has about as much strength as a newborn seaslug. You know, of course, that there are plenty of people who would rather sell to a naked Zulu with a spear and a ring through his nose than to a nice ordinary Jewish gentleman. That's why so many Jewish gentlemen change their names. Of course, you've got to look 'clean' to start with to get away with it. You don't look especially Jewish. Belle's right — you could pass for a shiksa any time."

"That's Daddy," I murmur. Judy is making me feel extremely uncomfortable, whether she means to or not. That's the sad part of it: every time I think I can trust her, Judy says something that pulls me back and slams the door.

"Don't feel bad about it," she says over her shoulder as she walks downstairs with a huge armload of revolting laundry stripped from beds and hauled out of the hamper. "It's nothing to feel apologetic about." Mrs. Tact.

Eventually, a family came along who wanted to buy the Londons' house, a dentist and his wife, with two very young children: the Axelrods. Dr. Axelrod took one look inside Sam's study and declared it suitable — with certain modifications — as an office. He told Judy he was a periodontist and that children seemed to prefer coming into a private home rather than an office. "Of course, we'll have to do some major plumbing work in here." I could just see the miniature dentist chair and the spit bowl and the gleaming instrument cabinet. The traces of Sam and Sam's heady labors would be swallowed by running water, buzzing drills, and the cries of frightened little kids. Serve him right. Sam, when he heard, announced that he couldn't care less, which was probably true: he was through with the place — what did he care how much blood was spilled in it? Typical. When I left, would he remember me for more than a day? I doubted it very much. Judy, on the other hand, might remember me for as long as a month.

I mentioned that Judy had an awful time throwing anything away. She asked me to help her sort and pack, but as it turned out she couldn't turn over any part of the job to me — she had to do everything herself. She picked up a looseleaf notebook with yellowing pages. "My botany notebook from college," she said, eyeing it like an old rival. "How can I throw this away?" She opens it and looks. "My God, did I really do this drawing? This is pretty good! But he only gave me a C-plus. I wonder what's wrong with it." She falls into a reverie. "There's nothing wrong with it," she says at last. "It's perfectly brilliant. He must have had a fight with his wife that day." She tosses the notebook into a carton. It will sit in the new house equally neglected, only the next time she looks the pages will turn to dust in her fingers. In the same way she couldn't get rid of a moth-eaten baby blanket ("Joey's first"), a hideous glass bottle she said was a wedding present from a dear friend, now dead, a pile of children's finger paintings. The only object I saw her get rid of was a suitcase that literally disintegrated as she picked it up and an old cheese box that smelled like shit. Her past, distant and near, lay on the crusty basement floor in cartons and trunks and cardboard boxes and all she could do was croon over it, caress it as if it were a sick baby she was afraid might die.

13

Water, Water
Everywhere

THANK GOD I MISSED the actual move. I went to my father's wedding instead.

The only other wedding I had ever been to was Freddie's cousin Dorothy's when she married her second husband Morton Freund a year or so after the war. The ceremony took place in Temple Joshu-a, the reception at The Club. Women like my cousin Dorothy wouldn't have dreamed of holding their wedding reception anyplace but The Club. Everybody felt, everybody always said, it was the ideal place for that kind of party: familiar but with plenty of *Lebensraum*. Besides, they did every thing so well at The Club. The service was impeccable, the food delicious, the privacy scrupulous. Why on earth would anyone want to hold a reception anywhere else? Other people might troop over to the Pierre or the Sherry Netherland. We went to The Club.

I remember the food at Dorothy and Morton's bash. That was what I generally remembered about a party. If the food was bad or scant I didn't have a good time. If there was plenty and it was good, I loved it. This time there were platters of smoked turkey and sturgeon, sliced and put back in the original fish shape. There were foothills of chopped liver, smoked salmon, and ham salad. There were hot hors d'oeuvres with cheese oozing over the edges and little hot dogs roasted inside pastry. All this was followed by a sit-down dinner served by waiters. I recall eyeing a slice of roast beef on my plate and realizing with a pang that I couldn't possibly finish it. I pocketed the macaroon that came with the sherbet. Mummy allowed me a couple of sips of champagne. There was no one else there my age except a weird-looking boy with black-rimmed glasses who looked at me like a detective and drove me uneasily back to my mother's side. Mummy said his parents had been lost in one of the camps. He was so thin I was sure he didn't like to eat. Anyone who didn't like to eat was on my weird list.

The wedding guests at Dorothy's behaved as if they had fasted for a week. Not Mummy, of course. She was different. She was obsessed with size nine. Size nine represented static youth; if she could stay a size nine she would never grow old. She might die, but she would never age. Women yearn for a skin without wrinkles, others need a grayless head. With my mother it was a body with no bulges, no flab. Sometimes I would catch her staring in the mirror. You might think she was pleased with what she saw, but she wasn't; she was as critical as if she were a size fifteen. She would frown and sigh and look away, tears brimming. Freddie teased her about it, but not as much as she deserved. She deserved to have her head examined. Poor mother . . . Her figure, perpetually nineteen years old and like something carved, was smashed and chopped up, burned, pulverized. What good did all that denial do? She should have eaten, she ought to have satisfied her hunger just once and died fat and happy instead of bony, always hungry. Always, Mummy eyed food as if it were the enemy.

At Dorothy and Morton's wedding everybody but Mummy ate like there was no tomorrow. They ate like people never before exposed to plenty. In went the liver, the chopped egg, the sturgeon, the shrimp speared on toothpicks and dunked in cocktail sauce. In went the roast beef, the string beans *amandine*, the tossed green salad. The sherbet. The macaroons. "Jews eat, gentiles drink," Sam told me once, rousing himself from his usual laconic self and getting a beer from the icebox.

"Why?" I said.

"Who knows?" he shrugged. "Why are there so many Chinese restaurants in Jewish neighborhoods?"

"Because it's cheap?"

"Maybe that's it," Sam said, stopping to think. Then he said, "See ya later," and slipped away again into his study. I hated that study more than I have ever hated any other place, including Dr. Fineberg's waiting room. I hated it because it said No and I was desperate for Yes.

Daddy's wedding was so different from cousin Dorothy's that an anthropologist from Mars would have been bewildered and would have concluded (with some justification) that two distinct cultures existed simultaneously within ten city blocks of one another.

The ceremony took place in the chapel of an Episcopal church on Madison Avenue. Lorna looked nice enough, if you went for her type. I noticed she had on Capezio shoes, flat like ballet slippers, and a satin dress, the same shade of eggshell white, passed down to her from some lace-loving ancestor. The dress looked to me as if mice had been gnawing at it for about a hundred and fifty years. Daddy was radiant. Lorna wore a frozen, permanent, toothpaste smile. The minister called on heaven and earth to witness and bless this divinely inspired union. Nobody mentioned Daddy's previous divinely inspired union. Only the first four or five pews on both sides of the aisle were filled, which surprised me — I had expected a mob. Somewhere from in back of me I heard a loudly whispered dialogue:

"Who is that plump child, my dear — the one sitting up front on our side of the aisle?"

"Fabia, I'm surprised at you. That's Willy's daughter — what's her name? — yes, Sarah. The child he had by that beautiful Jewess, Marguerite Baum. You remember, Sissy Colt was in her class at Seeley. I believe she married a publisher after the divorce."

"How dim of me. I recall now, the mother was lost in that frightful crash on the West Coast. Wasn't the child adopted by her stepfather? I find that somewhat odd, don't you, Bonnie dear, with Willy flourishing right here in Princeton?"

"Well, there's no use trying to guess why people do things nowadays. I gave that up some time ago. I believe her stepfather — I think his last name was Stein — was enormously rich. I suppose Willy wanted her to have more than he could give her."

"Willy's no slouch either, Bonnie. Not what you'd call on his uppers exactly," the one called Fabia said.

Bonnie laughed. "Ha," she said. "Now I ask you. Willy's first wife had a great deal of style, and look at that poor child. Why, she's as plump as a squab chicken. And not nearly so pretty as her poor mother. Isn't it a pity when a mother outshines a daughter? On the other hand, I suppose you could say it's a pity when a daughter outshines her mother. Oh my, what on earth am I talking about?"

"Heaven only knows. We shouldn't be talking anyway. Look, the bride's coming now. Who is that distinguished-looking man? Must be her father. My, isn't he splendid!"

"Hush!"

The words I heard burned inside me like hot soup. I wanted desperately to turn around and confront these two women, these awful people who did not have the sense to realize I could hear them. The thing I minded most about their conversation was not the part about Mummy being a *Jewess*, though "Jewess" was a word I loathed and was about as flattering as "Negress" (laundress) or "little lady" (wife). What I minded most was the part about how ugly I was compared with my mother. And if, by some miracle, I grew up to look half decent — I had no hopes of being the "beauty" my mother was — what satisfaction could I take in it? My mother had died convinced I was a blob, destined to be a blob for the rest of my life. Judy would have told me hotly that women spend far too much time and energy worrying about how they look, but I wasn't ready to listen to her. My mother's example was an influence too profound to be forgotten. And besides, I was so ugly I really needed help.

I was so hurt by the squab chicken analogy that I didn't even care what they said about Daddy's letting me be adopted by my stepfather; that particular remark went in one ear and out the other.

It was Lorna's first marriage (eventually she reached a grand total of three) and she played her role quite well, repeating her vows in a childish purr, looking at Daddy like a devoted pet, her musculature altogether camouflaged beneath the bridal satin and yards of antique lace. No bride looks normal. My father had on a dark blue suit and a silvery tie. He looked handsomer, more polished than I had ever seen him. Distinguished, a cross between polo player, successful politician, and Edward R. Stettinius. Nothing like what went on inside his head (as far as I knew, and I knew pretty far). I realized, for perhaps the first time, that my father, like Freddie, cared a great deal about how he looked, how his face came across to the world. In that respect they were just like women and maybe worse, because they weren't supposed to be vain, whereas it was okay for a woman to be vain. Not only okay but desirable.

When they walked back up the aisle — my father giving me a big wink as he passed — Lorna seemed to wrap her entire body around my father's arm. It made him look a little as if he were supporting her entire weight when in point of fact it was quite likely that the obverse was true. It had begun to sink in — although I made a million excuses for it — that my father was more or less perpetually stewed. Not falling-down drunk, not abusive, loud, maudlin, teary, or violent. Just constantly on the low boil, fuzzy around the edges, a little too soft and forgetful, slurry, confused. You would never have to scrape Daddy off the sidewalk or lift him back onto the couch or clean his vomit off the floor outside the bathroom.

The ceremony lasted about half an hour. Then we all got up and filed out to the street, where I got into a limousine with Lorna and my father and drove four blocks to the Fourbears Club for their reception. The emblem of the club was four dancing bears holding paws and dancing in a circle. But that wasn't what it was all about — it was about who your forebears were. And if they arrived any later than 1830, forget about applying for membership. So, the Fourbears was to WASPS what The Orange Club was to German and Spanish Jews. In that respect they were twins, though the Fourbears was founded almost a century before the Orange. Lorna's club was light and airy like an aviary — I expected to see birds flying around and fountains splashing. It was clean — it was so clean it didn't even need to be deodorized because no one who entered smelled like anything but the most delicate perfume or the most astringent aftershave lotion. The perspiration that dripped off the women in the massage room was immediately taken care of by fresh towels and running water. Bad breath was rinsed away before the mouth entered through the unprepossessing front doors.

The larger rooms in the Fourbears Club were furnished like a rich man's living room and the smaller, cosier rooms were furnished like libraries with real books in them. Judging from the state of their dust jackets you could see that very few people ever read the books in the smaller rooms. The ladies' lounge smelled like Mary Chess. Stationed in the lounge was a black woman who probably slept there as well. She wore a pink uniform with a crisp white apron, and after I peed and washed my hands like a good little girl (besides, I wanted to sample the soap), she handed

me a clean linen towel which she shook out of its folds just for
me. I wasn't supposed to tip her — there was a sign on the wall
admonishing about gratuities.

A spiral spine rose through the center of the four-story building, from the marble foyer to the glass roof. Voices were muted
by thick rich carpets the color of heavily creamed coffee. Every
one sounded happy and tinkly inside the Fourbears Club.

There's something about a club that brings out the best in men
and women like Daddy, Lorna, and Freddie. Here they are momentarily relieved of the disagreeable reminders of an anomalous
world. The Fourbears was like the Yankee Clipper hurtling past
tenements in Harlem and safely sealed off from sorrow, dirt, and
poverty. And there are shades in your drawing room to pull
down so you can concentrate on your Scotch and soda. The
Fourbears' shades were always drawn clear down to the bottom
of the window. This gave the members (and their guests) a nice
closed-in feeling and brought up the laughter quotient.

My father pounced on me as I came out of the ladies' and told
me I could stand with him in the receiving line. "You don't have
to if you'd rather not," he said, "I'll understand." I was uncon-
vinced.

"Do you want me to, Daddy?"

"Well, I think it would be very nice," he said, beaming at me.
"It was Lorna who reminded me. After all, wouldn't it look a
little odd if you weren't next to me?"

"Don't you think dark blue brings out the best in your father?"
Lorna says to me as she takes my other arm. I feel like a prisoner
being dragged off for questioning and possible torture. Trapped.
"You'd never know Willy was forty-two, would you, darling?
He's in such gorgeous shape. Why, he's got the figure of a boy.
Oh, I'm such a lucky girl, you two — this is the happiest day of
my life. I'm having so much fun. This is going to be the happiest
party! You dears!"

"Where's the bar?" my father says.

"Silly Willy, you can't have a drinkie now, you have to wait till the receiving line is over."

"Who says?" my father says.

Guess who wins? I'll bet Daddy was the only groom in history who greeted his wedding guests with a drink in his left hand. But it was so much in character for Daddy to have a drink in his hand that I'm positive no one but me and Lorna noticed. I noticed, I burned, I wanted to knock it out of his hand. I vowed to myself that I would never drink so long as I lived. I would teetotal totally.

The "small" wedding party turned out to be over a hundred people dressed to the teeth by the same dressmaker and clothier, each one a slight variation on the same theme. I stood next to Daddy, gritted my teeth, grinned fakely, and had my hand grabbed, pumped, squeezed, rattled, crushed, brushed, touched, mashed, petted, and yanked by at least one hundred men and women. Few of them had ever laid eyes on me before; several of them didn't know who the hell I was and were clearly embarrassed when Daddy introduced me as his little princess. One or two who did recognize me gave me the standard line about how I'd grown. They might just as well have told me how much I'd shrunk or informed me I was turning green for all it meant to me. Someone introduced to me as "You remember Charlie Hughes, don't you?" began talking to me about a house in Maine I didn't even remember, a place he said he had stayed in with me and my "mom" and how cold the water was and where did I go to school, the Seeley, wasn't it, and would I like a glass of champagne. I stared at him, blank, outraged by his prodding.

"Call me in five years," he said, slithering off to locate the bar. I felt like throwing up. The next in line was a woman who looked at Daddy with an expression of grief and regret. A girlfriend? I glanced at Lorna who, I could tell, was pretending not to notice.

You could ignore her about as easily as you could have ignored a pig roller-skating on its hind legs. She was all dolled up in a smashing Dior. How could Daddy make me do it? I looked at him, and he was smiling, swaying slightly, effusive, outgoing, slap-on-the-back Willy Sanderson, everyone's favorite drinking buddy. For a moment, the image of Sam London crossed my imagination and then retreated back where it belonged; it spent enough time, however, for me to make an instant — and disturbing — comparison.

The receiving line finally broke up into its human links. These drifted off in various directions, a good many of them to one of the three bars strategically located so no one would have to wait more than a minute or so for a refill.

Momentarily left alone, I began to look around for the food. I guess I expected to see tables sagging under the kind of platters we had at cousin Dorothy's wedding. I looked on one side of the room, saw nothing, crossed back — nothing again. I felt a pang of deprivation, my stomach growled and bunched itself into a fist, then relaxed noisily. Several people tried to get a conversation going with me, one of those thrillers that begin with "What grade are you in at school?" and end with "I knew you when you were a gleam in your father's eye." I was too preoccupied with my hunger to be polite, and they all looked for an excuse to get away from me before very long. Daddy had disappeared, and Lorna was terribly busy laughing hysterically with two enormously tall people who looked like gray-haired brother and sister but were probably man and wife. I don't know why it was so important to eat, but it was. It was as if filling my mouth and my stomach represented safety if not survival. And here it was only one-thirty in the afternoon and I had had waffles and sausages with Oma Lucy not four hours earlier. Well, I was addicted to food although I didn't know it then; I thought I was merely your ordinary "growing girl" with a large appetite.

Two black waiters in white jackets bore down on me balancing huge silver trays on their palms and murmuring for people to get out of the way. I felt they were sent to me by someone who cared. I stared at a tray. On it was spread a mosaic of tiny rounds of toast covered with pink cream cheese, a dab of egg salad, a whole sardine hanging over the edge of a piece of crustless white bread, a few strips of celery, some black olives, and a lot of unidentifiable smeary stuff. I was so disappointed I nearly cried. "Take two, Miss," the black waiter said to me. "They're pretty small." I nearly kissed him, he was so nice. I took one with a dime-size pad of black caviar and an egg salad thing, popped them into my mouth and swallowed. They were horribly salty and made me choke. I had to find something to drink. And there was Daddy, looking for me. "Where have you been, princess?" he said. "I've been looking all over for you."

"Right here," I say. "Could I have something to drink, please?"

"Of course, you can. You don't have to ask me that way. What would you like — a little champagne? This is a very special occasion, you can have a full glass of champagne."

"Thanks, Daddy, but I'd rather have a glass of ginger ale. I'm very thirsty."

"What nonsense," he says. "Here" — he swoops around and plucks one off a tray being passed by a waiter — "have a nice glass of bubbly. It's Dom Perignon '41. The Nazis got most of it. I bought up the rest. Now, isn't that wine something?"

"Yes, Daddy," I say, swallowing the stuff, gagging on it. "It's very nice."

"Are you having a good time, princess?"

"Yes, Daddy."

"Well, how about putting a smile on your face? You look as if you'd just lost your best friend."

Daddy told me he wanted me to meet "Lorna's dad." "He's the class of ought-eight."

Ought-eight sounded like Daddy was born in the eighteenth

century. Nobody talked that way. What was he trying to prove? I expected a Clifton Webb type and was surprised to see a small trim man with glasses and a neat paunch. His hair had drained away from his skull, leaving a thin grayish ring. He didn't look like my idea of a Yale man, but the moment he opened his mouth, his rocks-in-the-mouth accent confirmed it patently. That and his costume. He wore a pin-striped suit and a pearl-gray tie. His suit was cut so as not to pull or bulge over his abdomen. It occurred to me then that men after fifty often begin to look a little like pregnant women.

Ought-eight stares at me benevolently and pronounces me a "robust creature." "I understand you're a Seeley girl, eh? My late wife's cousin, Kate Reddy, was a Seeley girl. How did that song go — Seeley born and Seeley bred . . . ?"

"And when you die you're Seeley dead," I contribute, feeling stupid. "Only I don't go there anymore. I live in Brookline."

"Is that so?" Mr. Emerson says, unbelieving. He looks at me as if I had just told him I intended to devote my life to streetwalking.

"And I suppose you attend Winsor?"

"No, sir," I say. "I go to the public high school."

"Well, young lady," he says, taking off his glasses, whipping out a snowy handkerchief, and polishing the lenses furiously. "I must say you have a streak of originality in you, doesn't she, William? I say, your daughter is a real original." But Daddy has long since wandered away. The two of us stare at each other, curious and somewhat wounded. He pats my head and says, "Lorna will make you an excellent mother, child. She has a good heart, that girl. And she can teach you all you ever need to know about the game of tennis. And that's no mean trick, let me assure you."

I agree with him. He doesn't know that I'm as good at tennis as a sea lion. I just can't seem to make the ball go over the net. It's something Daddy never talks about. He takes it hard.

Lorna's mother was dead. I wondered what she died of. Ever since Roosevelt I had been extremely interested in the precise details of a person's death. If it was cancer that carried them off, that was enough to know. If it was something that could not possibly happen to me I wanted all the dope. Things like tuberculosis, frostbite, gunshot wounds, tropical parasites, malaria, syphilis — these I found riveting and wanted to hear or read about as much as I could.

When I asked Daddy how Mrs. Emerson died he said, "She killed herself, princess. Years ago. She was very sick." That gratified me. It had the right remote feel of dread to it.

I began to get bored on top of my hunger. I wanted to get away from these blue-haired old ladies and muscular young women, the men with professionally polished shoes and burnished hair. I had a date to see Nancy, sandwiched between the reception and an obligatory dinner with Oma Lucy. (After all, I couldn't just use her house like a hotel. I did really owe her the courtesy of showing up for a proper meal.) And Oma was too self-centered to ask Nancy to join us. So we had about an hour or two in which to become close friends all over again. I felt terribly cheated. And somehow, more of a waif than I had ever felt before. I could go here or there and be waited on, treated kindly, instructed to feel at home. But I had no home, not the house on Seventy-third Street, not Oma Lucy's, not the Londons', and not my father's in Princeton, N.J. I smiled at what even I could perceive as the irony. Water, water everywhere.

I found Daddy and told him I had to go. He made a big fuss of kissing me and giving me several rather painful squeezes. Then he apologized for not being able to see me off on the train the next day. "We've got plane tickets for Barbados on the five o'clock flight, princess. Otherwise we'd put you on that little old train ourselves."

"It's all right, Daddy. Have a good time on your honeymoon."

I didn't want to have to say the same thing to Lorna, because I didn't think I could make it sound sincere. In any case, I was spared the lie because no one could find the bride. I slipped away.

I was happy to be walking around New York again. If I didn't have a house to live in that I could call my own, at least I had a city. To a city child like me, the sidewalks are like a stretch of beach to a fisherman's daughter. I liked the stone under my shoes, the sound of my feet keeping up with one another. The noise of the cars and buses is the noise of the waves breaking over and over against the sand. I was agitated, high. My fingers and toes tingled. No one in the world except I knew exactly where I was at that moment; this gave me a feeling of immense power and freedom. But the feeling lasted only seconds. I was not quite ready to be set loose in the world.

I started running to the street corner where Nancy and I had agreed to meet. I saw her coming down the block in a new green coat with brass buttons. Her hair was longer and she seemed more grownup, brighter, prettier. I flew at her and we wrapped our arms around each other.

"Hey," she says. "You look terrific. You shed those five pounds?"

"Three," I say, fudging a little. "But I'm starving. I'm absolutely starving. I need a hamburger or I'll die. The food at the party was positively garbage. You should have seen it — wasn't fit for a slave!"

We rushed off to Hamburg Heaven where we each ordered double cheeseburgers, french fries, and Cokes. I forget everything in Nancy's presence. I loved her almost as much as if she had been a boy.

14

Nice Eyes

AFTER THE WEDDING I was depressed. It wasn't the same as when Mummy died. Then I suffered acute grief. Grief has an electric edge to it; there's always a slight tingle of terror and anticipation. But this was just low, lowdown, down in the dumps, hopeless despair; depression. It made me feel physically sick, heavy, the way you feel after you're had a high fever and the germ is taking leave at last. I attributed my depression to having seen Nancy and being immediately separated. It was probably that and a lot of other things as well, causes I knew nothing of directly and undoubtedly would have denied.

I liked my new room. It was Me. It suited me. I could go up there and lie on the bed, staring at the ceiling for hours and no one would bother me. Or, if I fetched the wood myself from the basement and carried it up in splintery armloads, I would build a fire, turn out all the lights, and watch the reflection of the flames move across the ceiling like giant moths. I pretended I was Jane Eyre, a girl I identified with fiercely — up to a point: the point being that I was Jane with no Mr. Rochester.

I pulled myself around school, just squeaking by in my courses. And I dragged myself around the house. Judy started in on me about going to see Dr. Fineberg if I didn't "perk up." I told her I'd take vitamins instead and she went and bought me a jar of capsules as big as my mother's engagement ring. For the sake of not being carried off to Dr. F. I made a great effort not to look as if I was about to pass out. I invented chatty little subjects to keep Judy off the subject of my health.

"Do you miss Sam when he goes away like this?" I say.

"Maybe a little," she tells me. "You don't really miss someone very much when you've been married as long as we have. Maybe you both even could use a little vacation from each other."

Good God! Does she realize what she's saying?

"What's he doing in New York?" I say.

Judy is lying singly in their double bed, her reading glasses on. There is a little gap between the frame and the bridge of her nose that makes me feel very uncomfortable, like when your bra strap slips down and you can't get at it to shove it back up. Judy's finger is the bookmark in a book lying on top of the blanket. I'm sure I'm bothering her but something keeps me there. It's late and the boys are in bed, but for a change I'm not tired. I'm not exactly frightened of the dark but if there's no good reason for me to go into the pitch-black living room I don't see why I should. Same with the dining room. Judy always keeps a light burning in the kitchen.

"Griffin business," she says. "Also he has an appointment with the ghoul."

"Mr. Snyder?"

"That's the one."

I feel guilty because it's my fault that Sam has to leave his work here and go see the ghoul.

"I always slip some Tums in with his toilet things when he has to see Snyder," Judy sighs. "I'm glad I don't have to see him. I'm not as polite as my husband. Imagine his going over every last household account as if I were some petty thief."

"I'm sorry," I say. "What are you reading?"

"It's a novel. By Jane Austen. It's called *Emma* and it's about an overconfident young lady who gets a gentle comeuppance.

This is my third go-around. I had a roommate in college who hated the book so much she called it 'Enema.' "

Enema. Yuk. I blush.

"Hey Sally," Judy says, apparently reading my second-to-last thought. "If you're worried because you think Sam has to go to New York on your account, forget it. He loves to go there — any excuse and he's off. Last time he went — that is, before you know — he had drinks with Dylan Thomas."

"Who's he?"

"A poet, child. What can I do for you? You still look worried." I wish she wouldn't call me child. It's so damn patronizing.

"Oh, nothing," I say. "I just wasn't very sleepy."

"It's spring. Everything's restless. All the little roots under the ground, all the tiny buds quivering, getting ready to burst into blossom." At this I turn to leave.

"You worry an awful lot about money, don't you, Sally?" she says in another voice. I want to trust her so badly it's sickening. The only grownup I ever trusted was Oma Lucy and I'm not sure I trusted *her* all the way, I mean the way she talked about Catholics. I adored Daddy but I didn't really trust him either — he disappeared too often. I feel that if I can tell Judy what I'm thinking, I will be able to trust her. "It doesn't seem fair," I say, making a stab at it. "That me and Roger have so much money and there are so many poor people."

She looks at me as if I were addled. "Fair? Have you really been taught that things have to be fair? Of *course* it's not fair — it's especially *un*fair. That's why almost half the world is Communist. *They* try to make things a little bit fairer. But listen, honey doll, there isn't a single country in the world where some people haven't more possessions than others. Not even Russia. Though it's not as bad there as it is here. It stinks here, if you really want to know. Don't look so shocked, Sally. Not all of it stinks — just the inequities."

She must absolutely despise me for being rich. "I wish I could give it away," I say.

"You can't fool around with your money now, not till you're twenty-one. But you probably can then, unless Freddie arranged to have it doled out to you every few years until you were forty-five or fifty. Maybe he did. We'll find out — we'll ask the ghoul."

"Twenty-one is a long way away," I tell her. "I have so much money I don't know what to do with it. I don't need it. I don't need anything."

"You poor little thing," she says, mocking me. "You, my dear, are what is vulgarly known as an heiress."

"I am not!"

"Hey, wait a minute. I didn't call you a cannibal. I said you were an heiress."

"Like Doris Duke? She's awful. And Gloria Vanderbilt? I don't want to be like *them*."

"Don't worry, pet, you're not *that* rich."

To be called an heiress was to be awarded the kiss of death. I can't figure out what Judy is up to. "Why can't you sleep?" she says, out of the blue. "Is there something else on your mind?"

Shall I tell her about Dereck Jolley, at school? Shall I tell her about two girls whom I like but am afraid to approach? Should I tell her that my plans are still vague, but that I will probably leave here and go off and live with my father and his bride? These are the things I obsess about, these and the money, my Jewishness, my fear of the dark, my nail-biting, and how fat and ugly I am.

"Not really," I say.

"Hand me those Old Golds over there, will you, Sally dear?" She points to the top of her bureau with a stubby finger. I hand her a collapsed package. She strikes a match like a man, lights up, and takes enough smoke into her lungs to choke a horse. She lets the smoke drift up through her tubes and out her nose. "Filthy habit," she says, looking at me watching her. I've tried it. Cigarettes make me dizzy, they make me feel as if I were going to pass out, they taste like dirt.

"Tell me, pet, have you ever been kissed?"

It's none of your business. My face pinkens again and my heart thuds. I shake my head. "Only on the cheek."

"Doesn't count," Judy tells me. "I'm surprised. I'm *really* surprised," she says, taking another massive drag. "I thought everybody from New York learned how to kiss along with the twelve-tables in arithmetic. Come to think of it, I was kissed when I was younger than you and I grew up in the Stone Age."

"A boy in dancing school tried," I say. "But I wouldn't let him."

"Why not?"

"I don't know. His pimples, I guess."

Judy laughs. "You could have closed your eyes."

"I tried. But I could still see them." Just talking about it brings them back to me, oozing and crusty. Vile things. Should I tell her that I burn with sexual desire, that I read dirty books and build orgiastic scenes in which a handsome man ravishes me again and again, where I am smothered with kisses which penetrate my lips. and made love to by a penis that reaches to my very soul? I would rather die than confess.

"Did your mother ever tell you about what are archly called 'the facts of life'?" Judy says.

Oh my God, she wants to tell me about the birds and the bees. I nearly laugh out loud. "I learned in school," I say. "In the sixth grade."

"I'll bet a nurse taught you and they called it 'hygiene.' Hygiene is washing your face and brushing your teeth, being clean. It has nothing to do with sex or babies or anything remotely like that."

"How did you know?" I say. In fact, it was the cleanest sex

course offered in the history of mankind. We sat for hours watching chickens hatch from eggs that had been sitting in a see-through globular incubator for six weeks.

"Because schools don't want to tell you anything disturbing or provocative. I'll bet you watched eggs hatch."

I nod. I hate her for always being one step ahead of me, for knowing the music so well she can sing it without the score. Well, actually my feelings swing so violently from one side to the other about Judy that I am constantly off balance — love to hate, trust to mistrust, accommodation to blank. Having very little control over my feelings, I am surprised ten times a day by what they feed me. I blame Judy for stirring me up. She has no right to try to enter my life.

"If I tell you something," I say, knowing that I am going through one of my soft phases, "will you promise not to laugh?"

Judy nods solemnly.

"I think," I say, taking the plunge, "that Mummy thought I was oversexed. It made me feel funny, like I'd done something I shouldn't."

She laughs. Judy laughs. I despise her — she promised she wouldn't, and now she's laughing. I am so angry I can feel my legs thrill with adrenaline and my fingers tingling.

"You promised not to laugh!"

"Oh, honey, I'm sorry — really I am. It was a mistake; I didn't mean to. It's only that you ought to know how silly that is. What makes you think she thought that?"

"I don't know. She was always asking me these questions about what I was doing. I don't know. I'm sorry I brought it up. I'm probably wrong anyway." I am fed up with the woman lying in bed with her horn-rimmed glasses — the lenses are smudged, disgusting — and her precious nineteenth-century novel. Why can't she read what the rest of them read — Norman Mailer and Betty Smith? Why does she have to show off with her Jane

Austen and her Wilson and her T. S. Eliot? If she tries to make my mother look ridiculous I am going to hit her. I'm stronger and I'm really going to haul off and hit her.

"You poor thing," she says, insulting me with her pity.

"Mummy wasn't silly," I tell her and stare at her in what I hope is a terrible way. "She was very happy; she never got grouchy." A lie, but now I don't care. "She could decide she wanted to do something and then just go ahead and do it. She had marvelous taste, she gave terrific parties. Everybody said how beautiful she was . . ."

"Sally."

"What?"

"I know your mother was a wonderful woman — you don't have to be defensive about her. I liked her, we all did. If you thought just now I was trying to say anything else, you're one hundred percent wrong. I only meant it was silly for you to think you were oversexed. That's all. Please try to understand." Her voice has wrinkles in it. We are both filling up on emotion, and it makes me extremely uneasy, nervous, hot, agitated.

"I don't believe you," I say in a tone that's surprisingly neutral.

"What don't you believe?" Judy comes right back.

"That you liked my mother. Anyway, you didn't really know her. You hardly ever saw her."

"Sally . . ." she says. She must think I've accused her unfairly, but she acts guilty as hell.

"You hated her," I say evenly.

"I did *not*," she says.

"You hated my mother and you hate me!" I cry. "And she didn't do anything to you and neither did I. I haven't done a thing you could blame me for. I've been *good* here. I've done all that stupid cleaning and housework and I never hit Roger even when he does awful things and calls me a shit. And I didn't ask to come here. I didn't have anything to do with it — they just decided behind my back and dumped me here. And I don't want to be here. I want to live with my father. He won't make me go to a public school . . ." I can't go on because my tears have caught up with me. They're pouring down my cheeks and slipping into my mouth. My chin is wet and sticky with them. I wipe my arm across my face. More tears follow. I feel as if I'm tied to a tree with my hands behind my back and Judy is peeling my skin off, strip by strip. For a moment we hang in the timeless space of mutual suspicion.

"My God," she says. "What am I doing?"

I stare at her, unable to accuse. There's just this enormous sense of injustice, a conspiracy against me, in which she has a major role. I can't tell her what she's done — she's done *every*thing.

"I ought to have my ass kicked around the block," she murmurs. I think her eyes are moist, but I can't swear to it. "You poor child."

"Why do you always make me feel stupid?" I ask. "You don't have to pity me — I'm okay."

"But you're *not* stupid," Judy protests. She is very unhappy.

"Then why do you and Sam act as if I couldn't read or write or have any idea how to take care of myself?"

"Do we honestly do that, Sally?"

"Yes, you do — you *both* do."

"I believe you're wrong. Stupidity is the last thing I think about you, I promise you, Sally. Oh God, I wish Sam were here to tell you."

"I don't. I know what he thinks. He's even worse than you. He thinks nobody but him can have an idea. He thinks I'm just a spoiled brat!"

"Sally!"

I feel terrific. It's all coming out in a gush. It makes me want to scream and yell and jump up and down. I'm letting loose and I don't care now what I say. "You all hate me," I shriek, "and the feeling's mutual!"

"Sally!"

Bleary-eyed Danny staggers into the room. "Mommy, why is she making all that noise? You woke me up." His pajamas have little red fire engines all over them, scattered every which way.

"Go back to bed, Danny. Here, I'll come with you." Judy gets out of bed, slips into her ratty old bathrobe, and escorts her little boy back to his room. You can imagine how I feel after my explosion — I'm like a fire that's been extinguished.

I debate whether to stay until Judy gets back and see no point in it, no point at all: there's nothing more to be said on my part, and anything she says I won't want to hear. I slip out the door and go down the hall to my lovely warm room where I quickly get into bed, turn out the light, and wait patiently for my eyes to get used to the flickers and shadows playing across the freshly painted ceiling.

After that night my feelings about Judy remained at this somewhat hysterical pitch. I went from hot to cold and back to hot again, never warm, never neutral. It took a lot of energy to keep up with my emotions.

Kathleen came into our lives. Judy claimed she hired Kathleen because of her Yeatsian name — Kathleen O'Herlihy — which I thought was pretty dumb of her. "She should be called Acne Annie," Sam said about the maid.

They didn't have the first idea of how a maid ought to act. I did, but it was really none of my business. As a matter of fact, I rather enjoyed watching her be what my mother would have unhesitatingly called a "slop." Kathleen wouldn't have lasted half an hour in my mother's house. She did things like this: wipe the bathroom basin with the same cloth she had just used to wipe off the toilet seat; dry a dirty spoon with a towel and casually drop it back into the silverware drawer; dust around — but not under — objects sitting on tables and other surfaces; dust the glass covering a picture by making a leisurely pass at it with a feather duster; take a perfectly straight picture and set it crooked; make a bed without hospital corners. It amused me that Judy wasn't aware she had hired a slop.

I wasn't Miss Sally to *this* Kathleen. I was just plain You. This suited me fine. I never liked being called Miss anyway. But while I could never tell what this new Kathleen was thinking (the old school: cover your feelings under a skin of subservience), it was quite clear what went on in her head. It was more honest perhaps, but it was also unnerving.

I didn't like Kathleen. She looked at me with slitted eyes and a sour mouth. When Judy went out she would sit at the kitchen table with a cup of tea into which she had dumped four heaping teaspoonfuls of sugar. Although she came in only a few hours a week and was paid by the hour, Kathleen would hold long telephone conversations with her friends in Gaelic. One day when I was home from school with a cold, I timed one of her calls: thirty-two and a half minutes. She was a nogoodnik, but she had brass. I was mean and told Judy about Kathleen's using the same rag on toilet and basin, in the wrong order. Also about the dirty spoon. I thought Judy would hit the ceiling, but she didn't — she just passed it off by saying, "I'd better talk to her about the toilet, hadn't I?" My guess is she never did. I don't think she liked having Kathleen in her house, not because of her personality but because she was an intruder. Judy was bad at doling out work to Kathleen. Either she was too abrupt or too apologetic. She never seemed to get the rhythm right.

Kathleen and Roger carried on a cold war. Kathleen had never seen the likes of Roger who was, of course, horribly spoiled. Also as rude as a masher. Kathleen would complain to Judy about Roger, and Judy would not quite know how to square it. How can you make someone feel better about a little boy kicking her in the shins and calling her "pimplehead"? In retrospect, I find it odd that Kathleen didn't give up and quit.

It made me wonder about Kathleen number one, who never complained about anything, though she had sufficient grievances. Why was my mother so special that no one would complain to her? Was she the Queen of Sheba? What were the unspoken threats, and why were they so powerful? If Kathleen had said anything in her own self-defense, would she have been fired on the spot? It made me very uneasy. How much did I really know about my mother's power over people dependent on her for their next meal and the one after that? And even over those whose lives she only brushed lightly from time to time. Come to think of it, how much did I *want* to know?

I don't need one tenth of what I own. My mother didn't need a thousandth, but she loved to collect possessions. She loved what was on display on alabaster pedestals and under spotlights, and she loved what was hidden in cabinets and closets. Judy didn't need a third, but she was always complaining about "too many *things,* there are too many *things* in this house." She was always going on about how people were so much more important than things, things tie you down and make you worry about them and getting them insured, and how the state ought to take everybody's things and money and reapportion them fairly. I would listen to her talk but somehow couldn't match the way she talked with the way she lived. If she was so damned concerned about things, why did she own so much junk? She came home after buying a new pair of pumps and pranced around in them, showing them off, just like my mother. She had copper-bottomed pots and pans in the kitchen and an electric mixer. The word "hypocrite" did not occur to me at the time, but the *notion* of hypocrite had swum fiercely to the surface.

There were other areas of mystery: the question of who, in my past, took care of what. Who shelved Freddie's books and kept them so beautifully dusted? Did Kathleen do it all alone?

Once a week, on Saturday morning at eleven, an ancient man with a shiny white shirt and trembling hands appeared at the door of our house. He carried with him a small leather instrument case like Dr. Einstein's in *Arsenic and Old Lace*. This old man, whose name I never bothered to find out, wound all the clocks in our house. He wound the grandfather clock with its three brass weights on iron chains. He wound the banjo clock with its moon that waxed and waned on the wall of Freddie's study, and he wound a nineteen-thirties clock which had its works ingeniously hidden inside glass and chrome housing, and he wound the ordinary clock against the brick wall in the kitchen (Mummy had brick walls long before it was fashionable to show the bare bones of a house). Why couldn't we wind these clocks ourselves? Who was this old man, where did he come from, how long had he been winding other people's clocks? There was another man, whose name I did know. It was Jimmy. Jimmy also appeared once a week. He came to paste-wax the banisters and the stairs. He also washed the windows with a sloppy chamois rag reeking of ammonia. Jimmy shampooed the carpets with an electric machine that hummed in a low key, and he moved the furniture around when the spirit moved Mummy, which was fairly often. Did Jimmy also help dust the books? Who was he? Where did he live? Did he have a wife and children? Did he have to come a long way, say Queens (somehow I had it in my head that people like Jimmy always lived in drab places like Queens)? How many other families did Jimmy work for? What did he do with Mummy's day after she died?

There were several anonymous men and women, plenty of Jimmys in the lives of my mother and stepfather, people who came and went like obedient slaves, oiling and turning the gears, polishing and priming so that we would run without breakdown, without letup.

You couldn't compare the Jimmys to Kathleen. She was a

horse of a different color. Most women, I now realized, did their own dirty work. Only a tiny fraction of the world's population would or could ask someone else to do it for them. I forced myself to think about women who never left their houses, never ate in a restaurant, not even a Walgreen's drugstore counter, never went to a movie or a baseball game because they couldn't afford the price of a ticket, owned maybe one old pair of shoes and stood over a steamy washtub all day trying to keep up with their family's dirt. Walker Evans people, *Grapes of Wrath* people, so destitute that when the money came in it was all used up in the same day. Thirty-year-old women whose teeth had rotted and fallen out and who didn't know what the inside of a doctor's office looked like. People who could make no distinction between Want and Need.

It hurt me that my mother bought so many things she didn't need. I would have liked her to sacrifice, not acquire. The list of my grievances against her was practically endless, perhaps because I idolized her and couldn't bear to name her faults nor see that she had behaved wickedly. I wanted to redo her image, remove the old furniture and bring in attractive new things.

There was something else bothering me, another secret that gathered questions to it the way a coat pocket gathers fuzz. I was, as a matter of fact, worried sick. I had been playing with myself at night, under the covers. The more I tried to stop my hands and keep them outside the blankets, as my mother had instructed me, the more they kept creeping under and making their way down to the place between my legs where it was warm and moist, soft and interesting. Somehow, with my fingers poking around and having a good time, my mind was set free and flew from memory to memory, from past to present desires, from vague longings to particular people, boys mostly, a boy, a particular boy named Dereck. I lay in a warm pond, floating on my back with the sun pouring hot on my eyelids. Dereck was usually there, swimming beside me, smiling. My hand created a rhythm whose echoes

cut across my consciousness like an old hummed song. I knew I
was doing something sinful and was ashamed. I read somewhere
that out of the masturbator's palm there grows a single long black
telltale hair. Every day I turned my palms up for inspection.

And what else was begging for answers? Worries about my
body, such as, what were those little raised dots all around my
nipples? Cancer? And what was that faint brown line connecting
my belly button to my pubic hair, a thin subdermal thread? Why
was it there? Did everybody have one? And finally, I couldn't get
used to my pubic hair. I hadn't had it long enough to feel it a part
of me. Every time I looked down or saw it in the mirror it
startled me. It was like a triangular black wound. I would squint
my eyes and it changed into a pointed beard, but where were the
chin and the mouth and the nose? I stood naked in front of the
mirror Judy had had affixed to the inside of my closet door and
stared at my boobs: they stared back at me, two wideset, dolorous eyes. Not laughing eyes, not bright eyes, but baleful eyes.
Then I took a short trip south and there it was: the kinky black
triangle. Why was it there? To keep my pussy warm? Wasn't it
too thick? I wondered about blonds — was theirs blond? Was an
old lady's white? The questions kept coming and were never
answered because I didn't have Nancy and I wouldn't use Judy
and there was no one else. Books you say? The only books I
could lay my hands on were so sappy my hands got sticky holding them. *My Body and How It Works*, written for unimagina-
tive cretins. *The Human Body*, trivial and irrelevant, skirting,
you might say, the only important issues. Novels with sex scenes
in them never got near such urgent matters as pubic hair and
raised dots. I conducted a no-stone-unturned search of the Londons' library and unearthed nothing more informative than an
encyclopedia with an anatomy chart in it, in color. No raised
dots, no pubic hair. Also no mention of what happens to you
when you masturbate.

I hated my body and I was afraid for it. I felt vulnerable and

ugly. I wanted to look like Rita Hayworth but didn't (too short),
Veronica Lake (too dark and round-faced), Katharine Hepburn
(hopelessly out of the question). People told me I had nice eyes.
That's what you tell people when you can't think of anything
else to say about how they look. Eyes are the last refuge of
desperate flatterers.

15

The Best
of Both Worlds

PEGGY PINCUS was a bony awkward girl who played the
flute, one rung below prodigy. She took lessons at the New England Conservatory and went to concerts almost as often as Oma
Lucy. Oma Lucy would have applauded our friendship on these
grounds, though hardly on the grounds of Peggy's Polish ances-
try. Her friend Annie Berkowitz was seeing a psychiatrist once a
week because she had some difficulty riding in enclosed spaces
like elevators and buses without practically passing out. Both
these girls were, like me, in the semimisfit class, that is, we had a
sufficient number of odd characteristics to keep us out of the
popular or "gang" category. When you're young you hate it;
when you're older you finally realize what a blessing it is not to
be swallowed up.

Peggy and Annie had been close friends, they told me, since
the seventh grade when Annie's family had moved to Brookline
from Mattapan. They opened up their tiny circle and cautiously
invited me in. I nearly swooned with gratitude.

We three were obsessed with how we looked. The shape and
style of your body was far more important than what went on
inside your head. And if you were unattractive that specifically
meant you were unattractive to boys. You were rarely what your
own destiny claimed for you — you were only identifiable from
behind the eyes of a boy. The ideal teen-age girl in 1948 had

pointy breasts, a waist the size of a neck (and belted by an eight-inch strip of heavy leather — it had to hurt to be good), long hairless legs, a bubble-headed smile pasted against a rosy and ex-pectant face, a smile that said both availability and untouchability — quite a trick if you could bring it off. Every girl desperately wanted to achieve this ideal, which found its embodiment in *Esquire's* Petty Girl. (The fact that I wanted also to look like Katharine Hepburn is clue enough to my oddness — Hepburn was much too skinny, sharp-boned, and aristocratic to be taken seriously by most women.) As for the Petty Girl riding in per-petual effervescence on an unanchored swing against an impos-sibly clean and blue sky, the three of us had as much chance of looking like her as Sophie Tucker did.

I thought Peggy looked like her flute, which she carried, broken down into three parts, inside a black leather case with a blue satin lining. *She* said she looked like a stringbean, with a chest like a washboard. She bought herself a brassiere and stuffed the tiny cups with Kleenex, which I guess fooled some people but didn't make her any happier. She had a pale soft fuzz on her cheeks and over her upper lip. This fuzz drove her crazy. Once every two weeks she would bleach her mustache with a murder-ous paste made of Ivory Flakes, ammonia, and peroxide. She smeared this on and wept quietly while it went to work. Annie Berkowitz came closer to the Petty ideal, but she thought she was ugly and that her tits, as she called them, were much too big, so what good did it do for us to tell her she looked great? Annie used to walk around with her arms crossed over her chest so that no one would look at her tits.

Peggy, Annie, and I consoled ourselves for our ugliness by pretending that we thought we were better than the rest of *them*. This actually helped us from becoming true misfits. What two of them had, in fact, *was* better, but since what they had was talent, not beauty, it didn't go very far in the morale department. Peggy played the flute, Annie wrote poems. She wrote poems the way other girls read *Modern Screen* and listened to Benny Goodman records. I don't know what I had except the slightly tarnished glamour of having lived in New York, gone to a Private School, and become half an orphan.

We consoled ourselves by sticking together, by being constantly with one another, whether it was at "my" house or one of theirs or on Beacon Street window-shopping or at the drugstore stocking up on calories in the form of ice cream and frappes. Peggy seemed to subsist on an all-carbohydrate diet. Though her parents were not really rich — her father owned the corner drugstore, the one patronized by Judy and half our neighborhood — they had bought her an expensive phonograph and given her all the money she needed to buy records of flute players playing the world's great flute music. She didn't often inflict this on us, however, and we would lie dreamy hour after dreamy hour on her bed or floor and listen to Artie or Gene or Benny or Stan (my favorite) on her terrific phonograph. While we listened we fantasized about boys, about love, about what we would do when we were grown up and released from the prison of adolescence. We were quite sure that the break between childhood and adulthood was sharp and absolute, like jumping over a chasm: you were either on one side or another, and there was no such thing as transition. And the same held true for losing your virginity.

I envied Peggy for being able to eat as much as she wanted without gaining an ounce. Peggy envied Annie her luscious tits. Annie, who wore glasses, envied me my clear blue eyes, and we all envied our glamorous classmate, Marcy Lifschultz, for being the living Petty Girl.

Annie had a copy of a book someone had smuggled in from India during the war. It described one hundred and thirty-two positions a couple could twist themselves into, like living pretzels,

during sexual intercourse. Some of these positions were illustrated with line drawings in an elegant, delicate Near East style.
First I was appalled. Then I learned to giggle. Annie's brother
knew someone who had tried each one, in consecutive order. I
didn't believe it.

"Who with?" I ask.

"Oh, different girls," Annie says.

"Anyone we know?" That's Peggy.

"Gloria," Annie says, smirking.

"I don't believe it," I say.

"Don't believe it then," Annie tells me firmly. She has a way of
getting aggressively to the top of things. I like her, but I like
Peggy better.

Peggy has a copy of *Tropic of Cancer* she stole from her
uncle's house. It was wrapped in a brown paper bag cut out to fit
over the cover. We took turns reading it aloud. Annie liked the
part about making love like the wolves do above the timberline.
She said that was poetry and tried to explain to us why it was
poetic and not just dirty. When it was my turn to read to the
others I invariably stumbled and blushed over "cunt." I couldn't
manage to get the word out of my mouth without a song and
dance. They laughed at me. Peggy and Annie were so used to
talking dirty that they could call a penis a "prick" or "dink"
without a pause. They tossed the words "asshole," "cunt,"
"cock," "shit," "fuck" around as if they had as much emotional
content as a theorem in math. It appeared, then, that although
everybody thought I was sophisticated and knowing, my traffic
with sex — verbal, literary, and actual — was light years behind
my friends' and quite possibly my classmates'. I was stuck at E or
F, they were at P or Q.

Annie, who was the sharper but also the less sensitive of my
two new friends, teased me. She said that there were men who
got their thrills from licking a woman's cunt.

"I don't believe that," I say, with a thrill of horror and embarrassment.

"It's true, dolly," Peggy says, crossing one bony knee over the other and tossing her head slightly to show it didn't mean a thing to her. "Isn't that disgusting?"

"Pretty gross," Annie says. "Though I can see, under certain conditions . . ."

I am agog. More than I can swallow, so to speak. "I'll never let anyone do that to me. No man is going to do that to me, I swear on a stack of Bibles. I'd rather kill myself." While I talk my mind is racing. What does it taste like? Mine? His?

"Wanna bet?" Annie asks. "Sooner or later you'll try it. Most women do."

"Not me," I say. "How do you know?"

"Get her," Annie says to Peggy. "I know because I've read about it. I also talked to this woman I know and asked her."

"What woman?" Peggy says.

"Just a friend of Mom's," she says. "She believes in sex education for the young." She follows this with a loud guffaw.

Peggy says, "Maybe I won't let a man do that either — how do I know?"

"Well, I'm going to try everything there is to try," Annie announces. "And maybe invent some things besides."

"Annie's going to burn her candle at both ends," Peggy explains. "She got that from Edna St. Vincent Millay."

"Yes," Annie says. "You stick-in-the-muds might learn something from old Edna."

We begin testing our limits. Annie announces that there are some men who "like to fuck you by sticking their dinks in your asshole."

"Only homos do that," Peggy argues. I am speechless.

"You're dead wrong about that," Annie says with confidence.

"Regular people do it. It's called buggery. Farmers do it to their sheep and cattle. In the city men do it to women."

"Please, spare us," Peggy says. She's smiling a little. Annie seems satisfied. My eyes are closed and my mouth is set hard. I am so innocent. I know nothing. I am being fed huge, gristly chunks of meat and I'm having a hard time chewing, let alone getting them down.

I thought about buggery. Is that what my mother meant when she quaintly referred to "making love"? It didn't sound much like making love to me. Did Mummy let Freddie do it to her? Judy, Sam? Instantly, I saw Judy as the victim of a brutish attack, which was the only way I could imagine it. A victim. I would from now on see Sam in a different light. Also, I might not be able to look Judy in the eye. I almost wish they hadn't told me.

Raw as their talk was, in some ways Peggy and Annie were as fragile as crystallized violets. When Peggy played her flute she was transformed from a stringbean into an Ariel. She made the hair stand up on the back of my neck — there was something so true and pure about the notes that they seemed to float on the air, like soap bubbles, before bursting into an echo. Mr. Turner was always asking Peggy to get up and play in assembly, which, much to my surprise, she was perfectly willing to do. While playing for an audience she had a remote, detached expression on her face which suggested that she didn't know where she was. Except when she played, Peggy was so shy with grownups that they probably thought she was a mute.

The foul-mouthed Annie wrote poems about shades of emotion so slight you couldn't feel them unless you peeled off a layer of skin first. She had dozens of notebooks filled with poems and scraps of poems and notes about subjects like the sense of loss, the sound of time passing, the special light in the eye of a lover. There was one about how a child feels when its father is killed in the war. "Seed buried deep, deep in her flesh . . ." and so on. I was profoundly impressed by Annie's poetry. I could never imagine myself writing anything so literary, so "felt." Most of my compositions for English had all the poetry of Fräulein in her oxfords clumping down the back stairs.

Our sex discussions accomplished little more than to turn us inside out. They excited us but filled us with dread at the same time. Annie insisted that love had nothing to do with sex and vice versa. Peggy argued that you could have love without sex. I told them what the minister had said to Daddy and Lorna while he was marrying them. "This marriage," he insisted, "symbolizes the marriage of Christ and His Church." I wondered which one was Christ and which His Church. Neither one seemed to fit in either category. But if I was just thick and if what the minister said was true, where did sex fit into this scheme?

Peggy and Annie — when they weren't talking about sex — swapped Jewish jokes. They told each other things that would have made a non-Jew turn aside in horror and shame. It seemed that there was a Jewish joke to suit every situation, personality, and human event — except concentration camps. For some reason, although you could tell a joke about a Jewish businessman who sets his own factory on fire —"Shhh, that's next week"— for the insurance, you couldn't tell a joke about a Jew in a camp. As a matter of fact, all the people in Annie's and Peggy's jokes were greedy, gluttonous, suspicious, pushy; they had filthy habits, loud voices, and insatiable appetites. Everything anti-Semites believed to be true. The two girls would fly into hysterical fits of laughter over a new joke. Annie was determined to catalogue these jokes by general topic, and she wrote them down in her notebooks under different headings: food, sex, adultery, etc. Whenever a joke contained a word in Yiddish, they had to stop in midstream and translate for me.

I was, it seemed, not only innocent about sex but also "pitifully ignorant of your heritage."

I tried to explain about the German thing, about people like

Lucy Stern and her son, people like Opa Teddy Baum. They just snorted.

"That's the most revolting thing I ever heard," Peggy says with a characteristic lack of precision. "Who do they think they are?"

"They think," Annie puts in, "they are the cat's pajamas." She pauses for the effect of the pause, not because there's a natural break in her thoughts. "I can't stand people who think they're better than other people. They make me sick." I am a little hurt, because she didn't know Freddie — nice, sweet, benign Freddie — and she doesn't know Oma Lucy, whom I considered someone worth knowing even if you didn't agree with her all the time.

"You should meet Oma Lucy," I murmur.

Peggy, who has heard of Oma Lucy — her name is attached to certain gifts in the world of music; she is after all a patroness of the arts — says, "Mrs. Stern is okay."

"Mrs. Stern," Annie says, looking at her friend in not the friendliest way, "would probably call your family *schnutzig Ost European* without giving it another thought. I hardly call that okay."

"She wouldn't," I say. "She's too refined."

"I'll bet she uses the word riffraff," Annie says. She is kind of relentless. Peggy and I decide, without saying anything about it, to shut her up.

"You don't know her," Peggy says. "So all you're doing is guessing. Why don't we talk about someone else?"

Doors opened inside my head at this point, and lights materialized at the ends of tunnels. What it all revealed was essentially this. For all their money (*gelt*, in the words of Annie Berkowitz), for all their social buoyancy, my mother, Freddie, and most of their Jewish friends acted as if they were hiding out from the Nazis. They covered their Jewish wrinkles, they shaved their Jewish armpits, they deodorized their Jewish kitchens, and they Pygmalionized their Jewish accents. What, *me* Jewish?

And here was Peggy Pincus, whose father's accent sounded like a parody of Mrs. Nussbaum in "Allen's Alley," whose mother had trouble with the English language, and Annie, whose parents kept a kosher house. Not only were they not ashamed to say what they were — they were positively *proud* of it. This paradox did not make it easier for me to be Jewish; it only confused me further.

We were sitting in the Londons' living room one Saturday afternoon, recovering from the exertion of watching Laurence Olivier make tormented love to Merle Oberon, when Peggy said, "Sally, there's something that's been bothering me for a long time. If you think I'm being too nosy, just forget it."

An auspicious opening. "Go ahead," I say. Annie looks mildly interested.

Peggy takes a deep breath and begins. "Well," she says, "ever since you came up here from New York, we — that is, Annie and I — have been wondering something." A quick look in her friend's direction for a corroborating nod.

She stops dead and looks down. She has a funny habit of starting sentences and not finishing them. It drives her teachers crazy. They're always saying, "Please Peggy, complete your thought."

Annie takes over. "What Peggy is trying to say is we can't quite understand what you're doing here. No, that doesn't sound right. We can't understand why you didn't stay in New York or go live with your father. Why up here of all godforsaken spots on the face of the earth? And with the Londons, who don't have nearly so much dough or class as you're used to. What it boils down to is, how come?"

"My stepfather said so," I say simply. "He decided he wanted Mr. London as our guardian. I didn't have anything to say about it."

"Yes, but *why* did he? Wouldn't it have made more sense to have you go stay with a relative or something in New York?" Peggy has found her thought again.

The things they are asking me now are the things I have been asking myself since it happened. "I don't know," I admit. "I can't figure it out either."

"Why don't you go ask London?" says Annie, cutting through to the heart of the matter.

"He doesn't like me," I say. "He probably wouldn't tell me. Besides, he never has time to do anything but work on his stupid book. Whenever I talk to him he acts as if he can't wait to get back to his work. No one can go in his study. He locks it at night."

"You shouldn't bite your nails," Peggy says with a smile. "If you let them grow they'd be really pretty."

"I can't help it," I say. "My mother used to put iodine on my fingers but it didn't stop me."

"Sadist," Annie says.

"How could he not like you?" Peggy asks. I could kiss her.

"You're sweet," I say. "But you'll have to admit he's not exactly the cuddly type."

" 'Put your arms around me, honey, hold me tight,' " Annie sings. " 'Cuddle up and cuddle up with all your might.' Brilliant lyrics. Listen doll, you wouldn't want to cuddle with him anyway. Mrs. L. might get jealous."

"Don't tease Sally," Peggy says, "It's not her fault. Mr. London is hard to get to know — even *you* can see that."

"I'm sorry," Annie says. When she apologizes I can see she means it. That's why she's my friend even though she's sometimes hard to get along with. "Is there any Coke in the icebox?"

I still feel funny about going into the Londons' kitchen and taking stuff out to feed my friends, no matter how often Judy reassures me, "This is your house, Sally. For heaven's sake, don't keep asking for things. Just take 'em." I don't feel comfortable about it. I feel as if I'm stealing.

"I'm sure there is. Judy says to take it. Don't you think that's nice of her?"

"Not particularly," Annie says. "You live here, don't you? You're paying for it too, aren't you? Come on, I'm parched."

We get the Cokes, uncap them, and drink from the bottle. My mother always made me pour it into a glass. She thought bottle necks had residual filth.

Annie returns to the mystery. "I know why your stepfather chose this place. It was the kosher butchers."

"No," Peggy tells her. "It was the B.S.O. They wanted her to be near Koussy."

"Or then again, it could have been Harvard. They wanted you to grow up and go out with Harvard men. 'Oh you can tell a Harvard man about a mile away, because he looks — boom boom — just like he'll fly away.' "

Peggy and I start to giggle. The idea of a college full of fairies is just too much.

"I'll go right up to Sam," I boast, "and say, 'Now, look here, Mr. Smartypants. How come I'm up here in the sticks eating macaroni and cheese when I could be strolling on Fifth Avenue in my minks and eating filet mignon for breakfast? What's the deal, buddy boy? Give it to me straight — no beating around the bush. Was Freddie really off his trolley, or did you blackmail him. Huh?' "

"Oh ha!" Annie shouts. "I'll bet you a million bucks you don't have the nerve."

Well, I couldn't ask him that night because they went out to dinner and a movie. And the next day, right back into the inner sanctuary where he stayed alone until three droopy men came to the front door, where he greeted them, then ushered them in with him. They stayed until dinnertime, at which point Sam was beyond communication — all he could do was grunt and ask for the catsup. By the next day I'd lost my nerve. It's a good thing Annie forgot her bet.

Dereck Jolley was a senior at Brookline High School. He was handsome with irregularities, the sort that usually reassure people: eyes that don't quite match, a mouth that turns up on one side, ears that stick out slightly. Dereck was the Renata Paul of Brookline High. For a number of good reasons, most kids kept a healthy distance between themselves and him. Lacking the experience that comes naturally with long exposure, I was wriggling on his hook from the first moment he talked to me. He used his eyes the way some people use their hands; often when he looked at me I had the eerie sensation that I could actually feel his eyes on my flesh, not moist like eyeballs should be but hot, like twin flames. Sex? Maybe, but something else too, something like power or the ingestion of one person by another.

First of all I was amazed that he noticed me at all, the fat girl. When I told Annie and Peggy that Dereck had spoken to me — had in fact asked me to have lunch with him — Peggy said, "Oh, *him*," and Annie told me I'd be better off having lunch with Donald Duck. Then they refused to discuss Dereck with me anymore.

Dereck, handsome, brilliant (early admission, Harvard), reminded me of the way Freddie looked, but with Sam's brains and Van Johnson's charm. Irresistible Dereck Jolley. I lived, slept, ate, dreamed Dereck. He even replaced my father. Dereck had put Daddy to sleep.

Dereck told me that as soon as he was old enough he was going to become a Catholic convert. He assured me that "Mom and Dad are going to have a shit fit, but tough titty, it's my life, it's my soul."

I passed this message along to the Londons one night. They

hadn't met Dereck. He was still only a name to them, but a name they were hearing with monotonous regularity. I would tell them a story about Dereck just so I could feel his name in my mouth.

Sam looked at me with his usual withering consideration. "He's been reading too much Hopkins," he said. "Or maybe Graham Greene."

"He's been reading T. S. Eliot," I say. "He understands every single reference in *The Waste Land*."

"Splendid," Sam says, stuffing his face with meatloaf. "Why doesn't your friend come and teach my class for me?"

"Sam," Judy says.

"Sorry," Sam says, about the time he swallows. "Most sensitive kids go through a Catholic stage. He'll probably recover."

I grind my teeth in fury. How come Sam knows so much about someone he's never even met? How come he knows more about my friend than I do? Dereck has given me books of poetry and instructions on how to read them, how to read them aloud to myself, how to solve an image or a metaphor, what to look for that isn't said. I had an agonizing time with *The Wreck of the Deutschland*. I understood about one phrase out of every twenty. It seemed hopelessly roundabout. Why couldn't he just come straight out and say what he meant? Nevertheless I assured Dereck I was moved by the poem, by those poor nuns drowning, by the rhythms and the language. Oh, what a lie I lived for him! I carried my Hopkins and my Eliot around with me the way a Jehovah's Witness carries her copies of *The Watchtower*.

Dereck liked to lecture me. I would furtively write down words I didn't understand, then look them up in the dictionary: sprung rhythm, enjambment, caesura, tetrameter, alexandrine. I don't know whether he assumed I could understand what he was talking about or was too involved to care. At any rate, he needed my ears more than my tongue because he rarely if ever asked me to contribute anything more than my lumpish presence.

Except when it came to my past. Then he was as hungry as I

was for love. My past, money, the German-Jewish thing — these topics held him spellbound.

"You know," he says, "I'll bet you think I'm not Jewish. I can tell from that suspicious look on your face."

"Are you?" In truth, I am surprised. He's got straight, light-brown, non-Jewish hair.

"Jolley was Jackowitz not so long ago. Ugly, isn't it?

"Jackowitz," I repeat.

"Yes, from Vilna. The Jackowitzes of Vilna and Brookline, Massachusetts, cordially invite you to attend the conversion of their son Dereck on Friday, the first of April, nineteen hundred and fifty-two."

"Why do you want to know so much about me?"

"I collect lives," he tells me. Naturally dumb, I don't believe him. His eyes are brimming with greed for my life. Dereck's head is shaped like a soccer ball; his eyes are green like a summer pond; his cheekbones stick out like a Korean's.

"Your boyfriend looks like a Slav," Judy tells me the first time she saw him. "Where are his parents from?"

"I don't know," I say. "Here, I think."

She lets it pass. But when I repeated to her the business about collecting lives she didn't smile the way I thought she would.

"If I were you," she said. "I'd watch out. He might just mean it. He writes, doesn't he?"

"Yes," I say. "He's going to be a writer for a living."

"That's nice. What does he write?"

"He hasn't really started yet — he says he's still collecting stuff. When he gets enough he's going to start with a few short stories, he says, to warm up. Then a novel." Oh, I was so impressed. "He'll probably start next year, when he's at Harvard."

"How nice for Harvard." She smiles a little to take the curse off her remark.

She starts to say something, stops, then changes her mind again.

"You know, Sally, I don't really buy that business about writers not writing. If they're writers, they write — if they're not, they don't. I mean, you can't talk a novel, can you?" If she's trying to make me doubt Dereck she's barking up the wrong tree. She'll only end up making me doubt her. For a smart woman she's awfully dumb.

Dereck and I meet for lunch whenever our schedules coincide. There's an unwritten rule that Seniors do not have lunch with Freshmen, but Dereck is not one for rules; he only obeys them when it suits him. He tells me that most people spend far too much time worrying about what other people think of them, which is fundamentally silly, because most people are too busy worrying about their own problems to make judgments. I wasn't sure I agreed with him, but I didn't dare voice my doubts.

Dereck was anxious to correct my faults. I've never known a person who could see so many things wrong: being with him was like sitting under a giant magnifying glass with hot lights shining on you. My faults were many, starting with nail-biting ("a revolting childish habit"), going on through errors in taste, judgment, comprehension, values, and attitudes, not to mention "an apologetic personality" and "not slim enough."

He ordered me to stop saying "I'm sorry." "You're always apologizing," he says. "It creates a very negative impression."

"I'm sorry." Oops.

"See what I mean, Sarah?" (He was the only person my age who called me Sarah.) "You come on soft and mushy. You should represent yourself as firm and confident, like Anna Karenina. She knew what she wanted."

"Didn't she commit suicide?" I ask.

"That's only because of the social mores, the pressures. Today she'd probably be a heroine." Dereck scraped a glob of orange mayonnaise from his salad. "Why do they feel they have to put this garbage on top of everything? It tastes like shit."

I'm not used to this sort of language, but I have to pretend I am. Also, I like mayonnaise. I've always liked the slightly lemony taste of it, and at home I used to spread it on white bread and eat it plain.

"How many original works of art did your parents own? Including the Calder and the Degas dancer, of course."

"I can't remember exactly," I say. "Maybe about twenty. I'm not really sure." He looks at me in disgust.

"What happened to them?" He isn't taking notes with paper and pencil, but he's got an excellent memory.

"Most of them went to the Museum of Modern Art," I tell him with a shrug. "At least the Kandinsky, the Klee, the Miro, and the Calder did. Oh yeah, the Braque, too. I think the Degas dancer went somewhere else, probably the Met. Mummy knew the director. We had a lot of small drawings — they were on the walls of the staircase. Mummy said people should have something nice to look at when they went up and down stairs. Isn't that nutty? Isn't it funny I never counted how many?"

"Not funny," Dereck says. "Typical."

"Typical of what?" When Dereck talks to me this way it makes my skin prickle. Only the blindness of my devotion to this weird boy kept me from hauling off and hitting him for treating me like a moron.

"Typical of your family's kind of money. You act as if it was dirt. No, that's not quite accurate. You act as if it were food in the Garden of Eden, there for the picking. You're hardly aware of its existence. I don't think art should belong to private individuals anyway — great works of art should be hung publicly so that everybody gets a chance to appreciate them."

"Yes, but what if somebody bought something when the artist was poor and no one had ever heard of him. And then he gets famous, and the picture or statue or whatever it is gets very valuable. What are you supposed to do then?"

"Was Braque poor and struggling when your parents bought his picture? In a pig's eye! Besides, I don't see any logic in your question. If the object gets valuable, the owner has to give it away, or maybe sell it at what he paid for it. He shouldn't be allowed to get rich off someone else's talent like that."

"You sound like Judy London."

"Unlikely," he says.

"I don't think the government would come in and force a man to sell what he bought on his own. Isn't that like the Nazis or Mussolini?"

Dereck strikes his fist against his forehead in a gesture of mock frustration. Mock or not, I don't appreciate the implication. "You think this country is perfect, don't you?" he says witheringly.

"No," I say. "I never said I did. And if you think I'm so stupid, why do you bother to have lunch with me so often?" This, from me, was a major challenge.

"Who's been talking to you about me?" Dereck says.

"Nobody."

"Somebody's been feeding you propaganda," he purrs, touching my arm ever so lightly but activating electric pulses along my flesh.

"I like you kid," he hums, close to my ear. His fingers do a little lighthearted dance on my skin. I feel like screaming.

"You just like my past," I say, pleading silently for him to deny the charge. "My past and my parents' money."

"Sure I do," he says. "How can one separate one's self from one's past? You are your own history — destiny is what you were born with."

"I'm not Mummy's money!" I cry.

"Oh, but you are. And the sooner you adjust to it, the better off you'll be. Your mother's and stepfather's money helped shape you — it gave you perfect teeth and a good complexion, it made your feet straight and strong, it shaped your attitudes, your personality, your character. Your money is as much a part of your personality and persona as your genes are."

"No," I say, aware, with a pang, that he might be right and that I can never escape my money any more than a poor man can escape the hunger he doesn't feel anymore.

"Yes," Dereck says, obviously amused by the form this conversation is taking. "And your face looks the way it does because your mother is a German Jew and your father's a bird — your father's an upper-class Christian gentleman athlete who went to Yale. The combination of *mère* and *père* makes your face more interesting than it would otherwise be, more suggestive. Crossbreeding generally brings out the best of both worlds. If and when you lose some of that baby fat you may be worth taking a second look at."

My face is burning. His compliment is so left-handed I can't even read its writing. "Where's my baby fat?"

"Here and here and here and here," he says, poking me in various spots. Several boys and girls at neighboring tables look at us.

"Well, thanks anyway for the compliment."

"I don't pay compliments," he says forking into his green Jell-O pie.

"Not even when you really mean it?"

"Most people, I've found, are insatiable for compliments. Give 'em one and they keep coming back for more. It's an addiction. It makes me sick!"

"Don't you like it when someone pays you a compliment?"

"It makes me feel like puking!" He shoves green pie into his mouth. "Ugh," he says. "It tastes like library paste."

"Remind me," I say, "never to tell you anything nice about yourself."

"You won't be able to resist," he says. I think he really means it. "How many pairs of shoes did Freddie own?" he asks, abruptly shifting gears.

It sounds very strange to hear Dereck refer to my stepfather as Freddie, as if he knew him. Is he "collecting" my family too?

"I don't know," I say.

"Would you say at least ten?"

"I guess so."

"And how many monogrammed silk shirts?"

"I don't know. I don't remember any shirts with monograms on them."

"No, of course, he wouldn't." Dereck shakes his head. He pats his mouth with a paper napkin that is still as clean and unwrinkled as when he unfolded it and placed it across his lap. Dereck has beautiful taste in clothes. Today he has on a dark green Shetland sweater over a pale pink shirt. Immaculate khakis. Loafers. He looks like a young man in an ad for sailboats. "How could I have slipped up like that?"

I can't answer, not knowing what he's talking about.

"I don't know any Jews who look like you," he says.

"I'm only half."

"You're kidding yourself," he says, shoving his chair back from the table. "If you're a sixteenth Negro you're all Negro in the eyes of the world. Same thing for Jews. Hitler was right."

"Oma Lucy said that too."

"Who's Oma Lucy?" New data.

"My stepfather's mother. We're very close."

"How come you didn't go live with her? Jesus, what a weird family!"

"She's too old, I guess."

"She's pretty rich too, right?"

I nod. I want to tell him about how Oma Lucy said that nuns only take baths twice a year but I am afraid of offending him. Instead I ask, "How am I different from other Jews?"

He looks at me clinically, shrugs, and says, "You ought to know. You look in the mirror, don't you? Let's blow this joint. The puerile atmosphere is beginning to depress me."

We walk out of the cafeteria, his arm just barely brushing mine. "I want to meet London," he says.

"Why?"

"He's a writer, isn't he? I want to see where he does it." I look sidelong at Dereck. I can't believe he's just seventeen. To me he looks ageless. He has the beauty of an ideal man set in motion, given blood and a heartbeat and still not altogether real. I can't imagine Sam responding favorably to Dereck — already there have been the snotty remarks and the skepticism.

"He doesn't write novels or stories," I tell him. He writes *about* things, about other people's work. He writes a lot for magazines."

"You mean journals," he corrects me. "And I'm perfectly aware of the sort of writing he does. It doesn't matter. The process is the same." He's making a C-minus student out of me; everything I say is dumb. I could cry.

At this point he puts an arm around my waist. "My, you're a big broth of a girl," he tells me, sexy as hell. "And don't let me catch you putting all that lovely flesh inside a girdle."

"Why not?" I say. I can't imagine what he's talking about. All fat people wear girdles — that's what keeps them together.

"Girdles are barbarous," he says in a voice that suggests he's really talking about something far more important.

I decided then and there that I would never in my life buy a girdle, even if I got as fat as the fat lady in the circus. Whatever he told me to do, I did. Whatever he warned me against, I avoided.

16
Quoth the Raven

FINALLY I TOOK Dereck "home" with me. To my considerable surprise he was crisply polite.

"How do you do, Mrs. London," he said, driving his arm out like a piston. She took it and they shook hands. "I'm glad to meet you. And I'm looking forward to meeting your husband. I've read some of his articles on James and I think they're first-rate, very incisive."

"James who? Oh, you mean *Henry* James. That's really very enterprising of you, Dereck. I didn't think they taught those things in high school."

"I read them on my own," Dereck says solemnly. Score points for Dereck. Take away points from Judy.

"Sally tells me that you're going to start at Harvard next fall."

"Yes ma'am."

If she's on to him, she's still maintaining a cordial style. How fortunate that everybody knows so well how to play the game. Judy and Dereck eye each other for a while, then Dereck looks restless. Judy suggests I get my friend something to eat or drink and retreats to the same old place herself to get dinner ready. Dereck pokes around the living room, scanning book titles and peering at pictures. He picks up a small bronze that looks to me as if someone put a perfectly round head through a clothes mangle. He says, "Okay."

"One of their friends made it."

"Not half bad," Dereck says. "I wonder how much it set them back."

"I think she gave it to them," I say.

"Lady sculptor?" he says, picking it up again. "She's got balls."

I blush, put my hand up to my face to hide it, but he's busy nosing around the bookshelves and hasn't noticed.

"Is your guardian home?" he asks over his shoulder.

"I don't know." Every time I hear the word "guardian" I jump. I hate the word — it makes me feel like an orphan. Just as I'm beginning to get used to the idea of living with the Londons, somebody has to come up and remind me that I'm an orphan.

"Why don't you be a good little girl and see if he's home. If he's not, why don't you show me where he works?"

Dereck, of course, is asking me to open Pandora's box, to taste the apple, etc. "I couldn't do that," I say. "He doesn't let anybody inside his study. Not even his wife!"

Satan must have overheard, for at this moment Judy appears at the door and says she's going to the store for milk. "We're fresh out," she complains. "I don't understand it. There were two whole quarts in the icebox this morning."

"Okay," I say weakly. She tells me the boys are out playing somewhere, including Roger, who has begun to tag along, though he hasn't yet joined in. So it's just us two chickens, as Dereck says the moment she closes the front door after her.

"How about it? Show me where the genius plies his trade."

"No," I say. "I told you, not even Judy goes in there. He's very spooky about it. Why do you want to see it anyway?"

"Seeing assists the imaginative process. I can fantasize what his workroom is like, but I want to corroborate my fantasy via reality. Visual rather than speculative evidence."

"Evidence?" I repeat. "It sounds like you were talking about a crime."

"My dear girl," he says, laughing but giving me a look to end all withering looks. "Why don't you just let me decide? Listen, suppose you open the door a crack, let me have a quick look, and then we'll close it up tight again. No one but you and I will ever know about the violation. I won't set foot over the threshold."

This sounds reasonable.

"And come to think of it, what kind of little Caesar is this guy London anyway? He's got all you females hysterical about going into his study. You're all scared shitless of him. What would happen if someone went in? Would they be struck by lightning? Would they turn into a stone or a tree? Jesus Moroni, it's just a lousy study. It's not a Kiva. It's just a room with a typewriter and some books. I'll bet it's a mess. I'll bet there are mouse turds all over the floor."

"I'll bet there aren't," I say, shocked to the roots. Dereck has a distinctive way of putting things. There's more sense to Dereck's argument than I can dismiss. Sam must be crazy. I mean, what sort of sane person goes around telling his wife and children that they are *forbidden* to enter his room? It's one thing to ask people not to mess around with your books and papers — I can understand *that* — but it's another to act as if your study was Mecca and heaven all rolled up in one. It's just nuts, that's how I see it. Dereck's right — we have been bullied.

"Maybe I could open the door just a crack . . ."

"That's my girl," Dereck says, clapping me on the back and grinning.

I step into the hall, Dereck following close behind. I can feel his breath on my ear, but I'm too nervous to be thrilled. "Maybe he works for the OGPU and he's got miles of microfilm in there," Dereck says. "Wasn't he a Party member at college?"

"I don't know," I say honestly.

"You don't know very much about the people you live with, do you? Don't you have *any* curiosity? Jesus, if I lived here, I'd know more about them than they do themselves. As a matter of fact, I'll bet I know more about them than you do." We stall in the hallway.

I turn. "How come?" I ask.

"Simple. I looked them up."

"Looked them up? Where?"

"The obvious places, doll. He's in *Who's Who*. He's got an inch and a half. But he's not going to report any Party membership in *Who's Who*." At this point Dereck shoves his hands in his khaki pockets and draws the fabric tightly over his parts. He sees me looking and smirks. "And as for her ladyship, she doesn't have a separate listing, but after a little digging I found something out. Did you know she worked for Everett Eisenstein before her children were born?"

"Who's Everett Eisenstein?"

"Surely you are pulling my leg," he says. He knows damn well I'm not.

"Oh, *that* Everett Eisenstein," I say lamely.

"You really don't recognize the name, do you?"

"Is that such a crime?" I say. My face has gone all hot again. He has humiliated me for the thousandth time. He's made me feel like a dummy. Just like Sam.

"No, I guess not," he says. He sighs deeply. "I guess I'm asking too much of you."

"Thanks a lot. Who is he?"

"He's a linguist. Why should you know?"

"Do you still want to go in?" I feel cool to him and his snooping. I'm beginning to wish he'd leave.

Dereck comes close and brushes my neck with his amazing lips and starts the whole thing up again.

"Of course I do," he says, caressing me. "Come on."

"All right," I say. "But remember, you promised — just a peek, no going in."

"A promise is a promise," he says reassuringly. I love him very much. I would do anything for him.

We cross the hall and stand outside the forbidden chamber. The door is wood, unpainted. The knob is brass and full of dents, as if it had been squeezed by an iron fist. "You open," Dereck orders.

I am trembling. I cover the knob with my palm — it is surprisingly warm. I turn it; push. The door gives a small squeal and slowly recedes.

"Pee-you," Dereck says, shoving past me and marching in. "Place smells like the men's can on the B&M!"

"Dereck!" I cry. "You promised!"

"Oh shit, Sally, how in hell can you look at a place if you don't go inside? Christ, what a shit heap. Will you look at this. I don't know how he can find anything in all this mess."

"Please, Dereck, come out — you promised you'd just look in from the doorway. That's the only reason I let you!" I am beside myself. This is all wrong. I am practically jumping up and down. "Come out, please!"

"Shut up," he says. "Boy, this is really interesting! Did you know London's got a first edition of the *Cantos*?"

Shut up, he said shut up. I am angry enough to cry. The agonizing awareness of having been used comes over me like a chill.

"Come out!" I scream.

At this moment, as my cry floats around the hall, striking doors and walls, dying slowly and with pain, Sam chooses to open the front door. He stands there looking straight at me. A question and its almost simultaneous answer are on his features, making them terrible. I would laugh at his anger if it wasn't directed at me: there is something so uncompromising about his anger, so credible.

He's standing there, in his long grayish raincoat, holding his briefcase, a thing that looks as if it was plucked out of the town dump, dripping water onto the scatter rug, his bare head sleek with rain and sinisterly black. "Who's in there?" he says.

My heart slams against my chest like a squash ball. My legs are overcooked spaghetti. I am the fugitive Jew, Sam the SS officer. He will drag me and Dereck off to headquarters where he will administer enemas of boiling oil, tear out our fingernails one by one, peel off our skin in thin strips, and then set us out in the sun for the ants to finish off. All I can do is stare at Sam.

"Who's in there, I said?"

I can't speak, my tongue is stiff, dead. I shake my head. Sam strides past me and goes into his room.

"It's just me, sir, Dereck Jolley. I'm a friend of Sally's."

"Is there something in particular you wanted in here?" Sam says in a voice so steady it could get a job doing a tightrope act.

"No, sir, thanks. Sally was just showing me where you work. You see, I want to become a writer myself."

"And you thought you'd like to see for yourself where the muse hangs out. Not such a bad idea, but essentially useless. It's all in your head anyway. May I have that book, please?" Sam extends his hand, an undeniable gesture.

"Oh, this," Dereck says. "Sure, sir. I was about to read something to Sally. A poem."

"Naturally," Sam says. "This is a book of poems."

Neither of them has so much as glanced at me. Never have I been so insubstantial. Dereck cannot realize the depth of Sam's control: he probably thinks Sam always talks in a dead monotone. The encounter is mercifully short. Tossing the book on his desk, Sam escorts Dereck out of the room and firmly shuts the door behind them both. He gives me a look it will take me three days to recover from. "Not many people go in there," Sam says to Dereck, his tone still peculiar. Dereck chooses to read it as spoken.

"I guess I should have asked first, sir. Still, Sally said it was all right."

Oh my God!

"She did, eh?"

Dereck gives my arm a little squeeze. I won't look him in the eye. Sam says "excuse me" and goes into the damn room again. I'm sure he's gone to check if Dereck has heisted anything else.

"You lied," I say to Dereck.

"Just a little white one, doll. Just an eeensy little one. I had to — it was the only way I could get into his room."

"And then you blamed me."

"No, I didn't."

"You did, you blamed me, you made it seem as if it was my idea. And you were going to steal Sam's book."

"If that's the way you choose to interpret me, I pity you, I pity you. You are nothing but a self-centered child. You have absolutely no conception of what life is all about. You have been petted and pampered until whatever few drops of vitality and originality you were born with dried up a long time ago. If you want to change, you will have to make a gigantic effort — to see the other side of things, to understand other people and complexities. You have a lot of growing up to do, Sally, my dear, and you better get started right away. And, oh yes, if you ever want to hold onto a man you'll want to shed about thirty pounds of that baby fat. You look like an overgrown marshmallow!"

He is a blur as he leaves. Talk about last words. The terrible thing is, I agree with him. It's true, black, living truth. I spend half that night thinking about how to do away with myself. Dereck was banished. My father, my sweet devoted father, stood out against my death, tennis racket in one hand, highball in the other. Only the smile I fixed on his face kept me alive. I had been destroyed. Love, as they said, was a fiction, words meant nothing: sadness, loneliness, abandonment, separation, grief — that

was what it was all about. I was too sad to cry, too hopeless to
wish for anything.

I knew even then that my father didn't have all my answers.
He was all I had, but he wasn't much.

It hit the fan the following night after dinner. "I'd like to have
a little talk with you, Sally," Sam says, turning on me the baleful
eye of authority. "Do you think you could skip the dishes tonight and spare a few minutes? Do you have homework?"

"A little."

"Well, this won't take long," he says briskly. "Boys, help your
mother with the dishes, please." They protest but do it anyway.
Sam has a way of getting things done without repeating orders.
He never washes up after meals.

"We'll use my study," he says. Irony of ironies! "That way we
won't be interrupted."

I have not noticed before how badly his shoes need reheeling
or his slacks pressing. Or his hair a good expensive trimming.
He's a model slob. As far as I am concerned, you can take this
entire person and send him in for repairs. Start with his heart.

Here I was, entering the forbidden city. The secrets of the
universe were about to be revealed and, like Dorothy, I discovered the fraud behind the curtain. It was nothing. It was just a
room with a lot of books and magazines lying around every
which way, stacked on the floor and the windowsills. The walls
are hidden behind bookshelves and the shelves hidden by books.
His desk is brown, dirty and larger than a bathtub. It too is
covered by books and papers. He sits himself down in an old-
fashioned swivel armchair, the kind Norman Rockwell paints
under a friendly old family doctor. There are more than a dozen
ashtrays lying around, all full to overflowing, and a couple of
pipes with their dead insides spilling out. It reeks of trapped
tobacco smoke and dust, pencil shavings, ink, old books, dirt with

no escape. There are a couple of pictures in the room but hung too close to the ceiling for me to see what they are.

Intimidated as I am, I am still alive enough to make a few observations. One, that there is no evidence in this room that Sam London has a life outside it, no pictures of wife and kiddies lined up like different-sized cans of soup on a shelf, no objects that could remotely be called "personal." I'm wrong, there is something. It sits next to a box of paper clips looking like a glazed dog turd. Is this the famous dog turd of philosophy I keep hearing about?

Sam sees me looking at this object. "A birthday present from Danny," he says. "He made it at school. What were you thinking?"

"Nothing," I say, blushing.

"Looks like something else, doesn't it?"

"I don't know," I say. I'm not going to get into *that*.

Now he's lighting his pipe. He looks at me over the flame — his face flickers. "Judy and I think you're seeing an awful lot of this young Jolley," he says.

I'm damned if I'm going to tell him I have no intention of seeing Dereck ever again.

"You do?"

"Yes, isn't fourteen a little young to go steady?"

"I'm not going steady."

"Do you go out with other boys?"

I won't answer.

"Sally, whatever you want to call it, don't you think you're cutting yourself off a little too soon?"

"Maybe," I say. I'm starting to perspire. I can feel the wet gathering in my armpits. Soon it's going to start trickling down my sides.

"Now, I can certainly see the appeal of this boy," Sam continues. "There is his brightness, his articulateness. And even I will admit, he's quite a good-looking young man. He's got unmistakable charm, I grant you. In a way I can't blame you."

"Blame me? What for?"

"Oh, Sally, come on. We're both talking about the same thing."

"What you really mean," I say, taking so bold a step forward that I nearly lose my balance, "is that you're mad Dereck came in here. You think I put him up to it. And you think he was going to take your stupid book!"

"No, I don't," he says, lying through his teeth. "I wasn't talking about that. Anybody can make a little mistake. And I don't want to talk about the book; I can't prove anything. Judy and I talked about this long before yesterday's incident"

If he calls it an incident he must mind it even more than I thought he did. And he *must* be lying about the book.

"You don't like Dereck," I say. "Judy doesn't either."

"That's not quite true," Sam says, leaving himself a small hole to wriggle through.

"My father would like him," I say.

"Are you sure?"

"Yes," I lie. "Daddy likes people like Dereck." Actually my father probably wouldn't like Dereck, but for other reasons. His pedigree. His religion. His side of the tracks. Furthermore, Dereck is aggressively intellectual and this quality does not go over great with Daddy.

"I think," says Sam, pausing to light his pipe again, "I think your father would find Jolley something of an arriviste."

"What's that?"

"Pushy." He laughs at a private joke I don't get. He takes his pipe out of his mouth and reams the inside of the bowl with a tiny dull knife. The noise sets my teeth on edge.

Then the most extraordinary thing happens: Sam begins a lecture, a lecture custom-tailored for me on New York style, as he calls it, and New York values. He refers to my marzipan life. He asks me if I have ever read *Madame Bovary*, which I consider an

unfair question to put to a not particularly precocious fourteen-
year-old girl who has an awful lot on her mind. Well, he says,
trying to compare New York's Upper East Side with Brookline,
Massachusetts, is like trying to compare Flaubert's Toulon with
Flaubert's Paris. He realizes, of course, that my not having read
the book makes the comparison somewhat academic, doesn't it?
By the way, sometime he would like to know a lot more about
Freddie's mother — didn't she absolutely typify her species? But
not now, this wasn't the time or the place. Getting back to what
was on his mind, it was natural that I would find the boys in my
class — that is, boys my own age — somewhat less sophisticated
than my New York friends. (God, he did seem to be hipped on
New York!) Nevertheless, don't I agree that perhaps I ought to
spread myself out a bit more, not simply concentrate on one boy,
and a boy so much older than me. He fiddles with his pipe again.
I wonder what he would do with his hands if he didn't have his
pipe to play with. Pick his nose? Clean out his ears? Make pup-
pets? They wanted me to be sure of one thing, and that is that
they do not consider Dereck to be a bad influence. It is just that
his sort of personality is hard to deal with, even for a girl as
sophisticated as I was. "I think," he says to me like the minister
who used to come to school assembly once in a while and bless us
for all the holidays or whatever, "I think that your friend Dereck
is more interested in what he wants than in what you do."

"But I don't want anything!"

"Ahah!" he cries. "But you should, don't you realize that?
Girls your age should want everything — you should want the
moon!"

"I don't want the moon," I say. I just want to go back three
spaces in time. I want my mother.

"I was exaggerating on purpose," Sam says, subsiding somewhat. It's not like him to get ruffled. "To make you see how
unequal your relationship with this boy is."

"He taught — he teaches me things," I say.

"Poetry? I'll teach you poetry, if that's what you want to learn. I didn't realize you were interested in poetry."

"I wasn't — before I met Dereck. *Now* I am."

"Oh, I see." Sam screws his eyes to the ceiling, he nearly loses the brown parts in his skull. "I told Judy," he mumbles, "that *she* should talk to you. Women are much better at this sort of thing."

I wouldn't know about that. All I know is that you're about as tactful as a starving bear.

"You must be aware that although I'm your legal guardian I have about as much control over you as the mailman does. I am legally responsible for you but I refuse to play the part of tyrant. As far as I'm concerned you could marry Tommy Manville."

"I'm not going to marry Dereck!" I cry, horrified the idea should even occur to Sam. Suddenly it all comes clear. They're far more worried that Dereck is going to knock me up than that he might be feeding me antisocial or even popish ideas. Of course that's it. The business about going into Sam's room was annoying but not a real threat. Dereck is a threat because he can make me pregnant. And I am too "unsophisticated" to resist. If they only knew how scared I was. How, like driving a car, sex is something to be deferred until I get my license, that is, until I grow up. I could no more have gone to bed with Dereck Jolley than I could get behind the wheel of the Londons' Pontiac and cruise to Provincetown.

"I never suggested you were," Sam says coldly. I'm certain that he would rather walk knee-deep in shit than meet my emotions straight on. He's that sort of man — calm and distant. He's like a large rock near the horizon, substantial enough but you're not going to get very far using him to tell your troubles to. "Who ever heard of a fourteen-year-old girl getting married? Aside from Juliet, that is."

"You never said anything about Dereck's going into your study," I say rashly. "Or taking the book."

"Do I have to?" he says. He's trying to catch my eyes now, but I'm not going to let him. I'd rather go blind.

"I guess not," I tell him. The explosion I expected, that I had readied myself for, is not coming. It's almost an anticlimax. "It wasn't my idea," I tell him.

"Then how on earth can you possibly see him again? Why, he tried to make me believe you put him up to it. What a low life! Sally, how can you possibly see that person again? He can't be trusted." His eyes hit THE book. He picks it up, turns it over, puts it down. I know what he's thinking.

"I'm not," I say, exulting in the last word. "If you'd given me the chance I would have told you I wasn't going to see him anymore."

"I'll be damned," Sam says, almost, but not quite, managing to smile.

"I have to go now," I tell him. "I've got to study for a history quiz." And with that I simply get up and leave his smelly old room. I wouldn't come back in here if T. S. Eliot himself issued me an invitation.

When I saw Dereck at school he pretended not to see me. I looked for pity from Annie and Peggy and found only that they were terribly relieved that I'd stopped seeing him. They called him a monster. They were less than no help. I kept dreaming about him. In my dreams he would meet my mother and they would go off together, leaving me at the door to our New York house with tears streaming down my face. They would turn and wave as if waving to a small child who is left behind to eat supper and go to bed. I had this dream over and over again. My mother's hand would be hooked into Dereck's arm. Dereck was alarmingly handsome and dressed like a banker. I would wake up weeping.

And yet, when I woke up, I would put my mother back on her

throne, manipulating her like a doll with flexible arms and legs and an inflexible smile.

One morning I was scolded for forgetting to put Roger and Danny and Joey to bed on time. They had paid me a dollar to be the sitter. What a laugh. They paid me! But I couldn't bear it when I did something wrong.

There had been a fight, a horrible thing between Joey and Roger. Roger had thrown something at Joey and cut his head. It was only a scrape but Joey made a revolting fuss and cried for almost an hour. Instead of sorting things out, I retreated to my room and shut the door. I couldn't handle it.

The next morning at breakfast Judy sighs and says, "Oh, Sally, what *hap*pened?"

"Who told you?" I am alarmed.

"Does it matter?" Judy says. All eyes — except Sam's — are on me.

"I thought you didn't listen to tattlers," I say.

"I don't usually," Judy says. "But this is different. I left you in charge."

"I didn't ask to be in charge," I tell her. I don't know what's happening to me: I could strangle her without a second's hesitation. "I'm frightfully sorry. I won't do it again." At the change in my tone of voice, Sam looks up briefly from his paper.

I see Roger smirking. "Rat!" I tell him fiercely. I'll take care of him too. All my enemies.

"You stink," he says to me. My own brother. My own half brother.

"Jesus Christ!" I cry, jumping up from the table and throwing my napkin down as hard as I can. "Nobody can make a little mistake in this stupid house! I hate it here. I hate you all. You can all go jump in the lake. I hope you drown." Sam looks up slowly from his paper again and arches his eyebrows. He gives me a look which says I've called the wrong thing stupid.

This soul-withering, spirit-killing, bug-squashing look of Sam's sends me hurtling out of the room and upstairs. Inside my bed-room I throw myself on the bed and try to commit suicide by smothering myself with the pillow.

I am cut short in this experiment by a knock on my door. "Sally!"

It's Judy. She knocks and calls again. I don't answer. "Sally," she cries. "Please open the door. I want to talk to you."

"I don't want to talk to you," I say, gasping for air, which feels pretty good. "I have to write my father a letter."

"Sally, what happened? Did something awful happen last night? I'm sorry I got angry. I shouldn't have asked you to do so much by yourself."

"Go away. I have to write to Daddy."

"Look, my pet, you can't scream bloody hell at everybody and then cut out. I want to know what's the matter. You really ought to explain things to me," she wheedles. "I'm your friend."

That's a laugh. She's my guardian. She's stuck with me.

"Please, Sally, I want to help you." The voice has turned a little. It must be hard for her to plead with me. Well, maybe I'll let her in. Just for a minute.

I pull myself off the bed and open the door. Instead of Judy I see the solid red face of Fräulein Kastern staring at me. I gasp and put my hand across my mouth.

"Have I got egg on my face?"

"No, it's nothing," I say. "I didn't mean anything . . ." The features of Fräulein are starting to melt back into Judy. I think I must be going crazy. "I don't feel good," I say.

"You look awful," Judy says, nodding. "Look, it's getting late. I've got to get the kids off to school. Why don't you lie down again, and as soon as they've left I'll come back up and we can talk. I'm sorry you don't feel well."

An unexpected holiday from school. I'm missing my favorite class, modern dance, but it's worth it.

Fifteen minutes later Judy comes bouncing back. But the more she comes at me, the more I retreat. It's just the way I am — I can't help it. If she would let me move first, it would be better. I wonder how much Sam told her about his talk with me: word for word, knowing *them*.

"Sam says you're not going to see Dereck Jolley anymore," she says, picking a piece of fluff off her skirt and examining it like a detective.

"He does?"

"Yes. How come?"

"Oh, I guess we don't really see things the same way. That's important, isn't it?"

"Yes," Judy says. I have the feeling she's waiting for me to spill some beans. But I don't have any to spill.

"He's always reading poetry to me out loud. I mean, I like it all right, but I like other things too. He thinks Stan Kenton is a creep. That's just too much, don't you agree?"

"Oh, yes," she says.

"Also, he makes me feel stupid, even stupider than I am."

"You're not stupid," Judy tells me. "I can think of lots of dumber people."

"Like who?"

"Well — me sometimes." Now I know she's faking me. She didn't have to say that. "Like when I don't get the messages you send me. It's not an I.Q. kind of stupid. It's being dense about other people. It's not seeing what's right in front of your eyes."

"Oh."

"Anyway, pet, I'm very pleased you're not seeing Jolley — what a curious name. It makes me think of "The House at Jolly Corner"— which wasn't very jolly either, for that matter. You're much too nice a girl to be pushed around by a boy like him. Yes, I'm very pleased. Even if I don't understand quite why. Bravo!"

When the school literary magazine, *The Raven*, came out later that month, it contained a story called "Flirting with Life" by

Dereck Jolley. I started reading the story without premonition, although I must admit with mixed feelings. (I wanted it to be bad because I couldn't bear the idea of it's being good, but I was proud because he had been my friend.) As I read, all unknowing, my blood ran cold. The story was so nakedly about me that no one could ever doubt it. I was all there, down to the last deposit of hip fat.

Specifically, it was about this girl who lived in New York with German-Jewish parents who were so rich they owned a Degas dancer, a Calder mobile, and a house in Maine for summer vacations. This girl — Susan, AKA Suky — was a perfect little snob, the sort of girl no one but a mother could love and sometimes not even her. She tortured her little brother Robbie and called the maid "worm" behind her mother's back. Before she shaved her armpits she lathered them with scented soap from England which she filched from her mother's bathroom. She ate the family's supply of gourmet goodies on the sly.

This Suky sounds like a caricature, but somehow she wasn't. Dereck had managed to breathe life into her, to make her real, pitiable and revolting. Dereck put himself in the story disguised as a kind of Hemingway adolescent: independent, courageous, wise, and horny. Suky was "plump and juicy as a peach from a Navarre orchard," as "blank-eyed and unquestioningly confident as a day-old sparrow." She was a bubblehead who asked everyone how much things cost and who Himmler was and who did not know the difference between "verse" and "stanza." I was seized with shame and horror. Everything he wrote about me was partially true. I felt as if I were a French collaborator dragged through the streets naked and with my head shaved. I took the magazine and tried to rip it through. It tore only partway. I hurled it across the room. It struck the side of the wastebasket and flapped open on the floor. I was wild. I could never go back to school. I could destroy my copy of *The Raven*, but every last student at school would read it and laugh.

Oh God, what am I going to do?

I sat down and wrote Daddy a long letter, sweet and sad, filled with longing, reporting my misery but not its cause.

Judy waved a copy of *The Raven* in front of my face. I turned white. "Have you by any chance read this?" she says guardedly.

I nod.

"Well," she says, the know-it-all. "I can't say I'm all that surprised." Is she *ever* surprised? "Although I must say I thought he was mostly gab and not much output."

"I told you he wrote," I said weakly.

"No, dear, you told me he threatened to be a writer. There's one hell of a difference." I think she's going to pause here, but she goes rushing on like a flood. "Now, this story of his, it's really not half bad, though it sounds like about ten other writers. One more echo and he'd be completely lost in it himself. I suppose it's okay for a beginning writer to sound like other people. What I really object to is using *you* that way. It's not fair at all. If I were you I'd be terribly angry."

"How could he do it to me?" I say.

"Well, sweetie pie, you might say you were asking for it. Remember when you came to me so proudly and told me this person collected lives. Ugh! It was so pretentious I didn't credit him with honesty. He meant it, he really *meant* it. What a creep! It's just too bad that he had to do it to you. You've had your share of trouble this year, haven't you?"

Now, there's a sentiment I can sink my teeth into. "I didn't ask for it," I cry. Nor did I ask for all my other "troubles." My defenses evaporate; I am the ultimate victim, the person things happen to — bad things. Passively I slide through life while people and events pummel me.

"This Dereck Jolley," Judy says, not bothering to contradict me, "is a bad egg — smooth on the outside, rotten to the core, if you'll forgive the mixed metaphor. You can tell by the way he looks at you, eyes up, chin down, like a flirt. He's so smarty-pants in his assumptions. He's much too cynical for his age — he ought to be eager instead of waiting to put everybody down. All the time he was hanging around you I had the strangest feeling he had his eye on something I couldn't see and that he thought he had superior wisdom. He even patronized Sam!"

"No!" I must be getting my sense of humor back.

Judy smiles wanly. "Oh yes," she says. "And if there's one thing that drives Sam crazy it's being patronized."

"I didn't know that," I say.

Judy continues. "I have a lot of friends who do things like paint and write and so on, and some of them are weird, but next to Jolley they're straight out of the executive training program at International Business Machines. Dereck is really gone. He always acted as if he were trying to steal something."

"Dereck *never* took anything! I swear."

"Well, that's a moot question, isn't it?" Judy says. "But in any case I meant that metaphorically, as if he were after Sam's brain or my blood or your past or whatever it is that took his fancy. He's a bloodsucker. He's like an actor who's a neb until he gets up on the stage and then steals a personality that belongs to someone else. Does this make any sense at all, Sally?"

"I don't know," I tell her. Maybe it's partly true, but she's missed something about Dereck that I sure didn't miss: his absolutely staggering sex appeal. Which makes everything else irrelevant. Do you worry about little things when you've got the A-bomb? Judy probably doesn't recognize sex appeal when it pats her on the ass. After all, she goes to bed with that grouch Sam London. Sam has little hairs growing out of his nose.

"He also went into Sam's study. And walked out with a copy of *Pomes Pennyeach*."

"I know," I say. "But he wasn't going to steal it."

Judy won't argue. "Sam was fee-urious. He hit the ceiling. He was ready to call the cops."

"My God," I say.

"Well, he wouldn't do that, would he? But I've never seen him so angry. I persuaded him not to take his anger out on you," she says.

"Thank you."

"There was some question about whose idea it was to go in there in the first place," Judy says.

"It was his idea," I tell her. "I swear it. He made me do it, and then he blamed me."

She seems to accept this without demanding proof. "Your friend really takes the cake," she says. "The thing to learn is how to spot the Jolleys and then avoid them like the plague. The awful thing is, the Jolleys are generally devastatingly attractive. It's as if God were punishing them for having overendowed them in the first place. I don't understand it myself, really, but will you believe me when I tell you I was once just like you?"

"No," I tell her. "I don't think so."

"I guess I don't blame you. But I wish I could tell you there was a quick and painless way to spot the Jolleys. I mean, wouldn't it be nice if they glowed in the dark or something, like decay under infrared lights? Or if they emitted high-frequency signals? But they don't. It's just a feeling you get after a while. Experience maybe. In the meantime, there's no harm in asking your friends what they think, is there?"

"I guess not." When she says "friends," does she mean people like Annie and Peggy or does she mean herself? What does it matter — because, as I cry, "I can't go back to school! I can't ever go back there. They'll all have read the story. I'm never going back. I'll have to find another school."

"Of course you can go back," Judy says. "You have to act as if nothing's happened. Or as if you're proud to be the main character in a published story. If you act like you're hurt, they'll make fun of you."

"That's not true," I say. "They *will* make fun of me. I would if it was somebody else. How can they help it?"

"You poor baby," Judy says, her eyes softening.

"I'm not a poor baby," I tell her. "It's just that he did such an awful thing. How could he do that to me? I'm not so bad as the girl in the story, am I?"

"Of course not, Sally. That's a caricature, not a real person. That's the girl he made by distorting you beyond recognition. That girl doesn't have a single good quality. All his male characters are appealing, all his female characters are rotten. I guarantee, if he ever writes another story, it will star the same stupid, vapid, and unattractive girls and the same brilliantly clever and attractive men."

"Oh, I don't care about that. I just know I can't go back to school, and I was just beginning to get used to it," I say without thinking. But, my God, it's true. I hadn't realized it, but it's true.

It's then that Judy, whom I have never kissed and have only touched by accident, rushes at me, a longlost sister, and takes me in her embrace. Temporarily we are glued together, her body softer and more meandering than my mother's, whose fleshless hipbones were like sharp weapons. Judy's body gives, answers. I feel passion rise in me and threaten to burst out. It is like heat and like motion but it is neither one. It makes me feel like crying or passing out. It has to do with the way I feel about this woman, something I did not suspect but which dawns on me as a revelation. Like the boys' battle, it is too much for me to handle. I have two choices. I take the easier and disengage, swallowing hard. "I don't think I can go back there," I say weakly. "But I'll think about it."

"Yes do," she says. "It's what you owe yourself."

17

Willy with
a Taste for Gore

ONE DAY not long after I decided to go back to school, stick it out, and face my humiliation like a man, I got a letter from my father. He told me he would be coming to Boston soon for a checkup. "I will be staying at the Lahey Clinic for a night or two. I would consider it an honor if you would join me for lunch the day they release me. Please do not be alarmed about my health, princess. I'm coming to Boston because that's where my sawbones, Dr. Foster, has decided to set up practice. It's somewhat inconvenient, but there's a silver lining."

"Is he sick?" Judy asked when I told her the news.

I explained about the doctor's moving. "Sooner or later all the good guys come to Boston," she nodded, smiling. "Hey, do you think he'd like to come out here and have dinner with us?"

I don't want him to set foot in the Londons' house. Disaster. He will look down his Episcopalian nose at everything. How am I going to keep him away?

"I don't know," I say. "He probably won't be able to."

"Why not? I think I'll write him a note. I'd like to get to know your father better. After all, the only time I saw him was at the funeral, and that's not exactly a propitious way to start a friendship." Does she think they can be friends?

Letters are exchanged. Daddy says he will be delighted to come for dinner. My heart grows heavy. I lose a couple of pounds, which is the one good thing about waiting for Daddy to show up. I've bitten my nails down so far my fingertips are bleeding.

"I want to make this a special dinner. What does your father like?" Judy says.

"I don't understand."

"What food does he like? Lobster?"

"I guess so."

"Great, we'll get some lobsters and one of Grossman's cherry cheesecakes. Asparagus. I can't wait," she says, her eyes happy. I ought to tell her that he doesn't care for food nearly so much as he cares for drink. I don't tell her how many times Daddy has left steak and strawberries sitting on the plate.

"He likes anything," I say.

"Well, we won't give him anything — we'll really lay it on."

"Oh," I say. "Please don't go to any trouble." The fact is that whatever Judy does, Daddy is going to see kikes. Kike kids, kike furniture, kike food (he won't even know that Orthodox Jews wouldn't touch lobster with a ten-foot pole). He'll sense kike values. He'll see kike the way some white people see nigger. If the Londons only weren't so Jewish . . . No, that wouldn't make the slightest bit of difference: he'd see kike anyway. My mother said that when he got mad Daddy would call her a kike. But I don't believe that. My darling daddy wouldn't do that.

As the day draws closer, I begin to feel as if I were going into the hospital for a horrible operation. Judy, on the other hand, is positively glowing with anticipation. She acts as if she's never served anyone dinner before. Out come the company tablecloth, silverware, plates. Things emerge from hiding that I've never seen before. She's acting like my mother, except that Mummy had someone to do the polishing for her.

I stand at the living room window waiting for my father's cab not to come. Behind me, in another part of the house, the London family is doing things. I can hear Sam's typewriter clicking away like a machine gun in his office. I have kept my past and present successfully apart so far. They mustn't come together.

There it is!

A yellow taxi swoops to a classy halt by the curb. Time stops dead. My dead eyes watch as the door opens slowly and a gray flannel leg pokes out, followed by the rest. There he is, loose-limbed, crew-cut, wearing an elegant blue-gray sport jacket and cordovan shoes. In one hand is a paper cone from the florist's and in the other a compact pigskin overnight bag. Daddy squints at the house, sizing it up. My father's no brain, but he's very good at sizing things up: he can make a quick evaluation of the house, the grounds, the neighborhood. Now he's looking straight at me but he cannot see me — the light hits the window, making me invisible. He executes a tiny gesture of impatience — where is Sally? — and starts to walk toward the house. My father is not the sort of man to question whether he's at the right house or not: he assumes he is. His coming toward me breaks the spell. I rush from the room and out through the front door. I don't stop short of my father but crash into him. I press my face against his murderous jacket (it's Harris tweed, there are little twigs embedded in it). Daddy pats my back as if he were burping a baby and says affectionate things into my ear. Darling girl, little bunny rabbit, my sweet girl, princess, I've missed you, and oh Sally, for good measure. Then he pushes me away and says the inevitable. "Let me have a look at you."

"You've grown up, Sally," he says in the bittersweet voice of a sentimental parent. "You're a young woman, not a little girl." This is all very silly, because he's seen me so recently.

"I haven't been a little girl since last year," I say.

"Well, well."

Daddy smells the same as ever: Scotch, tobacco, something expensive he pats on his cheeks after shaving. If there's sickness in him, it doesn't show on his skin or in his eyes. He's the picture of middle-aged health except that his black string tie and gray flannels, his athletic posture, make him seem far younger than he is.

"Come on inside, Daddy," I say, anxious to get it over with, tugging at his sleeve. He does something subtle to rearrange his body, to get ready to meet strangers. Not even Daddy looks forward to meeting strangers, in spite of the fact that he swims through life with the confidence of a man-eating shark.

"Right," he says. "I've been looking forward to meeting your guardians again." Maybe he expects them to be tiny, like Orientals. "Here, you take these," he says, handing me the flowers, freeing his hand to take mine the way he did when I was very small and he'd show up for his Sunday visit and take me to Central Park, where we would watch the bears roll on their backs and the baboons swaying their red asses at us. Sometimes he would be battling a hangover — his eyes runny, and his feet dragging like the victim of a stroke.

I ask him about his checkup. "The medics gave me a clean bill of health. Knew they would. There's nothing wrong with me — I'm strong as a horse. It was Lorna who insisted I go through the damn thing. I did it for her peace of mind. You can't have a woman worrying around you all the time." This brings us to the front door. "By the way, the apartment's almost done. Lorna's done a crackerjack job — you won't even recognize the old place."

We cross the threshold. "Well, now, I call this roomy," Daddy says. "Nice old place. Never could stand those cramped quarters your mother found so attractive. A fellow couldn't even swing a tennis racket in that house of hers without hitting the wall." Daddy's peering around. He's taking in the shabby entrance rug that some people wipe their feet on, the boots in the outer hall scattered around like small dead animals, the papers piled on the front hall table. (Whose papers are they? Everybody in the house denies ownership, yet there are always more papers to replace the ones Judy regularly throws away.) There's a cookie on the table with a bite taken out of it, a copy of *The New Republic*, a vase with nothing in it. I'm mortified. I thought Judy was going to straighten the house. Daddy's eyes shoot up the stairwell to the floral stained-glass window at the landing. The light coming through this window throws a mortuary pall over the entire hallway. "Was this place once a funeral parlor?" he whispers.

"Daddy!" I begin to giggle uncontrollably. It strikes me as the funniest thing I've ever heard in my whole life. My father is pleased with the unexpected success of his joke. He smiles like a kid. At last we are in concert — we have joined together on one side against the others. I love him for being so wonderfully silly.

At this moment Judy floats down the stairs like Tallulah Bankhead making the entrance everyone has been waiting an hour for.

"You must be Sally's father," she says in a strange voice. "I'm so glad you've come." I can hardly believe my ears. Is this the grubby, recalcitrant Judy who makes fun of everybody else's affectations? I gape. She stretches out her arm as if she expected her hand to be kissed. Judy is wearing a Pretty Dress, a silk print with flowers on a navy background, a dress that even my mother wouldn't have been ashamed to be seen in, although she wouldn't have worn it anywhere but to the dentist. Her hair is freshly laundered, and she's wearing lipstick, for once.

To Daddy, of course, Judy looks normal.

He's playing a part, she's playing a part. I'm the only one who isn't playing a part, although I have the feeling I've been thrust onto the stage and into the middle of the action. But they forgot to give me my lines.

"My husband will join us in a little while," Judy says, glancing at the closed door. The typewriter is silent — maybe he's fallen asleep. We go into the living room. "Will you have something to drink, Mr. Sanderson — Scotch, a martini?"

"A little Scotch and a splash of water will do splendidly — what a charming house you have here," Daddy says all in one breath.

"Thanks," Judy responds. "We like it. We've just moved. It's more space than we're used to but I'm sure we'll start spreading out."

Daddy is slavering for a drink. I'm sure they haven't exactly thrown a cocktail party for him at the Lahey Clinic. He must be going through ten kinds of hell.

"Sally," says Judy. "Will you entertain your father while I fix his drink? I'm sure you two have lots to talk about."

"Attractive woman," Daddy murmurs after she leaves.

"You really think so, Daddy?" I'm pleased. Maybe things will be all right. Maybe they won't hate each other.

"Damn right," he says. He seems surprised. Did he imagine Judy would be dressed in black with a babushka over her head and lots of hair on her face? "What's this?" he says picking up the piece of sculpture Dereck admired. He turns it over and over as if it were a take-apart puzzle.

"It's a head. One of the Londons' friends made it. Do you like it?"

"It must be a joke, princess," he tells me.

"No, it isn't. It's real."

"I wonder how much this reality is worth," he says.

"I don't know." I hope no one has overheard him.

"Frankly," he says, putting it down and looking at his hand, "I don't know a soul aside from your poor mother who's taken in by this sort of nonsense."

"Oh."

Judy comes back with a drink for Daddy, which I am sure is too pale, and one for herself. "Sally, dear, would you mind getting the plate of cheese and crackers I left in the kitchen?" Oh my God, they're going to be alone together. He's going to say something awful about the head. "Sure," I tell her. There's no way to avoid the errand. In the kitchen on the counter is a Jewish-type feast: cheese and crackers, chopped liver and black bread, nuts, carrot strips, herring spread. Daddy doesn't want to eat all this junk — he'll just look at it, then forget it. He'll think it's disgusting. Everything he wants comes inside a glass.

I pile the food on a tray and carry it into the living room. Judy beams. "Just put it down on the coffee table, please, Sally," she says, waiting for him to acknowledge her offering.

"Hmm," he says, picking up a carrot strip and nibbling at it. He sits back on the couch, drapes one knee over its partner, his foot hanging loose. His shoes gleam like the part of the saddle you sit on.

The one thing I'm most afraid of now is that they will talk about me, my future. Since my own mind drifts slowly from one safe port to another only to find it unacceptable for one reason or another, the mooring unsafe or the people unfriendly, I don't want either Judy or Daddy to think they "have" me. They don't have me, no one has me. The closest thing I have to a home is memory.

Trapped between Daddy and Judy, I hope for the best. If I can hope for the best, isn't that something to be pleased about?

"I think I hear Sam now," Judy says. Sam's study door has just shut with a polite slam; now he's walking across the hall and coming in here; no, he's running up the stairs. I'll bet he has to pee. Judy says, "I guess he'll be down in a minute." Nothing fazes my father. I notice that his drink has diminished to three tiny ice pebbles. He's looking at it as if it had betrayed him.

"Excuse me," Sam says, joining us at last. "I was tied up on a long distance call. *Mister* Sanderson, how do you do?" He's acting funny. One thing I've learned around this house is that Jews act differently with non-Jews than with other Jews. I know this is true, but you could never prove it to a non-Jew unless you made secret movies and showed him that way. Not that he'd care all that much. It's hard to describe what happens: a subtle shifting and gentle braking, a slight readjustment in style, a change of emphasis, putting your guard on notice. All this sounds abstract, but there it is and it's the best I can do. You always think they're ready to fight or shove and you're prepared for it. Like a weather forecast that predicts a tornado either may or may not hit your area. What would anybody in his right mind do?

The other side of this is that non-Jews don't act different around Jews. They're just happy if they can ignore them and not have to worry about their problems. Not "their." "Our." Me too, I'm one of us. Slowly I'm being dragged onto Sam's side. And I don't even like him.

"Would you like another drink?" Sam asks Daddy. What do you think my father says? My mother would have been horrified to hear how the offer was made. Her lesson to me: no matter how many drinks or how many servings a person has had, you never never use the word "another." If the person is falling-down drunk, you must still ask him if he would like "a drink." Okay, Mom, yours sounds better, but Sam's is more honest.

While Sam is out of the room getting Daddy's booze, Judy says she's sure Daddy would like to see Roger. Somehow she's got it in her head that Roger is important to my father. Roger is about as important to him as the London kids. If you'd ask him now, I'll bet he has trouble recognizing the name. But once Judy is wound up, there's no stopping her.

"Sally, do you think you could find your little brother and ask him to come down for a minute?" Another errand. She's really bossing me around this afternoon. "Sure," I say again.

"Come down," I snap at Roger.

"What do you want? Take your hands off me."

"We want you to meet my father. He's here for dinner."
Roger is cramming his head with Batman. He exists on comic
books and peanut butter.

"I'll meet him later," Roger says. "I don't want to meet him.
Why should I? He's not my father." Poor Roger.

"Judy wants you to. Come on."

"Piss pot." Roger sums up the idea.

"Please Roger, stop making such a fuss."

"Did he bring me anything?" Roger says.

"I don't know," I say, lying. I do know. He didn't.

The hope that he did is a sufficient lure. Roger is willing. But
when he enters there is an awful moment when it becomes clear
they've never laid eyes on one another and each couldn't care
less. Daddy does something odd. He gets up and walks over to
Roger and shakes hands with him. Roger is bemused.

"You look just like your mother, young man," Daddy says
solemnly.

"My mother's dead. I can't look like her."

"I mean," Daddy says, taking it in stride, "you look the way
she used to."

"Roger," Judy says, interrupting this morbid exchange. "Will
you do me a favor? You know where I keep the nuts for company, in that cabinet by the door, the one high up? You'll have to
drag a chair and stand on it to reach. Would you go out and
empty the jar of cashews into a little bowl? That's a good boy."
Her face is all grim, set lines. Her friendly feelings about my
father have apparently altered.

"I don't know where you mean," Roger says. He hates to do
anything for anybody except himself. He's still got his eye on my
father as if he wanted to prolong the conversation Judy is so

eager to stop. "You got plenty of stuff here," my brother says. "What do you want more stuff to eat for?"

"Come on," Judy says, jumping up. "I'll go with you — we'll find it together." She drags Roger from the room. Sam looks as if he hasn't heard a word that's been said. The coward.

"He's certainly an outspoken child," Daddy says, resuming his relaxed position on the couch.

Sam says, "Roger's been through one hell of an experience. It's been rough on him. He's beginning to come out of it a little. And we've got him in therapy. It seems to be helping, though of course there's no way of telling how he would have done on his own."

"You mean," says Daddy, aroused, "you've got that little boy going to a what's-its-name — a psychoanalyst? You must be joking."

"Not at all," Sam says matter-of-factly. "Once a week he goes off to see nice young Dr. Gabriel Mintz and play with his toys."

"Why that's absolutely astounding," my father tells us. "I don't think I've ever heard of anyone as young as that boy going to see a — what's the slang expression? — a head-shrinker. He looks perfectly all right to me. Of course, I only caught a quick glimpse, but he seemed a sturdy young thing. He's got good eyes."

"He's perfectly normal," Sam says in a monotone. "It's what happened to him that's abnormal. He's had quite a lot of trouble here. As a matter of fact, he can't seem to get along, my kids are afraid of him. Think he misses his parents . . ."

"Can't say I blame the child," Daddy says. "Still, a head-shrinker for a seven-year-old. Boggles the mind. Quite frankly, I can't go along with that infant sexuality business. Maybe I'm old-fashioned." Whenever anyone makes this disclaimer it means to me they think they're right up front. "But it seems pretty radical stuff to me."

"I don't think they get into sex very much," Sam says. I can tell he's masking a smile. "They do what's called play therapy."

"What on earth is that?" Daddy asks.

"Oh, I'm not quite sure. The kid plays with dolls — miniature adults — acts out his fantasies, works them through, something like that. It seems to produce the desired results."

"A little boy playing with dolls?" Daddy says. "He'll turn queer, don't you think?"

"Probably not — that's not the way it works." I think I can see Sam's sense of decency holding him in check. Thank God. Otherwise Daddy would undoubtedly be horrified. This cocktail hour or whatever you want to call it is running downhill fast, too fast for me. Everything is getting skewed: Judy out of the room, Sam and Daddy fencing but Daddy too fuzzy to hold the foil straight and Sam too devious to parry openly. They're talking around me as if I wasn't even there. Sam notices that my father's glass is empty again. Again an offer is made and again accepted. Sam gets up to make the trip to the pantry and grabs a chopped chicken liver thing on the way out. It's the only one eaten so far.

"He's a left-winger, isn't he?" Daddy says almost before he can be certain Sam is out of earshot. His eye touches a copy of *The New Republic* lying on the couch, then veers away. "I believe London's name was mentioned briefly during one of those House Un-American sessions. You knew that, didn't you?" Boy, Daddy can really shift gears. Does he actually expect me to know things like that? "Frankly," he goes on, looking toward the door, "I don't believe in witchhunts or guilt by association, it always seemed to me much too hasty. Still, you have to admit that sometimes the evidence makes it awfully hard to avoid conclusions. Oh, well." He lapses back into blandness.

"Do you mean they're spies for the Russians?"

"Good God, no. I didn't mean anything of the sort. I wouldn't have considered letting you live with them if I had the slightest kind of suspicion like that. No, they're probably what you'd call 'sympathizers.' I really don't understand how people brought up in America can allow themselves this kind of attitude. The strangest part about it is that this is the only country in the world where that sort of thing is tolerated."

I can't think of Sam or Judy as disloyal. It's a shocking idea.

"They're pretty nice to me," I tell my father. I don't want him to talk about them, and especially not about their being "sympathizers." "Judy's been teaching me how to cook and things like that."

"A useful art." Daddy nods. "Particularly when there's no domestic help. By the way, princess, I wouldn't mention what I've been talking to you about, not to them or to anyone else. These things have a way of getting blown up out of all proportion. Obviously, if they haven't said anything to you about it, they'd rather keep it quiet. Can't say I blame them."

Sam comes back. He's chewing on something. Judy is close on his heels. She apologizes to my father and explains that she's just served her kids and Roger their dinner in the kitchen. I wonder why she hasn't trotted out her boys for exhibition yet. It's not like her to keep them under wraps.

Daddy directs the conversation. Now, it seems, he wants to know all about school. It's a question-and-answer session between me and him with Judy trying to look alert and Sam drooping. He stares moodily into his drink, crosses and recrosses his legs. He's as interested in the curriculum at Brookline High as he is in the contents of my gym locker. Daddy asks if there is a tennis team. He acts surprised when I tell him yes.

"And I suppose the boys are knocking down the front door?"

"Not exactly, Daddy," I say, glancing at Sam.

"Well, I'm certainly not about to believe that!" my father says. His voice is muddy. Again, his drink is almost gone. I can't believe it. I have never known my father to refuse a drink, not even on the way to passing out. The Londons *must* be aware of his "little problem." What I pray is that they don't conclude this happens every night.

"You're probably getting hungry," Judy says. "Dinner will be ready in a minute."

"That's all right," Daddy says. He's looking at his glass again. I could die — he's so obvious. But Sam doesn't ask him if he wants another. Thank you, Sam.

Judy excuses herself to carry out last-minute preparations and asks Sam to light the candles. Once more Daddy and I are alone together.

"There's a hell of a lot of getting up and sitting down in this house," he observes. "I don't suppose London plays any tennis?"

"No, Daddy. I wrote you. Remember? He doesn't even own a tennis racket. The only thing they do is swim in the summer. They rent a place on Cape Cod. They say it's so primitive, there isn't even a doctor."

"I can imagine," Daddy says. "Swimming. How about sailing?"

"No, Daddy. They don't hunt grouse either. They mostly read." I'm so furious at my father for being tipsy that I don't even care how I sound.

"Pity," he says.

"*Why* is it a pity?" I say, almost in tears.

"Dinner's ready," Judy says, startling me. Her face is shiny from the kitchen heat. She's as happy as a young bride. Daddy gets up and tightropes a path from couch to dining room chair. The table looks as if the editors of *Good Housekeeping* had marched in during the afternoon and set it. Lace tablecloth, silver candlesticks with long white candles, daisies and jonquils in a

shallow bowl, yellow linen napkins folded ingeniously like a fan,
little dishes of nuts.

Daddy acknowledges Judy's labor by blinking rapidly and asking her with his eyes where he should sit.

"Please sit here by me, Mr. Sanderson," Judy says.

"Call me Willy, dear. Everyone calls me Willy, even my barber."

In a pig's eye his barber calls him Willy. If his barber calls him
anything, it's Sir.

Judy serves the first course, cream of mushroom soup made, as
she says, "from scratch." Anything made from scratch makes me
think of mosquito bites and scabs. I'd rather not think about it.
Still, the soup is marvelous, very rich and with a touch of sherry.
Daddy takes two spoonfuls and that's it. Sam slurps. I'm sure
Daddy is revolted, but Daddy doesn't notice: he wants to talk
about the war. He says, "I probably shouldn't admit this, but I'm
among friends, so I feel you'll understand. During the war I felt
more alive than at any other time in my life. Now isn't that
something?"

Judy's mouth drops open. She tries to catch Sam's eye, but Sam
won't play.

"Yes," she says. "That's really something."

My father asks Sam what he did in the war. Sam says he was a
foot soldier. My father looks disappointed. Later I found out that
Sam had been one of two surviving soldiers out of an entire
company and that this event had sent him around the bend for
several months. This he didn't tell Daddy. Sam hated talking
about the war. Once, still later, Judy told me that Sam had considered a CO status but had been dissuaded by a girl he had been
in love with. An icky story.

At the last minute Judy had decided that lamb would be better
than lobster. "Some people don't like that fishy smell on their
fingers." She cooked the lamb with a lot of garlic and was terri-

bly impressed with how rare it was. I didn't tell her I thought it was well done compared to the way my mother cooked it — it would only have hurt her feelings.

"The beef is excellent," Daddy says, poking it with his fork.

"Thank you," Judy says.

"It's lamb, Daddy," I tell him fiercely.

"That's what I said," he answers. I've been watching him carefully. He's only had three bites since the meal started. I feel sorry for Judy, who has been watching him too. Women do that, they watch people eat the food they've cooked. The only time they ever relax is when they're in somebody else's house or at a restaurant. Judy must feel awful.

Daddy is off and running every which way, there's no following his train of thought, but then nobody seems to be trying very hard. "Did you people know that this child's mother was a great beauty, a famous beauty?"

"I knew Fippy," Sam reminds him. "She was a remarkably lovely woman."

"Though if you'd ask me," Daddy bulldozes into Sam, "there was something about the woman which said her shoes were too tight, pinching her toes, eh? Not so with Sally — now, there's a sweet open look to her face, nothing tight about our Sally. She doesn't have the striking beauty of her old lady, but she has something better: love, softness, an inner glow."

"Daddy, please!"

"No 'Daddy please,' " he says, pretending to be hurt. "It's true. But your eyes are sad, girl. You've got a sad pair of eyes in your head." He goes on. "Now, I do think that sometimes it can be distracting for boys and girls to go to school together. Of course, nobody asked me, did they?" he adds with a rare flash of humor. Sam pours red wine into his glass. If I didn't know better I'd say that Sam was trying to get him even more oiled. "I know education isn't exactly my racket. Oh, that's a pun, isn't it? Racket.

Anyway, I'm no expert — you people must know far more about it than I do. Still, we're all educated men here and entitled to an opinion. Eh?"

"Precisely," Sam says. I'm beginning to think that Sam may be taking a perverse pleasure in getting Daddy to perform. Judy is dulled. Her glitter has definitely worn off.

"But about that school of yours, there's no better system in the whole goddamn country. I know, I checked with George Adams at the bank. He was reassuring. Brookline, he said, absolutely top drawer, sends half the class to Harvard and scatters the rest through the Ivy League and Seven Sisters."

Neither Sam, Judy, nor I want to disabuse my father. Let him believe it if it makes him happy.

Meanwhile, my father makes a pass at a lettuce leaf, misses it, stabs the plate. Oil splatters up and smears the side of his hand. He doesn't notice. Judy clears, brings in dessert. It is a molded apricot mousse. My mouth begins to water just looking at it. Daddy takes a token spoonful, twists his mouth around the unexpected sweetness, puts his spoon down, and leaves the rest on his plate. To make up for his lack of interest, I have two helpings.

"Coffee?" Judy says, maintaining to the end that this is a normal dinner and my father a normal guest. "I'll bring the coffee into the living room."

"Splendid dinner," Daddy murmurs, stumbling to his feet. The wine has turned his cheeks a feverish pink.

As we turn to leave the dining room, the London boys appear in the hall. They stare openly at this strange man who has taken their mother's arm and seems to be listing somewhat. "I thought I told you guys to get into your pajamas," Judy says. "This is Sally's father."

Sally's father sticks his hand out to be shaken but Danny and Joey stand limp, uncomprehending. "Shake hands," Sam growls.

"What's your name?" Joey says.

"Willy, just call me Willy," Daddy tells him. "Everyone does, even my barber."

" 'Willy with a taste for gore, nailed his sister to the door,' " Joey chants. My father's eyes widen.

Judy giggles. "He memorizes everything he reads," she explains. "Time for bed. Now you go up and when you're all ready I'll come and read you a story. Where's Roger?"

"In his room, reading comics."

The two kids run off toward the kitchen. " 'Mother cried with humor quaint, Willy dear, you'll scratch the paint,' " comes floating back. Judy laughs once more.

"I guess you could say reticence is not their strong suit," she says.

"You can say that again," Sam adds. My father, who is too foggy to perceive more than a fraction of what is going on around him, says, "Where's the loo?"

"It's under the staircase, first door on your right. Look out for the step," Judy says.

Miraculously, there's no crash as he closes the door after him. "First time I ever heard the word 'loo' actually spoken," she says to Sam.

"Then how did you know what he meant?" Sam asks.

"Used the old bean," she answers. "Besides, I've read Geoffrey Household and Evelyn Waugh."

"I'll help you clear the table," I say to Judy, to cover my embarrassment. "Daddy loved your dinner."

"You're sweet to say so, pet, but I don't think he enjoyed it as much as I hoped. Oh well, food isn't everybody's meat. I wonder if I should wash up now or wait till morning. Either way I lose."

"Why don't you wait?" I say, desperate to make amends for Daddy. "I'll get up early and help you before school."

"Will you really?" she says. "Now I call that nice. You're a nice sweet girl, Sally."

Suddenly exhaustion hits me a blow so hard it nearly knocks

me off my feet. I yawn and rub my eyes. My head droops. "I'm tired," I say. Big sigh. I don't think I can stay awake another minute.

But Daddy isn't ready to leave. Incredibly, it seems he wants to engage Sam in a discussion about who killed Edwin Drood. As I near the living room, I hear Sam saying, "There's no way of telling. Dickens didn't have the chance to finish it. We'll never know — that's about all there is to it." Daddy looks disappointed. I'll bet he's never read the book. He probably heard about it on "Information, Please."

What with coffee and then Scotch —"one for the road"— we are committed to a second round of sitting, attempting to reach a common piece of ground. So far I'm the only thing they share. Otherwise it is exactly as I wrote my father: they are *not* alike, they can't be friends, their styles don't mesh, they're interested in opposite things. Sam and Judy stand on one side of the great river, Daddy stands on the other, and they can shout and wave and make frantic gestures but they can't communicate because, for one, the dialect isn't the same, and, for another, the river's much too wide.

Daddy asks Sam if he subscribes to *The New Republic,* which he could answer perfectly well himself by looking at the address label on the magazine.

Not only subscribes, Sam tells him, but occasionally contributes. This makes my father squirm. I hold my breath, afraid he is going to deliver the superpatriotic speech. I ought to know better — he isn't nearly coherent enough to bring it off. Instead he amazes me by saying, "That's nice. It's always nice to make a little extra pocket money. I don't suppose even Harvard pays you fellows that good a salary."

"I'm afraid what I get from publishing is just chicken feed. And, by the way, I don't teach at Harvard. I'm at B.U. — Boston University."

My father gulps. "Daddy, I told you that," I say.

"Must've forgot," he says. He looks embarrassed, as if Sam had farted.

"There are some good people at B.U.," Judy says, but the damage has been done. Fed up, Sam says the unforgivable thing: "Very few Jews on the Harvard faculty these days."

"Oh well, I must say, that hardly seems fair, does it? Well, I must let you good people go to bed, it's getting late. I've got to be up at the crack of dawn myself. Sally, how about calling your old man a cab?"

Daddy wills himself to an upright position. There's a stain on his tie, his clothes suddenly seem to belong to someone else. He's gone from ripe Joe College to bum in four hours. The alcohol did it.

I run to phone for a taxi. Sam lights a smelly cigar and stands up. Judy makes busy motions. We're all thrilled to see my father go.

"Cab's here," Sam calls out. He's been watching at the front window.

"Damn quick service," my father says. "I want to thank you both for a delightful evening. You're a damn fine cook — has anyone ever told you that?" he says, reaching for Judy's hand. "And I must say I thoroughly enjoyed our discussion, London. Sally's a lucky girl to be living here with you. It's been a real pleasure." My father has used his last remaining words on this little thank you. He lurches into the night.

"Run, see your father into the cab," Judy says.

I dash out after him. "Goodnight, Daddy," I say.

"Goodnight, little darling," he says, rubbing my hair the wrong way. "You're going to meet me for lunch tomorrow, aren't you?"

"Yes, Daddy," I say. I'm almost in tears. Exhaustion and disappointment tie me in knots. I can't bear it.

"Get in, Daddy, he's waiting."

"Yes, of course," my father says. He can barely negotiate the motions required to place his body on the car seat. I slam the door, flash a fake smile, and wave. The moment the taxi starts to move off, I burst into tears.

With all my heart I wish my father was a normal, decent, sober man.

18
Bully
for Sarah

BACK INSIDE THE HOUSE, I find Judy padding around in her stocking feet, turning out lights, closing cabinet doors, recapping bottles. In the soft, dull light, she looks much younger, girlish. I trail behind her.

"Your father's quite a sentimental man, isn't he, Sally? He absolutely dotes on you. You could never disappoint him, you know that, no matter what you did."

"I know," I say. "Sometimes it makes me feel peculiar. Sometimes I think he doesn't see me at all the way I am."

"That's what love does to you," she says. "It distorts your perceptions. Love gives everything a high gloss." She stops as if listening. "Dammit!" she says. "There's a draft coming from the kitchen. Would you mind going out there and closing whatever it is. You're a doll."

The back door is slightly ajar. In New York my mother would have had seventeen different kinds of fit if this had happened. She had the house checked regularly by Burns Detective Agency. Here everyone leaves their doors unlocked, though not necessarily open to every night breeze.

For some reason I am now wide awake. I want to run, dance, leap high, turn somersaults, talk. I want to talk to Judy. I want to spill the beans. "Judy, could I talk to you for a few minutes?"

"Good heavens," she says. "Are you sure you wouldn't rather wait till morning? It's awfully late."

She wants to go to bed but I am too selfish to care.

"Well," I say, hoping this one word will do the trick.

"Come on, Sally, let's go sit in the kitchen for a few minutes. We've all got to get up at seven."

"Thanks," I say, wondering, all at once, why it is suddenly so important. Wondering why it can't wait.

Judy goes to the icebox and pulls out a bottle of milk. "Would you like a cup of hot chocolate? I'm going to have one. It's a great relaxant. My mother used to feed me Ovaltine. That's why I switched to Bosco."

"No thanks, I'm still full from dinner."

"My God," she says. "Does your father *ever* eat? I have the feeling I could have given him oatmeal and raw spinach and it would have been all the same to him. If I were a sensitive type I'd probably be brooding now."

"I apologize for him."

"No such thing," she says. "I won't accept it. You're not responsible for your father or for his appetite. But that's not what you wanted to talk about, is it?"

"Not exactly." But how to start? Dive right into the middle? "Remember the other day when we were talking about why some people get married? Well, something Mummy said after she got divorced from Daddy has bothered me ever since. She said that Daddy married her to make his father mad. She said my grandfather was as bad as a German. She called him The Old Nazi. He was an American, he was terribly rich and fancy, but he liked Hitler. And he hated Jews. He called them awful names and he said awful things about them. He would never even let one come into his house. Mummy says he thought they weren't quite human beings. You know, the way some white people think of Negroes? Well, Mummy said that when she and Daddy got

married, Daddy's father had a heart attack. A real one, not a fake.
He had to go to the hospital and be given oxygen. After that he
wouldn't see them. When he was dying he wouldn't even let
Daddy come into his room."

"Wrote your father off, did he?"

I nod. "But he left him some money anyhow. Maybe because
by that time Daddy and Mummy were divorced."

"And I'll tell you something equally awful. I have a friend, a
Jewish friend, who married a Catholic boy and her father went
to temple and said Kaddish — that's the prayer for the dead —
and hasn't laid eyes on her since. That was six years ago."

"Why?"

"Because she married a gentile. That's the same thing to him as
dying. Cute, isn't it?"

"Did she mind?"

"She claimed not to, but I think she must. I can't see her not
minding, at some level." Judy sighs. She lifts her mug of hot
chocolate and takes a sip, leaving a thin strip of brown over her
upper lip. She reaches for a paper napkin and wipes it off.

"Do you think a lot of Jewish people do things like that?" I
say.

"Not too many," Judy says. "But that's only because there
aren't that many mixed marriages."

"Oh," I say. "Opa Teddy didn't do anything like that to my
mother when she married Daddy."

"Of course not, he was probably pleased as punch. That's another story. Listen, honey pie, aren't you tired yet?"

"I guess I am."

We both get to our feet. Judy puts her arm around my shoulder. I like it. She gives me a little squeeze. This is okay too.
"Listen, Sally, I know you think your parents' marriage was a
horrible mistake. But there was one good thing to come out of
that misalliance."

"What?"

"Don't you know, you silly goose?"

I shake my head over and over again, but a little later, just as I was dropping off to sleep, the answer came, warming my blood.

"Put on a little lipstick, pet, you're not a baby anymore."

I have been secretly practicing with Tangee, which is labeled "colorless" but actually comes off orange. "Are you sure?"

"Sure," she says. "Why not?"

"Maybe people will think I'm trying to act like a grownup," I admit. I'm deathly afraid that people are looking at me, looking and laughing.

"You're acting your age, silly. Don't worry so much about what people think." Judy hangs around while I get ready to meet my father. New navy blue suit with a long, wide, gored skirt and short fitted jacket. A straw hat with ribbons down the back, red pumps, and a red purse to match. Nylon stockings attached to a garter belt that cuts into my hips. A swishy taffeta slip. I feel silly — I feel as if I were getting into a costume for a play. I'm not used to these clothes; they aren't Me yet. "Mr. Scott doesn't like the idea of my cutting math class," I tell her, as I attach my stocking to the little clip against my thigh.

"I'll take care of Mr. Scott," Judy says with a smile. "Now you really must stop fretting like this. It's important that you see your father."

"I've got butterflies," I say. "I don't know why."

"Okay," she says. She circles me to get the complete picture. "You look swell," she says. "Have you got a pair of white gloves?" Have I got a pair of white gloves? Is the Pope Catholic? I've got enough white gloves to glove the Dionne quintuplets plus their mother. I nod.

"It's your father you're having lunch with, pet — not the phantom of the opera."

I have to laugh. "Have you got any money for the cab?" Judy asks.

The funny thing is that although I have a trust fund so large I could spend a hundred dollars a day indefinitely and it still wouldn't run out — it is exactly like the goose that laid the golden egg — I never seem to have any cash on me. Judy gets her purse and gives me a greasy five-dollar bill. "This ought to do it," she says. "Yes, yes, of course, I'll keep track." I feel a need to apologize for being filthy rich and yet always needing pocket money. They say princesses never carry any money with them. Why should they? I want to apologize, but I don't know quite how — anything I say will sound stupid or insincere. Money is so emotional for me; if it didn't sound so insincere, I'd say money was my stigma.

"Hurry, I can hear the cab honking outside," Judy says. She's flustered. I dash out the door, forgetting my gloves. "And for heaven's sake, have a good time!" she adds. She sees the gloves and comes running to the taxi with them. "You forgot these. Have a good time!" she repeats. Just like a mother.

The back of Solomon Grossbart's head has a pale bald spot with brown polka dots on it. He's a good driver. He eases us through traffic like a worm in spring soil. For a moment or two I can relax, nobody will bother me. Peripherally aware that suburb is turning gradually into city, that grass and trees are giving way to concrete and cement, I force myself to think about money, my riches, my fortune, my bank account (the size of which I'm not at all sure of), of me wandering around loose like a gold statue with sapphire eyes. If he knew how rich I was, would Mr. Solomon Grossbart whisk me away to Chelsea or Charlestown, blindfold me, dump me in a deserted warehouse, and demand ransom? If I were him *I* would be tempted. The Lindbergh baby scared my mother so much she hired a detective to watch our place for a while after it happened. What do I need with a bank account and a trust fund, for Christ's sake. My money is like a heavy winter coat that drags on my shoulders and makes my back ache. I no longer want the things I have been used to, things I have given up for one reason or another: the pearly antiques — cherry wood married to burnished leather — mint-condition bills snapped from a Mark Cross wallet to pay for something I don't really need and probably won't like next week, double lamb chops cooked to order and wearing ruffled paper socks, liquid center chocolates in Sherry's violet tin box with its hinged cover. All gone, gone. I prefer Judy's ersatz Italian meatballs and spaghetti. I like Milky Ways and Babe Ruths much better than the bitter chocolates from the violet box. This may be hard to believe, but it's just as easy to get tired of filet mignon as melted cheese sandwiches. I know — I've had my fill of both. It is now perfectly clear to me, I can never fool myself again: most folks did not live like my mother and Freddie, they live more or less like the Londons — mostly less.

By any standard but my parents' the Londons were extremely well off. There were millions of families, for instance, who existed on no-meat diets and no-heat homes. Shacks. Christ, you don't even want to think about those people, just as, when you are hurtling into New York over the New Haven tracks, you don't want to look into Harlem through its uncurtained windows. Most people had horrible relatives staying with them and ancient crippled mothers who couldn't go to the bathroom by themselves, aged fathers whom you had to scream at to make yourself heard, mad or dopey cousins who were kept hidden when company came. Most people didn't eat something whole and fresh every night but instead, last night's meal made into tonight's, soft and gluey and held together by rice, noodles, or mashed potatoes. They darned their socks and patched their children's clothes. They borrowed books from the public library instead of buying them from Scribner's or Doubleday's on Fifth Avenue, and they went without phonograph records altogether. They sent their kids to a school half a mile's walk away and they didn't travel unless someone close to them was dead or dying. Fun was for somebody else, leisure pleasures had as much meaning for them as a spaceship. Sam said I lived in a marzipan world. And, oh, it was true. Oma Lucy ate imported marzipan like candy; marzipan, caviar, little cheese things from Fortnum's, cashew nuts, anchovy paste, Port Salut. I hated marzipan. It was so sweet it made my jaws ache, but everybody told me it was good and I ought to like it. It was a "delicacy," like oysters, and I ought to like it.

"You playing hooky?" Mr. Grossbart said.

"No, not really. I'm meeting my father who lives in New Jersey. I got permission."

"That's good. Wouldn't want to be cutting school," he says. Who does he think he is? My mother? My guardian?

He whistled through his teeth when I answered that what my father did was to be an investment broker. It was a whistle that expressed an appreciation of money. I couldn't blame him for doing it, but still it made me feel guilty. He probably lived in a basement apartment with his dying mother and five kids all eight and under. I was going to Locke-Ober's for lunch and he knew it.

"Is it much farther?" I say, noticing that we're near what I think is a museum.

"You late?" he says. I think I hear envy and disgust in his voice. "I can step on the gas if you're late for your big date."

We establish the fact that I am in plenty of time. The ride seems endless. Mr. Grossbart is a malignant force in the car with me. I want so much to get out that I clench my fists and cross my legs tightly, holding myself in a mass. I have to go to the bathroom, which makes it worse. That means I'll have to go even before we sit down to eat. I'm still a child. I have to use the bathroom in every building I go into. When will it end?

The city closes in. We are squeezed into streets that twist like intestines. I don't see how I can ever learn to get around this city by myself. New York is so logical in comparison, numbers following in an orderly progression, the up-and-down avenues easy enough to memorize. This city is a rat maze. It wants you to get lost or stay away.

"Here we are, girlie," Mr. Grossbart says in a surprisingly pleasant tone. "Just walk down that alley and you'll see it on your left. Men's bar downstairs — better not go in there. Take the steps up. My advice is order the scallops."

I take out my purse within a purse and overtip Mr. Grossbart, partly from nervousness, partly from guilt. Maybe he can buy his kid the hockey stick he's been asking for ever since he came down with polio. No overt sign that he wants to rob me or is merely waiting for the revolution. But if there is a revolution, won't Locke-Ober's disappear? Won't everything be like Chock-Full O' Nuts and Hayes-Bickford? Maybe the fanciest restaurant will be Schrafft's. Where does Stalin eat when he goes out to lunch? I'll bet he doesn't have egg salad on white or melted cheese and bacon. I'll bet he has sturgeon and caviar and eats like Oma Lucy even when he's all alone. God, I really *am* obsessed with money and food. I think about them all the time. Money is my yellow Star of David — I want to rip it off and step into the same boat with everyone else.

I pulled open the heavy door at the bottom of a flight of stairs and walked upstairs. Daddy sees me first, comes springing at me, inevitable drink in hand. "Princess," he cries, "how lovely of you to come. You look like Primavera — what a pretty hat."

What does he mean, how nice of me to come? Didn't we make a definite date? "Of course I came, Daddy," I say. "I told you I would last night. Did you stay here just for me?"

"Sure did," he says. "And for the soft-shell crabs. I wouldn't think of coming to Boston without having a plateful of Locke's soft-shell crabs." He sees me eyeing his cocktail. "I ordered a little drink while I waited for you."

"You don't have to explain," I say. The thing is, I know that no amount of "explaining" will ever make me understand his insatiable thirst. It's something beyond me, out of my experience, my comprehending. I chide myself for not being aware before now of how much liquor means to him. I almost think that if he had the choice of rescuing me from the lion's cage or giving up drink for the rest of his life, he might make the wrong choice — not because he wanted to but because he couldn't help it.

"I just heard that the Duke of Somerset — Old Goatie — is in town, princess, staying at the Ritz. I really ought to give him a ring. You know your Daddy and Old Goatie served together at Leeds not so long ago. Old Goatie would never forgive me if he heard we were in town at the same time and I hadn't checked in. I wonder what he's here for. Hope to God it's not the same reason I am."

"Go ahead, Daddy," I say. "I have to use the ladies' anyway." Daddy and I split apart. I can't believe he's going to call this Goatie person. It sounds too absurd. I navigate to the bathroom by asking three waiters. I always hate asking men the way to the john — it embarrasses me horribly. Just the way I hate to ask a man in the drugstore for Kotex. In fact, if there's a man behind the counter, I go to another drugstore until I find a woman.

Anyway, there's an old lady sitting in a straight chair in the ladies' room, keeping watch. She looks up briefly as I enter and I can see what's in her mind: Why aren't you in school, little girl?

I'm back first. I sit on the banquette and wait for Daddy and try to figure out what to do with my feet. I'm not comfortable crossing my knees and if I cross my ankles I'll look as if I were in dancing class.

"Is mademoiselle waiting for someone?"

"What? Oh yes, thank you. I'm waiting for my father."

"Very well, miss," the headwaiter says, and slithers away. He too wonders why I am not in school. I'm beginning to wish I was.

And irony of ironies, I'm not hungry. I'm always hungry. But
not now, not today. Today the idea of food makes me feel sick.

"He's left town," Daddy says, a cloud in his face.

"Is he nice?"

"Who, the Duke?"

I nod.

"I don't know, really — never thought about his being nice.
He's just himself, he's one hell of a good time. And rich. Listen,
princess, he has so many race horses that he's lost count. Owns
three castles. That sort of thing. People as rich as Old Goatie
don't have to be nice, if you know what I mean. He's there for
his own enjoyment. He's a damn good time, that's what Old
Goatie is."

By this time we are seated at our table, both of us with our
backs to the wall, so we can watch everybody else eating and
drinking. The waiter leans over us, bending from the waist. "May
I suggest the Oysters Winter Place?"

Not to Daddy he can't. Daddy's made up his mind what he
wants. He sends the waiter away for another "very dry martini,
Beefeater's gin, please, with a twist," and tells me he thinks putting salt, spinach, and bacon over an oyster and then baking it is
an abomination. Baking it, mind you, taking a perfectly good
little fellow and drying it out in the oven. For some reason
Daddy, who I thought didn't give a hoot about food and couldn't
tell the difference between ptarmigan and tarragon, has suddenly
become an expert in gourmet cooking. The menu is ample and,
thank God, mostly in English. Even though I've had five years of
textbook French I still can't read a menu in French. The waiter
comes back. Daddy asks him to bring us two orders of Cherry-
stones. If I had been hungry I would have ordered the shrimp
cocktail. "Now, what would you like for your main course? The
duck here is marvelous. Still, it's a pity not to take advantage of
the fish. What? I don't see soft-shell crabs on the menu. Oh woe!"

The waiter brings our clams. I won't say what I think they look like.

My father tells the man there are no soft-shell crabs on the menu. "No, sir," the waiter says."

"Will you go see if they have any, please?"

"Right away, sir."

"They always have a few things not listed on the menu," my father confides. He forks a clam, pops it into his mouth, swallows. A smile spreads over his face. "Beautiful," he says. "Eat up!"

Why does my father have to order the one thing not listed on the menu? I don't want my clams. I have never eaten one because of what they remind me of. I'm not sure I can get it down.

"Let me show you," Daddy says. "First, you put a little of this horseradish into the cocktail sauce, then you sprinkle your clam with a drop or two of lemon juice." He demonstrates. "Then you spear it with this little fork . . . and in it goes. Ah, delight!"

This is torture. I follow Daddy's directions to the letter, put the vile thing in my mouth, taste it for one split second, swallow, and almost gag. My gorge rises, will sends it back.

The waiter tells Daddy that the crabs are available. "Please tell the chef to broil them, not sauté them in a lake of butter. Yes, broiled lightly and served with a wedge of lemon. We'll have two orders of asparagus Hollandaise and two endive salads with vinegar and oil on the side. I'll mix the dressing myself." He orders a bottle of German white wine which we will share. "We'll see about the dessert later," he says, handing the menu to the waiter without looking at him. The waiter doesn't seem to think my father is being rude. Oh, it's terrible.

I want to know what Daddy thinks of the Londons but I'm afraid to ask. "How's Lorna?" I substitute.

"Now, that little bride of mine is a real marvel," he says. "She's got your apartment fixed up so beautifully you won't recognize it. She's so good at it that she's thinking seriously of going into it professionally — for her friends and acquaintances, that is. She doesn't want to have to go to one of those schools for certification or whatever it is you need to set yourself up in business. Besides, I'm not sure I'd like a wife in business. Marriages where the wife works — there's always some sort of trouble. But I must say I'm proud of that little girl. She's got imagination and stick-to-it-iveness. Some of the delays she's put up with you would simply not believe. But she never let a single feather get ruffled. No, sir, not my Lorna. I'll tell you a little secret, my dear. Can you keep a secret?" I nod, apprehensively.

"Well, Lorna and I would like a family, you know, a young man to keep the Sanderson name going. Mummies are valuable people — that's another reason I'm not giving too much encouragement to Lorna's idea of working. Children need their mummies. I made Lorna promise that the minute she gets pregnant she take a vacation and relax, really relax, have lunch with her girlfriends, go to the matinee, shop, you know — take it really easy. During those nine months every woman should be a queen. Your own poor mother — she went dashing around, getting a lot of damn fool artists to do something energetic for her favorite charity. I can't even remember now what it was all about. I got her father to tell her to stop doing so much — she was endangering your health!"

"Daddy, I never thought it was bad to work when you were pregnant." The word "pregnant" makes me feel slightly embarrassed. Besides, I think my father is much too old to be having children. It's revolting — he'll be old enough to be its grandfather. He's definitely what Nancy would call a dirty old man.

"It never hurts a woman to pamper herself during her term. It seems like a long time to you, I know, but when you think of a lifetime, sixty-five, seventy-five years, why, it's just a drop in the bucket. My philosophy is take it easy, have a good time, stay calm, eat well, be a queen."

Now he's switched subjects. He wants us to discuss the Lon-

dons' politics again. "Now this fellow Henry Wallace," he's saying, as he consumes another clam. "Smokes a corncob pipe. Who
does he think he is — Li'l Abner? I frankly don't understand how
he's managed to bamboozle so many people. Damn fools. What
this country does *not* need is a Socialist. Imagine stifling what
we're best at. By the way, I suppose London is a Wallace sup-
porter?"

I'd rather bite my tongue off (or swallow another clam) than
admit it. "I don't know," I say.

"Hmm," he says. "I predict — I'd be willing to bet a large sum
of money — that the man's name will be utterly forgotten within
five years." The reason Daddy wants to know whether London is
with Wallace or against him is that Daddy judges other men by
their opinions. Such as, if you think Thomas E. Dewey is the
cat's pajamas, you must be okay. If, on the other hand, you think
Harry Truman is an adequate Chief Executive, you're a nogoodnik.

"Third parties in this country can't cut the mustard," he informs me.

This is precisely what my history teacher at school told us the
day before yesterday.

"Aren't you going to finish those?" Daddy says, staring greedily at my uneaten clams. "I guess not," I say. "I want to save my
appetite."

"Well," he says. "You don't mind if I do, do you? I can't bear
to see them taken back to the kitchen to be chucked away."

"Have them," I say. He downs them in a second.

"You pay for the service here as well as the food," my father
says. "Some of the waiters have been here since the year one." At
that moment one of the elderly waiters walks smack into a serving
stand, capsizing a gravy boat and causing the sort of embarrassing
commotion that everyone tries hard to ignore. It is the sole light
spot in an otherwise tragic day. I start to giggle, watching the

poor old man mopping the goo off his black pants. My father —
somewhat harshly — tells me to stop laughing, I'm being rude.

Our waiter comes back with the crabs. There are three on each
plate. They lie under thin slivers of lemon and look like three
giant brown lice. I sneak a look at Daddy. He's slavering. "Very
nice," he says to the waiter.

"Wine isn't sufficiently chilled," he adds, twirling the bottle in
its chrome-plated bucket which the waiter has stationed by his
knee.

"Oh Daddy," I say, suddenly remembering something my
mother once told me: "Daddy needs to make a fuss in restaurants." I can't bear it. If he's going to make a fuss over the
temperature of the wine, I'm getting up and leaving. I can't possibly stay and listen. "Please don't say anything, it'll get cool in a
minute."

"There's no excuse," he says. He's cutting into his first crab
now, he's bringing the food to his mouth, he's opening, chewing,
smiling. "*Merveilleux*," he says. Thank God, the wine's fever is
forgotten.

I'm sure I won't like the crab, but I'm surprised to find it nice,
unfishy. "This is good," I say, my appetite perking up enough for
me to do a token job of eating. Given the choice I'd rather have
chicken salad, but it's not all that bad.

Our waiter brings the salad. The endives are lying under a film
of oil. My father draws back in horror. "They've dressed the
salad," he says.

"Yes," I agree.

"I asked for oil and vinegar on the side."

Now we're in for it: warm wine plus dressed salad equals fuss.
There's no way out. "I like it this way," I tell him.

"That's all very well, my dear," he says severely. "But I didn't
order it this way." Daddy peers around for the waiter, who is
gone into hiding.

"Please Daddy, don't say anything please!" I'm almost in tears.

"Princess," he says to me as if he were lecturing at the Library of Congress. "I want you to know the world as I knew it. I don't want you to accept disintegration as the normal way of the world. You must fight it all the way. I know it seems a trivial thing, but it's what it represents that counts. If Locke-Ober's lets down — just a little — the rest of society might as well give up. They're just supposed not to make mistakes here."

"Daddy please don't make a fuss about it."

"And stop saying that!"

A tear escapes and slides down my right cheek. Just one eye. Daddy glares at it, unbelieving. "I don't know what's wrong with you, what's happened to you. I want you to understand: I don't make fusses, as you put it. I only insist on getting what I pay for."

"For my sake," I say. Now the other eye has started.

"For your sake? I'd only *do* it for your sake. You don't think I really care about whether *they* pour on the dressing or *I* do?"

I get out my clean linen handkerchief with the S. S. embroidered in the corner and blow my nose. We have never fought before, never. I feel as if I had a big wound in the middle of my chest.

"Darling," he says. "Please don't cry. I won't say anything — I promise. Only I hate to let them get away with it. So help me, if it ever happens again, I'll have them crying for mercy." He grins at me to underscore his awful joke about crying for mercy. The two drinks and three glasses of wine have reached a crucial nerve center; pieces of his brain are melting and running together. "I guess I just expect service out of another era, a bygone time . . ." Oh God, it's the nostalgia game again.

"You're the youngest-looking father I know," I tell him.

"Do you really think so? You're an angel." I think he cares as much about his physical appearance as my mother did. Maybe more. It makes me sad to think so.

My father orders *marrons glacés* for me and a Napoleon for himself. "It's back to chopped sirloin and black coffee tomorrow," he says. "Today the sky's the limit."

I don't want dessert, but how can I hurt his feelings?

"I can see that you still feel like a stranger in the Londons' house," he tells me. "I can't say I blame you, it *is* another world. It must be a strain on my poor princess. Living like a house guest, neither here nor there, tiptoeing when you ought to be making as much damn noise as you please."

"I don't think that's the way it is," I say truthfully. "I thought I felt at home." This is not what my father either expects or wants to hear. "I can go into the icebox any time I want without asking."

"Bully for you," he says darkly. He brings his fork down across the pastry like an executioner: egg custard oozes out slowly; my stomach lurches. No one need ever point out to me the connection between mind and body, so intimate it is obscene. I have known about it vaguely from age six when I threw up hearing my mother and father fight in their bedroom. I know it now like a clout on the head watching my father eat. Daddy, you make me sick.

He doesn't want me to be happy with the Londons. Maybe he doesn't want me to be happy anywhere except inside his house, inside the room the wicked Lorna is preparing for me like the witch in *Hansel and Gretel*.

"Tell me, are all their friends Jewish?"

"Whose?"

"The Londons', silly — who have we been talking about? Sam and Judy London. My, that woman never does sit still, does she?"

"I don't know," I whisper. The chestnut feels like dry peanut butter in my mouth. I put down my spoon. "Most of them, I guess."

"It figures," he says. "Would you like a bite of my Napoleon? It's awfully good."

I shake my head, avoiding the custard with my eyes. "I'll be right back," I say and squirm out from behind the table. Daddy looks surprised.

"Little girls' room?" he asks. I nod. I'm going to throw up, I have that hot, stomach-doesn't-want-it feeling. I manage to make it out of the dining room. Thank God I know my way. I move as quickly as I can without attracting attention, shove open the ladies' room door, pass the attendant who looks up from her newspaper again, and do what I have to do. The fierce pain in my stomach fists itself and then opens up, disgorging, burning the back of my throat; the tears ooze from my eyes. I strain, pull, and heave, finally feeling the rush of glop upwards, then falling in a pink waterfall into the toilet. I have to watch.

I watch, half horrified, half relieved, as clam, cocktail sauce, crab, lemon juice, watercress, Coca-Cola, are released, homogenized. I am an up-ended bucket. I feel the perspiration drip down from my armpits and stain my blouse.

"Now, you just let it all come back up, dear, there's a good girl, that's right, that'll clean you out good. If it's going to come up, there's no use trying to keep it down." For a moment I can't imagine who is talking to me. Then I realize it's the old lady who guards the toilets. I heave again, a mighty wave of half-digested food fills my mouth and spills out again. The tears slide down my cheeks and follow the food. I flush the toilet with my foot and wait for the next installment. I'm afraid I'm making too much noise.

"There's a dear. Would you like me to come in and hold your head? I always held my kiddies' head when they threw."

"No. Thanks. Oh!" It happens again, but less this time. The storm's passing.

I can see her white toes just beyond the door. Someone comes in and uses the next john to mine. Her pee sounds discreet, like a child's.

I wait. It seems to be over. I wait yet another minute or so. My insides are resting. "There's a good girl — all done now?"

"Yes," I say weakly. I wait until the other woman washes her hands, dries them, and leaves. Then I open the door. The nice woman has a fresh washcloth in her hand. I let her sponge my face with it. There is a faint scent of perfume on the cloth. "Too much excitement for you," she croons, wiping my face gently with a soft towel. "Or maybe it's the rich food you're not used to. I wouldn't let my own children eat some of the rich food they serve here. Now, you won't tell a soul what I said, will you, darling? It isn't good for a body, all that butter and rich cream and sauces. There's a dear," she says. "Have you got a little brush so I can fix your hair nice again — that lovely thick hair you've got?" I shake my head. "I've got a comb." I hand her my tortoise shell comb and she runs it gently through my hair.

"Now a little lipstick and you're good as new. Nobody will ever know what happened except you and me. Now don't you go crying, there's nothing to cry about, it's perfectly natural, we all throw once in a while. I've been here a long, long time and believe me, you're not the first who came in here and did what you just did. Far from it. Now here, take this Kleenex and dry your eyes and go back to your people. Won't do to spend all day in here, would it? Like me?"

I shake my head. Who is this woman? "Thank you," I say. What I really mean is, I love you, but I couldn't say that, could I? "You're very nice."

"I'm just doing my job," she tells me.

"Well, thank you anyway." I reach into my purse and pull out a dollar bill which I try to give her.

"I can't take that, miss," she says.

"Yes, you can," I say. I reach for her hand. It's dry and rough like old leaves. I put the money into it. "Thank you again," I say and rush away before she can give it back.

I feel so much better I could scream. I walk boldly up to the table and sit down with confidence. "*All* the Londons' friends are Jewish," I tell Daddy. "Every last one of them is."

"Well, I must say I'm not surprised. Their kind are naturally shy of mixing. Dearest girl, it won't be too much longer. Just another month or so and then we'll be the family I've always dreamed of."

Oh hell.

I can't live with you. Judy washed her hair for you. She shaved her legs. She put on new stockings. She wore a fashionable dress. She polished the silver. Sam didn't make any dirty jokes. He didn't go off in a trance. He was polite as hell, for him. He let you talk about Edwin Drood.

How am I going to break the news to you, Daddy? What is Lorna going to do with her fabulous apartment, custom-designed and furnished for a rich, half-Jewish, overweight, teen-age orphan?

19

Seen

MAYBE FREUD WAS RIGHT, maybe certain people *do* enjoy their pain. Or, put the other way around, they don't allow themselves the pleasures of the thing done well or the triumph of good judgment.

Which means that as soon as I decided to stay with the Londons I began to have massive doubts. Was this really best, happiest; did Peggy and Annie really make up for Nancy? Were the boys at Brookline High any better than the kids of my dead parents' rich, snotty friends? Indecision had made me wretched, deciding seemed to make no difference at all.

Everything about the Londons disgusted me, as if I had never felt anything else. I must have driven Judy crazy.

"Why is Sam always so grouchy?" I ask her, knowing perfectly well that she can't answer this like an ordinary question.

"He's not," she says simply. "What makes you think so?"

"Well, he seems to be in a bad mood an awful lot of the time. He growls when you try to talk to him."

Big sigh from Judy, accompanied by ripple and shudder. Every time she does this I have the awful urge to punch her in the mouth. I twine my fingers together.

"That's just Sam. He's distracted, no doubt thinking about something difficult. I don't think he means to growl."

"How come you don't mind?" I persist. I am being a terrible little shit. We are folding laundry in the basement, folding and sorting shirts, jeans, towels, washcloths, sheets, underpants. I can't get used to the holes in the front of Sam's and the boys' shorts.

"Mind?" Judy says, looking up from a sheet with a gash in it. "I married it. It wasn't rich, it didn't have a title or even a job, it hated vacations and it worked like a dog. It didn't say very much. I must have liked it. Why else would I have got married?"

"I don't know."

"Of course you don't." She sticks her hand through the gash. "I feel like ripping this clear through." she says.

"Why don't you?"

"Waste," she answers. "I'll mend it and in two weeks someone's big toe will open it up again."

"Sam's different with you," I tell her.

"Really? How so?"

"Not so grouchy. He acts as if he doesn't like kids."

"That's not true!" Ah, I've hit her where she's mush. Maybe even frightened her. "He loves you, he loves all of you!"

"Well, he certainly has the funniest way of showing it!" I cry fiercely. I'm blaming her for his faults, which isn't fair, but doesn't she ask for it? Why does she always defend him?

"You haven't got the hang of Sam yet," she tells me. "It takes a while."

"He's not a frog," I say. "He's a person. Why should he be so special?"

Something I've said makes Judy smile. She holds a sock aloft. "Now where in hell is its mate? I can *never* find the second sock."

"Maybe he eats them," I suggest.

"Now that's an idea," she says. "Why didn't I think of that myself?"

How can you tear up a letter that isn't even written?

It can be done. I kept writing letters to Daddy inside my

head and ripping them up before they ever got to the pen and paper stage. It was the approach, the tone, which was giving me the most trouble. Head on? "Dear Father, I wouldn't come live with you if you were Cary Grant and T. S. Eliot rolled into one." Sideways? "Dearest Daddy, I don't think Roger is quite ready to have me leave him. So I thought I would linger here yet a while." Upside down? "Darling Daddy, I love Brookline High so much I can't bear to go to any other school." The unwritten letter hung over me unbearably. I couldn't ask anyone for help. My friends Annie and Peggy might have helped me compose something acceptable, but a deep sense of privacy restrained me from calling them in for consultation. And perhaps, too, I was afraid they might tease me about my money and my Princeton father.

I suppose I hoped the whole thing would go away and that my guilt over the fortune Daddy and Lorna had spent on my apartment would dissolve with time.

No matter what happens, unless you're dead you keep right on doing things. The Londons celebrated my fifteenth birthday by taking me, Annie, Peggy, Roger, Danny, and Joey to Chinatown for a feast. Judy ordered by phone ahead of time; the meal was fantastic, too large, delicious. There were duck and dumplings and shredded cabbage with pork that you ate in a rolled-up sour pancake and lobster disguised in tiny chunks and about eighteen other courses, all crowded together on the table. We ate like pigs except for Roger, who stuck to rice and spareribs and wouldn't touch anything else. Sam got pork grease smeared all over his chin. I was so embarrassed I couldn't look at him, but no one else seemed to notice. Even Peggy ate a lot. We staggered out of the restaurant. (I peeked at the bill — it was more than forty dollars and I wondered how much Sam would charge to me and how much to him, and then I realized what a pain in the neck it must be for him, keeping two accounts straight. And it had to be either straight or else crooked on my side, because I couldn't see

Donald Synder letting him get away with a single farthing. Poor Sam. Yet he had cheerfully taken the bills out of his soft, falling-apart black leather wallet and handed them over to the cashier, who grinned at him for having such a lovely big family who ate so much.) Out on the street Sam gave each child two dollars — and me five (whose money?) — to buy anything we wanted. I had to admit it was a nice idea for a party, much nicer than your usual magician, like the one who came to entertain Roger and ten of his little friends — turned out in gray flannel suits with short pants and knee socks and Eton collars — on his sixth birthday. I remember my Chinatown party as one of the best; I still have the small wooden box with a tiny brass clasp reeking of sandalwood I bought that night.

My other presents from Sam and Judy were a petticoat with three stiff layers and a copy of Frost's selected poems, one gift for each of the two sides of me, I suppose.

That night I went to bed a little less miserable than usual and determined to get up the next day and write that letter to Daddy. Write it, fold it, tuck it into the envelope, and walk down to the corner mailbox with it. I started composing, "Dearest Daddy, You know how much I love you and have been looking forward to living with you," and was slowly sucked up into the black straw of sleep before I could complete the perfect rejection letter.

No one in the London household realized there was anything wrong for a couple of hours. We ought to have sensed that Roger was not in the house when he should have been. But I suppose we were relieved not to hear him or see him. It didn't occur to us that the house was ominously calm. Anyone who has ever had to live with a "difficult" person will know what I'm talking about. It's not that you don't love them, it's just that they're so much trouble.

It wasn't until his supper was ready that Judy discovered Roger was missing. Judy was used to Sam's working late in his study each night; often she served the four of us kids first and then waited and had dinner with Sam about an hour later. She admitted it was twice as much work but she also said that hers and Sam's was a much more peaceful meal.

"Sally, would you mind seeing if Roger's in the garage. He's been fiddling around with some crazy machine out there . . ."

Roger wasn't in the garage or the cellar or the attic, his room, any of our rooms, hiding behind the shrubs in the back yard or, in fact, anywhere in the immediate area. He was "lost."

First Judy dispatched her children to go up and down our street and several nearby; then she began to call her new neighbors on the phone; she carefully avoided transmitting by mouth the worry that was clearly on her face.

"Roger's out somewhere playing in the neighborhood," she said. "You haven't seen him in the last half hour or so, have you? Well, thanks, Mary, if you *do* see him, would you mind telling him, please, that his dinner is ready? Yes, thanks." And hung up and called the next on her list.

One after another the neighbors reported that they hadn't seen Roger. It struck me as a useless kind of exercise because Roger wasn't that chummy with the neighborhood kids to begin with. He stuck pretty much to himself and his comic books and his engine in the garage. Joey and Danny came back empty-handed.

They had got the message. The drama reached them with none of the attendant anxiety. As far as they were concerned he was still the unwelcome stranger who had made their lives miserable. *They* had faced it: Roger did not have the gift of adjustment.

"Maybe somebody kidnapped him!" shouts Danny, jumping up and down and, for some reason, making gagging noises.

"Don't say that!" Judy cries. "It's not funny."

"Yes, but maybe somebody did!"

"Who would want Roger?" Joey asks soberly. "Anyone who stole Roger would dump him pretty soon. Who could stand him? His feet stink!"

"Why don't you two just get lost," Judy says. She's looking up another number in the phone book.

"Get lost?" Danny asks. "You mean like Roger's lost?"

"No, not like that, silly. Just stay out of my hair, beat it!" Judy dials the phone, speaks briefly, and hangs up. "No luck, he's not at the Wexlers' either. Sam!" There's a shrillness to her tone that I haven't heard before and this heightens the drama. "Sam!" she calls again.

I can hear him mumbling from behind the study door. "Sam, please, I need to talk to you!"

Sam comes out of his room, scowling. I am anxious to see what's going to happen. But Judy turns to me. "Sally, would you mind giving Danny and Joey their dinner. No sense their waiting. It's a casserole, in the oven — just spoon it out and make sure that they don't throw it at each other."

"Calm down Judy," Sam says, a phrase that's likely to give the calmest soul a nervous fit.

"I won't," she tells him. "Roger's missing, he's not anywhere, we've scoured the neighborhood, he's gone. We'd better call the police."

"Police?"

"That's what I said. Sally, please go on now and feed the boys!"

So I miss the best part, which is where she tells him what's *really* on her mind.

This is what I think: There are four possibilities to account for Roger's not being home. One, he's at someone's house and has either forgotten or deliberately decided not to come home. Two, he's been kidnapped (which would have been my mother's guess). Three, he's had an accident and is lying all over the street, bleeding from the ears, etc. And four, he's run away. Number one is unlikely; it's not his style and we've pretty much ruled it out. I won't reject number two, but it would be too bizarre for me to consider. Three is perfectly plausible, but one fatal accident per year per family is about all I can handle. Myself, I favor four; it sounds right.

"I'll bet he's run away," I tell Judy as she comes in to check up on me. Her forehead is squeezed together and her mouth is a tight, sharp line converged on by wrinkles. "Most unattractive," my mother would have said. "Worry ages people worse than cancer."

"Roger wouldn't do that," she says. "He told me just yesterday morning how much he liked our new house and the new swing set."

"Did he tell you without your asking him?"

"I don't remember," she says. "And really, Sally, it doesn't make all that much difference. Joey, eat your salad."

Sam walks in. "I've called the police," he says, heading for the liquor cabinet. "They're sending a detective over."

"Oh, dear," Judy says.

"I thought that's what you wanted."

"Well, I do and I don't. What are you looking for?"

"The bourbon," he says, shoving bottles around. "Where in hell is the bourbon?"

"If you don't see it then we're out," she tells him. "Try Scotch."

"You want one?" Sam says, holding up the bottle. "You look like you could use a drink."

"Well, *thanks a lot*," Judy says. "As a matter of fact I will. Oh Sam, where *is* he?"

"I don't know what good it does to speculate."

"That's all we've got!" Judy cries. "And anyway, isn't that what detectives do, speculate? Isn't that what Sherlock Holmes did?"

"Hardly," Sam says. He loves to correct her.

"Well, I don't see what harm it does to make educated guesses. Joey, where do you think Roger is?"

"The movies," Joey says.

I'm beginning to get an icy, sick feeling in my stomach. Numbers two and three become more solid possibilities.

Judy can't stand still. She sips at her drink greedily. She keeps running to the front door and opening it, peering out into the May dusk. The streetlights have come on and shed a bluish light over the new leaves, prettying them. "Oh, Roger, where *are* you, baby? Please come home!"

I think I know what she is feeling: I have lost a child entrusted to me, I have lost another woman's child. I am a freak.

I am reassured by the detective for the wrong reasons. His mechanical manner and his notebook, a cheap cardboard-covered affair that opens vertically and has a gaudy fake crest on the cover, make me think that, since he apparently knows what to do, he knows what he's doing. If anyone can, *he* will find Roger. He takes a black fountain pen out of his breast pocket and starts to write immediately.

The three of us sit with him in the living room —"You too, young lady," he instructs me, making me feel valuable — and get down to business. We sit there, Judy, Sam, and I, like anxious passengers on a boat that's headed into a certain storm. Sam keeps crossing and recrossing his legs, Judy clears her throat several times though there are no bubbles in it. I yawn over and over again.

"But where do you *think* he is?" Judy insists. She can't resist raising that silly question.

"Well, Mrs. London," the detective says. "That's something I was hoping we could all work on together. You folks know your son's habits and I don't. I was hoping you could tell me a little something about what kind of boy he is, who he hangs around with, where he plays, et cetera."

Sam breaks in. "He's not our son, Lieutenant O'Reilly. We're his guardians. His mother and father lived in New York, they were killed in an airplane crash earlier this year. You probably read about it in the *Globe*. Their name was Stern . . ."

The policeman's eyebrows shoot up together. "Is that so?" he says, scribbling to beat the band. "By the way, the name is O'Wiley, Lawrence O'Wiley. Funny, almost everybody makes the same mistake. So he's not your natural son, eh? But he's lived here since his parents passed away?"

"Yes, that's right," Judy tells him, clearing her throat again. "Roger's just like a member of the family, recently he had begun to really accept us, he was — is— getting along so well." With this the detective looks directly at me. I betray a little less confidence on this point than Judy. Detective O'Wiley reads me.

"Would you folks mind telling me then, Dr. London, or Missus, how you came to be the boy's guardian." He's released a brogue which he's held in check until this minute; he's warming to the subject. "I don't understand," Judy says.

"You mean how this has got any bearing on the present case?" My God, he sounds like a movie detective. Brian Donlevy. "Not that I blame you for asking," he adds. "Often when we have a disappearance, the background has more leads in it than the foreground, that is to say, the present, if you get my drift."

Sam looks gloomy. "Naturally we'll tell you everything you think relevant," he begins in a voice that sounds deadly, professorial. "But isn't it more urgent right now to be out looking for Roger?"

"My men are on the job, Dr. London," Lieutenant O'Wiley says, as if he were explaining addition to a slow first grader. "Now why don't you just start at the beginning?"

"On the job?" Judy says. "Doing what?"

"The things we do first: check the hospitals, the railroad and bus terminals, the airport. It takes a while, of course. But we're thorough," he adds proudly.

"That's good," I say — my first words. Hospitals — I don't want to think about it.

"Yes," Judy says. "Sam, please tell Lieutenant O'Reilly what he needs to know."

"O'Wiley, ma'am."

"I'm terribly sorry," Judy murmurs. "O'Wiley."

"By the way, Lieutenant O'Wiley," Sam says. "I'm not called Doctor. I have a Ph.D. in literature, not a medical degree or anything like that. I'd prefer Mister."

Jesus Christ, what's going on? Are they going to worry about what to call each other all night long? I am so mad at Sam for talking about his stupid Ph.D. that I go into one of my safety trances, a state designed to keep me out of trouble. When I come out of it minutes later I hear Sam say, ". . . as well as business associates. I know it's somewhat unusual for an academic like me to be involved in commerce, but this was a special case."

"As a matter of fact," Judy interrupts him, "my husband was more or less *invaluable* to Freddie Stern. Sam gave Freddie most of Freddie's good ideas — his publishing ideas, that is."

"Hmmm, is that so?" the detective says, scribbling furiously in his notebook, whipping over a page and scribbling some more. We're soaked in drama. If it weren't for Roger's being lost I would be enjoying myself quite a lot. "And can you tell me a bit more, Dr. London? The deceased and yourself must have had more than the publishing business in common for him to have left the raising of his children to you, I mean. It infers a lot more, don't you agree?"

The phone rings, sending shock waves through me. Judy dashes to answer it. It's inconvenient to have the phone in the hall, the one place no one ever stops. I hold my breath. The two men pause as if a stage director had told them: "Now the action ceases while suspense builds." Judy returns in two minutes, grim-faced. "It was that snoopy Mrs. Kaplan, wanting to know if we've found Roger. I hardly know the woman! My God, the vultures circle . . ."

"Easy does it," Sam tells her. "Maybe she meant well."

"Not her. The day Franny Kaplan means well I play flute with the B.S.O."

I think Lieutenant O'Wiley is a very patient man. "Go on, please, Dr. — I mean Mr. — London."

"Oh yes, of course," Sam says. He seems distracted by Judy's anger. Also, he seems to be enjoying this excursion into the past about as much as he would enjoy having his cavities reamed without benefit of novocaine. "Freddie Stern and I worked well together, we were on the same wave length. But it was compli-cated. The fact is, Alfred Stern, for all his money and social position and his critical success with Griffin House — that's his publishing outfit — all that, and the publicity he and his wife — Sally's mother — received, whether they sought it or not, didn't sit quite right with him. Either he didn't think he deserved those things or else he didn't really want them. I began to believe the latter . . ."

I realize I am getting some of my answers without ever having asked the questions. What incredible good fortune.

"He felt — don't we all? — that the grass was greener on the other side. With Freddie it was my side. Maybe he looked at it this way. 'I've got the money but Sam London's got the brains.' You couldn't have talked the guy out of it, an odd inferiority complex, but there it was. He admired my life when he couldn't see it clearly enough to describe its shape or color or smell or offspring. I suppose you could say he envied me. I know, I know, women are supposed to be envious and men anxious. But Freddie was envious — as well as anxious." Sam looks toward Judy.

"It *is* a better life," she insists.

"For *us*, maybe," Sam tells her. "But not necessarily for Freddie."

"Are you saying," I ask, "that Freddie was envious of *you*?" The second the words have left my mouth I realize how awful they sound.

"Strikes you as peculiar, does it, young lady?" Lieutenant O'Wiley looks at me with new interest. I have the feeling I'm muddying the waters just when they started to clear up. I look back at him bravely. How old is he? Thirty-five? Forty? There's a mean-looking palish hollow slanting across his cheek, nudging his jawline. An operation? A criminal's signature? No, probably a war wound. He's closer to thirty, then, than forty, but he dresses old — he's wearing a suit with a vest. Everyone I know, even Sam for God's sake, wears slacks and a sport jacket. This man has on a suit with sloppy pockets, like an old man.

"I'm sorry," I say truthfully. "I didn't mean it the way it sounds."

"That's all right, pet," Judy tells me. "Don't worry about it."

The phone rings. Judy dashes out again. "It's for you, Lieutenant," she calls from the hall. He lifts himself with surprising agility and goes to answer. Judy comes back, pale and fidgity. I can't look her in the eye because of what I have just said. "What do you suppose it is?" she asks Sam.

"Patience," Sam advises. "We'll find out in a minute."

"My men have checked all the hospitals between here and Worcester," Lieutenant O'Wiley says, coming back almost immediately. "We're in the clear there."

"Thank God!" Judy whispers.

But I'm not thanking God. Suppose Roger is lying inside the trunk of a car with his head chopped off?

"And how," Lieutenant O'Wiley says, seating himself in the same chair in the identical position, "and how did the young man react to the move? Did *he* feel like one of the family? You folks don't mind if I smoke, do you?" he adds, taking out a pack of Camels and not offering it around.

Judy shakes her head. "Of course not," she says. I wonder which one of them is going to tell the detective just how much Roger hated living here.

"To be quite candid with you, Lieutenant, Roger hasn't altogether adjusted to the change in his life," Sam says in a flat voice. "But no one could blame him for that. After all, he lost both his parents in one fell swoop, then he was removed from the one place he'd known all his life and dumped in with strangers in a town where he didn't know a soul. It's amazing the child is as pulled together as he is."

"He was spoiled at home," I say.

"And not here?" the detective says. He's very quick on the follow-through. He's going to get a promotion soon.

"No," Judy says. "At least I don't think so. We try not to." Is she going to tell him about the head-shrinker?

"Do you know if Mr. Stern ever told the boy about you folks? I mean what to expect if something happened to them?"

"No," Sam answers. "Since nothing *was* going to happen to them. When he asked me to take on this hypothetical responsibility Freddie lapsed into uncharacteristic romanticism. At least it was uncharacteristic to me — I hadn't seen it before. He thought he was after the life of the spirit. But he had no idea what really goes on in our house, the grubby part, the inconveniences. He despised his money — abstractly. Roger has become the beneficiary of his father's romanticism. It hasn't been easy." Pause. "For any of us." Sam sighs. Judy looks pained but relieved. The goddam phone rings again.

"I can't stand it!" Judy cries.

"Would you like me to get it?" Lieutenant O'Wiley asks.

"Yes," Judy says. "Oh, would you?" Out pops a grayish hand-kerchief. She must be about to turn on the waterworks. I feel pretty tense myself. Sam tells her everything is going to be all right. She looks at him as if he were speaking to her in Polish.

"Good news!" Lieutenant O'Wiley says, sticking his scarface in at the door and smiling. "They've located the boy. He was at the Greyhound terminal downtown, on St. James Avenue."

The waterworks go on. Judy collapses into herself, her sobs more like gulps from a swimmer who's been under just a shade too long. Sam jumps up. "Let's go!" he shouts.

"No need for that, Doctor," the detective says. "One of my men is bringing him here — they're on their way already."

"Oh, Sally," Judy sobs. "I was so worried."

"He tried to run away," I say. "I thought so."

"Happens all the time," Lieutenant O'Wiley says. Now that Roger has been found, the detective seems to have lost his power. He's just a stranger in our house who carries too much in his pockets and smells of dead cigarettes. We don't need him here anymore. He has, while sitting here, unraveled the mystery, and now what is he going to do with all that yarn at his feet? Will he scoop it up and toss it in the trash, will he keep it for his files — GREAT MYSTERIES I HAVE UNRAVELED? He hasn't done anything.

Anything, that is, but get Sam to talk about Freddie.

I wonder if we are to be charged for his services. If it was Mummy she would send him a "little gift," like a gold pencil from Tiffany. Judy is euphoric. She offers Detective O'Wiley a drink which he somewhat huffily refuses.

The first thing I noticed about Roger was how filthy he was. There was a large soot streak across his face, the shape of a hand. His little white shirt looked as if it had been dipped in mud. His legs were caked with dirt and his fingernails — well, I don't really want to describe them. Even his teeth looked disgusting.

He knew what he'd done.

When they walked in through the front door Roger was holding the policeman's hand, though of course who is to say? It might have been the other way around. But I chose to read it the first way, for it was clear to me that if he could possibly avoid a discussion with Sam London, Roger would. At that moment I was first aware that if responsibility frightens you, at least you know what it's all about.

I think I judged Roger accurately, but we were both surprised by Sam. As soon as the detective and his man closed the front door behind them and headed toward the next raveled mystery, Sam grabbed Roger and picked him clean off the floor, hugging him so hard I thought his little organs would come oozing out of his beginning and end like toothpaste.

Judy looks at me, makes a weird-looking face that says she too is surprised. I guess she doesn't know her own husband very well; it's not exactly her fault.

"You didn't have to run away, Rog," Sam murmurs. I'm glad I can't see his face, as it would embarrass me.

"I lost my suitcase," Roger says softly.

"We'll get you another one," Sam tells him.

"It had some of my good stuff in it," Roger adds.

"We'll fill it up again," Sam says. "I'll bet you're hungry. Judy's got dinner waiting. As a matter of fact, we were waiting for you so we could eat together."

"We ate already, Daddy," Joey says.

"Hi, Sally," Roger says, looking at me somewhat sheepishly.

"Roger," I shout at him, suddenly overwhelmed by my own fury, "don't you ever do anything like that again. So help me, if you ever pull anything like that again I'll kill you!"

"Sally!" Judy cries.

"I mean it!" I shout. "Look how worried we all were. And he just goes off like that and all he cares about is his stupid suitcase!"

"I'm sorry," Roger says and starts to blubber. His tears clear tiny paths through the grime on his cheeks.

"Come on, Rog," Sam says, reaching for his hand. "Don't you worry — Sally's just relieved they found you. People sometimes get angry after they've been badly frightened. But look, Roger, why don't you settle this thing for us: promise us, swear you won't try anything like this again. If you've got something big on your mind, you come and tell me or Judy instead of lighting out. Okay?"

"Okay," Roger says. From the look of him he must have been pretty frightened himself. I don't know if I would have had the nerve to do what he did at the age of seven. "I didn't have enough money for a ticket anyway. I only had two dollars and fifty cents and the man said it would cost three."

"Where to?" I ask.

"New York, dummy," he says.

Once we're at the table eating — the two London kids stare at our little wanderer as if he had sprouted a second head — Judy says, "Why did you feel you had to leave like that? Is it so bad, so *terrible* here?"

"I wanted to see Fräulein," Roger says. "She said I should come and visit her. And besides"— slitty eyes toward Sam —"*he* doesn't like me."

We all look at Sam. "I *do* like you, Roger. As a matter of fact, I might even love you." *Quel aveu*, as Mummy would have said.

"Then why do you always act so grouchy?" Roger finds the strength to persist when he wants to. Where other kids might back down he stands up for himself. I have to smile: blood, as Oma Lucy says, will tell.

"Well, I'm not sure I know how to answer that. You see, I'm damned if I do and damned if I don't."

Roger has scared the shit out of Sam, that's what. From now on he's going to behave himself. He won't be able to let his glooms, his dews and damps, spill over the rest of us and make everybody feel like turds.

As it turned out, Sam reformed as much as he could; he made it a point to ask us questions at meals. When he saw us in the hall or on the stairs he didn't look at us as if he'd never seen us before — he blinked and said, "Hi there." He started taking us places — the animal museum at Harvard, which I loved because it smelled like old fur coats, Plymouth Rock, The Rude Bridge, Brigham's for ice cream on Saturday afternoons, and the movies, which he got to enjoy so much he began writing fancy articles about them for *Commentary*.

Judy and I eventually sorted things out. I figured it was stupid to live with someone you're always suspicious of. I taught her how to shop for clothes; she acquired a style of her own which has aged nicely. More than that, I soon came to use her as I would a mother, which means that most of the time she gives out more than she takes in. But she claims she likes it this way. I am, she assures me, the warmhearted and loving daughter she always wanted but couldn't seem to produce herself.

ANNE BERNAYS was raised and educated in New York and has been writing for the past twenty years. She has written six novels, including *The Address Book*, *The New York Ride*, and *The First to Know*, and has contributed articles to the *Atlantic Monthly*, the *New York Times* and *Sports Illustrated*. The co-founder of the New England chapter of P.E.N., and the mother of three grown daughters, she lives in Cambridge where she is teaching the Fiction Workshop in the Harvard Extension Program and writing a full-length personal memoir.